Abandoned on Juracan

by

Earl T. Roske

Cover by: Mike Beckstrom

Thank You
Andrew's bottomless well of support.
Tim and Wendy for all the proofreading and feedback.
Linda K. & Ian T. for Beta reaind and feedback.

Mike for the awesome covers.

For my wife and daughter.

Never forgotten. Always remembered.
Judy, my mom.
Max, the cat.

01

"Go on, Castro, just say it."

Lieutenant Dewey Tyler and Staff Sergeant Diane Castro were walking the central corridor of the Hospitaller ship, Graevya. Having just left his quarters, they were now making their way toward the bridge. Dewey could feel SSgt Castro looking at him. He didn't have to turn his head to know she was smiling.

"I wasn't going to say anything, Lieutenant." There was mirth in her voice. Dewey could hear it clear as a klaxon alarm.

"You want to, though." The conversation paused as they passed several ship's crew in the corridor. The change of watch had just happened. These Hospitallers were likely on their way to the chow hall for their evening's meal.

"Lieutenant," they said, and saluted as they passed.

"Hospitallers," Dewey said to them, returning their salute. To SSgt Castro, he said, "Waiting."

With an exaggerated sigh, SSgt Castro said, "Well, it is true, Lieutenant."

"What's true?"

Dewey and SSgt Castro stopped and saluted as the ship's XO, Captain Bruce Gregory, stepped out from his quarters. There was a short section of corridor behind him. It was the last seven meters before the ship's bridge. Dewey assumed that the captain had been summoned, too.

"He was reading a book," SSgt Castro said.

Dewey wondered, fleetingly, how she could talk while supporting such a broad grin. He was certain, if nothing else, Castro was proud of her deduction and enjoying that fact.

"A book?" Capt Gregory had started walking to the bridge but just as quickly came to a stop. He turned back to Dewey and Castro. "Right, now I remember. Major Hughes joked about how we should confiscate the lieutenant's reader."

"I'll bet the major is regretting it only being a joke," said SSgt Castro. Her words preceded a chuckle that she failed to control.

They were crossing the threshold of the bridge entry hatch as Dewey said, "Let's not jump to conclusions. It might not be anything like last time."

"Last time?" asked Major Winston Hughes as Dewey and the others stopped to salute. "Last time, was there a distress call?"

"Last two times, Major," SSgt Castro said.

"Well, then it's exactly as before." The major, in Dewey's opinion, did not seem as amused as SSgt Castro. In fact, he seemed anything but amused. "How much do you know about lost systems, Lieutenant Tyler?"

Dewey knew quite a lot. He knew more now than before the mission on Wenshen. After discovering that Wenshen was more than just an uninhabited uninhabitable planet, he'd been reading many books on the subject. A lot of old books he found on old servers in government archives and university basements. And as Dewey never forgot what he read, he could recall a lot about lost systems.

"Any system in particular, Major?"

"How about the Cocijo system? Ring any bells?"

It did, but answers didn't come instantly. Dewey had to shuffle through all the retained information. It was like accessing the root directory of a ship's computer systems with all its layers and sublayers. Eventually, anything could be found if the searcher was patient.

The major was patient. SSgt Castro still seemed amused.

"Cocijo," Dewey said, "was discovered early in the first expansion but not colonized until their second wave. The habitable planet, Juracan, was settled by seven old Earth nations."

"I've never heard of it," said Capt Gregory. He had his arms folded, and the look on his face suggested doubt.

"Just before the Radial War," Dewey said. "And supposedly unrelated to it, Juracan had its own war. A nuclear war."

Major Hughes nodded. "A global nuclear war. They had to evacuate the entire planet."

"Oh," said SSgt Castro. She seemed to be the only one enjoying this conversation. "I bet not everyone was evacuated."

"Lieutenant?" Major Hughes had turned his full attention back to Dewey.

"All the books say it was completely evacuated." He paused as he sifted more information. "But there was some speculation that the Radial War may have interfered with the evacuation effort."

"They didn't have us." The conversation had been increased with the addition of Master Sergeant Stephanie Hill.

"No, they didn't," said the major.

"And that's where the distress signal is from?" Dewey asked.

"Yes, in a way," said Maj Hughes. "Oddly, the signal is being broadcast from a modern emergency beacon. And the beacon is telling us that a planet, lost for three hundred fifty years, needs help for its people. People that shouldn't exist."

"A modern-day beacon? With a cry for help from a missing planet? Could things get any more interesting?" Capt Gregory asked.

"I certainly hope so," said SSgt Castro.

Dewey noticed that MSgt Hill was grinning nearly as broadly as Castro.

"Lucky you, Staff Sergeant," Maj Hughes said. "Things are definitely going to get more interesting."

"We've been directed to investigate?" Dewey asked, even though he was pretty sure what the answer would be.

"We've already got our orders."

"One more time around the galaxy, eh, Lieutenant Tyler?" asked SSgt Castro.

Dewey bit back a groan. MSgt Hill and SSgt Castro seemed to be the only two people on the bridge deck to find amusement in their situation.

"Sergeant Stephens?" Maj Hughes turned in his seat to address the bridge duty NCO. "Broadcast it."

"Yes, Major," Sgt Bert Stephens said. He held the comm plunger over his mouth and tapped a button. Dewey heard the whispered click that came just before a ship-wide broadcast. "Unscheduled jump in thirty minutes. Repeat. Unscheduled jump in thirty."

As if the announcement were the starting gun, the bridge was suddenly animated by the crew at their stations, tapping at screens and communicating with other sections of the ship.

"You might want to brief your team, Lieutenant," Maj Hughes said. His gaze flicked over to SSgt Castro and then back to Dewey. "That's assuming they haven't already been apprised of the situation."

Dewey looked to Castro, who feigned shock at the intimation just before she burst into laughter.

On the barracks deck, Dewey's platoon seemed unimpressed by the visual of Juracan on the wall monitors. It had taken them a standard day and a half to reach the Cocijo system. Besides Juracan, there were several gas planets in the system, along with one rocky planet that was between Juracan and the system's sun.

"Well?" SSgt Castro asked as she scanned the rest of the platoon. "What were you expecting?"

Sgt Stuart Barrett shrugged. "I don't know. Maybe a green glow?"

"It's not a ball of radioactive isotopes," Cpl Kristen Chavez said. Chavez was one of the fireteam leaders in Sgt Barrett's squad. "It's a planet that had a nuclear war."

"Nearly four hundred years ago," added Cpl Victor Garner.

"Still," said Sgt Barrett, "I figured there would be something interesting."

"I see something interesting," said Dewey.

The platoon was sitting around several tables in the middle of their barracks deck. Most of them were facing or turned toward the large monitors. The ship was a unit transport, regularly used for moving entire battalions. As the rest of their battalion was already on station in the Wisakedjak system, they had the space to themselves.

"Would that interesting thing you see be a space elevator?" asked SSgt Castro.

"And it looks to be in good shape." Dewey knew it was there before they'd even made the first jump.

The message the ship had received came from someone claiming to be a citizen of Juracan. They'd also claimed they were on a space platform used for cargo and that they'd taken an elevator to get there. Along with the plea for help, the Juracanian had given the longitude and latitude for the elevator's planet anchor. Without that information, all the other coordinates that had been included in the beacon's message would have been useless.

"If it's in good shape, that means it's being used," said Sgt Christine Maxwell. She and her squad were new to the company and Dewey's platoon. They'd been picked up along the way to Wisakedjak.

"Someone's strip-mining the old cities," Dewey said. That information drew the attention of more of his platoon. "Someone found Juracan a few years ago. The message we received said these 'invaders' were stripping the old cities of metals and minerals. And that they were forcing the Juracanians to work for them as slave labor."

"The probe couldn't have been old," said Sgt Barrett. "And the tech to launch it would have to have been advanced."

"Or, they could have snuck aboard an elevator trunk," Dewey said. "And once there, they could have snuck aboard a ship and then used one of their probes. Which is what they did."

"Lieutenant Tyler? Do we know who these 'invaders' are?" asked Sgt Marion Parks, the last of the three squad leaders.

"We don't. And the Juracanian who sent the probe didn't seem to know either. He did say it wasn't a government entity, that it was some sort of company."

"So it's illegal," said SSgt Castro.

"Right." Dewey's comm beeped. It was Maj Hughes. Dewey stood and said, "But since the planet never aligned with any of the planetary organizations during or after the Radial War, the current ones, A.P., U.P., Freeworlds, aren't interested in what's going on here. The major has commed me. I'll let you know more when I get back."

There was a rustle of clothes and the sound of dozens of boots scraping the deck as Dewey's platoon stood to attention.

"As you were, Hospitallers," said Dewey before turning and leaving the barracks deck. He made his way to the bridge but was interrupted by the major's voice from an open hatchway.

"In here, Lieutenant."

Dewey paused and then turned to his right, entering Maj Hughes's ready room. He stopped, snapping to attention. "Lieutenant Tyler reporting, Major."

"Right, right, grab a seat, Tyler." The major was pouring hot water into two cups. Next to the cups was a still-open jar of Insta. "Haven't had time to restock my coffee canisters."

"I've never said no to a cup of Insta, Major."

Maj Hughes laughed and picked up a cup, setting it closer to Dewey. "Neither have I, Lieutenant. Neither have I. Drink while it's hot."

They both sat in silence through several sips of the steaming Insta. It tasted nothing like coffee and was one of many things the Hospitallers had invented for themselves. Most of the Hospitallers in the Orphan Corps had been drinking it since they'd turned thirteen. Most of them liked to joke about how awful it was, but they still drank it. There were too many memories in a cup of Insta to turn it down.

"I sent off a request," Maj Hughes said after a fifth sip. "This situation really needs more rank."

"And?"

Maj Hughes laughed. "Seems a major is all the rank we're going to get. There's too much else going on around the radial arm right now. We're just supposed to pop in and say hello, tell the bad guys to stop being bad, and then get back on the road."

"So, easy stuff."

"Right. Easy stuff, Lieutenant Tyler."

Which meant that it wouldn't be easy. Dewey had a hard time recalling when it was ever easy, and he rarely forgot anything. "So we should overpack for the journey."

"Just tell your NCOs to think paranoid."

"After our experience on Wenshen, I don't think that'll be a problem."

Wenshen had been a fluke. The planet was inhospitable to humans. The system had been declared a dead system. Yet, they were attacked soon after entering the system to rescue some faux-smugglers. The attack had forced them to land on the planet and live in their evac suits for weeks until help arrived.

"Read the reports," said the major. He downed the last half-cup of Insta and stood. "Quite honestly, I'd like the chance to see Wenshen and its citizens for myself. Anyway, you'll want to get everyone geared up and ready. I want you all on the planet in twelve."

Dewey knocked back the last of his Insta and stood, too. "Will do, Major."

Nine hours later, Dewey's platoon, distributed among three dropships, were buckled in and ready to drop into the Juracan atmosphere. Normally they could have used two dropships and even gotten away with one if they didn't have a lot of gear to carry. But they were packing for trouble which meant a lot of extra ammo, med supplies, emergency supplies, and more ammo.

As this was intended to be more an aid and comfort mission than a defend mission, they were bringing along the usual food supplies, clothes, shelters, medicines, and several large crates stuffed with toys and treats for any children they might encounter. Depending on where they were and who they encountered, each Hospitaller would be sporting a T-n-T bag filled with toys and treats for the children.

Hospitallers had a special affinity for children, which was likely due to their having grown up in orphanages where they were treated so well.

"Kids all buckled up and ready for the trip?"

Dewey looked up to see the dropship's loadmaster, Sgt Kent Thompson, coming down the aisle. The aisle here and on the other side of the dropship's bay was narrow, the central section being packed with crates and boxes. Thompson paused and looked down at Sgt Christine Maxwell, who was sitting to Dewey's right.

"All right there, Maxwell?" Sgt Thompson asked.

"All right, Thompson."

"New with Lieutenant Tyler?" Sgt Thompson nodded in Dewey's direction before speaking directly to him. "Hey, Lieutenant, making life interesting for us, I hear?"

Dewey chuckled and nodded.

Sgt Maxwell said, "Just transferred in. Missed all the earlier excitement."

Sgt Thompson snorted a laugh. "'Excitement'? Is that what they call it? I, for one, am happy without the excitement."

"How's that working out for you?" asked Dewey.

"It was going great until now, Lieutenant Tyler," said Sgt Thompson. "But, hey, that's what being a Hospitaller is all about." He turned toward the rear hatch and cupped his hands around his mouth. "Unlatching in sixty!"

"Double check, squad," Sgt Maxwell said. Her voice carried without the use of her hands. "Then check your neighbors."

Dewey checked over Sgt Maxwell's restraints.

"Fifteen, people!" Sgt Thompson was securing his own restraints. Next to him, a light on a panel went on. He set the last latch on his seat harness and grabbed a headset, settling it onto his head.

"Thank you, Sergeant Maxwell," said Dewey as Maxwell checked his harness.

"No problem, Lieutenant."

"Listen up," Sgt Thompson bellowed.

"Get ready," Dewey whispered just loud enough that only Sgt Maxwell could hear.

Maxwell responded in a similar whisper, "Ready?"

Dewey nodded as Sgt Thompson continued, "There's been a delay."

"A delay?" someone in the back asked.

Dewey bit his lip to stop the encroaching smile.

"Why's there a delay?" Sgt Maxwell asked Dewey in a whisper.

Dewey didn't have to answer as the gravity suddenly cut out and the dropship lurched. Several people shouted in surprise. Sgt Thompson laughed heartily. "Just kidding," he said.

The gravity came back online a moment later, causing a few more shouts of surprise. The Hospitallers on the other side of the dropship bay laughed at Sgt Maxwell's squad's confusion.

"Lieutenant Owen and Sgt Thompson do this every time someone new is on their dropship."

"That's what you meant when you said, 'get ready'?" Sgt Maxwell asked.

"Yes."

"Everybody comfy? Everybody ready?" When no one answered, Sgt Thompson looked in Dewey's direction and winked. "Let's go kick some dirt, Lieutenant Tyler."

02

It wasn't as easy as just dropping into the atmosphere and flying into the landing zone. Dewey had known that fact from the briefing. He was pretty sure that when Sgt Thompson suggested they were going to go kick dirt, he'd purposefully left out the big piece in the middle.

The ions in the atmosphere, specifically in the region where the troposphere and stratosphere overlapped, interfered with the electronics of any ship cutting through. It also seemed to affect communication. All of which they hypothesized as the reason the visitors had installed a space elevator. With the elevator, not only could they easily move stuff from the surface to space, they could also use it as a communication tether to the rest of the galaxy.

So, when the floor dropped out of the dropship, and everyone found themselves floating in their restraints, it was only Sgt Thompson who laughed.

"Did I forget to mention we were doing a Hi-Ho?" Thompson clapped one hand over his mouth and then said, "Oops. That one's on me."

High insertion, high open was a common method for dropping down toward a planet surface. It was used more often for worlds still in the terraforming phase. Those planets also had a lot of disruptive ions in the troposphere/stratosphere boundary. Just not as radioactive.

"Anyone pee their pants?" asked Sgt Thompson. "I warned you to go before we left."

Sgt Thompson's comment drew more laughs. Dewey knew it was a reaction to the relief in knowing they weren't all about to smack into the surface of Juracan. The number of times that it had happened during the Hospitallers' history could be counted on one hand. Still, the idea made even Dewey a little nervous.

His nervousness was quickly justified as the dropship lurched to one side and then seemed to slowly spin around an off-center axis.

"Thompson," said Dewey. He kept his voice steady.

Sgt Thompson had yanked the headset back on the moment the ship had done its non-normal maneuver. He had his hand cupped over the mic, but he seemed to be listening more than talking.

Finally, he pushed the mic boom away and said, "We lost one of the drop chutes. It's going to be like this for a few more minutes until we can power back up."

Several people groaned, clearly unhappy with the current situation.

"Look on the bright side," Dewey said. He spoke loud enough that his voice carried through the dropship bay. "We'll be first on the ground."

"Too right!" Sgt Thompson laughed and flashed a thumbs up to Dewey.

For his part, Dewey bit the inside of his lip to keep from smiling.

Down the row, one of Sgt Maxwell's squad, PFC Marc Webb, popped open a lunch bag. Lunch bag was the nickname the Hospitallers used for the barf bags occasionally deployed during a drop. Right before clapping the bag over his mouth, he said, "I knew I should have skipped seconds on breakfast."

As it turned out, the dropship Dewey was on landed ten minutes ahead of the others. The squad exited out the back, securing the perimeter in minutes. Dewey directed Sgt Maxwell to push them out further to clear the space for the other two ships.

While they waited, Dewey took some time to examine the terrain around them.

Based on what little Dewey had read, Juracan had been a thriving planet, even with its seemingly regular disputes among the nations that had colonized it. There were two continents and dozens of would-be-continents. Where Dewey's platoon had landed, following the directions given in the beacon, they were just west of the eastern coastline of the continent, Montego, and south of what had been a national capital, Atacama.

Dewey knew only about the history he'd read. He knew nothing of the current situation. All they had were a set of coordinates. As they'd come through the upper atmosphere, the dropship had collected images of the area below. In them, Dewey had seen several small towns with crop fields around them. The area they'd picked out for landing put them several kilometers away from the nearest town and several hundred meters from the nearest fields.

Had the people of the nearby villages noticed the dropships coming in? Would they come out to see who landed? Or would the people go into hiding? If the latter, Dewey's people would have to hike into town and hope someone was willing to open a door.

A beep from Dewey's comm distracted him from his thoughts.

"This is Lieutenant Tyler," said Dewey after tapping his comm to open the connection.

"Was that cheating, Lieutenant?"

"Of course not, Staff Sergeant Castro. Unless accidentally losing a chute is cheating." Dewey looked up. He could see the burners of the other two dropships as they slowly approached the coordinates. "But look on the bright side, the area's already secured."

"So, cheating and having all the fun," SSgt Castro said and then laughed. "Nothing from the towns?"

"Nothing, yet. Once you all get down here, we'll decide what to do next."

"Almost there."

Dewey tapped the comm, closing the connection. He scanned for and located Sgt Maxwell. He pointed skyward, saying, "Heads-up."

Sgt Maxwell acknowledged with a nod before turning to warn those near her to be aware.

Dewey went inside the dropship bay to check in with the pilot, Lt Horace Owen. He and Lt Maxine Walters were looking into several overhead hatches. Sgt Thompson held an electric torch to light their view.

"Sabotage?" Dewey asked.

Lt Owen laughed as he lowered himself from the hatch opening. "Ten drops away from being replaced and it retired early. Sorry about the surprise."

"I've been through worse," said Dewey. His mind automatically recalled the landing on Wenshen.

"Right," Lt Matthews said, apparently making the same connection. "You got to ride a spaceship into atmo. At the risk of sounding crazy, I'd like to experience that.

"I'll definitely never forget it," said Dewey. Then, shifting the conversation, he asked, "The lost chute won't affect the rest of your dropship systems? That right?"

Sgt Thompson was securing the overhead panels as Lt Owen replied. "No. But there will be a big red light on the ready board when we get back on the Graevya."

"And we won't be cleared for launch until the ship gets a full systems check."

Outside, the whisper of approaching dropships was building to an angry growl as they drew closer to the ground.

"We'll send you up as soon as we have information to pass along to Major Hughes," said Dewey. He paused as outside, leaves and other debris swirled past the open ramp at the rear of the dropship. Several leaves had made it into the safety of the bay and were drifting down to rest on the deck. "Right now, we need to find a local to make contact with."

"You want us to come with you?"

"No, Lieutenant Owen. I think you all can button up and hold fast here. Comms are working, so I'll communicate instructions and information to you when we know what to do next."

Dewey nodded and exited the dropship. Outside, the dust and micro-debris were settling to the ground. The back hatches of the other two dropships were slowly lowering.

"Welcome to Juracan," Dewey said as SSgt Castro and Sgt Parks exited the second dropship.

"Not exactly what I would have chosen for vacation," said SSgt Castro.

"You ever been on a vacation?" Dewey asked, amused because he knew the answer.

"What's a vacation?" asked Cpl Donald Mitchell as he moved past with his fireteam.

His comment earned a chuckle from everyone, Dewey included.

"So, what now, Lieutenant?" Sgt Parks asked.

Dewey turned to face the direction of the nearest town. He noticed as he pointed roughly north that MedTech Jasmine Chambers was making her way in his direction. "Soon as everyone does a gear check," Dewey said as he lowered his hand, "chokes down half a ration bar and some water, there's a town that way. We'll start there."

"Usually, we get a welcome committee," said SSgt Castro. "Or an unwelcome party."

"No one knew we were coming when we did," Dewey said. "And if they've dealt with invaders already, they might be concerned enough to stay hidden."

"Makes sense."

"Anyone hurt, Chambers?" Dewey asked.

"Not yet," said MedTech Chambers. She held up her tablet, which was strapped to a device about four times as thick. "But if we don't get blockers in everyone, we're all going to be dealing with radiation poisoning."

"We didn't do this before coming down," said Sgt Parks. "Was that also because of the interference?"

"What interference?" It was Sgt Stuart Barrett who asked. He was approaching in the company of Sgt Maxwell. They both saluted Dewey before Sgt Barrett added, "We have two squads on perimeter, Lieutenant."

"Good work, Sergeant Maxwell, Sergeant Barrett. We were just talking about radiation sickness."

"No thanks," said Sgt Barrett. "We getting an injection to help with that?"

"We are now," MedTech Chambers said. "Now that I have a more precise idea as to the rad levels we'll be absorbing."

Chambers opened up the front of a satchel she was carrying. Inside was a small machine made of plastic with numbered buttons, a small screen, and a window in which Dewey could see the small dispensing bottle. He watched as MedTech Chambers tapped in several strings of numbers and then the green button.

"Four hundred plus years," SSgt Castro had been saying. "You'd think that all the radiation - or at least most of it - would have dissipated or broken down. Something."

"A lot of it probably has," Dewey said. Then, "Arms or butts, Chambers?"

"Butts for this one."

"Right." Dewey started setting aside his gear. He planned on being first. Not because he was selfish or worried for his own well-being, but so that he was an example just in case anyone felt an urge to hesitate. "Undoubtedly, the radiation levels are lower than after their war. But there wasn't anyone to do remediation afterward, either."

"I don't understand why none of the interplanetary governments stepped in to offer," said Lt Owen. "They could have gained another system."

"No one saw the profit in it, Lieutenant," SSgt Castro said. She had dropped her gear and was unbuckling her pants. "And apparently, the Radial War distracted them."

Dewey waited while MedTech Chambers pressed the inoculation gun to his glute. There was a hiss from that direction. He felt a spreading of cold from the point of contact. Then the pressure was gone. After resetting his pants and buckling them, he said, as SSgt Castro stepped over to MedTech Chambers, "Someone felt it was worth the risk to come here now. Enough to set up an elevator."

Dewey pointed with his chin. He heard the click and hiss of SSgt Castro's inoculation. Those that turned in the direction Dewey'd indicated could see a dark, straight line that seemed to cleave the sky before disappearing into the clouds.

"Next," said MedTech Chambers as Castro walked back to her gear, buckling her belt along the way.

"Parks, you're up," Dewey said. He pointed with his thumb

toward Chambers. "When you're done, relieve Maxwell's squad. Maxwell, you'll relieve Barrett's squad."

"Yes, Lieutenant," the three sergeants said as one.

"Lieutenant Owen," Dewey added. "You and the rest of the dropship crews go after Sergeant Parks's team."

"No problem." Lt Owen turned to Sgt Thompson. "You want to pass that information along?"

"Will do." Sgt Thompson turned and jogged up the dropship ramp to comm the other ships.

SSgt Castro, now back in her gear, clapped her hands together and rubbed the palms vigorously against each other. "All right," she said. "Let's get these shots done and do some sightseeing."

Two and three-quarter hours later, standard time, the platoon was approaching the first houses. They'd passed several farms earlier, but a quick examination through magnified face shields showed buildings rotting from neglect. Here, though, the images had shown houses straight-standing and clean. Curtains fluttered in several windows, and at least one person had been seen ducking as Dewey looked too long in their direction.

"How's it look on point?" Dewey asked Cpl Merle Fleming. His fireteam had taken over less than a half-hour before.

"It's quiet, Lieutenant Tyler. We've glimpses of several people. It's weird, though."

Dewey signaled to SSgt Castro. She nodded and tapped her own comm. Several seconds later, everyone came to a stop and took up defensive positions.

"What's weird, Fleming?"

"The people we've seen," Cpl Fleming said. "They've either been kids or really old people. I'd expect they'd keep them safe and out of sight."

"Unless there was no one to look out for them," Dewey said. "Have your team pull back ten meters. Find a good place to hold up. I'll be there in a few minutes."

"Will do, Lieutenant."

As the comm went silent, SSgt Castro joined Dewey.

"What's going on?"

"More of the same," said Dewey. He was looking around to see who was closest as far as fireteams. "Young people. Old people. No one of military or middle age."

"Could this be some kind of trap? Pretty clever if it is."

Dewey shook his head. Then, seeing Cpl Victor Garner, he signaled for the squad leader to join him and SSgt Castro before saying, "I think what we're seeing is people either too old or too young for hard labor."

"Lieutenant." Cpl Garner saluted as he greeted Dewey.

"Garner. Check in with Sergeant Parks and let her know I'm borrowing you and your fireteam. Then, pick up your team and report back to me. I want your company to the front."

"On it." Cpl Garner saluted once more and then trotted off in the direction where Sgt Parks was watching.

"You're going to try and make contact?" SSgt Castro asked. She sounded doubtful.

On the other side of the road, Cpl Garner and Sgt Parks had finished talking. Garner was now moving along the road, drawing three people with him as he did.

"They know we're here," said Dewey. "And even if the children don't realize it, the adults have to know we know they're here. And we came here in response to a distress signal one of them is responsible for."

"Could we collect some data with a dozen eyes?" asked SSgt Castro. "Just to make sure we aren't being played?"

"Let's hold off on that," Dewey said. "Let me see how things look on the point. Then I'll let you know if we should."

Dewey clapped Castro on the shoulder as he moved past her. He motioned with his head and signaled for Cpl Garner to join him. Garner's fireteam joined Dewey, boxing him in as they each scanned their side of the box. When Dewey moved, they stayed with him.

Ten meters from where Cpl Fleming waited behind two narrow trees with drooping branches, Dewey paused to look at a sign. The sign was a series of wide planks strapped to uprights. Carved into the sign were the words, "Welcome to Puchuncavi."

"Not much of a welcome if you ask me," said Cpl Garner from behind Dewey's shoulder.

Dewey nodded in agreement. "Let's hope this is the worst of it."

"Don't sound so pessimistic, Lieutenant." Garner grinned and then added, "I'm sure it'll get worse."

"Thanks for lifting my spirits, Garner. Spread your team out and watch for anything that could make this worse."

Cpl Garner saluted and then turned to his people, signaling for them to spread out and keep watch. Dewey moved across the road and knelt beside Cpl Fleming.

"Anything new?"

"Nothing, Lieutenant Tyler," said Cpl Fleming. "I was thinking we should pop some eyes up and get images of the area ahead of us."

"You and Staff Sergeant Castro," Dewey replied.

The three dropships had collected data and images on the way down. That was part of the reason they knew the rad levels in the area. But even at maximum magnification, some of the imagery was fuzzy or missing. It also didn't take into account moving objects. That was part of the reason the eyes were so popular.

Over the decades and centuries, Hospitallers had developed many proprietary supplies, from the Insta they all drank to the eyes and hands used to collect data on the ground. The eyes had been around for decades but with improvements every few years. If enough data was collected from enough eyes, it was possible to create a virtual model of the scene. But even one eye was capable of collecting plenty of images that could be beamed directly to a Hospitaller's helmet for examination.

As they weren't sure what was ahead, but having been alerted by the few young and old faces Cpl Fleming and his team had seen, maybe Fleming and Castro had the right idea. A few more eyes to collect intel wouldn't be a bad idea.

"Wait," Dewey said. He'd been about to give the go-ahead to Fleming when he heard something.

"I hear it, too," said Cpl Fleming. "What is it?"

03

Dewey didn't know the sound, yet it managed to sound familiar. It was an undulating, pulsing, metallic screech. Nothing in his years as a Hospitaller sounded like it, but it did stir up a feeling of nostalgia, which he thought was weird.

It also continued to move closer.

And then PFC Eduardo Wallace laughed. The sound carried across the road. The metallic screech slowed for a moment and then returned to its previous tempo.

"Wallace?" Dewey asked over the comm. "You got eyes?"

"Yes, Lieutenant," said PFC Wallace. "It's an old man on a rusty bike."

When Dewey had first arrived at the orphanage of his youth, he'd been unsure and withdrawn. Then, he'd found an old tricycle in the tall grass near a shed. The wheels lacked rubber. The rust on the seat scratched at his backside. But it was his and unlikely to be taken by anyone else because of the state it was in.

He'd ridden it for days, circumnavigating the play area, the axles squealing a rusty squeal. When they went in for class or meals, Dewey would park it by the shed, adjusting the grass to hide it from anyone who might pass by.

This was the memory that had been stirred by the approaching sound.

"How far?" Dewey finally asked after a pause that caught Cpl Fleming's attention.

"Not even ten meters," PFC Wallace said. "You'll have visual in less than a minute."

With Cpl Fleming flanking him, Dewey leaned left to take in a wider view of the busted road. Seconds later, the sound was joined by the image of a man with a bloom of gray hair and dark skin making his wobbly way towards them. He was wearing loose trousers and a shirt that reached mid-thigh.

When he was within five meters, Dewey slowly stood, his arms out, palms forward. The old man ceased pedaling. The bike coasted two more meters before it wobbled uncontrollably, and he put his feet down to avoid falling over. Dewey motioned to the sides, bringing the rest of the point fireteam out from hiding. They, too, kept their hands and palms open and clear.

The old man earned smiles and a couple hushed chuckles when he mimicked the Hospitallers' hand positions.

"Greetings," he said.

"Greetings," Dewey answered. "We're Hospitallers. I'm not sure if you know what that means."

"It means you come from the sky. Like the invaders."

Dewey nodded. "Yes, from the sky, but not like the invaders."

"Right," said the old man. "You're here to help. They said you'd come."

Dewey looked at Cpl Fleming, curious if the fireteam leader had heard the same thing.

"Who?" Fleming asked out loud.

"My grandkids. Before they were taken."

"I'd like to hear more, but first, I'd like to bring the rest of my team forward. And I'd like to send a team ahead, just to make sure it's clear."

After a look over his shoulder, the old man laughed and shrugged. "You most certainly may, but you'll find nothing but the too old, the too young, and the too sick. If you're concerned about the invaders, you needn't be. They don't come this way unless provoked. And there's no one left to provoke them."

"Of course," said Dewey. "But we like to make sure, for our own satisfaction."

In response, the old man stepped off his bicycle and pushed it to the side of the road, leaning it against a bush. He looked at the bike as it sagged against the greenish-yellow plant before turning back to Dewey and saying, "It used to be a good bike. I've had it near a hundred years. Just don't have the materials and tools like I used to. Like we used to."

Dewey had signaled for Cpl Fleming to pull the rest of the platoon forward. As Fleming made the call over the comm, Dewey approached the old man and his bike. The man's dark skin looked different from what Dewey had ever seen. Well, that wasn't entirely true. The people of Wenshen had different skin, too.

"A hundred years?" Dewey asked, not sure if he'd been distracted by the texture of the old man's face and hands.

"Yep." The old man patted the seat, which had several tears in the cover and looked to have been repaired with plastic twine. "Was my tenth birthday present."

That would, Dewey quickly deduced, make him nearly one hundred ten years of age. Perhaps that explained the skin on the face and hands. He held out his own hand after removing his glove.

"I'm Lieutenant Dewey Tyler, Orphan Corps."

The old man seemed surprised by the greeting. Perhaps the invaders hadn't been as polite. But then Dewey realized the old man's eyes were locked on Dewey's hand. He rotated it so that the palm and then the back were displayed.

"They say we used to look like that." The old man gently took Dewey's hand and shook it. "I was named Luciano Munguia. Everyone calls me Luc, or Grandpa Luc, depending on their age, I guess."

"Pleasure to meet you, Luc." Dewey turned his hand so that Luc's was now on top. "I don't want to offend you, but may I look at your hand?"

"Sure, sure." Luc held out both hands. Dewey looked at them and then at Luc's face. His skin was gray and looked like it was made of hundreds, possibly thousands, of small flat pebbles.

"Does everyone look like this?"

Luc looked at his own hands. "Pretty much, yeah. Younger people have lighter skin. The mosaic isn't defined so much. Gotta keep it greased, though, or it bleeds in the cracks."

"Greased?" Dewey turned toward the sound of approaching footsteps. He gave a chin-lift greeting to SSgt Castro. "Can you find Chambers for me?"

Castro nodded and did a marching about-face, returning in the direction she'd come.

"Well, it ain't really grease, mind you," Luc was saying. Dewey turned back to him. "That's just what we call it. We get it from one of the flat-bean crops. Though, that's been a bit difficult to do of late."

"No one to tend the fields?"

Luc nodded and looked out to the fallow fields. "Pretty much. And no one to run the machines. No one to fix 'em, either."

MedTech Chambers appeared at Dewey's shoulder. "You asked for me, Lieutenant?"

Dewey nodded. "Luc, this is MedTech Chambers. Chambers, this is Mr. Luciano Munguia, but he says people just call him Luc."

"Or Grandpa Luc," said Luc.

"Hi, Grandpa Luc," Chambers said and then grinned. Her grin quickly faded as she seemed to become aware of Luc's skin. She started opening her medkit. "Chemical burn?"

"No, Chambers," said Dewey. "This is Luc's normal skin."

Chambers paused mid-search, her hands still in her medkit. "Normal?"

"Yes." Dewey turned and found Sgt Barrett. "Barrett? Take a fireteam forward and make sure that we have a clear path."

"On it." Sgt Barrett signaled to Cpl Chavez, who, in turn, motioned for her fireteam to move. As a group, they passed where Dewey was standing, sparing only the briefest of glances for Luc.

"Things were better before the invaders came?" asked Dewey.

Luc nodded. He held out a hand so that MedTech Chambers could get a closer look. "Greatly better," he said. "We had crops and family, and we were talking about working with the people at Soacha to bring the rail line out here."

"So, there are other towns?"

"Lots of them," said Luc. He paused as SSgt Castro approached. She nodded to him. He returned the nod and then continued, "But a lot less people than we used to have."

Dewey's comm pinged. "Excuse me," he said and stepped back.

SSgt Castro stepped into his place. "Your skin always look like that?"

"Go, Barrett," Dewey said. He could only watch the conversation as he gave his ear to Sgt Barrett.

"Looks clear, Lieutenant Tyler. Saw a couple kids, but an older lady called them back."

"All right, good work, Barrett. Have your team hold position. We'll be moving up shortly."

"We'll be here."

The comm connection clicked closed. SSgt Castro and MedTech Chambers were examining Luc's face. He seemed to be amused by their interest.

"And everyone looks like this?" SSgt Castro asked.

"For the most part, we do. I've seen people who'd traveled from far places. Their skin is always slightly different in color and pattern."

"But still patterned," said Chambers. She was holding a small medical device near Luc. Dewey could see large numbers changing on the machine's screen.

"I guess that'd be true."

"Tired of being prodded?" Dewey asked as he joined the group. Chambers showed Dewey the rad levels being emitted by Luc. It was enough to make anyone sick. Yet Luc seemed to be doing just fine.

"Not used to the attention," said Luc.

"Well, maybe we can find other people for Chambers to poke and prod. You said you had some grandkids who knew something about us? Maybe we can talk to them?"

Luc shook his head. He looked, in Dewey's opinion, forlorn. "There are others who you can speak at, but it won't be the grandkids. They're all gone. All taken."

"Taken?" asked SSgt Castro. "By who? The invaders?"

Luc nodded and then busied himself retrieving his bicycle. PFC

Lela Ramirez, from Cpl Fleming's fireteam, stepped over and gave him a hand extracting the bike from the bush.

"You know, sir, we got some lubricants that'll take care of that squeaking," said PFC Ramirez.

"That'd be nice," said Luc. He looked around and then back to Ramirez. "You wouldn't mind looking after it, would you? Seems rude of me to ride off."

PFC Ramirez laughed and nodded as she took control of the bike. When she looked at Dewey, he nodded a confirmation.

"Right," said Luc. He wiped his hands on the chest of his shirt and then waved one in the direction of town. "Come along then. I'm sure the others are all on pins and needles to meet you."

The town was more abandoned than occupied. Dewey noticed the number of homes that were shuttered with wood and plastic sheets outnumbered the occupied ones. It was also apparent that many of those left behind had begun to coalesce around the center of town, where there was a large roundabout.

The roundabout held a playground in need of a little preventive maintenance, a couple of small buildings with faded food signs, and several trees that provided shade. Along the road that encircled the roundabout were a dozen buildings. Most of them were commercial or government. Dewey easily identified the town hall, a series of shops, and a few homes. The homes were clean and showed evidence of occupation, even if the occupants all seemed to be absent. The shops, too, were being kept up.

"Things look nice here," Dewey said as they turned onto the roadway of the roundabout, heading in the direction of the town hall.

"Once everyone accepted that the young adults weren't coming back, those of us that remained decided we had to set a better example for the children. We spent a lot of time moping before then."

"Having your people taken hostage and hauled away would bring anyone's spirits down," SSgt Castro said.

Dewey nodded in agreement.

"So, we fixed up the center of town," Luc went on. "Seemed to make better sense to have everyone here rather than spread thin, lost among the empty homes. Most agreed. There's a few, though, that won't give up their homes."

They'd neared the town hall during the conversation. Dewey caught a glimpse of several people in the shadows of the open doors.

Luc continued, saying, "We got the school going, too. Each of us teaches the kids what we can. There's a cafeteria over that way where we cook group meals with what we have."

"Supplies getting thin?" Dewey asked. The people in the town hall had emerged into the dim light of day. There were four of them, three women and one man. All of them were of similar age to Luc.

"Getting thin," agreed Luc. "Hard to maintain the fields at our age. And the little ones are too small to offer much help."

"Well, we have supplies," Dewey said. "Those might help for a while. These are the rest of the elders?"

Luc took a second to scan the stairs leading up to the town hall doors. "Not all, no. There's others. Some are in their homes. Those who want to help are with kids. Ivan's sitting with Bennie this morning."

Dewey caught SSgt Castro's look. Whoever Bennie was, they'd been separated by name from all the other people referred to. But before Dewey could inquire, the other elders had reached the sidewalk where Luc and the Hospitallers now stood.

"Greetings," Dewey said.

The four elders nodded and then looked at Luc.

"Hospitallers," Luc said. There was a relieved look on the faces of the elders. Then, Luc made introductions. "Lieutenant Tyler, this here's Jacobo. That's Maria. And then Constanza and Valentine."

The elders nodded to Dewey, their greetings a mixed jumble of words.

The one identified by Luc as Valentine spoke, saying, "Do they have a doctor?"

"Not a doctor," said MedTech Chambers, stepping forward. "But I have training."

Dewey pushed a laugh back behind pursed lips. He smiled and then said, "Chambers is a medical technician. Might not mean much outside the Orphan Corps, but our MedTechs have as much training as most general practicing doctors on any world."

"Is there something I can help with?" asked Chambers.

"Benjamin, my grandson," said Valentine. "He's real sick."

"Bennie came back from the invaders' base," Luc said. "He managed to slip out and get back here. Unfortunately, he's got something. Now a few of the others have it, too."

"Some have died," said the other male elder, Jacobo. "Young and old."

Dewey turned to MedTech Chambers. "Sounds like a contagion."

"We'll want to quarantine whoever's come in contact with him until I can run tests," said Chambers. She turned after receiving a nod from Dewey and spoke to Valentine. "Let's go see your grandson."

04

The town had an infirmary which, while having several rooms with beds, didn't look like it was meant for long-term care. The room where they found Bennie was cramped with the addition of a second bed where one of the elders apparently slept at night. For now, the elder was sitting in a plastic chair. He had an open, printed book in his hands.

"Not sure if you should have anyone staying in here," said MedTech Chambers as she removed a compact rebreather from her kit. "The whole room might be a contagion zone."

"The only two elders that come in here are Constanza and Ivan," said Luc. The elder in the room, who'd been sitting near Bennie, looked up as Luc talked. His face flashed surprise and then quickly returned to an emotionless mask. "They've been sick and survived. So we figured they were strong enough against the sickness."

"Good point," said Dewey. To Chambers, he said, "We'll wait out here for now."

"Be right back, Lieutenant." MedTech Chambers hefted her medkit and crossed the threshold.

Bennie was awake, but his eyes were half-shuttered. He seemed to be completely drained of energy. As Chambers approached, his gaze drifted in her direction.

"How long has he been like this?" Dewey asked as he, Luc, the other elders, and Fleming's fireteam stood in the hallway.

"Since he came back. It's been two weeks." Luc indicated the other elders with a hand. "We recognized the signs and kept him away from everyone who hadn't been sick before."

"Is this common?" asked Cpl Fleming from further down the hall.

"This illness?"

Luc shook his head and chuckled. "It may shock you to hear this, but no one really gets ill on Juracan. At least, not from what we've learned from other towns. Certainly not here."

"But you recognized the signs," Dewey said.

"Only because it's come through several times in the last few years," said Valentine. She was pressed against the door jamb, her eyes on the activity inside the room.

Something occurred to Dewey. "So, no one was sick until after the invaders came through?"

"That's about right," said Luc. "Contact with the other towns seems to agree with what you're saying."

"Each time," said Jacobo, the other male elder, "people died. It was worse the first time, not so bad the second time. Third time, we started isolating the sick. Like this."

"How many people died?" asked Cpl Fleming.

The silence that preceded the answer was long enough and heavy enough that Dewey almost wished he hadn't asked. But the information was important to know. They were on a new world for the Hospitallers. A world that seemed to be more than just a radioactive danger.

"Half, the first time," said Jacobo.

Valentine scoffed as she turned around. "Half? Who taught you counting, Jacobo? No, it was more than half. A lot more."

"The second time, we lost half of those who'd survived the first time," said Luc. "We had no idea what was happening. We thought maybe the invaders had done it on purpose."

Dewey surmised that the Juracanians had lost close to seventy-five percent of their population. He was beginning to consider pulling everyone back from the town when MedTech Chambers approached. She'd removed her mask.

"Chambers?"

"We're good, Lieutenant," said Chambers. She looked over her shoulder and then back to the group crowding the doorway. "Influenza. We're all inoculated. Still, with our natural defensive systems, it wouldn't kill us."

"But it's killed the people here."

MedTech Chambers had taken out a small tube and squeezed a bead of gel onto her hands. She rubbed them together. "I did a quick blood test. The Juracans are different from us. Not a lot, but just enough that they lacked the ability to fight off the virus."

"Centuries of isolation," said Dewey. "And the adaptation to a radioactive environment."

Chambers nodded. "That'd be my guess, too. But if we could get the lab people down here, they'd have a better answer."

"Hey, Chambers." It was Cpl Fleming. "Could you give them the immunization shots we all get from time to time?"

"Absolutely. There's a printer on the ship. If we get that down here, we can start printing all the doses we need."

"And what about Bennie?" asked Valentine. "And anyone else that's sick?"

"Yes," said MedTech Chambers. "I already gave Bennie an antiviral. It won't cure him, but it'll help him recover."

"So, he'll live?"

"Based on his current state, yes," said Chambers, who suddenly found herself in a hug from Valentine.

"Thank you," said Valentine as she released an amused looking Chambers. She looked into the room and then back to MedTech Chambers. "Can I go in?"

"Were you sick before?" When Valentine shook her head no, Chambers echoed the movement. "You'd be better waiting for the immunization shot and then a short waiting period."

"Mask?" asked Dewey. He could see that Valentine was hurting.

MedTech Chambers's eyes widened. "Right, yes. Thanks, Lieutenant Tyler."

Chambers went back into the room and opened a compartment in her kit. She returned with a light-gray mask and handed it to Valentine. Valentine studied the mask for a second and then slipped it over her head. She looked at Chambers. Once Chambers flashed a smile and a thumbs-up, the elder woman slowly entered the room, making her way to Bennie's bedside.

"I'd like to stay here for a while, Lieutenant, if that's okay?"

"Permission granted, Chambers. Comm us if you need anything."

MedTech Chambers saluted and returned to the room and Bennie's bed. Bennie already seemed to be responding to the meds given to him.

Dewey turned to Luc and the other elders. "I'd like to know as much as you can tell us about the invaders. Also, if there's a place we can use for supplies and a temporary bivouac? We have several dropships we'd like to unload."

Luc nodded and turned to the others. "School gymnasium is still in good shape."

"Water works, too," Maria said. She received a non-confirming shrug from Jacobo. "Okay, well, it worked last time I was in there, about six months ago."

"It's got a roll-up door at one end," added Constanza. "Should make it easier to put supplies in there."

"Sounds good," said Dewey. "May we continue this outside?"

Luc nodded and waved Dewey to proceed. Outside of the clinic, the rest of the platoon was waiting. Dewey noticed that they were in a defensive posture.

"Everything okay out here?" Dewey asked SSgt Castro.

"All clear, Lieutenant Tyler," said Castro. "Just keeping it that way. How's the sick local?"

"Flu. And they don't have immunity against it." Dewey paused and looked around at the town. He'd seen abandoned towns before. Most of the time, they'd been battered by war and fire. This one was different, having been eviscerated by a virus so common that any chem printer in any home could print the immunization and the medicines to minimize the effects.

SSgt Castro must have followed Dewey's eyes as they scanned the empty town. "How many did they lose?"

"Most of them," said Dewey. He pursed his lips and nodded to himself, briefly. "But we can help. First thing, I need you, Sergeant Barrett, and Corporal Fleming's team to go with Jacobo here to inspect the school gym. See if we can use it for a base of operations."

"Will do." SSgt Castro turned to Jacobo. "Which way?"

Jacobo pointed to a street on the other side of the roundabout.

"Sergeant Barrett?" said SSgt Castro. "Shall we?"

Sgt Barrett and Jacobo led the way. In a few minutes, they were gone, and Dewey was down a fireteam and a platoon sergeant.

"Sergeant Parks," said Dewey. "You and Sergeant Maxwell. Take your teams back to the dropships. Tell Lieutenant Owen I'd like everything unloaded and the crawlers prepped."

"You got it, Lieutenant Tyler," Sgt Parks said. Her squad was already forming up for the march back to the dropships.

"Also, let Lieutenant Owen know I'll need one dropship to go topside with a report as soon as I have it done."

Sgt Parks saluted and turned to the two squads waiting to march. "Let's move."

"Corporal Chavez, I haven't forgotten about you," Dewey said. "I need your fireteam to make sure the area remains clear. I need to find a place to sit and work on a report."

"I know just the place," said Luc as Cpl Chavez saluted her response to the orders given. "There was a restaurant that is now the cafeteria. Plenty of seats."

"That should work. And then maybe you can also give me a quick briefing on what's been happening since the invaders arrived."

For the next hour, Dewey learned that the invaders had arrived once before. They'd come in a smaller ship with only a handful of crew. That had been north of the old city. Luc's people didn't learn about this first visit until after the larger contingent arrived several years later.

The invaders had come in half a dozen ships, larger than the Hospitaller dropships, disgorging several hundred armed men and several tens of laborers and engineers. The soldiers had kept the curious among the Juracanians away from the old city as the invaders built the base anchor for the space elevator.

Construction of the elevator seemed to have been stalled as many invaders became ill with radiation poisoning. Radiation blockers, like Dewey and his platoon had used, weren't cheap, but they were effective. Only someone who put profit over employees would scrimp on something so important on a planet like Juracan. So the elevator construction came to a stumbling halt.

Then, a day came when the town was visited by a platoon of masked and armed soldiers. With them came a man in a hazmat suit. He wanted to hire people from Luc's town to come and work for them. Collectively, they agreed to not offer help to the invaders. The presence of the armed soldiers and the man in the suit wasn't wanted, and they should just go away. With the basic radio communication they had on Juracan, the news spread and the agreement with it.

The invaders maintained their guard around the elevator anchor but seemed to go quiet besides that.

Then people started to get sick. And then people began to die. Like a scythe through a field of grain, the sickness wiped out large swaths of the population. Some towns fared better. Others fared worse and ceased to exist.

Around the same time, the invaders returned, this time with trucks and weapons pointed. This time they didn't ask. They rounded up those who were young enough and healthy enough for hard labor. Some resisted, some died resisting. Others went. Most had yet to return.

Every once in a while, someone would make it back to town or pass through, hoping to reach their home. Often, like Bennie, they were ill. In the first years, no one understood the source of the illness. These travelers were looked after, resulting in a new outbreak. From those who'd managed to escape, Luc and the others learned that most of those who had been taken away were dead. Dangerous work conditions and the illness chewed through the population of forced labor.

It was just over ten years, now, that the elevator had been in existence. The invaders had been observed tearing down the old city, smelting the metals, crushing the rock and crete, and shipping it all up to the spaceport on the other end of the elevator cables. And every six months or so, the invaders would come through scrounging for laborers. They rarely found them as those who seemed likely candidates for forced labor either went into hiding just before the invaders arrived, or they disappeared before anyone knew why or even where.

These days, Dewey learned, the invaders drove past Puchuncavi on the way to towns that still had populations to draw from.

"Well, I can tell you that all of this is illegal." Dewey signed off on the report and sealed it with a code that Maj Hughes had and could use to unlock the report. "What's happened here is even beyond the actions of most of the Dark Worlds' more corrupt systems."

Luc exchanged a glance with Maria that, in Dewey's opinion, shone with hope.

"You mean you can do something to help us?" Luc asked.

"Yes," said Dewey. Movement off to his side distracted him. SSgt Castro was outside the cafeteria. "I need to send my report to my CO. He'll make calls. If the other governing systems don't want to help, we will. That's part of our mission."

As the conversation paused, Dewey waved for SSgt Castro to approach.

"Good sized gym," Castro said after she saluted. "Showers work, but we'll need to figure out how to get the boiler operational. Room for most of the supplies, but I imagine we'll distribute a lot of it pretty quickly."

Dewey turned to Luc. "How far away are the towns nearest to Puchuncavi?"

"Well, Romeral is about a two-hour walk west of here. About the same time north takes you to the city. South, three hours walking, is Corral. Towards the ocean, two hours, Puerto Chile and Puerto Argentina."

"So, we'll have the supplies with us for a while," said Dewey. "Maybe we can disperse some to the other towns in a couple of days."

"What we can't fit inside the gym, we can leave on the crawlers and bolt down," SSgt Castro said.

Dewey stood, tapping his tablet to close the files he'd be sending up to Maj Hughes. "I don't think we need to worry about thieves, Staff Sergeant. Let's get back to the crawlers so I can push my reports over to the dropship returning topside."

He left Sgt Barrett and Cpl Fleming with his fireteam in the town. SSgt Castro had informed him that the children, though still being kept away, were becoming bolder. She'd even been waved at a few times. Before leaving for the walk back to the field and the dropships, Dewey had Cpl Chavez's team pass over their T-n-T bags, just in case the children grew bolder still.

They moved faster, returning to the dropships in half the time it took to reach Puchuncavi. All of the crawlers were out from the lower holds. The supplies that had been on the upper deck with the Hospitallers and those stuffed around the crawlers in the lower hold had been unloaded. Most of it was already on the crawlers, too. Cpl Chavez's fireteam hurried to help, not wanting to be left out of one more thing.

"Sergeant Parks," Dewey said as the squad leader approached with a salute. "Did you bring out the extra T-n-T crates, too? The children in Puchuncavi seem eager to make our acquaintance. We wouldn't want to disappoint them."

Parks laughed. "Oh, yes, Lieutenant, we're making sure to load those last. They'll be easy to access if needed."

"Good. Give an update to Staff Sergeant Castro. I need to speak to Lieutenant Owen."

"Will do. Lieutenant Owen is in Lieutenant Haynes's dropship." She pointed to the middle craft.

While Sgt Parks caught SSgt Castro up on the status of the supplies and crawlers, Dewey made his way to the second dropship. The four lieutenants that piloted the other two dropships were gathered near the access hatch to the pilot's cabin. They had several tablets open and were studying the screens.

"Anyone bored?" Dewey asked.

Lt Owen looked up and grinned. "You know us pilots. If we aren't flying, we're dying to be flying."

"I have just the thing." Dewey waved his own tablet. "But you'll have to draw straws or something. I need one of you to take my reports to Major Hughes since we can't beam a message up."

Though they were all lieutenants, Owen outranked the others based on time served in rank. He was also the flight XO.

"Oh, I'd like to pull rank on this," said Lt Owen. He had a wistful smile on his face. What he'd said had been true. Dewey's orphanage friends who'd gone on to flight school were never the same afterward. "But Lieutenant Haynes needs more flight time, especially atmo to space."

Lt Haynes looked excited and nervous at the same time. This was more than just flight time. She wouldn't be flying as part of a flight. She'd be solo for this mission.

"Okay, Haynes," said Dewey. He tapped his tablet and then executed several commands before sliding his fingers across the screen in Lt Haynes's direction. "I need those taken to Major Hughes."

"You got it, Tyler." Lt Haynes was on her feet. "Come on, Hall, let's find Sergeant Simon and prep for takeoff."

Second Lieutenant Cynthia Hall jumped up and followed Lt Haynes, who was already on the ramp and scanning for Sgt Vincent Simon, their loadmaster.

"You want us to remain here?" Lt Owen asked.

"You can," said Dewey. "Or you can come to town. There's plenty of room. And lots of kids."

"Kids? Well, that settles that." Owen was now on his feet. "Lieutenant Haynes, secure your ship. Let's get ready to march."

A half-hour later and the two dropships staying behind had been locked down and coded for reentry. At least Lt Owen and Lt Gray wouldn't have to risk their hands to an acidic environment to access the ships when they needed to enter. This wasn't Wenshen.

The crawlers were already on the road when the engines on Lt Haynes's ship roared with the eagerness to take off. Dewey and the other officers joined the caravan of crawlers. They'd put enough distance between them and the field that they wouldn't be abused by the debris hurled about during lift.

Lt Owen tapped his comm and said, "Okay, Haynes, you can go."

Dewey wasn't on the comm, so he didn't hear Lt Haynes's reply. However, just as Lt Owen nodded and tapped his comm, the dropship roared louder and lifted from the field. The caravan paused as most of the Hospitallers turned to watch the dropship climb higher and begin to come around for its departure angle.

"Lieutenant Tyler?"

Dewey turned. Sgt Maxwell was pointing into the sky, but not in the direction of the dropship. Dewey followed her pointing finger. As soon as his eyes registered what Sgt Maxwell was pointing at, he hit the comm.

"Lieutenant Haynes, you have an incoming missile."

05

As Dewey and the rest of the Hospitallers watched, the missile burned its way across the sky towards the dropship. It seemed that Lt Haynes was unaware of what was approaching. Dewey reached for the comm, intending to call the dropship again when it spat out countermeasures before banking hard to port.

"Too early." Lt Owen had joined Dewey. His voice was a frustrated whisper.

The dropship made a second hard bank to starboard, coming around one-hundred-eighty degrees. Still behind it, the missile drew closer. The countermeasures had dropped from the scene seconds before the missile passed through where they'd been. "Does she have more countermeasures?"

"No," said Lt Owen. "She dumped them all at once. Not uncommon for someone who's never been in a situation like this."

"Nothing we can do?" asked Sgt Maxwell. She sounded as frustrated as Dewey felt. There was nothing quite as painful as watching something terrible about to happen while knowing he could do nothing about it.

"Not us," Lt Owen said. "But Haynes has a few tricks up her sleeve. If she remembers them."

In the sky, Lt Haynes's dropship had begun to climb. The climb took a lot of energy, and there was a perceptible slowing of the ship's speed. Behind it, the missile climbed after the dropship, drawing closer with the benefit of less weight to push.

"Bad move?" asked Dewey. It seemed like it from where he stood.

"Again, too soon," said Lt Owen. "But I think she's figured it out."

The dropship banked once more and then pushed its nose toward the ground. Below it, the missile corrected its own trajectory. Dewey now understood. If Lt Haynes had waited a couple more seconds, the missile wouldn't have corrected in time and would have over-shot the dropship. But she hadn't, and the missile struck.

The explosion from contact rocked the dropship.

"Yes!" Lt Owen clapped his hands together and high-fived Dewey, who didn't understand the elation. "It was a glancing blow on the side rather than a direct hit."

"They've lost an engine," said SSgt Castro from behind them.

Dewey nodded in agreement. He could see the trail of smoke stringing out behind the dropship as it spiraled in long loops groundward.

"Yeah, I see that." Lt Owen seemed less elated now. "We practice this kind of thing all the time in sims. If no one in the cabin is injured, she should be able to control the landing."

What Dewey wondered now was where the dropship would land. It had already been kilometers away when the attack occurred. Would Lt Haynes attempt to return to the fields where they were standing? Would she be able to control where she put the ship down? It would make things even worse if they dropped their ship on top of the other two still on the ground.

In the sky, the dropship was closing with the surface. It was also clear that it would not be landing anywhere near where the Hospitallers watched or where the other dropships waited.

Dewey lost sight of the dropship just before it made a hard landing.

"Someone mark that direction," said Dewey. He tapped his comm. "Lieutenant Haynes? Do you copy?"

Lt Haynes did not respond. Dewey attempted a comm connection with 2nd Lt Hall. When that failed, he tried for Sgt Simon.

"Comms could have been damaged in the crash," said Lt Owen.

"Either way," Dewey said, "we're going to have to go after them."

"I'd like to go with you."

"No problem, Owen," said Dewey. He turned to Lt Gray, who'd

been watching the attack from several meters away. "Gray. I need you and Staff Sergeant Castro to accompany the crawlers back to Puchuncavi."

Lt Gray nodded. He moved to join SSgt Castro, who had started back toward the crawlers.

"Sergeant Maxwell, your squad's with me."

"You got it, Lieutenant Tyler," said Sgt Maxwell. She turned and signaled to her squad to move.

"Castro, Gray, we'll contact you as soon as we reach the dropship."

"We'll be ready if you need us," said Castro. Lt Gray echoed the sentiment with a sharp nod.

Dewey turned his attention back to Sgt Maxwell. "You know the direction?"

"Got it, Lieutenant."

"Take us there."

Sgt Maxwell turned to her squad. "Corporal Wong. Your team in front. Let's move."

Cpl Lena Wong waved her fireteam forward even as she jogged into position. "Russell, on point."

Pvt Russell took the point position and began a quick march across the field. The rest of the fireteam followed after she'd taken a ten-meter lead.

"Okay, Owen," Dewey said as he followed Cpl Wong's fireteam. "Let's go find them."

It took them just under two hours to reach the dropship. They'd been forced into several detours. One had been a deep, steep-banked creek. The other had been the remains of a factory of some sort, long ago destroyed, long ago abandoned.

Dewey was ready to find the ship a broken hulk on the ground. He was even ready to find the crew dead. It was a sorry way to start off a new mission. There was little comfort in the knowledge that it wasn't the worst start.

What Dewey wasn't ready for was what they actually encountered.

The ship was nose down in the dirt. A tree lay across the top, the bright white of snapped and exposed wood a stark contrast to the ship's weathered hull. The back hatch had been opened and held in place by several braces from inside the loading bay. The crew was outside the ship. They were not alone.

With Lt Haynes and her crew were twenty or so civilians. Some of them were children. The children were playing with toys from T-n-T bags. The crew and civilians were sitting on the ground, talking. It also looked like the crew was sharing food from several emergency ration packs with the civilians.

Sgt Simon was the first to look in the direction of the approaching Hospitallers. He leaned past an elder civilian and tapped Lt Haynes on the knee. Haynes looked up and smiled. As she stood, the civilians joined her. The children, clued by the motion that something else was happening, looked toward the approaching Hospitallers.

The children shouted a high-pitched shout of joy, waving their toys in the air.

"Lieutenant Tyler," said Lt Haynes. They shook hands, then Haynes repeated the action with Lt Owen.

"Good save, Haynes," said Lt Owen.

"It also looks like you didn't need a rescue after all," said Dewey.

Lt Haynes looked over her shoulder at the civilians. Turning back to Dewey, she said, "They appeared shortly after we managed to get out of the dropship. They said they'd gotten a call from someone called Jacobo. He'd told them we were friendly and might need help."

Several of the civilians had slowly approached during the conversation.

"Thank you for saving our people," Dewey said to the civilians, and a wink to Lt Haynes to let the lieutenant know it was all in jest.

One of the civilians laughed. "They as sure didn't need any help from us. Except when maybe the kids saw they had toys."

"It was a dangerous moment," agreed Lt Haynes with a follow-up chuckle. "Fortunately, there was plenty to go around."

"Well, we appreciate you looking after them until we got here."

Dewey offered his hand. "Lieutenant Dewey Tyler, Hospitallers."

"Horacio Tercero, Romerol town council."

"Word gets around?" asked Dewey. He also noticed that he was the focus of several children. He reached for his T-n-T bag, only to discover he didn't have one. Looking around, he caught Sgt Maxwell's attention and pointed at the children. He signaled to her that he was out of ammo.

"Not much, actually," Horacio said as Sgt Maxwell approached, waving several pieces of hard candy that attracted the children's attention. "We don't normally communicate over the air with each other. Tends to draw the attention of the invaders. If it's not urgent, we'll send someone on a bike."

Dewey nodded as he watched the children being guided away by a sweets-wielding staff sergeant. "If they fired a rocket, are they going to follow up with a ground sweep?"

"Can't say. We've never had anyone else but the invaders come in from off-planet."

"Right, good point," said Dewey. He paused and looked around. The children were running around with several toys, their lips stained with candy color. The Hospitallers were amusing the children while still keeping eyes on the surroundings. It was also getting dark. If they left now, they might be able to reach Puchuncavi an hour or so after sunset. That might or might not be a dangerous thing.

"Lieutenant Owen," Dewey said. "How's the dropship team look? Any life-threatening injuries?"

Lt Owen had a child on his shoulders as he galloped several meters to reach Dewey. "Scratches, bruises, and some busted pride. Nothing more."

"Good. I don't think we'll be leaving here tonight. Any chance we can right the dropship, so we have shelter for the evening?"

"No need for that, Lieutenant Tyler," said Horacio. "We've a lot of vacant homes. You're more than welcome to make use of several of them."

"We'd also like you to join us for dinner," said another elder civilian.

"This is Rebeca Chapa," Horacio said. "She's on the council, too."

"I'm under the impression that supplies are tight at the moment."

"At the moment, Lieutenant?" asked Rebeca. She shook her head, a tight smile on her face. "They've been a problem for years now, and getting worse since we lack able bodies to do most of the fieldwork."

"There are lots of machines to do the heavy lifting these days," said Sgt Maxwell. She had wandered over with a child of three or four years of age in her arms. The child was clutching a plastic rocket and a floppy-limbed lion.

"Not on this planet," said Horacio. The child had reached out for him, and he was now accepting the transfer.

"I'm sorry," Sgt Maxwell said. "I meant that it's likely possible that we could get those to you. Right, Lieutenant Tyler?"

"Absolutely," Dewey said. "Once we can get off the planet without getting shot at."

"You could talk to the invaders about that," said Horacio. He had a mischievous grin on his face, clearly aware of how easily that task would be accomplished.

"That we'll worry about tomorrow," he said. "For now, we gladly accept the offer of quarters for the evening."

"And the meal," said Rebeca. Her voice made it clear that it wasn't a suggestion and was no longer just an offer.

"And the meal," Dewey said. "Sergeant Maxwell, let's get everyone rounded up. I'm taking you all out for dinner."

Sgt Maxwell laughed. "Your generosity exceeds your rank, Lieutenant Tyler." She then turned and cupped her hands over her mouth. "Hospitallers! Form up!"

"Lieutenant Owen," said Dewey as the Hospitallers converged on Sgt Maxwell and formed a line facing her. "If it's possible to button up the dropship, I'd like to see that taken care of."

"Shouldn't be a problem," said Lt Owen. "Getting back in again might be another issue."

"At least we'll know where to find it."

"Right." Lt Owen waved at Lt Haynes, catching her attention.

"Give us twenty, Tyler, and we should be ready to march."

"Maybe we can leave a few civilians as guides?" Dewey asked Horacio and Rebeca. "And the rest of us can proceed to town?"

"We can do that," said Horacio. "I'll take care of that now."

"And I'll show you the way to town," said Rebeca.

Dewey turned to Sgt Maxwell. She now had a line of Hospitallers and, right in front of them, a line of giggling children making a poor showing of being serious. "Maxwell. Let's move out."

Romerol wasn't much different from Puchuncavi. The homes on the edges of the town were boarded up. Some, Dewey noticed, had suffered fire damage. Most of the occupants seemed to have retreated to the homes and businesses close to the town center. There wasn't a large roundabout like the one in Puchuncavi. It was smaller, with a single tree. On the outside, though, there were two parks on opposite quarters of the circle. The other two quarters were the town hall, shops, and a primary school.

Just behind the southern park was a large home that looked older than the rest of the town. It was here that Rebeca and the others led the Hospitallers.

"Family that lived here, the Patinos," said Rebeca, "they moved east before the invaders appeared. We'd thought we'd use it for a museum or a hotel."

Dewey nodded and said, "But then the invaders came."

Rebeca nodded. "Yep. Then they came, and the world changed. So, plenty of room. The Patinos left most of the furniture. And it's in good shape, the building. They'd been the founders of the town a good two hundred years or so ago."

The inside of the home did have furniture. Despite that presence of furniture, it still felt abandoned. Sgt Maxwell's squad quickly organized the rooms and set out eyes and hands to help monitor the exterior for movement. Maxwell then set up two duty rotations between the fireteams.

"We can go with short shifts so that everyone can have a chance to eat," Sgt Maxwell explained.

"That reminds me," Dewey said. He tapped his comm. There was a little more static with the increased distance, but he was able to connect with MedTech Chambers. "Is it going to be hazardous to eat the local cuisine?"

"I was asked the same thing here about a half-hour ago," said MedTech Chambers. "I've scanned the food and the raw ingredients. The rads are higher than what we'd call normal, but with the blockers in your system, you'll be fine. We may want to consider a regular booster, depending on how long we're here. And I don't think we should be here any longer than necessary."

The question Dewey asked himself after thanking Chambers was, how long was necessary going to be? They had two dropships left. Granted, they could all fit snugly in one if they left the crawlers behind. So that meant, what? They could try to push the other one past whatever air protection system the invaders had?

No, he wasn't willing to take that chance. There was a smarter way to handle the situation. Dewey just needed to understand the situation in more detail. Which meant he needed time. How much time he would get depended on how desperate the invaders were to keep their actions secret.

"Lieutenant Tyler?"

Dewey turned to find PFC Pablo Armstrong in the arched passage between the bare-shelved sitting room and what Dewey knew from reading to be a main or fancy dining room.

"Armstrong? What's up?"

"Company." PFC Armstrong pointed with a thumb over his shoulder. "At the door."

Company turned out to be Lt Owen, Lt Haynes, and the rest of the downed flight crew. They were in the company of Harcio and a younger woman who Dewey didn't recognize. From the look of her, though, she was either a sister or daughter of Rebeca.

"I've come to show you the way to our dining hall," said the young woman.

Horacio laughed and said, "It's nothing fancy. We're using the school cafeteria."

"But we have appropriately sized seating for adults," the other woman added.

Dewey laughed. "I'll gather the troops."

Hours later, Dewey lay on a sheet-covered mattress borrowed from one of the other uninhabited homes. Sgt Maxwell had, with permission, scouted through several boarded homes for a couple more beds, and linens to at least cover the bare mattresses.

The food they'd been served had been plain. The people of Romerol had attempted to make a feast, but Dewey had been adamant that they not waste resources. He could bring them supplies, but that wouldn't be until they could make contact with their ship. The Romerolians had reluctantly, but gratefully, agreed. Despite that, everyone seemed to have enjoyed the company, especially the rest of the town's children.

It was the children that puzzled Dewey. If the invaders had come in the last five years and taken all the able-bodied citizens, there shouldn't be any children younger than five. And yet, Dewey had seen two toddlers who were barely three years of age. He'd inquired several times to different people. Each time, they'd deftly parried the question and drawn his attention to something else.

There was a secret there. A secret Dewey hadn't yet gotten an answer for. And a secret that followed him into sleep.

Sleep did not last long. The sky had lightened with the prospect of dawn when Dewey heard the comm in his helmet buzz for attention. He quickly sat and pulled the helmet on.

"Lieutenant Tyler. Go."

"Sorry to wake you, Tyler," said Lt Gray through the whisper-crackle of the comm. "But, we just had company."

Dewey stood and started for the doorway that would lead to the stairs and then down to the foyer. "What kind of company?"

"From the looks of it? Mercenaries."

06

Dewey yanked open the door to the room. He lost his grip on the knob, and the door banged against the dressing table behind it. The door bounced back, striking against Dewey's heel as he crossed the threshold.

"Mercenaries? You're sure?"

In the hallway, Pvt Wade Pratt stood guard at the top of the open staircase. Dewey signaled for him to rouse the others. Without hesitation, Pvt Pratt banged on the doors where the other officers slept, making his way to the rooms where the rest of Sgt Maxwell's squad were bunked.

"Pretty sure," said Lt Gray. "Once we knew you weren't coming back, Staff Sergeant Castro asked if she could put out some eyes and hands. I thought it wise to not argue with her."

Dewey laughed. "You're wiser than me, Gray. So, how many mercs?"

"Not quite sure," said Lt Gray. "A squad. Might be more, but not much. They were being careful. We had all the officers and NCOs keeping watch through the VR. Everyone was pretty consistent on the numbers they were seeing."

"Okay, so a squad." Dewey stopped by the top of the stairwell. Lt Owen had stepped into the hallway. Behind him, Lt Haynes appeared, rubbing the sleep from her eyes.

"Trouble?" Lt Owen asked.

"Maybe," Dewey said. "Let's get everyone outside and ready to march, ASAP."

Dewey bounded down the stairs as Lt Owen started bellowing reveille and announcing formation in ten.

Outside, Dewey continued his conversation on the comm. "No contact with the mercs, Gray?"

"None," Lt Gray said. "I went out with Sergeant Barrett's squad. But by the time we reached the mercs' furthest point into town, they'd already started pulling back."

"They knew you were there."

"Turns out, yep. We did a scan and found several cams and ground sensors. We disabled them. They know we're here, so we can't hide that fact. But we can make it difficult for them to know what we're up to."

"Good thinking," Dewey said. He was watching as Sgt Parks's squad began to appear outside the house. "Do you still have eyes on them?"

"Affirmative," said Lt Gray. "I left Sergeant Barrett and his squad to shadow them."

"Right. How far did you tell Sergeant Barrett to follow the mercs?"

"They're to remain within town limits," Lt Gray said. "Didn't think it was wise to get drawn out into the open."

"Good decision," said Dewey. "You should also have Staff Sergeant Castro work on securing the town perimeter. The mercs might attempt to penetrate from a different direction."

Lt Gray laughed. "The staff sergeant is already on it."

"Of course she is. All right, Gray. Thanks for the update. We'll be leaving soon. I'm going to ping Sergeant Barrett."

"Understood. See you when you get back." Lt Gray chuckled and then said, cryptically, "The surprises just keep coming."

The comm went silent. Dewey tapped for Sgt Barrett. While he waited for Barrett to respond, Dewey looked around him. The sky was red to the east and still dark with clouds to the west. Most of the Hospitallers had exited the house. Dewey moved away after returning several salutes.

"Lieutenant Tyler?" asked a voice over the comm.

"Sergeant Barrett? How're things?"

"Interesting, Lieutenant," said Sgt Barrett.

"So I've heard. Can you tell me about the mercs?"

"I can tell you lots," Sgt Barrett said. "They've got top-of-the-line gear. They're seasoned. They moved like they've done this enough times that it's second nature."

"Past tense, Barrett?"

"They're gone, Lieutenant. They had an APC waiting for them. One squad and an officer."

"Okay, stay in place," Dewey said. "If nothing changes in the next couple of hours, send some hands forward, post a fireteam, and then pull everyone else back to the center of town."

"Will do."

"See you when we get back." Dewey tapped the comm and ended the conversation.

On the roadway in front of the house, Sgt Maxwell's squad was forming into two lines. Off to the side, the lieutenants, Owen, Haynes, and Hall, kept out of the way. Sgt Simon, Lt Haynes's loadmaster, shadowed Sgt Maxwell. Dewey felt for Simon as he didn't currently have any responsibilities and likely didn't know what to do with himself.

Sgt Maxwell waved Dewey's attention to her and then pointed in the direction opposite the house. Dewey looked in the direction indicated and saw Horacio approaching. He waved at the approaching elder, who waved in return.

"I've been sent by Rebeca," said Horacio as he neared Dewey's position. "I'm to see if we can tempt you with breakfast. We do have some productive chickens in town."

"Thank you, Horacio," Dewey said. "That is very tempting. Unfortunately, the invaders sent a small team to check on us. I need to deal with that as priority."

Horacio's expression turned sour. "Be careful, Lieutenant Tyler. They're cruel."

"Always careful in the face of the enemy," said Lt Owen, who'd joined the conversation. To Dewey, he said, "Something come up?"

"Down, actually. Mercs. They came looking but left before we could properly introduce ourselves."

Horacio laughed. When Dewey looked at him, puzzled, he said. "Not much of an introduction needed. They come into town, say they have orders from their C.O.O., and then start grabbing all the able-bodied people they can find."

"C.O.O.?" That wasn't one Dewey had heard used by a mercenary company before. They typically followed a ranking system used by other military forces.

"Chief Operations Officer, whatever that is, but his name is Ernest Thayer."

"You've met him?" Dewey asked. He was watching his people. Though they stood in formation, they were no longer alone. The children of Romerol had managed to find them and were now working their charm on the Hospitallers, securing more sweets and at least one more toy.

"No, never met him," Horacio said. "But word travels. A few people have seen him. He used to come out with the soldiers. Not anymore. They say he's afraid of our air."

"Radiophobia," Dewey said automatically. He'd read it in a book somewhere, and like everything else, hadn't really forgotten it. "Fear of radiation."

"Seems like the wrong world to come to if you're afraid of radiation," said Lt Owen.

"Credits can often help a person overcome their biggest fears," Dewey said. Turning back to Horacio, he added, "Thank you for helping at the landing site. And for your hospitality. As soon as we can clear a way back to our ship, we'll be sure to get you some supplies."

"If you could get rid of the invaders, that would be thanks enough. Just be careful."

"Thank you, we will." Dewey turned and called to Sgt Maxwell. "Sergeant? Let's move out!"

Departing Romerol was easier said than done. The children, who'd clearly enjoyed the presence of the Hospitallers, were reluctant to let them go. But with the promise of another visit, and a couple more sweets as bribes, the Hospitallers were able to get away. They force marched out of Romerol until they were past the site of the down and busted dropship. Only then did Dewey ease up on the pace.

"How much do you have left?" Dewey heard Cpl Wong ask PFC Marc Webb, one of her fireteam members.

"One piece." PFC Webb held up a single white candy in clear cellophane. "And that's only because the little one hanging on my arm didn't like the other coconut candy I gave him."

"I've three lemon drops," said PFC Juanita Bryant, also in the same fireteam.

"You saved those for yourself," Cpl Wong said.

PFC Bryant's response was to unwrap one of the lemon drops and pop it into her mouth. "I'm a sucker for lemon drops."

"I think the children managed to obtain nearly every piece of candy we had," Lt Owen said from behind Dewey.

Dewey nodded. "When we finally get access to air space, we'll have to have them bring us dental supplements. That or risk being another group of people the Juracanians are unhappy to see on their planet."

The rest of the march back to Puchuncavi was a mixture of silences punctuated by bursts of conversations. The conversations ranged from funny moments in past operations to Lt Haynes's misadventure in the sky.

During the original outward march, Dewey had been too concerned to give the countryside much attention. Now, even though there were the invaders to deal with, he found time to look at the world around him. He couldn't say for certain, but he was sure that the world he was looking at now was much different from the way it was before the nuclear war.

After that war, based on other readings Dewey had done, there would have been a nuclear winter. Those that had survived had supposedly been evacuated from the planet. And yet, there was a thriving population. Correct that, had been a thriving population until the appearance of the invaders.

Those abandoned on Juracan must have had some technology or

access to it to keep them going. The going had to have been hard. There should have been a spike in cancers, stillbirths, and birth defects, not to mention abbreviated lifespans. They'd managed to survive despite all that. They'd also seemed to have adapted to the changes in their world, considering their skin and the ages of at least Horacio and Luc.

So, before the invaders appeared, there'd likely been millions on the planet. Millions spread out over millions of square kilometers of land, banded together in small towns, a long way from the bustling, prosperous planet that was part of the first expansion.

Dewey wished he could have seen images of that world before they pummeled it with nuclear weapons. Were the greens of the grass and leaves greener than they were now? Or were they always this yellowish-green? Was there still wildlife? How had it fared? There were so many questions that Dewey would have liked to see answered. But he was only here to find answers to a different subset of questions. Who were the invaders? Why were they here? Why had they taken the locals as slave labor?

He was pretty sure he already had the answer to the second question. The licensing and fees to operate mining interests on worlds were astronomical compared to asteroid mining. Finding a viable world to mine without being noticed was near to impossible. Finding one with the metals already separated from the ore and just begging to be taken off world was a one-in-a-billion chance. Add to that the world being lost and not on anyone's radar, and Juracan must have seemed the greatest gift the universe could bestow upon an organization willing to skirt the laws.

The answer to the third question was likely connected to the second. If someone was willing to skirt the laws to avoid the fees and licensing, it probably wasn't much further of a step to employ forced labor. And while that much of an answer was plenty enough, Dewey wondered if there might be more to it than just greed. Most mining work was done with autonomous machinery, which, while initially costly, worked around the clock and for decades without tiring or falling ill or dying of diseases.

Dewey would have pondered the thoughts and problems further, but he was suddenly aware of a rare but familiar aroma. He turned to look at Lt Owen.

Owen, who was already looking at Dewey, asked the question. "Is that coffee I smell?"

Dewey nodded and then noticed that he and Lt Owen weren't the only ones who'd identified the aroma. Sgt Maxwell's squad was chattering amongst themselves while simultaneously sniffing the air.

"From where?" Dewey asked himself. He checked the treetops for a breeze. The direction was a surprise. "From Puchuncavi? Sgt Maxwell, where do you think the scent is coming from?"

"Straight ahead, Lieutenant." Sgt Maxwell laughed and then looked serious. "That'd be an elaborate ambush lure."

"We would have heard from Gray or Staff Sergeant Castro if something had happened."

"Agreed," Dewey said in response to Lt Owen's observation. "Still…"

Dewey signaled for the squad to split up and leave the road. He sent Lieutenants Owen and Haynes with Sgt Maxwell and Cpl Wong's fireteam. He signaled for 2nd Lt Hall and Sgt Simon to join him and Cpl Lopez's fireteam.

Both fireteam leaders put a person on point and slowed their pace for the final kilometer into Puchuncavi. As they entered the town, Dewey's concerns were erased by the appearance of PFC Don Horton.

PFC Horton saluted when he saw Dewey and the other lieutenants. "Glad to see you back, Lieutenant Tyler."

"Everything okay here?" asked Dewey after returning the salute.

"So far," PFC Horton said. "I'm assuming you know about the mercs that came snooping."

"We do, thank you."

"You smell anything funny, PFC?" asked Lt Owen.

Horton seemed confused at first, but then he nodded and chuckled. "Right, that, Lieutenant. We've been given strict orders not to ruin the surprise. But I can tell you that it's coming from our base at the school."

"Smells like coffee," Lt Owen said. He was watching PFC Horton closely.

"It does, doesn't it, Lieutenant?" Then Horton pinched a finger and thumb together, zipping them across his mouth. He wasn't going to say anything more.

Dewey laughed before giving orders for the squad to form up. The lieutenants and sergeants formed a loose gaggle to one side. When Dewey nodded to Sgt Maxwell, she started her squad in motion toward the old school and whatever surprises it might contain.

Dewey wasn't sure what to expect when they came around the back of the school. They'd crossed paths with several other members of the platoon who were patrolling the empty streets. None of them surrendered the secret that they were directed to keep. They all smiled and shook their heads before suggesting that Lt Gray might have the answer.

"I'm absolutely certain that Gray didn't have possession of coffee beans on the Graevya," said Lt Owen.

A shrug was all that Dewey could offer. There were plenty of smells that could be mistaken for others. Coffee, though, was distinct, especially to soldiers.

When they came around the corner of one of the classroom buildings, they had their answer. It wasn't an answer Dewey would have considered. Yet, here it was.

Several two-hundred-liter barrels were being rotated over pit fires in the open space between the gym where they had set up base, and the nearest classrooms. That was surprising enough. But then Dewey saw Lt Gray and his cargomaster, Sgt Christy George, directing several other Hospitallers and locals as they worked to keep the barrels moving.

Dewey signaled for everyone to stay back as he approached.

"Lieutenant Gray?"

Everyone working with and around the rotating barrels jumped. The Hospitallers snapped to attention only to be chastised by Lt Gray.

"What are you doing? They'll burn! Keep turning, keep turning."

The Hospitallers, Pvt Foster, Pvt Becker, and Pvt Wells, looked at Dewey, clearly unsure what to do.

"You heard Lieutenant Gray," said Dewey. "Don't burn the beans."

"Yes, Lieutenant," they all said as one before turning back to the barrels, putting them in motion once more.

Dewey turned from watching the barrels to the approaching Lt Gray. "Is this going to be a good story?" Dewey asked.

"They're growing like weeds all over the place," Lt Gray said. He had a blissfully happy look on his face. "It's not even the right elevation or weather, but there they are."

Dewey signaled for the others to come in. The two fireteams moved in from around the school building, joining the other Hospitallers already present.

"Where?"

"Everywhere, Tyler," said Lt Gray. "Like weeds. In fact, that's what they treat them like. They clear it to put in grain and bean crops. They were showing us their few active fields. I thought maybe we could lend a hand. They just waved and said, 'We have to clear all these weeds to get in a good planting.' Weeds! Can you just imagine? The Grand Mother at Dreux would have been mortally offended.

Dewey nodded. Now, it was clear about Lt Gray's attitude and his suddenly revealed skill of roasting coffee. Dreux was the orphanage on Wiraqoca. Wiraqoca was a mountain-pocked planet that was well known for its varieties of rice and its coffees. Dreux was also one of the few orphanages where Insta wasn't the preferred beverage.

"And they didn't know what they had," Dewey said.

"No!" Lt Gray threw his hands skyward in exasperation.

A thought occurred to Dewey. It was a natural thought considering where they were. "Is this going to be safe to drink? What with the rad levels and all?"

Lt Gray laughed as he stepped away to grab a small branch with leaves on it. "Are you ready for this? The rad levels in the beans are normal. Our normal. Off-world normal. The leaves, though? Don't put them in a salad. Not that you would anyway."

Dewey found that to be very interesting. The coffee bean plants were growing in non-traditional areas. That could be a condition of adapting to the world's elevated radiation levels. And it made sense that the leaves took up most of the radiation in the soil. But for the beans to be at acceptable rad levels or lower? That was some serious adaptation.

"Hey, Gray," said Lt Owen as he approached. "Where'd you get the beans?"

"Everywhere!" came the chorale response from the Hospitallers and civilians manning the turning barrels. They broke into laughter at their own action, followed by Lt Gray.

"I take it they've heard you say that a few times?"

"Indeed, Owen, indeed."

"And when will the beans be ready?"

"Soon," said Lt Gray. "In fact, I need to pull another sample right now."

"All right," Dewey said. "We'll leave you to it, then."

"Hang on," said Lt Owen. "How do you plan to grind the beans when it's time?"

"Old fashioned way." Lt Gray grinned and then added, "With mortar and pestle."

07

"Got to admit," said Luciano, "this tastes weird."

The rest of the elders of Puchuncavi nodded in agreement. The Hospitallers laughed. All except Lt Gray, who seemed wounded by the response. What he might have failed to notice, but was clear to Dewey, was that the elders kept sipping the freshly roasted and brewed coffee despite the claimed weird taste.

Dewey, Lt Owen, and the rest of the team who'd been in Romerol had taken some time to refresh themselves. At the same time, SSgt Castro and Lt James caught Dewey up with the information they had on the mercs. They'd not only been well-armed, the equipment they carried was top of the line for what mercs could lay their hands on. In none of the images they pulled from the eyes SSgt Castro had laid out could they see any badges or other indicators of the mercenaries' origin.

By the time Dewey had been fully briefed, news had come back that Lt Gray's roasted beans had been ground and were now in several large pots in the former restaurant turned communal cafeteria. There weren't any percolators and definitely no presses. This was going to be coffee the old school way.

Lt Gray had beamed with pride as he and his cargomaster had ladled out cups of steaming, dark brew. Dewey had been surprised by how good the coffee tasted. He was pretty sure the rest of the Hospitallers agreed. That was probably the reason why they'd all laughed when Luciano had pronounced his verdict.

"Would you like another cup?" Dewey asked Luciano as the laughter died off.

Luciano had looked into his cup and found it empty. He smiled and held it out to Dewey. "Oh, definitely."

The laughter had then been twice as loud. But this time, Lt Gray was once more beaming with pride.

After the initial exposure to the newly rediscovered brew had waned, Dewey was able to bring everyone back around to the current issue. That issue was not, as Lt Gray had surmised, how to harvest and roast the beans quicker.

"None of you have ever been to the city?" Dewey asked. Next to him, SSgt Castro was listening, her hands cupped around her coffee.

"Been to the edge," said Jacobo. "I was younger then. Never had a reason to go since then."

"I've been there," Constanza said. Dewey noticed she seemed a little jittery. Probably three cups of coffee for their first time was a bad idea. "Couple years back. I was – "

Her words were buried by a mutual coughing fit between Luciano and Valentine. Constanza looked surprised but quickly recovered.

"Well, I was there," she continued. "It's an ugly place."

"You plan on going there?" asked Luc. Dewey noticed that Luc's hands were definitely shaking.

"I'd like to get a look at the elevator," Dewey said. His own cup was half full. He resisted taking another sip. "Hopefully, some of the city buildings can provide a nice scouting post."

"If they don't fall down on our heads," said SSgt Castro.

"Buildings should be all right," Valentine interjected. "They've been standing for centuries."

"Lieutenant Tyler? You have maps of the city?"

"I do, Staff Sergeant," Dewey said. "But they don't have known dates. So they could be from early in the city's construction or nearer to when the war started. Does anyone know the status of the bridges?"

The city of Atacama straddled a river of the same name. From there, the city expanded outward in a series of rings. According to Dewey's maps, each ring crossed the river twice and had bridges at both points. That was, except for the center of the city, where there was a single bridge that connected a road bisecting all of the ring roads, perpendicular to the river.

Constanza looked at Luciano and Valentine. When they remained motionless, she shrugged and said, "It's been a while, and I don't remember where exactly I was. But I think the one at the center of the city is still there. I think I recall seeing another bridge, upriver, that was still intact. But I can't say for absolute certainty."

"What about going around the city?" Lt Owen asked. "If all the bridges are down?"

"Could, I guess," said Constanza. Again, she shot a furtive look at Luciano before continuing. "But it would add hours to a journey."

"If we had comm, we could request a bridge truck be sent down," said SSgt Castro.

"Could," agreed Dewey. "If we had comm."

At other tables nearby, Sgt Maxwell's squad was leaving for guard duty. In a few moments, Sgt Parks and her squad would be arriving for lunch and some of the coffee they'd likely been looking forward to. Based on how the civilians were acting, Dewey was considering having Lt Gray limit the quantity of coffee Parks' team drank. He needed them well rested for the morning.

"The person to ask would be Bennie," said Luciano. "He's been there most recently."

"Good luck getting past MedTech Chambers," SSgt Castro said.

Dewey nodded in agreement.

"Same for Ivan," said Valentine.

The other civilians concurred.

"Well, maybe we can approach that problem in the morning." Dewey waved away Sgt Simon, who'd been approaching with a small cooking pot of coffee. Luciano and the other civilians looked to him as if they'd already taken in too much caffeine. Instead, Dewey stood, stepping over the bench as he said, "As for now, I need to do some planning and check on the perimeter. I'll see all of you in the morning. If you're awake."

It had been Dewey's thought that the elders would have stayed up late from the excessive caffeine and then slept in late the next morning. However, in the pink light of sunrise, he found Luciano and Constanza had come out to see him and Sgt Parks's squad off.

"Oh, we were up late, all right," said Luciano after Dewey expressed his surprise. "But the children weren't."

"And the children must be tended to," added Constanza. She punctuated her comment with a long yawn that infected several of the Hospitallers who'd been watching the interaction.

"Is this the side-effect of the coffee that SSgt Castro told us about?"

Dewey looked around and located SSgt Castro in conversation with Sgt Parks. Castro was remaining behind with the flight crews and the other two squads. Based on previous experience in similar situations, Dewey knew SSgt Castro had told Sgt Parks to keep an eye on him. As if he had less combat experience than Castro.

He turned back to the elders. "The body adapts to the caffeine in the coffee over time," he said. "If you drink it regularly."

"That so? Well, until then, any chance there's more? I could use a little boost of the energy I had last night."

Luciano's comment raised a chuckle in Dewey. He and Parks's squad had already eaten a breakfast of ration bars, enhanced by Lt Gray's coffee. Lt Gray had been up several hours before the other Hospitallers, grinding the beans and prepping the water in the school's cafeteria kitchen.

"You'll find Lt Gray inside," said Dewey. He pointed toward the open doors. "I'm sure he'll have plenty of coffee to help your day improve."

The good humor on Luciano's and Constanza's faces faded for a moment. Luciano offered a hand. "Good luck out there."

Dewey accepted the handshake. He hadn't yet put on his tactical gloves, so he felt the hard, fractured skin of Luciano's hand as they shook. On Wenshen, the people had been forced to adapt to the acidic atmosphere. Part of that adaptation resulted in reddish skin tones and eye vision that put twenty-twenty eyesight to complete shame.

After noticing the Juracanian people's skin, Dewey had spent random moments wondering in what other ways they'd adapted to their radioactive world. Besides their skin, the only other thing seemed to be longevity, but he'd only been on planet for little more than two days.

"Are you going to talk to Bennie before you go?" asked Constanza as Luciano stepped back.

"Did," said Dewey. "Briefly. It's early, and he was a bit groggy. Seems the best bet is to just stay on the main road. It's broken and uneven, but the bridge is supposedly safe to cross. It'll take us straight through the city, and we'll have the elevator line to guide us as we get closer."

The space elevator cable was visible from Puchuncavi, but only if the sun's light was at a specific angle. With his visor down and its magnification dialed up, Dewey had been able to identify it. Once on the other side of the river, the cable should be visible without enhanced viewing.

"All right, then," Luciano said.

Dewey noticed that the elder man's eyes kept flitting past Dewey toward the doors leading to the cafeteria. He held back a laugh as he said, "Right, then. We'll be leaving in a few minutes. You can check in with SSgt Castro if you would like an update. I'll let her know you'll ask. Just in case."

"Thank you," said Constanza.

Luciano had already given a wave-salute and was meters ahead of Constanza. She shook her head and chased after him.

"Already addicted?"

Dewey turned to an approaching SSgt Castro. He nodded and said, "Yes, Staff Sergeant, it would seem so. But, I would imagine it is more appreciated than the flu."

"I appreciate it." She grinned when Dewey looked her way. "Not saying I don't appreciate Insta. Just that of the two, I'll still go with coffee if available."

"Good to know. Sergeant Parks ready to roll?"

"Ready and eager," SSgt Castro said. "Now, you sure you just want the one squad? You could take two. We'd still be okay here. We have the dropship crews to draw on."

"I'd take everyone, but I don't want to make the mercs nervous." He paused. "Well, more nervous."

"They did shoot down one of our dropships."

Dewey agreed. "But we don't know that it wasn't an automatic system. And if it was intentional, we don't know why. They can't be ignorant to the fact they are doing something illegal. And they likely didn't know who we were until they came calling."

"You mean that maybe they thought we were competitors?"

"Something like that, Castro. And if we go in guns blazing, we learn nothing."

"Fair enough."

"Thank you," said Dewey. "Now, if the civilians ask for updates, you have my permission to share, using your discretion. Is there anything else?"

SSgt Castro pointed at herself. "From me? No, I'm good, Lieutenant. Be safe."

Dewey returned the salute she offered and then walked over to where Sgt Parks and her squad waited. They were formed up on a black crete-like surface. The lines for different sports were still clearly visible. It reminded Dewey of his days in the orphanage. They'd played all sorts of games. Some of them were obscure. Others were played on school grounds across the second radial arm of the galaxy. Few didn't involve teamwork.

From their earliest years, they'd been steered toward teamwork and relying on each other. Dewey had met officers from other forces that admitted admiration for the level of dedication the Hospitallers had for teamwork, and how well they worked together in difficult situations. It was understandable to Dewey, being an everyday part of their lives since they could all remember. It was what kept most of them alive in dangerous situations.

Situations like now.

"Ready to roll, Sergeant Parks?"

Sgt Parks saluted. "Ready, Lieutenant Tyler."

"Put point at fifty meters until we're a few kliks from the city.

Back them to twenty after that. Rotate frequently. We've a long way to go, and I don't want anyone losing focus because they're bored."

"You got it, Lieutenant." Parks turned to her squad. "PFC Arnold, you got point. Fifty meters. Comm me when you're out. Everyone else. Right face."

As PFC Nora Arnold jogged ahead to create the fifty-meter gap, the rest of the squad made a right face move. They were now facing the back of the person who'd been standing to their right.

"Forward march," Sgt Parks called.

The squad began marching. Sgt Parks and Dewey marched to the side of the squad. They maintained the formation order until they reached the edge of town. PFC Arnold had commed her distance shortly before.

"Parks? Let's spread them out for patrol."

"Both sides of the road, Lieutenant?"

The road here was fairly smooth and made of a material similar to the playground at the school. The shoulders of the road were choked with bushes and tall grass. They'd make for great cover, but they'd also hide a waiting enemy.

"Let's do that," said Dewey. "I'll take the right side if you don't mind?"

"Of course," said Sgt Parks. She called Cpl Mitchell and Cpl Garner by name and then signaled for them to take to the sides of the road.

Without further guidance, the squad separated by fireteams and then spread out so that they weren't walking too close to each other. Pvt Becker took up a position five meters behind Dewey.

"We expecting trouble, Lieutenant Tyler?"

"Expecting it? No, Becker. Planning for it? Every time."

Two and a half hours later, PFC Burke signaled for a stop. He'd been on the right side of the road, which was worse looking the further from Puchuncavi they'd come. He'd stayed to the side of the road as it climbed a short rise about five meters in height. His signal had come just after he'd taken a stealthy look over the top.

Sgt Parks gave her own signal. The rest of the squad had spread out, covering the area around them. She and Dewey then made their way up the slope to join PFC Burke, who was now prone, his head just barely higher than the crest of the hill.

"What do you have?" Sgt Parks asked as she and Dewey joined Burke on the slope.

"The view," said PFC Burke. "It's sort of flat and wide open from here. It's also interesting."

"Interesting?" Dewey asked. He got on his belly and crawled forward, shifting his face shield so that it was down to protect him. He doubted there was a sniper waiting, but that wasn't any reason to relax his guard. With his first look, he said, "Interesting is a good word for it."

"What?" Sgt Parks belly crawled up the hill to join Dewey.

Lacking any detailed history of Juracan or its society four hundred years ago, Dewey could only make assumptions. But, he had a sense from other cities, other worlds, that he was looking at what had once been the suburbs of the old city. He was basing this on the few bits of steel and crete that still stood.

The flat and wide area PFC Burke referred to spread out just past the rise. It undulated naturally. The surface was mostly gray. Dead, stunted trees poked up here and there. What Dewey was assuming had been homes had been obliterated by some force, centuries ago.

"Tactical nuke?" Sgt Parks asked.

Dewey nodded. "I would think so," he said. "But whoever used it must have really been mad at the enemy. This would have been where civilians lived. Homes, schools, parks."

"Maybe they'd had a chance to evacuate."

Dewey knew that Sgt Parks was trying to sound hopeful. Not that it really mattered. The war was centuries in the past. Anyone who'd survived was long dead. And, clearly, some had survived.

"Most of the population was evacuating the planet because of the nuclear attacks," Dewey said. "This could have happened after an evacuation. Either way, it's still terrible to see."

Planets still had nuclear weapons. Especially the First Expansion worlds that had shared the world with people with whom they might not have agreed. The current Second Expansion was allowing homogenous groups to establish colonies. When they had to share a world, everything was done to find a similar or like-minded population. It didn't always work out, but no one had waged all-out nuclear war in that time.

Dewey turned and sat, pushing up his face shield and pulling out his tablet. "Sergeant Parks," he said as he thumbed the tablet awake. "Let's pop a couple eyes up so we can have an overhead view. Make sure to run thermals and IR."

"You got it, Lieutenant."

Sgt Parks pushed back from the crest of the hill and then trotted back down to the flat. As she signaled for two of her people to join her, Dewey flicked through several more files in his tablet. Before they'd left the Graevya for the surface, Dewey had managed to find the book where he'd read about Juracan. There were several maps in the book. Unfortunately, they lacked enough detail to be of much use.

He had been able to determine the name of the old city, though. Atacama, named after the river it had been built across, had been the Basoalto region's capital. It was upriver from a smaller port city, Puerto Calama. There'd also been a spaceport, Piso Grande, in a location about where the space elevator was now anchored. Perhaps the old spaceport was the reason the elevator had been placed there. Maybe Dewey would ask if the opportunity presented itself.

"Keep watch, PFC Burke," said Dewey. He put his tablet away and stood to a crouch.

"Will do." Burke moved forward several more centimeters, improving his view.

As Dewey made his way down the hill, he heard the familiar whomp of grenade launchers propelling eyes into the sky. He'd soon have an overview of the area. While he doubted they'd find the mercs lurking nearby, like lowering his face shield against unlikely snipers, he wasn't taking chances.

"Rest and water everyone, Sergeant Parks," said Dewey. He took a

Sgt Parks nodded and passed along the order for rest and water. She signaled for PFC Arnold to switch positions with PFC Burke.

Five minutes later, Dewey's comm beeped. He looked around and found Sgt Parks watching in his direction. She tapped her helmet when he caught her eye. The images were ready. When Dewey dropped his shield, a signal at the top right of his vision alerted him that he had received a file.

The file showed a bird's eye view of the suburbs of Atacama. The roads were partially buried beneath centuries of falling and wind-blown debris. The one exception was the road they were currently on. It looked to be fairly clear all the way through the image. Perhaps, Dewey mused, the Juracanians had used the road before the appearance of the invaders.

Most importantly, there weren't any thermal signatures for lurking mercenaries.

Dewey closed the file and raised his shield once more. "Okay, Sergeant Parks, let's go sightseeing."

08

Dewey had plenty of experience with war-battered landscapes. He'd been looking at them since he was eighteen, but none of them were as eerie as here in the suburbs of Atacama. Though it had had four hundred years to wipe away the memory of nuclear war, the signs were still evident. Partial walls stood alone like macabre tombstones. The ground was a littered mixture of wind-eroded brick and crete, slowly being subsumed by layers of dust and dirt.

The backdrop to the suburbs wasn't any more cheerful. Atacama had been a business center, being so close to the old spaceport. Towering skyscrapers had jutted high into the air, signaling their importance. Now, they were as broken as the barren tree boles Dewey had already seen.

Perhaps the only thing that could have been seen as a sign of revival was the nearly invisible space elevator, cutting a narrow line in the sky. Unfortunately, it was being used to rob the planet of resources and was implicated in the death of many of the civilians of Juracan. If the stories they'd been told were true.

"Seems strange."

Dewey brought his gaze down from where the elevator faded into the clouds to look at Sgt Parks.

"What seems strange?"

"I've been watching the elevator since we had a good view of it," she said. "Not every second, but you'd think I'd have seen at least one trunk shuttling cargo up to the docks."

It hadn't occurred to Dewey until now. There'd been something that had bothered him, but he hadn't been able to put a pin in it. Now he could.

"You're right, Sgt Parks," he said. "There hasn't been any action on the cables."

"Maybe they left?" Sgt Parks sounded like she doubted her own idea.

"Or they're waiting for something?" Dewey suggested.

"Surely not us," Sgt Parks said and laughed.

Dewey shared the laugh but with more reserve. "No, definitely not us. There could be plenty of reasons, but I'd hazard that it has something to do with the lack of ships. There wasn't one when we took orbit. Major Hughes would have made contact with them. The station at the end of the cables was little more than a loading dock. There wasn't room to store tens of trunks."

"So they'll wait until a ship docks and then start sending them up."

"Seems likely. Maybe we can ask if we get a chance."

By this time, the landscape had transitioned to the remains of apartment buildings, light industrial, and warehouse structures. Here, too, Dewey was basing his opinions on the shapes of what remained and the information he'd pulled from the old texts about Juracan. The buildings were separated by wide roads that formed the concentric rings around the center of the city.

Atacama looked in surprisingly good shape for a city abandoned and nuked four hundred years ago. It was true that many of the buildings were worn. Their upper levels and much of their facades littered the streets. Despite that, what stood looked stable to Dewey's experienced eye. Of course, that also meant there were likely many places that an enemy could lie in wait.

"Stick to the buildings as much as possible," Dewey said as they crossed the first ring road. "Let's not make ourselves into inviting targets."

Sgt Parks passed orders to her squad. Whenever the opportunity presented itself, they moved through the lobbies and storefronts rather than remaining exposed on the roadway. They continued in this manner until they reached the last ring road and the city center. Dewey knew this to be the center of government for Atacama and the outlying region.

There were four short, wide buildings at the feet of the three towers that made up the city center. The rest was a park-like setting that had long ago gone wild. Of the buildings, two of the towers were on Dewey's side of the river.

"What do you think, Lieutenant Tyler?" asked Sgt Parks. She had allowed him several minutes of quiet observation before speaking up.

Dewey pointed to the two towers. They had at least fifteen good floors. There were five to six more above that, but they'd have to be tested before climbing higher. Most importantly, they were taller than the broken tower on the north side of the river, and taller than any other buildings between them and the space elevator.

"Let's investigate those two buildings," he said. "If we don't have company, we'll put a fireteam up each and establish watch posts in both before we pull back."

"You don't plan on exploring further?" Sgt Parks sounded disappointed, which only made Dewey smile.

"Oh, we will, Parks, just not right now. Let's get an idea of what we're facing before we jump into the dark."

"Understood."

"Good. Send your squad in. Act like you're expecting a hostile greeting."

Sgt Parks laughed. "After Wenshen, that's the only way I operate." She turned and started giving assignments. When she was ready, she turned to Dewey, who nodded for her to proceed.

They crossed the ring road one at a time and then proceeded into the wild park. PFC Wong was on point, shortening the distance on Sgt Parks' command when she momentarily disappeared amongst the bushes and weeds. Unlike Wenshen, the plants here didn't slice skin.

Bracketed between the two fireteams, Dewey watched with the same caution, his own weapon ready if needed. He had a gut feeling they weren't going to encounter the mercenaries here. At the same time, his gut implied it was only a matter of time.

When PFC Wong neared the entrance to the wide bridge that made up the city's bullseye, Sgt Parks signaled for her to stop and then pull back to one of the shorter, broken buildings that stood off to the side. The building's northern side backed up to the river, providing a clear view of the bridge and the other side. The bridge was wide, even with the sides chipped and broken. Rusty, bent lines marked the tracks where trolleys would have sped citizens to and from work in the pre-war days.

The squad took fire positions in the debris along the edge of the road. They could watch the buildings across the way while shielded from above by the wreckage they'd slipped into. With Cpl Garner's fireteam monitoring the way they'd come, Dewey and Sgt Parks slipped forward to join PFC Wong.

"How's it look?" Sgt Parks asked.

"Weird," said PFC Wong. "I know I haven't been doing this long, but this place just seems more unusual than any I've seen before."

"You're not alone," said Dewey. He gave Wong a clap on the shoulder before slipping past her to move closer to a two-meter tall slab of rebar-pierced crete that marked where the northwestern corner of the building had been.

While the building was close to the river, there was still space for a wide footpath between the river bank and the building's side. Several visible benches faced toward the river. One was broken and slumped to the side. The other was covered in yellow-leafed vines. The path had probably been smooth when it was still in use. Now, it was a bent and twisted ribbon with several faded yellow lines running down the center. Most importantly, there wasn't any place to hide there or on the bridge. Not for mercs, not for Hospitallers. Anyone crossing was going to be exposed for forty or fifty meters. It was a long distance and a long way to travel.

"Parks."

"Yes, Lieutenant?"

"I want you to take Corporal Mitchell's fireteam and work your way as high as you can in this building. I'll go with Corporal Garner's team. We'll cross the street and go up that tower."

"You got it, Lieutenant."

"The higher, the better," said Dewey. He smiled and then added in a warning tone, "But that doesn't mean putting yourselves at risk."

"We'll play it safe."

Dewey clapped Sgt Parks on the shoulder. He knew she'd keep her people safe. "Good. Let's go."

While Sgt Parks pulled Cpl Mitchell and his fireteam together, Dewey moved back to where Cpl Garner's team was watching the direction they'd come from.

"Must be a holiday, Lieutenant. All the shops are closed."

Dewey honored the joke with an honest chuckle. "Too right, Corporal Garner. Maybe we'll have better luck on the other side of the street?"

The look on Cpl Garner's face shifted from amused to serious. He looked across the street and then back to Dewey. "You're coming, too, Lieutenant Tyler?"

"I promise I won't get in the way."

Cpl Garner signaled for his team to gather. "It's not that, Lieutenant. It's just that we'll be exposed for a good ten meters. You sure you don't want to just wait here?"

"I trust you to keep me safe, Corporal. And Mitchell's team is already moving up. You going to let them beat you?"

PFC Nora Arnold stuck her face into the conversation. "They get a head start?"

"They'll need it," said Cpl Garner. The seriousness of his words was tempered by a grin. "Okay, team. Burke, you're on point. We'll guard your three, six, and nine while you hustle across. Then Becker, followed by the lieutenant. You and me, Arnold, we'll shut the door."

When they all nodded, Cpl Garner turned back to Dewey, who nodded, too.

"Okay, then," said Cpl Garner. He clapped PFC Burke on the side of his arm. "Let's go check the view."

The crossing of the road to the opposite tower had been as uneventful as the march into Atacama. Once across, they'd quickly found a stairwell and climbed twelve floors. Dewey followed Pvt Becker and PFC Burke out of the stairwell onto a floor layered with the debris of time lightly layered across it.

Though the facade had long ago fallen away, some of the interior remained. There were rusting desks and the skeletal remains of chairs. Several interior walls still stood but were pockmarked with large and small gaps that exposed wiring and metal tube studs.

"My dorm father would faint if he saw how they kept this place," whispered PFC Burke.

"Why are you whispering?" asked Cpl Garner, who'd come onto the floor last.

PFC Burke shrugged. "Kind of feels like a place you should whisper in."

Dewey agreed. Though there was likely no one to hear them, the place had a tomb-like quality. It was a rusty monument to the power of human aggression, and he could have spent a solid hour just observing the hinted-at memories of the long-abandoned place. Unfortunately, all he could spare were a few quick glances which were mostly to assure him they didn't have company.

"Okay," said Dewey as he pulled his attention back to the task. "Let's find some good positions for the eyes."

Cpl Garner nodded and said, "You got it, Lieutenant Tyler." Then, he paused as the building vibrated from the concussion of a nearby explosion. "That wasn't an earthquake."

"No, it wasn't," agreed Dewey. He was pretty certain what it was.

PFC Arnold pointed as she spoke. "Here, Lieutenant, Corporal Garner! Someone's firing on the building with Corporal Mitchell's fireteam."

"Keep back from the edge," Dewey ordered. He moved close enough that he could see a dust cloud billow up from the road. He tapped his comm. "Corporal Mitchell?"

"Here, Lieutenant," Mitchell responded over the comm. Another explosion shook the building. "It's the mercs. I think. They're firing from the other side of the river."

"Understood. Anyone hurt?" Dewey signaled to Cpl Garner to locate the source of attack.

"No one's hurt. Just surprised."

"I want you to pull back immediately, Mitchell. Get everyone out of the building and move south, out of the city center. Set up a defensive position. We'll join you shortly."

"On it," said Cpl Mitchell. The comm went silent.

"Garner, what do we have?"

Cpl Garner had his face shield down. On the floor, crawling over several rotting ceiling tiles, a hand with an eye attached to it was nearing the raw edge where the wall had long ago fallen away.

"I have thermal running," said Cpl Garner. He paused as the hand reached the ragged line between floor and sky. Across the street, another rocket struck the other building.

"Lieutenant Tyler," said Pvt Becker. "I think they're trying to knock the building over."

Dewey tore himself away from watching Cpl Garner and the hand perched on the building's ragged edge to pay attention to Becker. "Why do you think that?" he asked.

"All three impacts have been at the base of the building." Pvt Becker pointed in the direction without approaching the edge and exposing himself. "At the same corner. They're chipping away at it. Like taking down a tree."

As if to emphasize Becker's observation, another rocket slammed into the other building.

"Corporal Mitchell," Dewey said into his comm. "Tell me you're out of the building."

After a crackling pause, Cpl Mitchell said, "Not quite. The stairs we came up with are damaged. We're looking for another set."

"Understand. Keep me posted." Dewey turned back to Cpl Garner. "Anything, Garner?"

"Yes," Garner said. "I've got a lock on their position. "If only we had rockets."

They'd come to observe and collect intel. So, no, they hadn't brought rockets. But they did have grenades.

"Send me the data," Dewey said. He waved at Pvt Becker to follow him as he ran for the stairs. "Then set up several more eyes on hands and get ready to pull back."

Without waiting for a response, Dewey was up the stairs with Pvt

Becker hustling to keep up. They went up two more floors to an exposed roof. On the roof, Dewey slowed to a cautious walk. He changed out the barrels on his weapon and loaded a magazine of grenades.

Behind Dewey, he heard Pvt Becker mimicking his actions, replacing one barrel for the other. On Dewey's shield, a small icon indicated he had incoming information. Dewey reached out to tap the icon in VR, copying it and sending it along to Becker.

"That's our target," Dewey said to Pvt Becker. "Keep back out of sight. Fire when you have a lock on the target."

Dewey was already shouldering his weapon. He linked it to the VR of his face shield and began adjusting his angles until the red crosshairs went green. He pulled the trigger, adjusted for the recoil, and fired again when he had the green for go. Near him, Dewey heard the throaty thunk of Pvt Becker's weapon launching grenades, too.

When they'd both emptied a magazine of grenades, Dewey waved Pvt Becker back. The first two grenades had just struck and exploded. Dewey doubted they would deter the mercs for long.

"That'll do, Becker. Head back down and tell Cpl Garner I said to exit, now. It's an order."

"On it, Lieutenant." Pvt Becker dashed back to the stairwell. Dewey could hear his boots heavy on the stairs.

Before making his own exit, Dewey took the time to place two more eyes onto hands and set them loose on the floor. As the other grenades landed and exploded, he accessed the VR's controls to set the hands and eyes on perimeter duty. They would walk the edge of the floor, allowing for multiple views until their batteries were depleted, which was about ten days.

With the hands and eyes set, Dewey hurried toward the stairs. As he passed the floor where the rest of the fireteam had been, he was gladdened to see that they had already left. If he paused and listened, he might have heard their boots thundering down to ground level, except that he was already breathing hard with exertion. Across the street, he heard another rocket explode against the building. He could only hope that they'd bought Cpl Mitchell's fireteam the extra time they needed to find a second stairwell and reach safety.

Dewey's comm beeped. He tapped it as he rounded a landing, heading to the next floor down.

"Lieutenant Tyler." It was Cpl Garner. "You'll need to hurry."

"That's what I'm doing." Dewey was breathing deep as he switched to jumping halfway down each flight of stairs. The smell of crete dust was strong in his nose.

"A little faster then, Lieutenant. The other building's started to fall, and it's falling this way."

09

The idea of being struck by a falling building was just the energy boost Dewey needed. He jumped down flights of stairs after the first two steps, using the rail to swing him around to the next flight. He stumbled just once, striking his knee hard enough to make his leg wobble for several steps.

"Continue past the ground floor, Lieutenant Tyler," Cpl Garner said in Dewey's ear. "There's a parking garage. The exit is to the south."

"Got it." Dewey's answer was a ragged pant. He was two floors away. While he was worried about his own safety, he was more concerned about Cpl Mitchell and his team. It was Dewey's orders that had put them in harm's way. And though being in harm's way was part of the daily duty of being a Hospitaller, it wasn't something that he or any leader took lightly. The fewer names that had to be etched on the CO's wall, the better.

As Dewey touched the landing of the ground floor, the building shook more violently. A brief glimpse to his right, as he swung around for the next flight down, showed him that the sky was dark with shadow and falling bits of debris. With both hands on the rail, Dewey flew down the last two flights, crashing into the door, which was open, held up by its bottom hinge.

Ahead, he saw daylight and Cpl Garner's fireteam. Despite the pain in his knee, Dewey pushed harder, sprinting for the exit. Behind him, he heard a symphony of destruction following in his wake.

"Go!" Dewey waved at the others who had started running toward him. He realized, as they hesitated and then followed his orders, that he was running with an awkward gait, favoring the knee he'd banged on the stairs.

There was going to be a lot of dust when the building collapsed. Dewey tugged at his jacket's inner collar, pulling the gas mask layer up over his mouth and nose. Breathing would be warmer, talking a little more difficult, but it was a better option than lungs full of crete dust. Ahead of him, he could see the others doing the same thing at Cpl Garner's directions.

As Dewey burst from the garage, a billowing of crete dust appeared on the periphery of his vision. The fireteam was already across the street. Dewey didn't stop running, even as he joined them. PFC Burke and PFC Arnold had to catch him so that he didn't collide with the pile of rubble behind them. They were all under the eaves of a shorter building. Looking up, Dewey saw that the building he'd been in was still standing. Though now it was supporting the extra weight of the tower from the other side.

"Sergeant Parks, you copy?" Dewey took two steps towards the direction he'd assumed Mitchell would have gone. "Mitchell?" He tried several more times before turning to Cpl Garner. "Did you try to contact Sergeant Parks?"

"Soon as we were out," Garner said. His voice was muffled by the gas mask present over the lower half of his face. "Corporal Mitchell, too. All I got was static."

Dust was still settling in thick clouds, billowing along the street. The fallen tower now blocked the bridge. It would take time for anyone to find their way through the debris. Hopefully, they would have enough time to find Cpl Mitchell and his fireteam before then. Hopefully, they were still alive.

Dewey turned to give his orders to Cpl Garner but was interrupted by the groan and screech of twisting metal. He turned back around to see that a section of the fallen building was calving from the rest. It fell sideways onto the main street, effectively blocking access to the other side.

Finding Sgt Parks and Cpl Mitchell's fireteam had just become more difficult.

"Corporal Garner," Dewey said. "We need to find a way to the other side of the street. We may have to go back a block and come around from behind."

"Understood," said Cpl Garner. He turned and just as quickly came to a stop.

Dewey saw it, too.

Dewey responded to a comm request from PFC Burke. "Ours or theirs?"

"Don't think it's either, Lieutenant. I think it's a local."

"Defensive positions, now." Cpl Garner's command moved the other members of the fireteam. They formed a protective ring with Dewey in the middle.

The civilian, who Dewey noticed was dressed in worn clothes and a ragged-edged bandana across the lower part of their face, was approaching from the west. They walked slowly, their hands out with palms forward, and their eyes moved continuously. They seemed to scan from Dewey's position to the building that the fireteam had escaped from and then back to where Dewey continued to observe their approach.

"Anyone else," Dewey said through the comm.

"Nothing," said Pvt Becker.

"Same here," said PFC Arnold.

"Except for the debris, everything looks clear," Cpl Garner added.

Dewey did a quick visual of the area surrounding the fireteam. They were in the shadow of a smaller building, across from the tower they'd put the eyes in. Debris from the fallen building now blocked their access to the other side, but it looked like the road back to Puchuncavi was still open. And then there was the road west that would take them to another bridge across the river, if the bridge still stood. That was where the civilian was.

It was clear it was a civilian. Dewey had used the magnification on his face shield to verify. On any other planet, it would have been difficult to tell a civilian from a soldier except by their attire. Dewey found it unlikely, though, that the mercenaries had recruited Juracanian locals into their service. Nor was it likely that they had disguised themselves with the pebbly skin of the people of Juracan.

The civilian had approached to within twenty meters and slowed.

"You want me to order them to stop, Corporal Garner?" asked Pvt Becker.

"Lieutenant?" Cpl Garner turned to Dewey as he asked.

"Another five meters, Becker," said Dewey.

While the rest of the fireteam kept their eyes on the perimeter, Dewey observed over Pvt Becker's shoulder as the civilian continued their approach. They looked, by Dewey's estimation, to be nervous to the point of being terrified. Considering that the only interaction the people of Juracan had with off-planet visitors had been negative to the point of deadly, Dewey could understand the concern.

What Dewey wondered, even more, was how had the civilian come to be here in the supposedly abandoned city? And from where did they come? Since Luc had mentioned that the skin patterns differed depending on where someone was from, Dewey had been observing. The approaching visitor's skin was lighter in pigmentation. The pebble pattern was larger on some of their visible features, looking more like thumb-sized river rock.

"Far enough, thank you," said Pvt Becker.

The civilian halted. "I'm unarmed."

Dewey could hear the tell-tale quiver in their voice. They were afraid.

"Ask if they're alone," said Dewey.

"Where's the rest of your team?" asked Pvt Becker.

The civilian started to turn, as if to point back the way they'd come, but froze. Slowly turning back to the Hospitallers, he said, "Back that way. Two blocks."

Dewey figured the civilian didn't want to reveal the other Juracanians' location. Smart. "Why are you here?" Dewey asked.

"To help." They sounded unsure.

"Come on in." Dewey stood and waved the civilian forward.

The civilian looked unsure at first but then moved toward the fireteam, still keeping their hands open with palms forward. Once they were past Pvt Becker, Dewey waved them to a kneeling position that would make them less of a target if the mercenaries had moved into the area.

Dewey held out his hand after removing his glove. "Lieutenant Dewey Tyler, Hospitallers."

The civilian hesitated for a second and then accepted Dewey's hand saying, "Alexander Arriaga. I'm from up north."

"You're a long way from home."

Alexander chuckled. "A lot of us are."

The comment surprised Dewey. "How many are you?"

Alexander's face, which had shown a spark of amusement, went flat, like a mask dropping into place. "I'm not sure I'm the one to give that information," he said. "But when we get to safety, maybe someone else can answer your question."

"Safety?"

Alexander started to point again but stopped. "We have a place where you'll be safe from the invaders. I was sent to bring you in."

Dewey paused and looked around. The fireteam, with their eyes on the perimeter, were clearly lending ears to the conversation. "We'd be glad to go with you," Dewey said, "but we have another fireteam we need to recover."

"We know about them," said Alexander. "We were going to find them, too, but the invaders were already in the area."

Around Dewey, the fireteam gripped their weapons a little tighter. They sighted down the barrels, ready to engage.

"Then we need to rescue our people," Dewey said. He started to turn with the intention of giving Cpl Garner orders to prepare but stopped when he felt Alexander's arm on his.

"The invaders will take them hostage," Alexander said. "They'll be safe, and we can show you how to rescue them later. If you go now, they might capture you, too. Valentine said you would trust us if we came to you."

"Valentine?" More questions and more mysteries that Dewey hoped to get answers to. When Alexander nodded, Dewey spoke to Cpl Garner. "I think we're going to have to trust Alexander here. We'll get the other fireteam first chance we get."

Cpl Garner nodded while still keeping his eyes on the

surroundings. "Sounds like it might be the best plan, Lieutenant. No need to get us all captured. Who'd know to come and rescue us?"

Dewey grinned as he looked at Alexander. "Oh, I think someone would know quickly enough."

Still, there wasn't any need to give the mercenaries more of an upper hand than they were already getting.

"Can we go?" asked Alexander.

"Corporal Garner, let's move out. Safe and secure."

"You got it, Lieutenant Tyler." Cpl Garner reached out and tapped PFC Arnold on the shoulder. "You got rear guard, Arnold. Burke, you're on point with the civilian. Private Becker will follow Burke."

There was a ragged chorus of acknowledgment. Then, PFC Burke moved next to Becker before turning back to Dewey and Alexander.

"Sir, if you'll show me the way," Burke said.

Dewey gave a head tilt in PFC Burke's direction. "He means you, Alexander. He'll stay with you as you guide us to wherever it is we're going."

"Of course." Alexander stood and then just as quickly bent at the hips, lowering his profile. He followed Burke onto the sidewalk. Burke put a hand on Alexander's arm, stopping him long enough for Burke to get a good view of the street. He then nodded to Alexander, who started down the street with a hurried gait. PFC Burke stuck close to him.

Pvt Becker followed several meters behind, also pausing to check the street before continuing. Dewey moved with Cpl Garner, making their own pause before also moving onto the street.

"Who do you think they are?" Cpl Garner asked Dewey as they kept a distance between them and Pvt Becker just ahead.

"You mean besides just being Juracanians?"

"Yes."

Behind them, PFC Arnold stumbled, kicking a fist-sized chunk of crete so that it skittered across the road. She raised a hand to signal she was okay when Dewey turned to look. He nodded and continued moving with Cpl Garner.

"If Benny was able to escape when he was sick," said Dewey, "I imagine that others have also done the same. As to whether or not the mercs know or care, that remains to be learned."

"If they escaped, why not return to their homes? Why stay here?"

Ahead, PFC Burke was signaling that they were turning left. Cpl Garner returned a signal of acknowledgment. Dewey held his thoughts until they checked the corner in their turn and followed, still keeping meters between them and Pvt Becker.

"Perhaps to help others who escape," Dewey said. He'd been pondering the situation from the moment they'd seen Alexander approach. Along with who they were and why they were here, he was curious about how they moved around without being seen by the mercenaries who were equipped for war. Ahead, Alexander and PFC Burke had come to a stop. "I suspect we'll have our answer soon."

They were on a side street that connected the main boulevards that ringed the city. It was a wide street with broken benches, stunted but resilient trees, and several large debris piles. Alexander was waiting next to one of the piles while PFC Burke circumnavigated it.

When Burke came around the other side of the small hill of debris, he nodded an all-clear.

"Are we meeting them here?" Dewey asked.

"Yes. Sort of."

The answer was cryptic. But before Dewey could interrogate further, a section of the rubble shifted and rose on hidden hinges.

"Talk about déjà vu," Cpl Garner said.

Dewey nodded in agreement. The last time they'd seen a secret entrance, it had been on Wenshen. It, too, had been created by locals who shouldn't have existed.

In the gloom of the open passageway, several more Juracanians appeared. They scanned past Dewey until they reached Alexander. Only then did they nod and wave for everyone to enter. When Dewey looked at Alexander, the Juracanian indicated that Dewey should proceed. It was a trust issue. Did Dewey trust them enough to enter first?

Dewey nodded a greeting to the faces below and entered the passage. The people below moved back as he advanced. The steps were wide and old, with rusted strips of metal embedded for traction. To the sides, once past the faux debris, Dewey saw tiles and frames where posters might have once been.

Ten steps down, there was a meter-wide landing and then more steps. Dewey paused to look back. Pvt Becker, PFC Arnold, and PFC Burke were close behind. Still at the entrance, Cpl Garner waited with Alexander. Everyone looked safe if a little nervous. Dewey was, too, but he reminded himself that Alexander had invoked Valentine's name. That had to count for something.

Ahead of Dewey, the Juracanians continued to move backward, keeping space between themselves and the Hospitallers. Dewey also noticed that there was light behind the Juracanians. After three more narrow landings, the Juracanians and Dewey were at the beginning of a tunnel. The light came from glass domes in the ceiling. They weren't electrical. They were light tubes. Somewhere on the surface, likely built into the sidewalks, were the other ends of the glass tubes. Dewey was now sure they were in a subway. The tiles, the lights, the empty frames were all familiar hints.

"Hello," he said to the waiting Juracanians as Cpl Garner's fireteam joined them.

They appeared to ignore Dewey and looked past him. He looked over his shoulder to see Alexander and Cpl Garner.

"That all of them?" asked one of the other Juracanians.

"Yes."

"This way then." The Juracanian, a tall woman with dual braids hanging down her back, waved at them to follow and started walking.

The three Juracanians remained in front, one of them repeatedly checking over their shoulder. Dewey walked in the middle of the fireteam with Alexander as company. Dewey had questions but thought it prudent to wait a little longer. It was hard to ignore the fear and distrust emanating from the Juracanians ahead. When they got to their destination, he was sure some of the answers would be obvious.

The tunnel exited into a large open area. There were neat piles of brick and crete scattered around. Turnstiles were still in place, but the gates had been removed. There was a kiosk bracketed by the gaping turnstiles. Sandbags created an extra layer across the kiosk's front, and the roll-up shutters that covered the windows were in place. Small gaps in the shutters hinted at signs of movement.

Several seconds later, ten more Juracanians appeared from the right. Half that number appeared from the left. Four more appeared from behind the kiosk, separated from the Hospitallers by the turnstiles. All of them carried truncheons or long-handled sledgehammers.

"Stand down," Dewey said in a soft voice, just loud enough for the fireteam to hear. He was confident that the people around them were more afraid of the Hospitallers than the other way around.

"This all of them?" one of the four beyond the turnstiles asked.

"Alex says it's all," said the woman with the braids.

The four past the turnstiles had a brief, whispered conversation. The other Juracanians to either side remained in place, their weapons held loosely but at the ready. The one Juracanian who had asked about the Hospitallers separated from the other three, slipped through a turnstile and approached.

Alexander moved forward. "Sam, this is Lieutenant Tyler."

"Lieutenant Tyler," Sam said. She held out her hand. "I'm Samantha Barrientos. I'm the leader by vote."

Dewey shook Samantha's hand. The pebble texture of her skin was more like squares with rounded corners. "Leader of what?"

Samantha laughed as she looked around, her hand still in Dewey's. "For lack of a better word? The resistance."

10

Dewey took a moment to look around once more. Again, he saw the truncheons and long-handled sledgehammers. There wasn't any sign of rifles or pistols. Not a hint of them. Dewey slowly returned his attention to Samantha, leader of the resistance, not even attempting to hide his doubt and confusion.

For her part, Samantha responded with a rueful smile. "I did say, 'for lack of a better word.'"

"You did. How have you fared against the mercs?"

"Well, we haven't had to do that," said Samantha. Dewey noticed the nervous looks of the other Juracanians around them. "Mostly, we've been helping to free those still slaving in the salvaging operations."

"We try to keep track of those who died, too."

Dewey looked past Samantha to the older man with dark-pebbled skin who'd spoken.

"This is Franco Rodarte," Samantha said. "He was one of the first to escape. He keeps the ledger."

"Ledgers," said Franco. He put a hard emphasis on both syllables. Dewey imagined a stack of thick real-paper ledgers with names printed in small tight letters, thousands of names cataloged within them. It reminded him of the names on the office wall facing every CO's desk.

"A lot of people died even before Franco and some others got away," said Samantha. She paused and looked around before seeming to make some internal decision. "Come, we should move in case the invaders discover the entrance here."

She turned away from Dewey and slipped back through the

turnstiles, where she walked further into the gloom. Like water, the other Juracanians followed, leaving the Hospitallers with Alexander to catch up.

Once Dewey received a nod from Alexander, he turned to Cpl Garner. "Move out."

Garner, doubt on his face, saluted and then turned to the squad, waving them to follow. He took up the rear position as the fireteam followed the civilians.

It only took another ten meters before Dewey realized that the darkness was increasing. The light tunnels in the ceiling were gone now. The only light in the space came from behind. Instinctively, Dewey reached up and turned on his task light to illuminate the area.

He just as quickly turned it off when several of the Juracanians cried out in dismay, several more in anger.

"What happened?" Dewey asked. The brief moment of light had affected his vision, and now he was standing in complete darkness.

"We don't need artificial light," said Alexander.

From the darkness, PFC Arnold asked, "Then how do you see?"

"We just see," Alexander said.

Another voice came from the darkness, close to Dewey. "You're like the invaders. You need assistance to see when the sun is down?"

"Yes," Dewey said. "And you don't?"

"No. Though the seeing is different, we still see."

Dewey now had the gloom of the distant light tunnels to highlight some of the people closest. Several of them were grumbling about off-worlders and their vision.

"Do you know how it is that you do see?" Dewey tapped his night vision. It enhanced the limited light available, providing more detail than his unaided eyes in the dim light. He imagined that this wasn't how the Juracanians were actually seeing.

"Don't know." This time Dewey was able to see Samantha shrug. "It's something we've always been able to do."

"Came in handy giving the invaders the slip," said someone else nearby.

"Until they caught on," said Franco. "Now they've ringed the barracks in bright lights."

"They have no idea how much that light hurts," said Alexander. He sounded bitter.

"I doubt they would have cared," said Cpl Garner.

"Lieutenant Tyler?"

Dewey turned. "What do you have, Becker?"

"Infrared, Lieutenant," said Pvt Becker. "I think they see in infrared, but far to the edge."

"Really?" Dewey switched from enhanced vision to infrared. At first, he didn't see much more than before. But when he adjusted the system from seven hundred nanometers to one thousand nanometers, the space around him glowed with light. He could see the faded directional signs hanging from the ceiling, other tunnels, and a distant second set of turnstiles.

"Hey, cool," said PFC Arnold. Dewey turned to see that she was turning in a slow circle, obviously seeing what he saw.

"You don't need your artificial lights, then?" asked Samantha.

"Not the ones that hurt you, no," said Dewey. "So, please, lead on."

Samantha gave a curt nod to Dewey and waved at the others around her to move. Several of them cast curious looks at Dewey and the fireteam. Still, they just as quickly acquiesced to Samantha's motions and turned away and walked toward the distant turnstiles.

"You think this is what they see?" Cpl Garner asked from his position next to Dewey.

"Not sure." And Dewey wasn't. He'd read about artificial vision enhancements. He knew that the Hospitallers had experimented with them and other senses close to a century ago. Unfortunately, the enhancements only lasted for a short period of time. Worse, decades later, the volunteers suffered from rapid macular degeneration that defied the standard treatments. The Hospitaller leadership had banned further testing in vision enhancements and looked with a caustic eye upon any other suggestions.

Dewey also knew that he couldn't just show one of the Juracanians what his helmet saw and ask if it was the same thing.

Their own vision would have an effect on how they translated the view through the helmet shields. It would have to be a mystery left for the Hospitaller scientists who would be as excited as orphanage children on Founders' Day.

For now, Dewey would just have to remain curious as he followed the Juracanians through the second set of turnstiles and then down another tunnel. There seemed to be a lot of tunnels and stairs. Some led down, others led up. A good many were blocked by fallen debris, but some looked as if they'd been purposefully cleared. That generated another question of when and by who it had been cleared. Dewey chuckled to himself as he realized he'd squeezed two questions into one.

"Everything okay, Lieutenant Tyler?" Alexander asked.

"Not really," Dewey answered. "But I'm personally fine. Just a funny thought. So, Alexander, are there spaces like this under the entire city?"

The tunnel they were in was now sloping upward.

"In the center of the city, yes. But past the second ringway, it's more spread out. Outside the city, it's just tunnels and stations."

"Past the city?" asked Cpl Garner. "How far past?"

"I probably shouldn't say much. I'm not in charge, you see? But, I'd heard that before the big war, the tunnels had trains that went all over the continent. There was even supposed to be one that went under the water to Mamara and the city that was called Segou."

"What do you think, Lieutenant?"

Dewey knew what Cpl Garner was asking. He'd read about the train system, but the books he'd read hadn't mentioned them being underground and spanning the small continents. But what Cpl Garner was specifically wondering without saying was if the train tunnels reached Puchuncavi. Dewey would need to know if there was a town there before the nuclear war before he could even suggest the likelihood of such a thing. But if it did, it might explain one of the other mysteries he'd become curious about.

Maybe Dewey would get a chance to interview someone like Samantha or Franco. He'd have to keep an ear peeled for such an opportunity. For now, he would have to wait. The tunnel had terminated at a flight of steps that hinted at a spacious lobby. The Hospitallers became silent as they took the steps and found themselves in more significant company.

A quick mental count brought the number of Juracanians to fifty-one. Was this all of them? Were there more? Again, the moment wasn't allowing Dewey to find answers. Samantha was speaking.

"This is most everyone," she had said with an introductory wave as she partially answered Dewey's unasked questions.

Dewey noticed PFC Arnold give a little wave that several of the Juracanians returned in kind.

"You have people out on posts?" Dewey asked. It was a natural question for him as it was what he was trained to do and would do.

"Guards? Yes. But others are elsewhere." Her answer gave Dewey the impression that she didn't want to give out all her intel at once. Again, the same thing that Dewey would have done.

Some of the Juracanians who'd been with them on the short walk were now among the others who'd greeted them. There were some whispered conversations, of which Dewey could hear the occasional syllable. And he would have enjoyed the opportunity to continue listening, but he had more pressing problems.

Dewey indicated the man next to him as he spoke. "Alexander told us the mercs will have captured our people. Can you help us get them back?"

Samantha, who'd easily replied to all other questions, hesitated before saying, doubtfully, "Yes."

Her tone wasn't reassuring. Dewey spared a glance for Alexander, who gave a micro-nod. Dewey took in all the information. Either Alexander was overconfident, or there was more to the situation than just a rescue mission.

"Are you holding our people hostage, too?" Dewey asked. He could feel the tension of his own people ramp up. The Juracanians might not have realized it, but each of the Hospitallers had, by habit, had taken a grip on their weapons and were, like Dewey, assessing the opposing force. It wasn't something Dewey had intended. It was just their overly cautious nature.

"We didn't take your people," someone behind Samantha said. Their voice was defensive.

Samantha turned to look over her shoulder, pushing down any zealous action with a pat of the air with her hand. "I don't think that's what the Hospitaller was saying." She turned back to Dewey. "I hope that wasn't what you were implying."

"Of course not," Dewey said. "But you want something."

"Help."

"Of course. That's why we've come to Juracan."

"A couple dozen of you?" Samantha laughed. "They have more than twice as many soldiers on the other side of the fence. You need more soldiers if you want to rescue your people."

Now Dewey understood. "Speaking of my couple dozen people, I'd like to check in with them if I may? Then we can talk? And maybe not standing in the middle of a large, open space?"

Dewey raised his hand to his helmet, his fingers hovering over the area he would tap to make contact with SSgt Castro. Once Samantha acknowledged the request with a nod, Dewey tapped the comm. He waited for a response but only received popping static. He gave it another half-minute and then tapped the comm to close the unanswered request.

"I'm not able to make a connection here," he said. "I probably need to go up and out. If you don't mind. We'll come right back."

Dewey now felt himself being scrutinized by Samantha and probably everyone else on her side of the room. They lacked the knowledge of the Second Expansion and the history of the Hospitallers. If they had all that information, Samantha would know that Dewey's word was as reliable as the sun rising.

"Your whole team?" Samantha asked.

By which, Dewey understood that she was concerned they would attempt to leave without helping them in any way. Instead of being disappointed or acting unsurprised, Dewey shook his head and said, "At least one of them should come with me. If one of them doesn't, Cpl Garner will break out in hives."

"It's true," Cpl Garner interjected, accompanied by soft laughs from his fireteam.

"So, if you don't mind, I'll take one person with me. You can send a couple people along, too, as I don't know where we are." Dewey was confident that Samantha had every intention of sending people along. It would probably take some time to earn their trust, even if people like Valentine vouched for them.

With her eyes on Dewey, Samantha motioned with her hand for several people to come forward. "Rodrigo. Juan Sebastian. Maria. Show the Hospitaller officer to the street."

"Burke," said Cpl Garner. "Stay with the lieutenant."

"No problem." PFC Burke moved over to stand just behind and to the side of Dewey. Dewey knew the position was so that Burke could see Samantha and the three Juracanians she'd called forward.

There was a silent stand-off where the three chosen by Samantha stared down Dewey and PFC Burke. Then, one of the three looked at the other two. The two shrugged. The first one nodded and turned. "This way," he said and started walking.

The other two Juracanians followed right behind.

"We'll be back in a bit, Corporal Garner."

"I know you will, Lieutenant."

Dewey marched after the three Juracanians with PFC Burke like a shadow just behind him. They passed by most of the other waiting Juracanians, whose eyes Dewey could feel studying him. They'd all been tricked and abused by the mercenaries and their employer. Now, along came another group of people from off-world. They might not have a lot of experience with other people from the galaxy, but the galaxy had already started off on the wrong foot.

Past the larger group of Juracanians, the other three led Dewey and Burke to an inoperable escalator. The gratings of the stair treads were packed with the dirt of centuries. Several stairs were askew. Dewey noticed the Juracanians stepped over them. Dewey copied their actions, looking back to verify that PFC Burke did the same thing.

The three Juracanians waited for Dewey at the top of the escalator.

He wondered if they watched to see how he and Burke would fare on the busted stair steps. Rather than being disappointed, the leader of the three nodded. Then, they turned without a word and started walking once more.

They were now in a wide corridor with several doors at the far end. There should have been six, but two were missing, and one hung by only its top hinge. The others were at different degrees of openness. The Juracanians slipped through the open spaces and continued. Dewey and PFC Burke continued in their wake to find themselves in a thirty-meter tall lobby.

The exterior wall of the lobby was missing all of its glass. Only the metal and plastic grid that had held the windows remained. The ground was littered with debris. Most of it was metal and glass, but Dewey noticed some leaves and one good-sized branch. Here and there were sections of furniture that one would expect in a lobby. The material that covered them was mostly gone, leaving rusted springs and cracked plastic.

"This good enough?"

"Should be," said Dewey. "Thank you."

Dewey was about to tap his comm when he received an incoming request. It was not Sgt Parks, though Dewey had wished it so before seeing the icon in his face shield. He tapped his helmet to open the line.

"Hey, Owen," he said. "I was just about to call you."

"What a coincidence, Tyler. We've been trying to contact you for the last hour. Something's come up." Owen paused, releasing a short laugh before adding, "Well, down, actually."

"What do you mean?" Dewey took several involuntary steps toward the street as if that would be enough to quickly bring the answer.

"Something's entered the atmosphere," said Lt Owen. "It's heading in our direction."

11

"Something, Lieutenant Owen?" Reflexively, Dewey was scanning the section of sky that he could see. "We don't know more than that?"

Next to Dewey, PFC Burke had his face shield down as he, too, scanned the sky. It amused Dewey to see the Juracanians doing the same thing.

"We're working on answering that," said Lt Owen. "I sent Haynes and a fireteam double-timing back to the dropships."

There was nothing Dewey could do from here inside Atacama. Lt Haynes would have already scanned the sky with the dropship's equipment long before Dewey could return.

"Okay, Owen," he said, lowering his eyes so that he was no longer studying the empty sky. "Keep me up to date on that. We have our own odd set of problems here."

"Oh? Is everyone okay?"

"We think so." Dewey gave Lt Owen an update of the situation with Sgt Parks and Cpl Mitchell's fireteam and the discovery of the Juracanian resistance.

"That might explain the sudden change in behavior of Luc and the other elders here," Lt Owen said. "Valentine came over to where the others were on their fourth or fifth cup of coffee. She whispered something to them. Then they all got up and trotted off. I figured it was serious as they hadn't even finished the cups they were drinking."

The comment was worth an involuntary laugh. Dewey easily remembered how Luc and the others had commented on the coffee's strange taste but were eager for another cup. So, yes, if they were willing to abandon their cups, they had to understand the seriousness of the issue. Dewey signaled to PFC Burke that everything was okay. The Hospitaller looked concerned after Dewey's sudden burst of laughter.

"There's still a lot we don't know," Dewey told Lt Owen. "Hopefully, when I speak to Samantha, she'll answer some questions, asked and unasked. First, though, I need to see what we can do about getting Sgt Parks and the others back. Then we'll be heading back to Puchuncavi."

"Understood," said Lt Owen. "We'll keep you posted when we learn more about what's coming down. You let us know what's happening there."

"Always," said Dewey.

"Stay safe."

The comm clicked and went silent. Dewey turned to the three curious-looking Juracanians. "Okay, I'm ready to talk to Samantha."

Rodrigo, or Juan Sebastian, Dewey hadn't determined which was which, waved for everyone to follow. He led the way back to the inner space where everyone was still waiting.

"Everyone okay back at base?" asked Cpl Garner.

Dewey nodded and then turned his attention back to Samantha. She'd said she wanted help and was amused by the idea that Dewey's platoon was of any use against the number of mercs present on the planet. Either there were more of them than Dewey was guessing, or she, like most of the second radial arm, underestimated the Hospitallers.

"Have the invaders dropped anything into the atmosphere since they started using the elevator?" asked Dewey.

Samantha turned and looked at Franco.

"Not since. No," said Franco.

"Why?" added Samantha.

"Because something has entered atmo." Dewey paused and looked around. He hadn't made an exact count, but his memory was exceptional. Half, or thereabouts, of the Juracanians were missing. "I'm assuming it's ours, but I wanted to make sure."

"Your people are sending more soldiers?"

"We're not soldiers," Cpl Garner said quietly. "We're Hospitallers."

Technically the same when it came to combat, but Dewey didn't feel like going into the particulars. There were other things much more important.

"Corporal Garner? Can you run a quick survey and see how many of the eyes we put out are operational and what kind of data they're pulling?" That would give Garner something to concentrate on. To Samantha, Franco, and the other Juracanians listening, he said, "Let's talk about how we get my people back."

"Help us," said one of the younger men standing a meter and a half behind Franco, who was near Samantha's left.

"Right," Dewey said with a slow nod. "That's sort of why we came here. But I'm getting a feeling that you want more than just food and medical supplies."

"We need to learn how to fight," said Samantha. "And we need the supplies to fight."

Dewey had noticed the odd tools the resistance Juracanians had armed themselves with.

"We don't normally train civilians to be fighters."

Before he could continue, Alexander spoke, saying, "I don't think this is normal. I mean our world. Juracan. The invaders."

"Invaders are somewhat common, unfortunately," said Dewey with a dismissive chuckle. "But, yes, normally there is some sort of military or defensive force that could give the attackers a fight and maybe even repel them."

"There hasn't been a military force here since the war," Samantha said.

Franco added, "Everyone who'd survived the war was too busy trying to stay alive to be bothered with more war."

"My great grandfather said everyone had lost the taste for war," said Alexander. He looked around, and most of those present nodded an agreement.

Dewey thought it was a shame anyone had a taste for it. "As

Hospitallers, we prefer to avoid military conflict if we can help it. There are times when we have no choice." He paused and looked in Cpl Garner's direction. The corporal still had his face shield down. He was manipulating unseen controls with his right hand. The rest of the fireteam had formed a triangle around their leader. Dewey turned back to once more face the Juracanians. "We can help train you, but there are two problems."

"Just two?" Around Samantha, the other Juracanians laughed reservedly but were clearly amused.

"Two for now." Dewey smiled and then said, "We don't know how much time we have to train you. More time would be better, but we may need to settle for hitting just the basics."

"That's one?"

"That's one," said Dewey. He'd turned to answer Franco's question and noticed that the telltale light along the edge of Cpl Garner's shield was gone. He was out of VR. "The second thing is weapons. We have extras, but not enough to arm all of your people."

"We might be able to help you there," said Samantha. Around her, several people had developed predatory grins. "We know where the invaders keep their guns and stuff."

It wouldn't be as easy as walking in and taking them. Still, Dewey liked the idea of having a bead on the enemy's munitions. If he could access those, he'd be able to arm the Juracanians. It would also deprive the mercenaries of their reserve weapons and munitions.

"Any chance that you also have their business calendar?" Dewey asked. He earned his own reserved laugh from the Juracanians.

In a more serious tone, Samantha said, "We don't know when the ship will come. It depends on how many of the containers they've managed to fill."

"They've more than enough," added Franco.

Dewey turned to acknowledge Cpl Garner's approach as he said to Franco and Samantha, "So, the clock's ticking."

"Found them all," Garner said with a salute. "Then I found more."

"You found more?" That was an interesting development, in

Dewey's opinion. "Where?"

Cpl Garner motioned off into the distance. "A block past the building that came down," he said. "The eyes Sgt Parks and Mitchell put out are buried in the rubble. The one I found was set to record. It's still recording. I didn't look at it."

Dewey could look at it later. If it had been set to record, Sgt Parks must have had a reason. To Cpl Garner, he asked, "You said more? I assume that means more than one?"

"Just one more." Cpl Garner looked surprised as he added. "It's inside the mercs' base."

Dewey snapped his face shield down and activated the VR to start the menu for available eyes. A map resolved itself on the shield. It showed a hundred-meter radius from Dewey's position.

"What's he doing?" asked Alexander.

"Looking," said Cpl Garner. "The helmet has a computer, and it allows us to see stuff differently."

With his left hand, Dewey pulled back the view. He did it slowly so that he didn't lose his balance.

"Like how we see in the dark?"

"Not quite," Dewey said in response to Alexander's second question. "It's complicated. Cpl Garner can show you."

Dewey couldn't see beyond his face shield, but he heard Cpl Garner removing his helmet and assisting Alexander.

"Burke? Becker? Maybe you can show Samantha and Franco?"

"Yes, Lieutenant," they replied in unison.

While he waited for the Juracanians to join him, Dewey located the eye that had been recording. He tapped the virtual menu and found the recording. With his right hand, he manipulated the controls only he could see. The VR image shifted. The eye was on the ground. Bits of rubble blocked some of the view. It looked to Dewey like someone had hidden the eye. He stopped the recording and tapped a button to return it to the beginning, where even more of the eye's view was blocked by someone's leg. Then he touched the virtual pause button and waited.

Simultaneously, as two markers appeared on the top edge of

Dewey's face shield, he heard dual gasps of surprise. Samantha and Franco had joined Dewey in VR.

"What is this?" Samantha asked. Her voice was more apparent now that she was in a helmet.

"This is a recording from an eye. An eye is a device that sees and then sends us what it sees."

"Pictures, then," said Franco.

Dewey could hear Cpl Garner chuckle in response.

"It's more than that. Stand by." Dewey reached out and tapped the button to start the recording playing. The leg in the view shifted and opened more of the space. Dewey could see Pvt Foster and PFC Gonzalez. They had their hands on their heads, and their multi-use weapons were missing.

Someone had been talking before the video recording had begun. It picked up with someone finishing a sentence. "- of you?"

Sgt Parks responded. "There was," she said. "But we're the only ones that made it out of the building."

"This is happening now?" asked Franco.

Dewey tapped the pause button. "It's a recording. Based on the timestamp, this happened about the same time that we entered the subway station." He tapped the virtual button that started the recording once more. As he'd only been able to identify three of the fireteam, Dewey was anxious to know that Cpl Mitchell and Cpl Wong were okay, too.

"So five of you," said the unknown voice. "All right, get up."

"Where are we going?" It was Cpl Mitchell. That left just one unknown for Dewey to discover.

"Well, you aren't going home," said another unknown voice.

"Shut it, Green," barked the first unknown voice.

"Of course, Sergeant Cook." Dewey couldn't mistake the insolence in Green's voice for anything else. Apparently, neither did Sgt Cook. "You're on point, Green. Go."

Then, the sound of boots scuffed the ground followed by some muttering that failed to earn a response from the mercenary sergeant. As the boot steps faded, the sergeant spoke again, but this time it wasn't to a surly teammate. "Up, Hospitallers," he said. His voice sounded calmer than the last few seconds. "You're coming with us."

It wasn't until Sgt Parks said, "Corporal Mitchell," that anything happened.

Cpl Mitchell stood, finally visible in the eye's view. He looked around, his gaze pausing on either the eye or the person partially blocking it. Dewey assumed it was Sgt Parks. When his gaze moved on, he said, "Fireteam, up."

Dewey could see Pvt Foster and PFC Gonzales as they stood. Then another person rose into view. It was Cpl Wong. Her helmet was off, and she had a compress strapped to the side of her head. The whole team was now accounted for.

The view from the eye was momentarily blocked. The leg that had covered the lower half of the view moved upward and then away. Dewey now had a clear view of Sgt Parks. Her left arm was in a temp cast, cradled in a sling. Some of them had taken injuries, but they were all alive.

A mercenary approached Sgt Parks, waving a hand towards the left of Dewey's view. It was the mercenary sergeant. "All right, all right," he said. "Follow Barnes, there. Get moving."

When the mercenary passed out of view, Sgt Parks looked directly at the eye. She winked and then limped away, out of the screen to the left. Dewey let the recording run a little longer. The mercenary sergeant appeared with one other of his team. They stooped to pick up weapons and gear they'd made Cpl Mitchell's fireteam unload. Then they walked left and out of view.

To be sure, Dewey set the recording to continue at double speed, and he watched it for several more of his minutes. When nothing happened, he tapped the button to stop the recording and then the one that ended the VR. Near him, someone cried out as they staggered.

"Easy there," said Cpl Garner.

Dewey lifted his shield, looking to his right. Cpl Garner and PFC Arnold had Franco by his arms, helping him to stand. Once he was stable, they helped him remove the helmet. Samantha had already removed hers and handed it back to Cpl Garner once he was done assisting Franco.

"Corporal Garner said there was another of these eye devices inside the invaders' camp?" Samantha asked.

"It is," said Dewey. He reset his shield and called up the other stray eye. As Cpl Garner had described, it was in some low grass with branches obscuring some of its view. One of Cpl Mitchell's team must have tossed it there when no one was looking. He set it to record on motion detection and exited once more. He turned to Samantha. "There's nothing on it yet, but it might come in handy later. What I would like to do now, which we lost the chance to do earlier, is get a better view of the elevator compound."

"We can do that," said Samantha. "I know just the place."

12

Dewey, followed closely by Cpl Garner's fireteam, proceeded in the wake of Samantha and Franco. After her declaration that she knew a good place to observe the space elevator, Samantha had turned and started across the open space and down a different set of stairs. Only a half dozen of the other Juracanians followed the Hospitallers.

"Where are we going?" Dewey asked Alexander as he signaled for Cpl Garner to keep an eye on those coming along behind them.

The Juracanian, who was walking next to Dewey, shook his head as they reached the next level down and another subway tunnel. Several light tubes glowed weakly in the ceiling. "Can't say for sure. We have a few watch posts to make sure the invaders don't try to sneak into the city. Samantha must have a specific one in mind, though."

The tunnel opened onto a subway platform. Samantha and Franco were already halfway across it. On the other side was another set of stairs that split to go up or down, as one needed. Dewey also noticed that the tracks here were clear of debris. If there'd been time, he would have gotten Cpl Garner's impression. There appeared to be a shine on the tracks that implied they'd been used recently.

Instead, Dewey asked another question that had occurred to him after Alexander answered the last one. It seemed that the Juracanian resistance had eyes everywhere. "So, you were aware that the mercs had gone to investigate our presence in Puchuncavi?"

Alexander looked embarrassed. It turned out not to be the reason Dewey assumed. "No," Alexander said. "Our watch post in the center of the city fell asleep."

Behind Dewey and Alexander, Dewey heard Cpl Garner and PFC

Arnold snort with amusement. Dewey signaled for them to stand down.

"Are the mercs aware that you're here?" asked Dewey. If so, he conjectured, the mercenaries would have made an effort to slip through unnoticed. Then, asleep or not, the lookout might never have seen the mercenaries. The conversation paused as they took a flight of stairs down to another station perpendicular to the one they'd just crossed. There were several more light tubes here, but the glow from them was even weaker.

"We think they know a couple of people are here," Alexander said. They continued to follow Franco and Samantha. "But they haven't made any effort to come into the city to look for us. Samantha thinks they don't care, so long as we don't give them a reason."

"Like attacking their outpost," said Cpl Garner.

"I guess that would make them mad." Alexander grinned after his comment.

Dewey could well imagine the desire to make the mercenaries and the company they served pay for enslaving and then indirectly killing the citizens of Juracan. His thoughts and considerations were put on hold as they approached Franco and Samantha. The two were standing in place at the end of the platform. Here, a short set of narrow steps led down to the tracks. The metal of the tracks was well coated in rust, very much unlike the tracks one level up.

"We have to go this way," Franco said. "There isn't any light down here."

"But you can see down here?"

Samantha nodded. "It's a little dim, Lieutenant Tyler, but we do fine. Will you be able to use your helmets?"

Dewey had his doubts. The night vision required some light, and the UV required a UV source. "I'm not sure," he said out loud. "If not, maybe we can use a weak light source to provide us some illumination without hurting your ability to see."

"Let's find out," said Franco. He turned and led the way down the stairs and onto the tracks.

Samantha followed Franco, with Dewey close behind her. He'd

already pushed his face shield down and had the night vision system running as he stepped onto the track. There was still enough light to make the night vision work. He was able to use it to walk a few more meters down the tracks. However, it was clear that past those first meters, he was going to be blind.

"Are you seeing?"

Dewey turned to look at Alexander. In response, he said, "Some, but I'm using light enhancement. That's about useless now. Corporal Garner? How's IR looking?"

On the stairs, Cpl Garner paused and reached out to touch a virtual control. "Same as earlier," he said. "The far edge of infrared is still working down here. I wonder if it has anything to do with the radiation?"

"Or it's just the planet," said Dewey. "The number of nuclear weapons that would have been required to irradiate the planet this deep wouldn't have left a city to be discovered." He switched to IR and adjusted a virtual dial before turning and identifying Samantha and Franco. "I think this will work. I'll let you know if things change."

He watched in the light of IR as Samantha nodded. She turned and started walking. Franco was quickly on her heels. Once Dewey was assured that the rest of the Hospitallers could see, he followed after the two Juracanians. They walked for another fifteen minutes. They went through one station before the track tunnel dipped. It went on a long incline that Dewey decided was taking them under the river. When the track tunnel leveled out, they were walking through knee-deep water.

"We got a pump working," Samantha said over her shoulder. "Uses solar power. Stuff we stole from the invaders. But it takes a while for the batteries to charge. Fortunately, the tunnel fills up slowly."

They were in the water for several minutes. It was enough time for Dewey to notice that it was reasonably clean water, not the stagnant he'd expect to find in a long-ago abandoned tunnel below a river. After that, the tunnel began to rise, almost leveling out when they came to a Y branch. Franco and Samantha took them down the left tunnel, eventually reaching a station that was as dark as the tunnel they'd walked through.

"We go up from here," said Alexander. He spoke in a hush and nodded with his head to indicate their direction of travel.

Dewey looked around. The IR wavelength provided some illumination. It was still gloomy despite the assistance of the augmented face shield. Even so, he could see that the two stairwells at either end of the station were pitch dark. It was a simple conclusion that the stairs were blocked. The building could have collapsed long ago, or the exits could have been sealed for other reasons. No matter how he looked at it, there wasn't any way they would be going up the stairwells. That meant there was another way.

"Here we go, Lieutenant," said Cpl Garner. He was motioning over his shoulder toward the wall opposite the platform.

Three of the other Juracanians who had followed behind had now hurried ahead. They were shifting a large panel with a faded map, lifting it off the wall. Behind it was a service door. Two of the Juracanians then lifted the third so that she could open the door and pull out a ladder whose feet landed with a crunch on the grime-coated gravel. With the ladder in place, they stepped aside.

"This used to be the station for an apartment building," said Franco. "It was as tall as the ones downtown. Now, it's half as tall."

"But it's still standing?" Dewey figured that might explain the blocked stairwells if the building had partially collapsed. But if it was partially collapsed, it would also be less stable.

"Well, enough," Franco said. "I lived here when I first escaped. I'd watch the goings-on over there."

He'd pointed with his thumb over his shoulder.

"It's mostly ladders," said Samantha. The grimace on her face gave Dewey the impression she'd made the ascent enough times. "But when you get to the observation post, you'll have a clear view."

Dewey turned to Cpl Garner. "I'll take one team member with me."

"Great," said Cpl Garner. "I love a good climb."

He stepped forward. It was evident to Dewey that Garner wasn't going to be dissuaded from his decision to join Dewey up to the observation level. Dewey nodded in agreement before turning to Franco and Samantha. "Let's go then."

Franco laughed. "Oh, I'm not going. Neither is Samantha. We leave that to the young these days."

Two of the Juracanians that had worked to reveal the opening turned and started up the ladder to the access hatch.

"After you," said Alexander. Even in the gloom of the weak IR light, Dewey could see Alexander's grin.

"Arnold," Cpl Garner said. "You're in command until we get back."

PFC Arnold nodded in acceptance. Cpl Garner returned the nod before stepping over to the ladder and starting up. He was followed by Alexander. Dewey went next, with three more of the young Juracanians following.

Though the group had to go manually up to the top of the building, the first part was the worst. The service tunnel went left and right, but they weren't in it for long before proceeding up another ladder. This one went up for thirty meters to a small room. In it was another ladder leading up through a rough-hewn hole. This put them in an air shaft with ladders secured to one wall.

"The bottom levels are impassable," said one of the Juracanians leading the way. He was breathing heavily with the exertion.

Fifty meters more and they were able to step through a meter-tall service hatch and onto a landing. A placard on the face of a door indicated this was the fourth floor. From here, it was all emergency stairwells. Dewey's legs already ached from the ladder climb. Fifteen more levels had his thighs and calves burning. When they came out of the stairwell on the nineteenth floor, Dewey was met with a jumbled view of crete and twisted steel.

"This way," the lead Juracanian said. He began to climb over and through the maze of debris.

The Juracanians and Hospitallers passed through in the same order they'd arrived. The debris in the passage they clambered through was worn smooth. Dewey presumed it was from numerous others who'd come here to observe.

When he emerged from the debris, Dewey stood in silent admiration. He was standing in as good an observation post as any Hospitaller would have built. The outer facing wall looked like a random pile of fallen debris, but he could see the spy-holes with smooth ledges for resting elbows on while watching. Between the spy-holes and where he stood, there were seats, several makeshift bunks, a door with a clearly defined signage for a lavatory, and a small kitchen with a portable stove. Next to it were several cases of field rations with markings for Allied Planet and United Planet forces. Likely all purchased through the black market for the mercenaries across the way and stolen by the enterprising Juracanian resistance.

"What do you think?" asked Alexander. He and the other Juracanians watched Dewey closely like nervous orphans waiting for their dorm father's approval.

Dewey scanned the area a little more, slowly adding a nod so that they knew what to expect. There were barely hidden smiles on their faces when he said, "This is a well-built observation post. I'm not sure we could have done better. What do you think, Corporal Garner?"

"I think I'm jealous," said Garner.

The Juracanians shared grins with each other. Then one of the unnamed Juracanians waved Dewey over to the spy-holes. "You can see the buildings where the invaders live from here. That last opening shows the elevator-thing."

"These ones show where they grind the metals down, and the loading yard," added one of the others.

"Thank you," Dewey said. To Cpl Garner he added, "Let's see if we can wedge a couple eyes in the debris so we can check in later."

"On it, Lieutenant."

While Cpl Garner pulled eyes out of pouches, Dewey moved in for a closer look through the spy-holes. The buildings built by the invading company were prefab stackers that went up four floors on the largest building. Two others were half that height, and then one other some distance away from the trio. It was only a single story high. Using his face shield, he was able to magnify the image of the outbuilding. It had warning signs on it that marked it as the armory.

Dewey shifted to the middle spy-hole, bumping into Cpl Garner, who'd been fixing an eye to a space above the hole that Dewey was not looking through. Here Dewey could see the salvage yard. Several large machines were grinding massive girders and rebar into thumb-sized nuggets. People were shoveling the nuggets into wheelbarrows that were then wheeled over to several mobile ramps. The people were thin, and their clothes were worn ragged at cuffs and hems. Teams of three stood at the top of the ramps and used ropes to pull the wheelbarrows up. The contents were then tilted into top-fed trunks. The process was being repeated by long lines of poorly-dressed workers.

There was no mistaking the workers for anything but Juracanians. Their pebbled skin was impossible to miss, especially through a magnified face shield.

The third spy-hole showed Dewey the space elevator, its shadow drawing a dark line east in the late afternoon sun. The elevator had three tracks that splayed across the ground like the foot of a gigantic bird. The equipment used to load the trunks onto the rails that would run the trunks up to the station sat idle. Dewey also noticed several specialized trunks near the base of the elevator. He was about to comment on them when a call signal appeared on the edge of his vision.

After stepping back from the spy-hole, which was immediately occupied by Cpl Garner looking for a place to secure an eye, Dewey reached out. He tapped the call icon to enlarge it. Enlarging it pulled out the data so he could see who was calling. His breath caught momentarily.

"Something wrong?" asked Alexander.

"Lieutenant?" Cpl Garner was approaching. "You get a call?"

"Yes," said Dewey. As he tapped the button to engage the comm, he said, "It's Sergeant Parks's signal."

The comm clicked, signaling a connection.

"Hello? Hello?" A woman's voice. Nervous.

"This is Lieutenant Tyler, Hospitallers," said Dewey. He hadn't been surprised to not hear Sgt Parks's voice. That would have been hoping for too much. "Who am I speaking to?"

"What? Me?" The voice sounded surprised. "Ms. Tegan Lerner. Mr. Thayer wishes to speak to you. Hold, please."

13

There was a long pause in which Dewey didn't hear the usual tell-tale clicks that told him he was on hold. Instead, he listened to the uncharacteristic sounds of fingernails on carbon-reinforced plastic. That and some indistinguishable grumbles clued Dewey in that Ms. Lerner did not know her way around a military helmet. Or a Hospitaller helmet at least.

"Um... excuse me?"

"Yes, Ms. Lerner?" Dewey shrugged as Cpl Garner looked at him with a questioning look. Dewey had his own questions, but not for Ms. Lerner. All of the Juracanians, except Alexander, were giggling near uncontrollably.

"How do I put you on hold?"

"Triple tap the right side of the helmet," Dewey said. "Fast."

Ms. Lerner exhaled, sounding relieved. She said, "Please hold," in a professional manner. Then, Dewey heard the clicks that indicated he was on hold.

He tapped his own helmet and then reached out to the virtual controls. Several quick taps and slides with his finger, and another icon appeared at the top of his face shield. Not far away, Cpl Garner paused and then made eye contact with Dewey. Garner nodded as he tapped the side of his own helmet.

Cpl Garner would now be listening in on the rest of the conversation. As soon as Dewey was taken off hold.

In the meantime, while he waited for Mr. Thayer to come on the line, Dewey turned his attention to the Juracanians. They were still giggling, and despite their pebbled skin, it was clear Alexander was blushing. The spaces between the pebbles of the skin on his face were bright pink. Dewey had yet to see that color on any of the Juracanians before.

"So, what gives?" asked Cpl Garner. Despite the moment spent connecting with Dewey over the comm, he appeared to be equally curious about the Juracanians' behavior.

"You want to tell them? Or should we?"

"It's not important, Jazmin," Alexander said.

"Oh, yes, it is," said one of the others. "Maybe you should tell them, Jazmin. It'll be more sensitive that way."

"What's that supposed to mean?" Jazmin seemed angry by some implication that slipped past Dewey.

"How about someone just blurt it out?" Dewey suggested.

"Alexander is infatuated with Tegan," said one of the two male Juracanians.

"Stop," said Alexander.

"And it's reciprocated," Jazmin added. There was a spark to her eye that seemed to jump to the eyes of the other Juracanians present. All except Alexander.

"That's how he escaped."

Alexander lifted his head, defiance in his eyes now. "That's how you escaped, too, Damian. So be thankful for that."

The third Juracanian nodded, a little less playful in his actions. "She's helped a lot of us since she met Alexander."

"It's still cute," said Jazmin. Though the humor in her eyes hadn't diminished, Jazmin seemed to have developed a more serious tone.

Dewey would have liked to ask more questions about the escapes and Ms. Lerner, but Mr. Thayer chose that moment to come on the line. Sort of.

"Hospitaller? Can you hear me?" The voice was distant and sounded like it was being shouted. "Hospitaller?"

"I can hear you," Dewey said. "Barely."

"I'm sorry," said Ms. Lerner. Her voice was clear. "Mr. Thayer says the helmet has too much radiation."

There was hardly any radiation. Dewey knew that they were subjected to higher than healthy doses on Juracan. Still, the material of the helmet was designed to reflect harmful rays of many sorts. If Mr. Thayer was going to make things difficult, it seemed Dewey would have to work with it.

"Ms. Lerner? Do you have the helmet on? Is the face shield down?"

There was a pause, and then she said, "It's down now."

"Good. If you'll reach out and touch the green dot at the top right, please."

There was a pause. Then, "Got it. Oh, wow."

Dewey knew she was responding to the sudden expansion of a menu of commands that had suddenly appeared before her. It had been the same way for Dewey and all the other Hospitallers when they'd first tried on a helmet back at the orphanages.

"Good work," he said. "Now, tap the command line that says external. From there, tap for microphone and speaker."

Dewey did the same thing with the speaker on his side so that the curious Juracanians could hear, too.

"Sure thing," said Ms. Lerner. There was a pause, and then Dewey heard her say, "Try now, Mr. Thayer."

"Try what now?"

Dewey heard the words much clearer, though they still sounded as if something was interfering with the communication. Perhaps it was the walls?

"Talk, Mr. Thayer," Dewey said. "I can hear you now, and you can hear me."

"I can. Now, tell me why you're on my planet?"

"Your planet?" There was no denying the message of the eye rolls of the Juracanians. They'd heard this before.

"We've already filed our claims for the mineral rights here."

Dewey shook his head. "Was that before or after you learned people still lived here, Mr. Thayer."

"What would you know about that?"

Dewey shrugged even though Mr. Thayer couldn't see it. "Only what I've read."

Of course, what Dewey read stuck with him, no matter how long ago he'd read it.

"Doesn't matter. Now, we need to make arrangements for you to evacuate. How many of you are out there?"

The Juracanians and Cpl Garner watched Dewey during the conversation. He signaled Garner to use the eyes and scout the area in case they were being stalled on purpose.

"I'm sure you saw us come down. Three dropships. I don't doubt that you know how many people they carry."

"Excuse me," said Ms. Lerner. "How do I mute the mic?"

"Touch the mic command you touched earlier," said Dewey. "That takes care of the external. Wipe the command window up, and you'll reach the general controls. Tap the mic you'll find there."

"Yes, I see them. Thank you. Give me a second, please."

A hard silence filled Dewey's ears. Rather than muting his own mic, he switched it to speak directly to Cpl Garner.

"How's it look out there?"

"Quiet," said Cpl Garner. "I've zoomed in and stitched the vids together so that I have a panoramic of their base. They've got a reinforced guardhouse at the road, and vid watchtowers. The only movement inside is the workers shoveling scrap."

"Thank you, Garner. Keep a watch out. And on the Juracanians. I don't expect trouble, but I am curious how they're reacting to the conversation with Mr. Thayer. I might use some subterfuge, and I don't want them panicking."

"You got it, Lieutenant."

Dewey switched the comm mic back to Sgt Parks's helmet. The silence remained for another half-minute. Then, Ms. Lerner was back.

"Hospitaller?"

"Lieutenant Tyler, if you don't mind," Dewey said.

"Of course. Lieutenant Tyler. Mr. Thayer is back."

Again Dewey shrugged. "All right."

"A fourth ship dropped in," said Mr. Thayer. His voice still had the strange sound of separation that shouldn't be there.

"Yes."

"Well, explain that."

What Dewey wanted to do at that moment was tell Mr. Thayer it was none of his business, but his actions were familiar. This was often the way that civilian leaders spoke to Hospitallers. They wouldn't be as bold with space marines.

Instead, Dewey said, "Supplies that wouldn't fit inside the first dropships."

Cpl Garner flashed a thumbs up and caused Dewey to grin. He actually had no idea what had been sent down. He was guessing that Maj Hughes had sent a trunk down to the planet. After several days of comm silence, Dewey would have done the same thing. Hopefully, Lt Owen would have that answer soon enough.

"Well, you'll have to leave them behind when you go. You're short a ship."

"Which you shot down." Dewey began to pace, frustrated with the conversation. He'd understood quite clearly when he'd accepted officer candidate training that there would be times like this. Times where he'd have to deal directly with people with whom he would be at odds. At those times, he would have to find common ground with them or even acquiesce to their position. It was a very different situation than being an NCO who occasionally had to deal with a civilian who wasn't there to assist. He could imagine what majors and colonels went through, but he chose to shy away from the mental exercise.

Mr. Thayer was chuckling. It made Dewey dislike him even more.

"Yes, about that." Mr. Thayer paused. "Bit of an accident with that. Some of the soldiers were a little on edge. No one is supposed to be here, so you can see how they might have taken your actions as a threat."

"No, not really," said Dewey.

"Doesn't matter," said Mr. Thayer. His voice had gone icy even with the strange filtering. "You have enough ships to lift off-planet. You need to do that now."

"You have five of my people."

Even Cpl Garner paused as the conversation turned.

"You can have them back. Once you're off-planet, we'll shuttle your people up to the loading docks, and you can pick them up there."

Dewey had his doubts about Mr. Thayer. If he was willing to let hundreds to thousands of locals die with little interest or concern, how much would he actually care about five Hospitallers?

"It'll take me some time to get everything and everyone loaded," said Dewey. Standard tactic: stall.

Again Mr. Thayer laughed. "I wouldn't wait too long, Hospitaller. The clock is ticking."

There was a moment of near-silence in which Dewey heard Ms. Lerner ask in a whisper, "What? What? Yes, of course, Mr. Thayer."

Then the comm line went silent. Dewey tapped his helmet even though he was sure that Ms. Lerner and Mr. Thayer weren't eavesdropping.

"Any of you know anything about Mr. Thayer?"

Three of the Juracanians turned to look at Alexander.

"He's paranoid," said Alexander. "He rarely leaves his offices and apartments. Tegan says the walls are insulated against radiation. When he does come out, he's in a special suit to protect him. In fact, when he was talking, he was probably on the other side of the glass wall that separates his part of the office from Tegan's."

"Sounds paranoid," said Cpl Garner. "And crazy. Why come to a radioactive planet if you're so afraid of it?"

"Credits," said Dewey. He turned to the Juracanians. "We've left eyes here. They'll allow us to check in on the facilities across the way. So, there's no need for us to stay here anymore. I'd like to talk to Samantha and Franco about returning to Puchuncavi."

There was a ragged array of nods before Damian started back through the debris maze. Jazmin followed. Alexander and the other Jurcanian waved for Dewey to proceed. Cpl Garner was close behind as they began the trip back down to the tunnels.

Hospitallers trained nearly constantly. If they weren't providing aid and comfort somewhere, they practiced combat skills on other planets and in mock towns. They were always moving. For that reason, they were considered to be in excellent physical shape. But up and down stairs and ladders for fifteen-plus levels? That took a toll on anyone. So, Dewey was relieved when they finally stepped out of the service hatch where Samantha, Franco, and the other Juracanians were still waiting.

Dewey noticed that the rest of Cpl Garner's fireteam, who'd set themselves at the ends of the platform, came to attention as Dewey dropped down to the gravel and rusted tracks. He signaled for them to stand easy.

"Enjoy the view?" asked Franco. He'd been sitting cross-legged in a circle with some of the others. They'd been bouncing small, thick sticks on the ground between them. A game, Dewey assumed.

"Worth the climb," said Cpl Garner. Dewey wasn't fooled. He could see the sweat on Garner's face. He'd felt the labor as much as Dewey did.

"Received a phone call from Mr. Thayer," said Dewey.

That silenced the group for several seconds.

"What did he have to say?" Samantha asked.

"He asked us to leave," said Dewey. "And the quicker, the better."

Franco and Samantha exchanged looks. Some of the other Juracanians looked angry. Some looked lost. Dewey understood why. It was based on the simple fact that the Juracanians had no knowledge of the Hospitallers other than what Dewey and his people shared in conversation.

"And what will you be doing, then?" asked Franco.

"Leaving," Dewey said. He hoped his grin gave away the joke before he continued. "But when we're ready."

The Juracanians as a group seemed to sigh with relief.

"They still don't get it," said Cpl Garner. Dewey wondered until Garner grinned if he really was saddened by the notion.

"We're not beholden or responsible to Mr. Thayer," said Dewey. "We came here to offer help and aid to the people of Juracan. And we've barely even started."

"Would that include military training?" asked Franco.

"It will. But for now, I need to communicate with my people. Preferably face to face. And the sooner, the better."

"I'm not sure we'll make it back before nightfall, Lieutenant Tyler," said Cpl Garner.

"It may not take as long as you think," said Franco. He had a smile on his face that made Dewey suspect a secret was about to be revealed.

"Either way," said Dewey, "I'd like to get going."

"Okay, everyone," said Samantha. She clapped her hands to draw the attention of the few people not watching the conversation. "Back we go."

The Juracanians and Hospitallers marched back the way they'd come. This included through the water, which was several centimeters deeper. Dewey made a mental note to find some other power sources the Juracanians could use to keep the pump running. He knew of several that were in the supplies they brought. What he knew they didn't have in the supplies was a pump. But maybe they could do something about that, too, if things dragged on that long.

As they continued back the way they'd come, Cpl Garner briefed the rest of his fireteam with the information they'd gleaned through observation and conversation. That included Ms. Tegan Lerner's reciprocated affection for Alexander.

"Is that even possible?" asked PFC Burke. "She has to take radiation blockers to be here. And she's inside buildings protecting her from radiation."

"We've been able to see each other a few times," said Alexander. He nodded and added, "But, yeah, we have to limit her exposure."

"What if he left Juracan?" asked PFC Arnold. "Would Alex become less radioactive?"

"I'm not sure anyone would allow him on their ship or station," said Cpl Garner. Then to Alexander, he said, "No offense, Alexander, but you'd set off radiation alarms wherever you went."

In a way, by Dewey's reckoning, the situation was much like it was for the people of Wenshen. Yes, they were all human, Wenshens and Juracans. But there were just enough genetic differences that it would be fatal to them or to others if either group were to leave their home planets. And that had Dewey wondering how many other lost places had shoved humans onto different genetic paths.

He wasn't able to wonder long. As they came out of the tunnel to the next to the last station, things had changed. There was something on the tracks now, which explained the absence of rust he'd seen earlier. It was a pair of oversized handcars. They'd been worked on recently and had more than just the seesaw pump that turned the wheels. There were several rows of seats along the sides.

Based on the number of people on the platform, the handcars had been occupied by more than just a couple people. Stacks of emergency rations from the dropships were also piled on the platform. As Dewey scanned the people and supplies, a woman stepped forward.

"Hello, Lieutenant Tyler."

14

Dewey took the steps up to the platform as he greeted the unexpected guest. "Hello, Valentine. I'm surprised but not surprised to see you here."

"What about us?" said SSgt Castro as she stepped out from behind the stack of ration cartons.

"Not once I saw the rations," said Dewey, returning the staff sergeant's salute. "But, I am pleased to see you and Cpl Fleming's fireteam."

The Hospitallers laughed, shaking hands with those who'd been with Dewey.

"I guess I'll have to settle for that, Lieutenant," SSgt Castro said. She became more serious as she asked, "What about Sergeant Parks and the others?"

"Still being held," Dewey said. He relayed what had occurred at the watch post so that SSgt Castro and Valentine knew where things stood.

"But you're not going to leave," said Valentine, and it wasn't a question.

"That's right. I don't trust Mr. Thayer with my people, and he's not why we came here. Now, if the people of Juracan want us to leave…"

Valentine shook her head. "Clearly, I can't speak for all the other towns," she said. "But I think I know them well enough to say they'd want you to stay and help us."

"That's good to know." Dewey then turned to SSgt Castro. "You didn't just come along for the ride. Any of the remaining squad leaders could have handled this."

"No, there's a reason," admitted SSgt Castro. "And we could have waited to comm you, but it seemed a good excuse to come see the city."

"So, what's the reason?"

Dewey spared a glance for the other Juracanians. They were being educated on the emergency rations by the rest of the Hospitallers. Likely, Dewey considered, they were telling the Juracanians which meals were the best and which were the ones to avoid unless they were desperate.

"It's the trunk that the Graevya dropped down. It's got a security lock on it." SSgt Castro grinned. "It needs your handprint."

"And no clue what's in it?" When SSgt Castro shook her head no, Dewey turned to find Samantha and Franco, who'd joined Valentine. "Looks like I need to return to Puchuncavi."

"Fortunately for us," SSgt Castro said from behind before the others could speak, "we discovered that the people of Puchuncavi were keeping a secret."

A quick glance back showed that SSgt Castro was holding back her typical good nature. He turned back to the trio of elder Juracanians and waited for an explanation.

"Should we lay all our tap-sticks out for you to see?" asked Franco.

Dewey had no idea what tap-sticks were, but the implication was still obvious. They were still working on building trust between the two groups.

"No," he said after a pause. "And no one blames you. But now that we know, can I get a ride?"

"Of course." Valentine appeared surprised by the politeness of the request. Considering how Mr. Thayer and the mercenaries had been the very opposite, Dewey couldn't blame her.

"Thank you." Dewey turned back to SSgt Castro, who was now her usual smiling self. "Castro, you get to do more than just see the city."

"I get to blow stuff up?"

While the other Hospitallers laughed, the Juracanians looked shocked. Dewey expressed neither emotion. Like any member of the Orphan Corps, SSgt Castro liked a good explosion, especially if they were the ones to set it.

"Maybe later," Dewey said. He waved Franco and Samantha over. "These are the leaders of the resistance."

"Staff Sergeant Castro," said the staff sergeant as she offered her hand in greeting. "I promise not to blow anything up without permission."

Franco grinned as he shook hands. "That's a relief."

"They are the leaders of the resistance," said Dewey as Samantha shook hands with SSgt Castro.

"Elected leaders," corrected Samantha. "We lead until someone calls for a vote."

"Sounds messy," said SSgt Castro. Then, "But fair."

"I'm glad you think so," said Dewey. "Because you are going to stay here and give some basic training to the resistance."

It was SSgt Castro's turn to look shocked. "Train civilians?"

Behind her, Dewey could see the other Juracanians beaming. There were some worried looks shared among the Hospitallers.

"I know it's not how we normally do things," Dewey said. "But this isn't a normal situation. And I know that you're the best person for the job."

"The lieutenant has a way with words," SSgt Castro said in a mock aside to Samantha and Franco. While the Juracanians chuckled with amusement, Castro asked Dewey, "What and how much do I teach them?"

Dewey had been considering this as he'd returned from the observation. He didn't want to just keep them busy and out of trouble. That would only anger them, and that wasn't helpful for anyone. He also wasn't going to teach them how to attack an armed encampment. That kind of training would take years, and they likely only had weeks, maybe even less. But they needed to learn something useful for the moment.

"Basic team drills," he said after his pause seemed to be growing long enough to worry the Juracanians. "Weapons. Basic urban situations. Clearing spaces, defending spaces."

"How to establish a kill zone," added SSgt Castro.

"Yes. The things they'll need to defend against the mercs and keep them bogged down."

"Sounds fun," SSgt Castro added.

While the younger Juracanians looked eager, Dewey noticed that Samantha, Franco, and a few of the older members of their resistance suddenly looked doubtful. Likely, SSgt Castro's mention of the kill zone drove home the seriousness of their request.

"I know you're eager, Castro," Dewey said. "But start with basics and simple stuff. Pick out those with the most promise and escalate their training. No one has to participate."

"Just like the orphanage."

"Yes, Castro," said Dewey. "Just like the orphanage."

Not every orphan enjoyed the games they played when they were young. A well-aimed marshmallow gun could leave a mark. Dewey had been caught in a crossfire just once. Not only had he spent an hour trying to wash the marshmallows out of his hair, he had a black eye from a particularly stale marshmallow. And not every orphan became a member of the Orphan Corps. That was volunteers only. There were thousands of other opportunities to serve with the Hospitallers that didn't require a weapon, and there was no shame in it. Everyone learned to respect everyone, no matter how menial the job seemed. Without them, there wouldn't be uniforms, logistics, research, and a host of other things that supported the Orphan Corps' work.

"Do I have help?"

Dewey smiled and nodded towards Cpl Fleming, who had an eager look. Apparently, he had been listening in. "You have a fireteam of help, Castro."

SSgt Castro looked in Cpl Fleming's direction and got a thumbs up from the fireteam leader. She turned back to Dewey. "Should be fun."

"Not too much fun. We don't want anyone to get hurt." He turned to Valentine as SSgt Castro chuckled amusedly. Dewey said to her, "Shall we go?"

Valentine nodded and turned back to a set of wood stairs placed halfway along the platform. Dewey turned to Franco and Samantha, shaking their hands before following Valentine. Behind Dewey, several of the Juracanians followed. Cpl Garner's team jumped off the platform and met Dewey and Valentine at the handcars.

"It's dark in there," Cpl Fleming said from where he was standing near the supplies. "And Valentine wouldn't let us use task lights."

"Next time, try IR, far end of the spectrum," said Garner as he hefted himself onto the forward car and took a seat.

The Juracanians manned the seesaw handles. Valentine pulled on a lever as she waved goodbye to those still on the platform. SSgt Castro saluted as the cars moved into the darkness of the tunnel. Dewey returned the salute as the cars picked up speed, carrying them into the tunnel.

The trip through the train tunnels had been the dullest experience Dewey'd had since being on Juracan. Even with the IR providing illumination, there was nothing to see but crete walls and the occasional subway platform. Most of them were dark and showed a complete lack of use. A few others looked like they'd been accessed at some time since the war that ruined the planet.

Though ruined might not be the right description. People were still alive on Juracan. And though they'd been changed by the radiation and lived hard, they'd been thriving. But the galaxy had found them. Unfortunately, it had been the greedy part, and that had come with a price.

These were the sorts of thoughts that kept Dewey company during the short trip back to Puchuncavi. Even a brief turn on the handcart's seesaw handles didn't help dispel the gray thoughts of the state of the people of Juracan.

"And here we are," said one of the other Juracanians who'd come with them back to Puchuncavi.

They slowly rolled into a station that was dimly lit with evening light from several light tubes overhead. The station was clean. If there'd been any debris, it had been removed long ago.

The handcarts screeched as they jerked their way to a stop, lining up with a narrow set of wooden stairs, much like the ones at the beginning of the journey. Valentine beamed with pride.

"Perfect stop," she said as she stepped from cart to stairs to platform.

Dewey and Cpl Garner's team followed Valentine up a long flight of stairs. It was darker in the station than below. The building's windows were boarded over. But, when they pushed through a large wooden door, Dewey understood why.

The station was about seventy meters from the center of Puchuncavi. It was surrounded by fields, most of them fallow, and several other outbuildings. When Dewey turned around, he didn't see a subway station. It wasn't because of the long evening shadows. It was because if there had been a subway station, it had been replaced with an old barn.

"Clever," said Dewey.

"It's new," Valentine said as they began the short trek into town. "Once we realized the invaders weren't friendly, we thought it best to keep our ability to move about a secret. The barn used to be over there. We took it apart and rebuilt it. That was while we still had the younger people to help. And we did it at night, which you now know isn't so dark for us."

"Impressive," said Cpl Garner from just behind them. "Same building, different location. The mercs probably didn't even notice."

"I noticed the track went on," Dewey said. He also saw the task lights from a group of Hospitallers leaving the town and coming in his direction. He began walking to shorten the distance as he asked Valentine, "Does the track go to Romerol?"

Valentine nodded as she took long steps to keep up with Dewey. "Yes."

"Other places?"

Valentine stopped, forcing Dewey to do the same thing. "It does and doesn't. The tracks haven't been completely cleared. But most of what we've seen is in good shape. The barn where all the train cars were kept was destroyed."

"And there's no electricity to run them," said Dewey.

Valentine started walking again. "We haven't been able to generate enough. Not yet."

"Can you reach the towns near the ocean?" Dewey asked as he kept pace with her.

"One."

The other Hospitallers, having come within fifty meters, had turned down their task lights' luminosity and were now identifiable. Lt Owen and Lt Matthews were approaching in the company of Cpl Lena Wong's fireteam. Trailing them was Sgt Thompson, Lt Owen's loadmaster.

As he waited for them to get close enough to hail without shouting, Dewey asked Valentine another question. "And what about north of the city?"

"North?" Valentine chuckled. "That's a bit more complicated. There's debris no one's moved yet. You have to walk a section and wait for another handcar to arrive from the other side. Just so you don't have to ask, we can reach six towns from here."

"Lieutenant Tyler. Welcome back."

Dewey returned Lt Owen's salute. "Thank you, Owen."

"Lieutenant," said Cpl Wong. She saluted in turn.

"Wong. Everything secure?"

"Buttoned up tight," said Cpl Wong. Her eyes shifted to Valentine. "Unless there's more secrets."

Valentine grinned. "I'll never tell."

Dewey laughed. "Fair enough. Now, Owen, where's this trunk that needs my handprint?"

Lt Owen pointed several degrees west of Romerol. "About an hour walk that way."

Dewey tracked the sky for the sun. "We still have a couple hours of daylight. Let's get there and see what's so important it needs me to be present."

"I'll skip this part of the adventure, Lieutenant Tyler," said Valentine.

"I understand." Dewey turned to Cpl Garner. He could see the eagerness to continue the adventure in the corporal's eyes. But they'd been through a lot already. He had, too, but he was needed. "I'm giving you an order, Garner. Get your team back to base. Clean up, eat something warm. Maybe Lieutenant Gray has some coffee for you."

"Oh, he's got coffee all right," said Lt Matthews. She grinned as Cpl Wong and her fireteam laughed. "Unless the elders drank it all."

"There you go, Garner. Better hurry before it's all gone."

"Will do, Lieutenant," said Cpl Garner as he saluted. When Dewey returned the salute, Garner waved for his team to follow. They walked around the group of officers, giving a nod to Cpl Wong as they passed.

As Cpl Garner's fireteam and Valentine resumed the walk back to town, Dewey turned to Lt Owen and Cpl Wong. "Let's get moving while we still have daylight."

"On it, Lieutenant," said Cpl Wong. She turned and signaled to her team, singling out PFC Marc Webb for point. He nodded and quick-marched until he was twenty meters ahead. PFC Juanita Bryant went next before Cpl Wong waved for the lieutenants and Sgt Thompson to proceed. She then brought up the rear with Pvt Marlene Russell.

The journey, though short, took them across a variety of terrain. Past the fallow fields by the subway was a stream that they crossed via a log that looked like it had served this purpose many times before. There were several ruins along the way, too, their chimneys serving as headstones. After several abandoned fields, they crossed through a wide stand of trees before coming out into an old parking lot that had slowly been repossessed by nature over the centuries. Rusted and bent light poles dotted the open space, made stark by the task lights everyone was now using to illuminate their path.

On the far side of the parking lot, just visible in the pale wash of task lights, the trunk waited with all the patience of any inanimate object.

"We've been speculating on what could have been here," said Lt

Owen as they approached the trunk. "There's no substantial ruins of any kind. I thought maybe an arena."

"Or an airport," said Lt Matthews. "But something had to have survived to this time. Control tower, maybe?"

Dewey looked around. It did look like a parking lot in the middle of nowhere. He wondered if it could have been a train station like one used by commuters. Or perhaps even a subway. The city wasn't that far away. The list of unanswered questions was growing faster than the ones with answers.

"Unfortunately, we're not here to explore," he said as they reached the trunk.

With the help of several task lights, Cpl Wong was unbolting the cover for the trunk's access panel. The trunks weren't generally locked with a palm print. Most of the time, all they had to do was push the green button to unlock it. But there were occasions where the Hospitallers didn't want random people accessing the materials inside. Even then, a simple six-digit pin would have been employed.

Requiring a palm print meant that Maj Hughes was absolute that he didn't want the contents to fall into the wrong hands. If someone managed to force the trunk doors, it would ignite phosphorus flares down the length of the trunk. If the thieves weren't prepared or didn't expect it, the fire would destroy most of what was inside.

Fortunately, Dewey was still alive and still had his hand. He tapped a code to wake the palm reader and pushed his hand against the glass surface.

"Let's see what kind of goodies the major sent us," he said as the screen flashed green.

15

Lt Matthews and Sgt Thompson pulled on one of the doors as Dewey and Lt Owen pulled on the other. Cpl Wong had moved back to watch the perimeter with her fireteam. The doors came open slowly but moved on well-maintained hinges. They pushed the doors the last one hundred eighty degrees until they locked against the trunk's sides.

Back in front, his own task light panning across the dark interior, Dewey took a moment to examine what he could see. Next to him, Lt Owen and Lt Matthews had added their own task lights, illuminating more of the interior.

"That's a pleasant surprise," said Lt Owen.

Dewey agreed. "And a welcome one, too."

At the front of the trunk, its broad, slightly angled face staring them down, was a RapRes. The RapRes, like the crawlers, could go over just about any terrain, take a beating, and keep going. Unlike the crawlers, the RapRes were designed for rapid response and could go much faster.

There were several rubberized buttons on the back of the door with the security lock. Dewey pushed them. After a brief delay, bar lights down the middle of the trunk's ceiling snapped on.

"Owen? Can you operate a RapRes?"

"I think I was born in one."

Dewey laughed at the hyperbole. "Great. Climb in. Let's see if we can get that thing out."

"It's kind of packed in there, Lieutenant," said Sgt Thompson. His task light was highlighting the space to the right of the RapRes.

Lt Owen had stripped off his gear and was already climbing over the boxes and containers that looked as if they'd been shoved into every available space. Owen wouldn't be able to get the back hatch open, but if he could reach the top hatch that they would have left open for this very reason, he could snake his way in. After that, if he tried to move the RapRes, he'd damage or destroy the gear stowed around it.

"Good point, Thompson." Dewey signaled for Cpl Wong. "Four eyes on the trunk, Corporal. Then you're on VR duty while the rest of the fireteam works with Sergeant Thompson."

"On it, Lieutenant Tyler," said Cpl Wong. She signaled to her fireteam. They began opening pouches, pulling out eyes.

"What about me?" asked Lt Matthews. She had a grin on her face.

"You?" Dewey asked in mock surprise. "What about me?"

"I guess we could inventory the gear as it comes out," suggested Lt Matthews.

Dewey was already pulling out his tablet. "We're lieutenants. It's what we do."

They stepped back as Sgt Thompson began tugging free the closest containers. Thompson set the container on the ground just to the side of Lt Matthews. Cpl Wong's fireteam came around the trunk's sides as the sergeant turned back to fetch another container.

"You two take that side," said Sgt Thompson, pointing at PFC Webb and Pvt Russell. "Put that stuff off to the side of Lieutenant Tyler. We'll put this stuff on the side with Lieutenant Matthews."

Inside the trunk, Dewey could hear Lt Owen still scrabbling across the top of the RapRes. "You okay, Owen?"

"Almost there." Owen's voice was breathy with the effort he was putting into reaching the hatch.

Dewey turned his attention back to the slowly growing stack of supplies. There were more emergency rations, along with dried and dehydrated civilian foodstuffs that were more palatable. There were bundles of clothes and already several emergency shelters. Some of the items, like the shelters, weren't going to be needed as far as Dewey knew. But as they hadn't been able to communicate with the Graevya, Maj Hughes had no idea what they needed. It made sense in that situation to send a broad spectrum of supplies.

And the supplies kept coming. Sgt Thompson had the fireteam carry the supplies further and further out from the trunk so as not to impede the RapRes when it was free to move. Cpl Wong had found a sturdy crate to sit on. Dewey had checked in on her several times. She was doing well, and there wasn't any sign of trouble.

"Lieutenant Tyler?" Sgt Thompson's voice drew Dewey's attention from a toys-and-treats crate. When he looked at Thompson, the sergeant pointed toward the RapRes. "I think Lieutenant Owen made it."

Grinning and waving, Lt Owen could be seen in the cab of the RapRes, the panel lights illuminating his smile.

Dewey tapped his comm and used the virtual buttons to locate and connect with the RapRes. "Owen? You hear me?"

"Loud and clear," said Lt Owen. "We ready to roll?"

"Sergeant Thompson, are we clear?"

Sgt Thompson held up a finger to pause his answer as he looked down both sides of the RapRes. From where Dewey stood, he could see PFC Webb backing out of the space between the trunk wall and the RapRes. Once Webb was out of the way, Sgt Thompson stepped into the gap. When he turned around, he shook his head.

"Couple more minutes, Lieutenant."

Dewey nodded and then said to Lt Owen, over the comm, "Couple more minutes. Anything behind you in the back of the RapRes?"

In the cab, Lt Owen was nodding. Over the comm, he was laughing. "It's like a bunker back there. Shoulder-fired-rockets, mortars, grenades, and more cases of ammo than you'll ever need."

"Let's hope so," Dewey said out loud but for himself. "Okay, Owen. Stand by a few more."

"Will do. Oh," Lt Owen held up a tablet. "This was in here. It's got a security lock on it. I can't open it, so I think it's intended for your eyes only."

"Understood. Don't break it."

Five minutes passed before Sgt Thompson gave Dewey the all-clear. Dewey passed the information to Lt Owen, giving him the green light. Everyone stepped back as the RapRes hummed to life and then slowly rolled out of the trunk. Sgt Thompson guided the vehicle forward, stopping it twenty meters out so that it wasn't in the way of the as yet unloaded supplies.

The back gate of the RapRes whined to life, slowly lowering to create a ramp. The interior lights were on, and Dewey understood what Lt Owen had meant now that he could see it for himself. Owen had been forced to turn sideways to reach the back opening. There was little space for movement. Dewey hoped that he never needed that much ammo ever.

"Guess you'll all be walking," said Lt Owen as he stepped down the ramp, straightening his uniform as he went. "I'm lucky they left a gap up front, or no one would have gotten in."

"Someone had to get out," said Sgt Thompson. "Makes sense they'd have left a gap."

"Right you are, Thompson," said Owen. He gave his sergeant a hearty shoulder pat. "What else is in there?"

The trunk was large enough that it could have carried another RapRes. Instead, it was filled with more supplies. Dewey turned on his helmet's task light again as he entered the trunk. He identified the markings for medical supplies, extra uniforms, and a case of multi-use weapons. Mixed in were all the sorts of equipment they normally used to provide aid to people displaced by war or nature.

"Who's going to carry it all?" asked PFC Bryant. She grinned at her joke.

"You are," said Cpl Wong.

Dewey tapped his comm. There were worse problems to have.

"Hey, Tyler," said the voice over the comm.

"How's the coffee coming along, Gray?" asked Dewey. There were nods of appreciation from those within earshot.

"I'm in my element, as it were," said Lt Gray. "Just finishing up the last batches for the day. I've got to have plenty to satisfy the elders of Puchuncavi. But you didn't call just to chat about coffee. Is there a problem with the trunk?"

"We have been blessed with an abundance of supplies, Gray, and no way to get them all back to town." Dewey turned as he spoke, having heard Lt Owen say something to Lt Matthews. Owen was carrying a tablet in his hands.

"You'll want a couple crawlers, I presume," Gray said. "And people to help load."

"If you could pass the word to Lieutenant Haynes. Have her send Sergeant Maxwell and the rest of her squad, along with two crawlers, that'd be great."

Lt Owen held out the tablet, which Dewey accepted.

"Making it happen now," said Lt Gray.

"Thank you," Dewey said and tapped the comm line closed. He turned his attention to the tablet he'd taken from Owen. It required his personal code to access it. That was one way to keep private whatever was on it.

Dewey called up the keypad and tapped in his fourteen-digit number. The screen flashed briefly, revealing the main menu. There was only one file on the entire tablet. Dewey shared the screen with the others around him.

"I'm not going to lie," said Lt Matthews. "That's weird."

"Well, if Major Hughes didn't want anyone to know what was on the tablet," said Lt Owen, "then the security code made sense. And if you didn't want anyone to know anything more than the message, should they manage to access the tablet, wiping it of everything else takes care of that."

"Bit paranoid," said Sgt Thompson.

"That's okay," Dewey said as he tapped the file to open it. "I'm feeling a bit paranoid myself."

The file was audio. Dewey could have connected it to his comm so only he could hear. But he reasoned that the information wasn't something to keep from his team, just from others like the mercenaries and Mr. Thayer.

"Greetings, Lieutenant Tyler," said the voice on the recording. It was Maj Hughes. "We haven't heard from you. Not sure if there's a problem. I'll wait another twenty-four hours before sending someone down to investigate. In the meantime, just in case you are well, I thought I'd send you some more supplies. Not sure what you might need, so we sent you a variety and hope that we got some useful stuff for you. If you can get a message back up to us, that'd be great. If not, well, twenty-four hours, and we'll come looking for your bodies."

"Ever the optimist," said Dewey as he closed the file and deleted it. He looked at the tablet for a few seconds, turning it over and then back again. Then, he held it out to Lt Matthews. "Can you unlock this permanently? And then, can you upload everything you have that might be useful to the Juracanians?"

"Like history stuff?" asked Lt Matthews as she accepted the tablet. Like Dewey, she turned it over several times as if maybe it would answer the question for her.

"Yes. And anything else that might be useful that wouldn't be considered sensitive information."

Lt Matthews stowed the tablet with hers. "I can do that. Maybe I should survey the other officers to see what they have as well?"

"I have a bunch of books on construction," said Sgt Thompson. "I'd been thinking about transferring over to engineering on my next contract."

"Perhaps after the officers, you talk to the NCOs," Dewey said. "And then the enlisted. Who knows what gems we'll find? I'll send you everything I have when there's time. For now, I'd like you to stay here with Corporal Wong's fireteam and then oversee the loading of the crawlers when they arrive. Set a new passcode on the trunk, empty or not, and secure it before you leave."

"Will do."

Dewey turned to Lt Owen. "How about a lift back to town?"

The town was silent when they rolled into it. Local time put it close to midnight. So, the children who'd been much more active with the presence of the Hospitallers were asleep. Their absence gave the town an eerie feel, compounded by the dark sky.

Dewey hadn't had time to look skyward in the evenings since

touching down. He'd been in talks with the people of Juracan or asleep or too busy to look anywhere else but forward. Now, though, with the brief moment of near solitude, he looked skyward.

Every habitable planet had an aurora, the northern and southern lights. They were an artifact of the magnetic field surrounding each planet, and Dewey had seen them a few times on different worlds. But a person usually had to be further north or south. The auroras on Juracan were unlike the shimmering curtains Dewey had seen on those other planets. Here, they were more like Cirrus clouds, long and wispy but glowing in the night.

Perhaps these weren't the result of the magnetic fields near the poles. Maybe it had something to do with the radiation still in the atmosphere. The same radiation that made it impossible to communicate with the Graevya. Either way, they were mesmerizing. Dewey watched them dance across the sky until the RapRes jerked to a halt.

Sgt Barrett and Cpl Chavez were waiting by the rear gate as it whined its way to the ground. Barrett fought back a yawn before they both saluted Dewey and Lt Owen as they stepped out of the RapRes.

"Welcome back, Lieutenant Tyler. Lieutenant Owen," said Sgt Barrett. "I hear we have new toys."

"And things that go boom," added Cpl Chavez. Her eyes twinkled with enthusiasm.

Dewey hooked a thumb over his shoulder. "Lots of things that go boom, but we need a place to keep them safe."

"There's a playing field out behind the school," said Sgt Barrett. "And a service shed on this side of it. We can clear it out and then sandbag the exterior."

"We have ballistic shields in the trunk, too," said Lt Owen. "We could layer those between the walls and the sandbags. Extra precaution."

Dewey had seen the ballistic shields. They also had them in narrow compartments at the rear of the dropships and the RapRes. They unfolded like square umbrellas and could stop standard munitions and shrapnel.

"Okay, Sergeant Barrett. You and Corporal Chavez's fireteam can empty the shed, and Lieutenant Owen will back the RapRes up to it. You don't have to unload it tonight, but you'll want to put a guard on it just to be safe."

"You're not worried about the mercs, are you?" asked Sgt Thompson.

"No," Dewey said. "But the children here are curious. We don't want them getting dangerously curious."

"I'll drive back there now," said Lt Owen. He waved Sgt Thompson to join him.

"I'll get my team," Cpl Chavez said. She saluted and jogged back toward the school.

"Anyone else up?" Dewey asked as he and Sgt Barrett started walking.

They were crossing the center of town with its wide roundabout. The town's cafeteria had a few lights on. Dewey thought he saw some movement inside the building. Somebody was awake.

Sgt Barrett, who'd also been looking toward the cafeteria, chuckled. "We told them not to drink the coffee so late at night. I don't think they've ever had caffeine before."

Dewey had read plenty of history about colonies that had gone centuries without alcohol or other substances, only to develop an intolerance for them. Sometimes, the results were fatal. Not just for an individual but for the entire planet. Dewey would have told Sgt Barrett these things, but an alarm suddenly began beeping in his helmet.

The virtual controls winked on as Dewey pulled his face shield down. Sgt Barrett looked around, pulling his shield down before bringing his weapon to his shoulder. Dewey tapped through the controls to find the source, though he had a pretty good idea what it was based on the alarm tone. And for that reason, he was hoping he was wrong for a change.

Unfortunately, he wasn't. He tapped his helmet, silencing the alarm. The HUD went blank. Dewey was left temporarily blind until his eyes adjusted to the gloom of night.

"Lieutenant Tyler? I don't see anything."

"Up, Barrett." Dewey lifted his face shield as he pointed skyward.

"I don't see anything," Sgt Barrett said.

"Way, way up," said Dewey. He couldn't see it either. Not yet. But he knew what to look for. One of the Graevya's escape pods had entered the atmosphere.

16

The RapRes bounced across an open field, cutting as direct a line as possible toward the escape pod's landing position. Dewey sat in the cab with Lt Owen, whose attention ping-ponged between the view out the windshield and the screen on the dash. An orange light pulsed halfway between the top of the screen and the middle. In the middle of the screen, a green light glowed steadily. That was the RapRes's position.

The two dots drew closer as the RapRes bounced up a sharp rise in the land.

"Would have been more comfortable if they'd dropped it in the daytime," said Lt Owen. He'd paused halfway through his statement when it felt like they'd gotten the RapRes stuck going over the hillock.

"How fun would that be?" Dewey asked, even though he too silently wished the escape pod had dropped in the daytime. The Graevya had been that considerate with the trunk, and that was also why Dewey was worried.

The comm buzzed for communication with the back of the RapRes. Dewey tapped it, leaving Lt Owen to concentrate on not rolling the RapRes as they neared the target.

"Everything okay back there, Sergeant Barrett?"

"Private Wells says he has to pee," Sgt Barrett replied. "So if you could aim for the bumps, we have a betting pool going on."

In the background, Dewey could hear Pvt Wells's exclamation of alarm.

"I'm afraid that was the worst of it," Dewey said. "Who was betting on him holding it the entire way?"

Sgt Barrett laughed. "Oh, definitely Private Wells."

Even Lt Owen laughed. Then, he bit it off at the same time as his foot eased off the accelerator. He leaned forward as if it would improve his vision. Except for the glow of the screen with the two dots a hair apart, the cab was in darkness. Unfortunately, the outside was just as dark.

Dewey glanced at the screen to verify their location before saying, "It's here, Owen."

"Yeah, but where? I don't see the beacon."

A series of white strobes pockmarked the exterior of the escape pods. They should have started when the chutes opened, and they should have been visible even now. Dewey had noticed the lack of them when the pod was still earthbound but had kept that concern to himself. It could mean the pod was damaged and anyone inside was dead.

It could also mean the Graevya was concerned about the pod's discovery.

"Throw on the externals."

"You sure?" Lt Owen's hand hovered over the rubber-coated button that would engage the floodlights on the front of the RapRes. Pushing it would bring daylight to a forty-meter radius half-circle. It would also broadcast their location to anyone looking.

"We're southeast of Puchuncavi," said Dewey. "Maybe the mercs have vid feed on the elevator. Even if they did, they wouldn't be able to respond in time."

"And maybe the civilians would let us know if they were coming."

"Right. Or Staff Sergeant Castro."

Lt Owen nodded. He squeezed his eyes shut and said, "Sounds good. Might want to close your eyes."

Dewey closed his eyes. The next instant, they were backlit by a harsh brightness. He waited a few seconds before slowly opening them while looking down at his feet. Again, he gave it a few seconds and then lifted his head to look into the sterile light. He smiled and nodded.

"Good thing we stopped when we did," said Lt Owen. He was

flicking switches with one hand while releasing restraints with the other.

Less than ten meters ahead of them sat the escape pod. It was as half as wide as the RepRes was long and nearly as tall. The parachutes glowed under harsh light, flaccid and trailing out on the other side of the pod.

Dewey pulled the release of his restraints and tapped the comm. "Sergeant Barrett. We're here. The floods are on up front, FYI."

"Got it, Lieutenant," Sgt Barrett replied. "Give us a minute. We'll secure the perimeter."

"Thank you, Barrett." Dewey turned to Lt Owen. "Can you give us a three-sixty on the monitors?"

Lt Owen tapped the screen where the orange and green dots had been. A menu flashed into view. Owen tapped through it, and finally, the monitors above it faded on, revealing the sides and rear of the RapRes. Dewey could see several members of Cpl Fleming's team moving out and to the sides.

Dewey continued to watch as the team sent several eyes aloft. Another minute and Sgt Barrett commed the cab to let Dewey know everything was clear.

"Well, let's go see what all the secrecy is about."

He led the way with Lt Owen close behind. They passed through the empty rear compartment. They'd hastily unloaded the weapons and ammunition back at Puchuncavi. Outside the RapRes, Sgt Barrett was kneeling on the ground to the left of the ramp. He had just tapped his helmet, and the blue edge glow of VR was fading from his face shield.

"Anything at all?" Dewey asked.

"Nothing," said Sgt Barrett. "Not even on IR."

"Good work, Barrett. Let's keep everyone on watch until you and I see what's with the pod."

"You want me to stay with the RapRes?" Lt Owen asked.

"Just in case," said Dewey.

Lt Owen nodded and returned to the cab. Dewey, with Sgt Barrett a meter behind, made his way to the escape pod.

Under normal conditions, anyone inside would have blown the hatch and started securing the area. They'd be safe inside, too, but would have less control over their situation if they did. That wasn't something a Hospitaller would do unless they were severely injured or dead.

So many questions.

More questions were raised in Dewey's mind when he uncovered the access panel and punched the green button to release the hatch. The pad flashed red.

"It's locked?"

"So it would seem, Sergeant Barrett." Dewey pulled off his right glove and pressed it to the panel. Light pulsed beneath his hand several times before finally turning green. The light was followed by a loud clanking sound, and then the hatch unseated itself from the escape pod's frame.

"A hand, Barrett?"

Together, they pulled the thick door open. Escape pods received annual maintenance. Judging by the stiffness with which the door moved, this one was probably nearing its scheduled overhaul. That wouldn't be happening now, of course.

"Hello?" Dewey called into the dark interior. Not even the emergency lights were on.

Had there been a power failure? It seemed unlikely, as the chutes had deployed. Dewey reached in and found the panel for interior environmentals. A manual switch brought the panel to life, which initiated interior lights.

"No one's home," said Sgt Barrett from over Dewey's shoulder.

"It's a costly way to send a message," Dewey said as he stepped over the threshold and into the escape pod. "We can recover a trunk, but this is a one-off."

Inside the pod were enough seats for a squad. The restraints were still held in place by break-away ties. Based on Dewey's observation, it looked like no one had entered the pod before it was ejected from the Graevya. Again, more questions.

Perhaps the pod's systems had an answer. Dewey crossed the

space and tapped at the terminal that was angled toward one seat. He sat, observing Sgt Barrett watching outside the pod with occasional glances inside to where Dewey sat. It took several minutes for the system to wake. When it did, it requested a password, which wasn't standard SOP. Still seeking answers, Dewey entered his code and waited as the screen flashed a green of acceptance. Seconds later, Maj Hughes's face appeared. He had a stern look on his face. It was a recorded message.

"Lieutenant Tyler," said the recording of Maj Hughes. "My apologies if sending an escape pod seems overly dramatic for a message. However, calling directly doesn't seem to work." Here, the major flashed a smile before continuing. "We have company in the system. Three ships. Details are in the pod's systems. One of them is registered with the Dark Worlds as a materials transport. The other two don't have a registration, so you probably know what that means. They are armed and locked on. Our surrender has been requested."

Maj Hughes looked away. Someone was speaking, but Dewey couldn't hear them.

"I only have a few more seconds to load this. We'd have left, except they caught us unawares. I'm going to get a lot of grief from my fellow captains." Again, the brief flash of a smile. "The critical part here is that I can't send you any more help, and I can't call out for help. Did I mention we're being jammed? I think I did. No time for playback.

"It's on you right now, Lieutenant Tyler. If you can access the comms on that elevator platform, maybe you can call for help. If not, try and stay safe for six more days. When HQ doesn't hear from us, they'll come looking. Right, got to send this. Stay safe."

The screen winked black before the general menu came back online. Dewey tapped through it for recent uploads and found data on the three ships, including images taken of them.

Dewey tapped his comm. "Lieutenant Owen, could you come here to the pod?"

"On my way."

While Dewey waited, he opened several compartments. As he suspected, everything was still in place. He found the emergency rations, shelters, coveralls to replace damaged uniforms, the small weapons cache, and medical supplies. He'd have Sgt Barrett and Cpl Fleming strip the pod of everything before they left.

"What's going on?" asked Lt Owen as he appeared, climbing into the pod.

"Enemy ships in the system," said Dewey. "Not just cargo transport. Warships."

"You know what type?" Lt Owen took a seat as Dewey pulled the images back onto the screen.

"I think I do. But there's been modifications. So I'm hoping that we can arrive at a conclusion between what I know and what you know."

Dewey pulled the images up one at a time. They only had a single point of view, almost head-on with a narrow view down one side. The first one was obvious to Dewey as there weren't any modifications.

"Materials transport," said Lt Owen.

"Agreed."

Dewey switched to the next ship. It was smaller than the first ship but had evidence of armament modifications.

"Troop transport," Lt Owen said. He reached forward and touched several places on the screen. "Looks like we have railguns here and here, where there should be dropships."

"Right. It's an older United Planets' ship. Forty or fifty years old. With those mods, it'll be carrying fewer troops."

"If any."

Dewey nodded, though he doubted Mr. Thayer's company had sent an empty ship. The Juracanian resistance leaders in the city had said the company rotated out the mercenaries on a regular basis. Made sense to Dewey to schedule rotations at the same time as the transfer of raw materials.

"And this one." Dewey pulled up the last image. It was the largest of the three ships by about half. "Cruiser, but old."

"Real old." Lt Owen chuckled. "I don't think even we keep anything that old. Five generations out?"

"Probably more." Dewey had stared at the image for several minutes before he'd been able to place the ship.

It was an early Allied Planets' ship. Something designed more for in-system patrols. It was the modifications at the aft end of the ship that had thrown Dewey for a second. Someone had cut off the old engine compartments and bolted on something more substantial and more powerful. Something that could make it to jump speeds quicker.

The ship might have been old, but it was still a fighting ship. The railguns were bristling along the port and starboard sides. Rocket launch tubes dotted the nose. Along the top were several missile batteries that looked half as old as the rest of the ship.

"Crew?" Dewey asked. He didn't imagine they were running with the same size crew as the Allied or United Planets forces operated their ships with. It wasn't about ability but cost. Large crews ate into profits, and mercenary forces were companies. Companies survived on profits.

"If they've automated a bunch of the systems," said Lt Owen, "they could get away with a crew in the tens. I'd guess twenty-five?"

"Less on the troop transport. Not counting the combat mercs."

"And not more than ten on the cargo ship," said Dewey. It wasn't a lot of people, but it was more than twice what he had.

"What are you thinking?" Lt Owen asked. He'd leaned forward and was looking directly at Dewey.

What was he thinking? He was thinking something crazy, and it all depended on time and what they could get done in that time.

"I need to talk to the Juracanians in the city," Dewey said. He shut down the pod's computer systems. They wouldn't need them now. "But first, we need to strip out everything we can from the pod and load it into the RapRes. I'll try and comm with Lieutenant Haynes while that's happening."

He climbed out of the escape pod with Lt Owen close behind.

"That's the plan for this moment," said Lt Owen. He stopped.

Dewey did, too, turning back to face Lt Owen. "But what's the big plan?"

Dewey didn't respond. He looked at Lt Owen and then over at Sgt Barrett. In Lt Owen's eyes, he could see the light of understanding beginning to dawn.

"You're going to go after the merc ships?"

"No," said Dewey, even though his grin didn't leave his face. "We are."

17

Dewey's intention to speak with Franco and Samantha in Atacama was stymied by the early hour of the day and the related fact that the elders of Puchuncavi had been indulging in late-night coffee. None of them were awake. There were a few adults up and about as the sun was peeking over the horizon. However, none knew anything about communicating with the people in Atacama or the other towns.

It would have been easy to assume they were keeping secrets. The elders had done precisely that without batting an eye. But there was a look as they spoke and how they carried themselves that Dewey took to be signs of their honesty. Nor was he going to start calling people liars. That never benefited anyone.

While he waited for the elders, he grabbed a cup of coffee himself. It was poured by a proud Lt Gray.

"The Juracanians have really taken to coffee," Gray said.

"Like an addict to Synth-X," Dewey replied. He gave Lt Gray a wink so that he would know that Dewey was just playing.

"I'd like to think my coffee is a little more benign," said Gray. He took a sip of his own before continuing. "So, now what are we doing? About the mercs, I mean."

Dewey had caught Gray up on the situation once they'd returned from recovering the emergency pod. Lt Owen was supervising the unloading as well as a second task. They had every Hospitaller except Lt Gray and Sgt George, Gray's loadmaster, loading two of the crawlers. He wasn't sure if he'd get the chance to send them, but he wanted to be ready just in case.

"Secure them," Dewey said. He paused and sipped the coffee again. Maj Hughes would swoon over the flavor. Dewey would have to make sure they saved the major some of the roasted beans. "Either before or after we recover Sergeant Parks and the others. And I think the clock is ticking. Once they start loading the trunks onto the elevator, it'll only be a matter of time before they bring the replacement merc unit down."

"Then we'll have twice the work," finished Lt Gray.

Dewey nodded. "And we have enough work already."

"Well, I think you can finally make that call." Gray pointed his chin to an eye-rubbing elder making their way to the town's cafeteria.

The elder, male but otherwise a mystery, continued to rub at his eyes, clearly attempting to push the tired away. This also explained why he appeared to be making a beeline for the cafeteria and Lt Gray's coffee. It was something the lieutenant anticipated, and he was already prepping a cup.

Just inside the doorway, the elder stopped and finally ceased rubbing at his eyes.

"Ah, Jacobo. Good morning." Gray set the cup of coffee in front of the nearest seat to the elder.

For his part, Jacobo grunted and then sat. He pulled the coffee closer, inhaling its aroma. He slowly sipped it, getting past the first scalding touch. When he set the cup back on the table, he looked like a different man.

"I thought this stuff was supposed to energize you," Jacobo said. He looked at Lt Gray as he spoke but seemed to suddenly realize Dewey was also present. "Good morning, Lieutenant Tyler."

"Good morning, Jacobo. And yes, it does energize you, so long as you don't abuse it. When did you stop drinking it yesterday?"

"It was dark out. That's all I know," said Jacobo. "You're saying I shouldn't drink this all the time?"

"Perish the thought," said Lt Gray through his grin.

"You were raised on it, Gray," Dewey said. He moved to sit opposite Jacobo. "I'd suggest not drinking once it's past noon."

"Pity."

Jacobo's comment brought a bark of laughter from Lt Gray. Dewey accepted the word with a smile and then moved on. "I need to contact Samantha and Franco. Can you help me with that?"

Jacobo nodded while drinking his coffee and managed to not lose a drop of the liquid. He smacked his lips as he set the cup down. Then, he looked into the cup and then looked up at Dewey and Lt Gray in surprise.

"Is there more?" he asked, holding out the empty cup.

"I'll need to brew some," said Lt Gray. "Maybe you can help Lieutenant Tyler while you wait?"

"Help?" He looked surprised. Then he seemed to remember. "Right! You want to talk to Franco. We have to go over to the town hall."

Dewey drained the warm coffee from his cup and set it on the counter. "We'll be back, Gray."

"I'll be brewing."

Jacobo, now with a cup of coffee coursing through his system, appeared to be more energetic. Rather than the slow walk he'd made toward the cafeteria, he strode across the roundabout with purpose, compelling Dewey to take longer steps to keep up. At the town hall, Jacobo fairly bounced up the stairs, with Dewey following just as quickly. Once inside, Jacobo took an immediate right toward a hallway off to the side. It was short, ending at a windowless door. Beyond it was a stairwell that led down.

"You do know I was hoping to call them and not take the tunnels back there?"

With a laugh, Jacobo answered. "The tunnels don't pass near enough. Patience, Lieutenant. You'll see."

The basement was clean but empty. The corridor they'd entered did a quick right and then a left turn. There were doors here, concealing spaces behind them.

"These were meeting rooms," Jacobo said. "Clubs met here in the evenings. I was with the drama club. We did plays, you know? Until they came."

Dewey assumed that Jacobo was referencing the mercenaries and the company that hired them.

"Now it all just sits empty," said Jacobo. "Not enough people to put on a play or have a heated conversation about books. Stuff like that."

He'd come to a stop at a door halfway down the hall. Unlike the other doors, it did not have a window allowing a view into the room beyond. From around his neck, Jacobo pulled out a chain on which hung a key. He inserted it into the lock and turned.

"Four of us have access to communications," he said. "We didn't used to lock it, you know? Never felt it was necessary. Now, though, people get worried that Mr. Thayer and his merry band of invaders will destroy it if they see it."

"They might," said Dewey. "If they thought it would help them keep control of the planet."

"Well, they haven't." Jacobo opened the door to reveal a small room with several desks. A small window high on the opposite wall was the only source of illumination. And as it was still early in the day, it only provided the weakest amount of light.

Dewey switched on his task light, throwing sharp shadows across the room. He reached up, adjusting the light so that it pointed toward the ceiling, diffusing the light and softening the shadows.

To the side of the desk on Dewey's left, there was a metal table with casters. Strapped to the top was a field phone that looked to be hundreds of years in age. But when Jacobo threw the latch and pulled the front panels open, the shine of glass, the sheen of rubber-covered buttons, and brass frames around meters all had the look of something younger and well maintained.

"There is, or was," explained Jacobo, "a factory up north. They were rebuilding old phone sets that had belonged to the military. The long-term goal was to get a phone in every house. I think they had them in their shops in the northern towns. We were set to get one for the restaurant and the clinic, but then the invaders came."

"What about the one in Atacama, with the resistance?" asked Dewey. He was watching Jacobo adjust switches. Several dials lit up, suggesting that there was power to the basement. Dewey saw the switch and crossed to it. When he flicked it, nothing happened.

"We still haven't gotten much in the way of lighting," Jacobo said.

"It's candles and lamps or nothing, except in a few places like the clinic. As for Atacama, the people who built this one also put one in the city to call when they were close to here or on their way back north. We had to call and ask about it when the first people escaped the invaders."

"Convenient."

Jacobo looked at Dewey and tapped his helmet. "Not as convenient as those."

"Agreed, but you have the longer range. Any luck?"

"Calling now." Jacobo had a headset over his ears and a mic on a stand whose position on the table he adjusted near constantly.

There were several analog meters that Dewey watched. The needle on one of them remained still while the other one jumped like it had hiccups. After a few mesmerizing seconds, both needles jumped. Jacobo leaned forward, his lips close to the mic. Dewey could hear the buzz of another voice leaking from the headphones.

"This is Jacobo of Puchuncavi," Jacobo said into the mic. "I need to speak to Franco or Samantha."

"Or SSgt Castro," Dewey said. He raised his voice to be heard through the headphones.

"Or that staff sergeant will do," Jacobo said.

The voice buzzed through the headphones once more.

"Right. Standing by." Jacobo sat back and pulled the headphones down around his neck. He looked over at Dewey. "It'll be a few minutes."

"I'll be right back." Dewey paused just long enough to get a nod of confirmation from Jacobo before leaving the room and then the basement.

Outside, Dewey started back across the roundabout. He tapped his comm to connect with all of the other lieutenants for a check-in. It was pure chance that he was not only the platoon leader but the lieutenant with the most seniority. It did make the chain of command easier. Perhaps that was what it was like being the company commander. Or the battalion commander. Dewey smiled as he recalled having the same feeling when he'd been made squad leader.

Lt Owen had the RapRes unloaded and had started loading two of the crawlers. The other lieutenants were busy with other tasks passed along by Owen, who was second in seniority. Third was Haynes. Fourth was Gray, and he had another urn of coffee ready to go.

"If the place wasn't radioactive, I'd resign from the Corps and move here. Imagine being the first coffee baron?"

Dewey nodded. He'd been a few places that made him question his life's path. But never enough to resign.

"Speaking of radioactive, Lieutenant Gray."

Both Gray and Dewey turned to a saluting MedTech Chambers.

Dewey returned the salute. "You have words about the radioactivity?"

"Your absorption is up, Lieutenant Tyler." She accepted the cup of coffee.

"I need a booster?"

"You should get one before you start tearing across the countryside, Lieutenant. But the problem is bigger than that. I've made flu inoculations for Puchuncavi and for Romerol. I figured it would be okay because we'd get more chems from the Graevya. But Lieutenant Matthews said there weren't any in the trunk."

"I saw boxes of med supplies," said Dewey. "I assume then that you needed a specific box."

MedTech Chambers nodded. "Base chems. They come in tubes for the synth box. If I hadn't made all the flu shots, we'd be okay."

"Don't beat yourself up, Chambers," Dewey said. "I would have suggested you do exactly the same as what you already did. How long before we have a problem?"

"Depends on the exposure," MedTech Chambers said. "If you're in hotspots too long, you'll need a booster sooner. Puchuncavi seems to be a low exposure area. I think you picked up the additional exposure when you went into the city."

"We're all going there soon."

"Oh." Chambers took a sip of her coffee, nodding approvingly, which put a grin on Lt Gray's face. "In that case, Lieutenant Tyler, I'd say the less time we are there, the better. Unless it means we're going to the Graevya soon after."

"We are." Dewey accepted two mugs of coffee with paper covers over them. "In a roundabout way."

Back in the town hall, Jacobo was pleased to see Dewey was carrying two mugs of coffee.

"Drink fast. It's already cooling."

Jacobo moved from the seat in front of the field phone. "I'll drink. You talk."

"They been waiting long?" Dewey sat and picked up the headphones.

"Couple minutes."

While Jacobo took the first of many noisy slurps of coffee, Dewey put the headphones on. He pressed the button on the microphone stand. "This is Lieutenant Tyler, over."

"Lieutenant Tyler, what is this coffee that Jacobo was going on about?"

"I'll explain later, Samantha," said Dewey. "For now, how are things with the mercs and the company?"

"Same as before. And your staff sergeant isn't making friends. Some of the young people are complaining she's too demanding."

"I see. What's your opinion?"

"If what she is doing keeps most of them alive," Samantha said, "then she should be a little harsher. I think she's pulling her punches."

"She may well be. Listen, Samantha, there's been some events you need to be made aware of."

"Have there?"

Dewey succinctly laid out the events since his return to Puchuncavi. He put all the cards on the table as there wasn't any reason to be holding back. Not when he was relying on the Juracanians for their assistance. He hoped that Samantha and the other leaders would see what he was doing and reciprocate on a level playing ground.

"Well," Samantha said after a short pause following Dewey's

explanation, "we knew they'd be coming eventually."

"But you don't know if they always came so heavily armed?" Dewey would be more comfortable if this was Mr. Thayer's company's S.O.P. rather than being an unusual case.

Unfortunately, Samantha's answer offered neither reassurance nor concern. "We've only gotten one person up the elevator," she said. "He didn't make it back. In fact, until you arrived, we weren't even sure he'd managed to send out the message."

"That's too bad," Dewey said. "About your man and about the ships. Two of them I can understand. But the warship, that seems like overkill, even for a company running an illegal operation. I think I'm going to assume this is an extraordinary case and that Mr. Thayer got a message out to his people, and this is the response."

"So what do you plan on doing now? Assuming they've taken your ship."

Dewey was distracted by Jacobo, who was pointing at Dewey's coffee. He hadn't drunk any of it since the conversation started. The paper over the top was wet from the steam. With a nod of understanding, Dewey slid the coffee cup over to Jacobo. The elder took it eagerly. He was going to be on edge all day, now.

Turning his attention back to Samantha, Dewey said, "We are going to go get our ship back. But to do that, we'll need the elevator."

"To get to the elevator, you'll have to go through the soldiers."

"Right. But before that, we need to secure their comms so they can't communicate with the ships topside. I believe you, or Alexander, have someone inside that might be able to help?"

"We can try."

"Do that. In the meantime," said Dewey, "we're going to start pushing ammo and weapons your way. But I don't want to bring them overland. I'd like to use the subway tunnels. How many handcarts do you have?"

There was another pause. Dewey thought he heard another voice behind Samantha's.

"We have a couple in each section. The debris could be cleared in a few hours if we have enough help."

"Well, I have two squads here and a fireteam with you."

"And we have about thirty able-bodied men and women."

"So, a couple hours?" Dewey asked. That was assuming that everyone worked together.

"Yes, but then you'll want to hurry up with the next part of your plan."

The edge to Samantha's voice was an alert to Dewey. He leaned forward, his lips almost touching the mic. "Why?"

"They've started loading trunks on the elevator."

It would take hours to load them and then several hours to reach the port at the top.

"They normally exchange the mercs at the end?"

"Usually."

"Then you're right. We'd better hurry."

18

Jacobo accepted the headset as Dewey pulled it off his head and passed it to the elder. As Dewey stepped away from the field phone's box, Jacobo asked, "Things getting interesting?"

"They've started loading the trunks on the elevator," Dewey said. "So, yes, things are getting interesting. Maybe a little too fast."

Dewey grabbed the two empty mugs and left the town hall, stopping by the cafeteria. He set the mugs on the counter, drawing Lt Gray's attention. "Gray, is there a civilian who can guard your beans? I need all the officers to meet me at the school."

"I'll find someone and be there ASAP."

"Sooner, the better."

Dewey quick-marched to the school. He commed the other officers and gave them the same request he'd given Lt Gray.

"Attention," barked Sgt Maxwell. It was just her and PFC Donald Allison. They were moving some of the company gear toward the doors.

"Carry on," said Dewey. Then, "Heads up, Maxwell. All the other officers are en route."

"Thank you, Lieutenant Tyler," said Sgt Maxwell. She moved faster, saying, "Double-time, Allison, unless you want a cramp in your right arm."

Dewey chuckled as the two Hospitallers hurried out the door. Close behind their exit, Lt Owen appeared with Lt Matthews on his heels.

"What's going on, Tyler?" asked Lt Owen.

"You mean besides our ship being captured? That would be enough, but the mercs' employers have started loading trunks onto the elevator rails."

"So we need to hurry," Owen said.

Dewey nodded but waited to make further comments as Lieutenants Hall, Haynes, and James entered the building. Behind them, crossing the open space at a jog and carrying a plastic tote, Lt Gray was bringing up the rear.

"We'll do details as soon as Gray gets in and pours coffee."

"How do you know he has coffee?" asked Lt Haynes.

Lt Hall laughed. "Ever since we found those beans, Gray always has coffee."

Lt Gray entered the room to a round of laughter. "What'd I miss?"

"Nothing," Dewey said, smiling. "You can pour, and I'll talk."

The idea of pouring coffee must have distracted Lt Gray's curiosity because he turned his attention to the crate, removing cups and a jug wrapped in towels.

"It was all I could find to keep the coffee warm for the trip over," he explained.

"As long as it's hot, Gray," said Dewey. "Now, here's what we have. The Graevya has been compromised. The invading company has three ships in orbit. And now they've started loading the trunks onto the elevator." Dewey paused long enough to accept a cup of coffee from Lt Gray. He took a sip, pleased to find it still hot, and continued. "From what we've learned from the Juracanians in Atacama, the company's mercs will rotate out once the trunks are on the cargo ship."

"How fast does the elevator run?" asked Lt James.

"That I don't know," said Dewey. "But I gather from what Samantha and Franco have said that it's a couple of hours one way. And there are tens of trunks to load."

"Won't they have come with empty trunks, too?" asked Lt Owen. "To replace the ones they're taking? That should slow down the process and give us more time to do what we need."

"Depends on the trunks," said Lt Haynes, who was already looking to Lt Gray to get a top-off on her cup. "If they're using trunks with built-in runners, and the trunks are empty, they can send them down as fast as they load them."

"And if it's all automated," said Dewey, "it'll go fast."

"So the clock is running," said Lt Owen. He'd been holding out his cup for a refill and nodded his thanks to Lt Gray. "What do you have planned?"

Dewey explained the plan. They needed to get as much of the supplies as they could into Atacama. They had to do it using the subway tunnels, which was going to make things complicated.

"The track isn't clear all the way through," Dewey said. "I think they left some of the debris in place to keep anyone else from using the tracks."

"By which you mean the mercs," said Lt Matthew.

"That's my impression."

Once they had supplies to Atacama and set up a distraction, Dewey wanted to secure the communication system so Mr. Thayer couldn't use it to warn the ships or call for reinforcements. And they had some inside help.

"Can this person really shut down the comms?"

"I'm not counting on it, Owen," said Dewey. "So, we're going to have to secure it."

"We have to get inside first," said Haynes. "And that's going to set off alarms."

"Perhaps," Dewey said. He paused for a sip of his coffee. He tried not to grin as the other lieutenants leaned in expectantly. "But I plan on being inside the fence before that happens."

"How?" several of them asked as one.

"The subway."

"Oh, yeah," said Lt Owen. "The space elevator is built on the site of the old spaceport. And a subway system that served the area would surely have run to the spaceport."

"Is it still intact?" asked Lt Gray.

"I don't have confirmation, but I have a feeling that it would explain how some of the Juracanians managed to escape. Like most of the information they have, the Juracanians aren't exactly dumping it all on the table."

"Best way to find out would be to go and ask," said Lt Owen. He punctuated his comment with a cup-emptying gulp of coffee. "So, let's get going."

"Are the two crawlers on their way to the subway station?"

"They are."

Dewey nodded and then downed the last of his coffee, too, before saying, "We'll need to send one fireteam ahead to start clearing the track. We'll rotate fireteams so that when everyone else arrives at the obstruction to finish clearing, a fresh fireteam will go forward to the next section and start clearing."

Lt Hall raised her hand and asked, "What about moving the supplies? Are the crawlers going to fit?"

"Is there a way to get them down there?" asked Lt Owen.

"Not at this station," said Dewey. "And it would take time to reach a station that could. Even then, I'm not sure they would fit. No, we're going to have to move it all by hand to the platform. From there, we'll load it on hand carts. There are carts in each section, so we'll have to transfer cargo several times, sending the empty carts back for the waiting supplies."

"That's a lot of work," said Lt Matthew.

"We could try using a dropship," said Dewey. "But not only do we risk it being shot down, it would also give the mercs a warning I don't want them to have."

"So we should get moving?" asked Lt Gray.

Dewey nodded. "Get moving."

Lt Haynes was put in charge of moving supplies from the crawlers down to the subway platform. Lt Gray would assist once he'd given quick instructions to some of the elders on how to handle the cooked beans and how to make their own cups of coffee.

Dewey couldn't be everywhere at once, which was disconcerting. As much as he trusted the other officers and his own platoon to do their jobs correctly, he still felt the compunction about being there, just in case. But, he had to be someplace else at the moment.

It had been a tough call for Dewey. He would have preferred to bring along at least a fireteam with him and Lt Owen. The work in the tunnels, though, would go quicker with more people employed there. So he proceeded toward Atacama with Lt Owen and Sgt Thompson as the only crew in the RapRes.

They'd loaded a dozen crates of ammo and weapons into the vehicle and strapped it in. If anything happened, if the mercenaries somehow managed to learn of their approach and set up an ambush, it would be just the three of them to offer resistance.

"Do you really think they'd come out on a preemptive strike?" asked Lt Owen as the RapRes rolled down the road toward Atacama.

"Have we ever left things to chance, Owen?"

Lt Owen's silence was confirmation that they didn't. But that didn't mean things still couldn't go wrong. Hospitallers weren't necessarily pessimists, but they made a habit of expecting the unexpected. That was why they were rarely caught off guard.

The rest of the drive, with the sun rising behind them, was mostly silent. Several times, Sgt Thompson would ask in a mock, childish voice, "Are we there yet?"

When they finally entered the outskirts of Atacama, Dewey tapped the comm for SSgt Castro. The response was quick.

"I was beginning to think you forgot me," said SSgt Castro.

"Sorry to leave you hanging, Castro, but I'm bringing presents."

Next to Dewey, Lt Owen guffawed and nodded.

SSgt Castro must have heard the noise. She asked, "Is it the kind of presents that go bang and kaboom?"

"Is there another kind?"

"Well, there's kapow and boom." SSgt Castro mimicked the sounds and then chuckled. Then, soberly, she asked, "You're aware of the trunks going onto the elevator, I take it?"

"That's why we're hurrying. How are the Juracanians taking to Hospitaller training?"

The response was a snort and then a laugh. "Nothing that ten years of doing everything together couldn't fix."

That was the difference between the Orphan Corps and the other systems-wide forces. Hospitallers had grown up together, played war games together, cleaned latrines together, since they were old enough to hold a peashooter and a toilet scrubber. They knew each other and understood each other. Top those years off with two years of combat training where the camaraderie was refined to a razor's edge, and you had a force that moved and acted as one. The Juracanians had none of that for now.

"You don't have ten years," said Dewey.

"I don't even have another ten hours," added SSgt Castro. "But they'll be useful as long as we don't ask them to lead the charge."

That was something Dewey would never allow the civilians to do, no matter how much they might insist. It was in contradiction to the Orphan Corps mandate of aid, comfort, and defend. Instead, he'd prefer they not be involved at all, but he also knew that was impossible.

"They should be helpful in a diversion, though," said Dewey. "And we'll need a big one."

"I'll make sure they're ready."

"Good. Now, we need you to guide us in."

An hour later, the RapRes rolled into an underground parking garage. It was three hundred meters from where Dewey had first met Samantha and Franco but closer to the watch post. The RapRes barely fit on the garage's first level, chipping crete and tearing empty water pipes as it entered.

"I may have scratched the paint," Lt Owen said. The broad grin on his face made it clear that he'd enjoyed the task.

"Good thing it's ours, then." Dewey stepped away from the copilot seat and through the hatch that separated the cab from the rest of the vehicle. "Okay, Sergeant Thompson, let's go say hello."

Sgt Thompson had repositioned himself by the back hatch. He punched the button that unlocked the hatch and lowered it to serve as a ramp. Just beyond where the ramp would touch down, SSgt Castro, Franco, and several other civilians waited. Everyone but SSgt Castro had a curious look on their face. Castro was smiling.

"Welcome back," she said as Dewey came down the ramp. She

followed her words with a salute that Dewey returned.

"I thought there were more of you," said Franco as he accepted a handshake from Dewey.

"They're with the rest of the supplies," Dewey said. "We came ahead with enough to wet your whistle and keep the shine in SSgt Castro's eyes."

"It's going to be fun."

Based on the looks Castro received from the Juracanians with Franco, they had a much more sedate idea of the definition of fun.

"Well, it'll be interesting," said Franco. The twinkle in his eye said that he appreciated SSgt Castro's enthusiasm.

"And where would we find Samantha?" Dewey asked. "And Corporal Fleming's fireteam?"

"Corporal Fleming is with Samantha," said SSgt Castro. "She's showing them a possible location for a base of operation for the distraction. You want to go take a look?"

"If there's time." Dewey turned back to Franco. "We need a staging point for the equipment that's coming in. Someplace safe."

"If we bring it all into the central junction, we can move stuff down to the lowest level."

"Can we reach that from here, too?"

"We can, Lieutenant."

Dewey nodded and then indicated the back of the RapRes with a sweep of one arm. "Then let's get all this down there and get ready to greet the rest of my people. They should be here soon."

Franco turned to the Juracanians with him. "Help the Hospitallers. Follow their lead."

A ragged collection of affirmatives preceded their movement to the back of the RapRes, where Sgt Thompson was waiting.

"You want me to wait here with the vehicle?" Lt Owen asked.

"No," said Dewey. "Once all the supplies are out, secure it, and we'll come back for it if we need it."

There were enough Juracanians and Hospitallers that everyone had one box to carry. The boxes were heavy, so it was fortunate that they only had to cross the garage, go up a level, cross a street, and down three levels. The only one who still seemed to be having fun was SSgt Castro, and even she seemed relieved to be able to set her crate of four MUWs with extra barrels onto the deck of the station platform.

Dewey had been checking the maps in his head against the markings still visible on the subway system walls. He'd placed his crate of grenades with the other ammunition before turning to locate Franco. He joined the Juracanian close to where the others had congregated, rubbing biceps and wiping brows.

"That's the line to the old spaceport," Dewey said, pointing into the darkened tunnel.

Franco hesitated before nodding.

"And that's how most of you escaped from the company and the mercs."

Again, Franco hesitated before nodding.

"How close does it put us to the comm building?"

Before Franco could hesitate or nod or whatever he was inclined to do, another voice answered.

"Less than twenty meters from the exit to the front of the comm building." Dewey turned to see Samantha with Alexander and Corporal Fleming's fireteam. Her eyes scanned the area before adding, "It looks like you've brought weapons."

"And ammo," said Dewey. "There's more coming."

"How much more?" asked one of the other Juracanians. Likely he was visualizing having to carry the crates great distances like he'd already done.

"A lot," Dewey said. This time he shared a grin with SSgt Castro.

At that moment, Castro also pointed behind Dewey to the tunnel that led away from the spaceport. Dewey turned. He could hear the whispered groan of the hand carts approaching and saw flickering illumination diffusing the darkness.

SSgt Castro laughed and said, "Looks like there really is light at the end of the tunnel."

19

Dewey hopped down onto the tracks. Behind him, SSgt Castro joined him in the same manner. The Juracanians took the wooden stairs. The light in the tunnel was approaching, growing brighter.

"Douse the lights," said Dewey after making a comm link with the approaching Hospitallers.

The lights went out a few seconds later. A moment after that, the ghostly image of an approaching handcart, accompanied by its seesaw crank's muffled squeak, made itself known. Seconds later, Dewey could see people operating the seesaw handles and several people sitting on the cart's forward end. As well, he could now identify a few more standing and looking past those operating the handles.

Three seconds later and the first of the handcarts entered the station, slowly rolling to a stop with Hospitallers leaning on the handles to slow the cart faster. They came to a halt five meters from where Dewey stood. On the front was Lt Gray. He jumped off, coffee cup in hand.

"Greetings," he said, quite jovially.

"Lieutenant Gray," Dewey said, a small smile on his face. "Everything good through the tunnel?"

Gray pointed over his shoulder with the cup. Nothing spilled from the motion. Dewey realized it was empty. "All the debris has been set aside. One of the carts broke an axle, so we had to move it off the tracks. Other than that, everything is moving smooth as can be expected."

"Where are my people?" asked Samantha, stepping forward to join Dewey.

Lt Gray looked taken aback and looked to Dewey.

"The Juracanians that were helping you."

"Oh, yes. Them." Gray grinned broadly enough that Dewey thought the lieutenant's face would crack. "They were looking a little tired, so I gave them some coffee. Now they're back there transferring crates in the dark. They said our lights hurt their eyes."

"It does," Samantha said. "And what is this coffee everyone has been talking about?"

With another face-cracking smile, Lt Gray called over his shoulder, "Sergeant George? Coffee if you please."

"On it, Lieutenant," came the muffled voice of Sgt Christy George, Lt Gray's loadmaster.

"We have about a quarter of the supplies here with us," said Lt Gray. "Another quarter is en route. The last half will be here in a couple hours."

"Good work," Dewey said, slightly distracted by the approaching figure carrying a twelve-quart pot in their mitted hands. Behind them, another Hospitaller carried a small tote that clinked and clanked as it rocked with each step taken.

"Here we go," Lt Gray said. "Put it there, Sergeant George. Cups there, Private Russell. Thank you."

Gray passed his cup to Sgt George and then squatted to remove the lid and quickly scoop coffee into two cups before returning the lid to its place on top. He stood and brought the cups to Samantha and Franco.

"It's hot." Lt Gray passed the coffee to the elders and stepped back. He looked at Dewey as he said, "Sergeant George wrapped copper wire around the pot and applied a current to it."

Samantha and Franco took the cups with caution, clearly mindful of the heat they could feel through them. Samantha was first, and with Franco studying her, she sipped the steaming liquid. The sip was noisy and short as Samantha seemed to realize that Lt Gray wasn't joking about the heat. Then she took another sip. And then another.

"Well?" Franco asked.

Samantha looked at Dewey. "You drink this? All the time?"

"Not all the time." Dewey laughed. "We drink Insta more often, but we do like coffee when we can get it."

"Tastes strange," Samantha said. But like Luc and the other elders in Puchuncavi, it didn't stop them from taking several more sips. "Probably have to develop a taste for it."

"That's one way to put it," said Dewey. "Now, while you drink your coffee, Lieutenant Gray will move his pot of brew out of the way, and we'll stage the supplies on the platform. Staff Sergeant Castro?"

"Doing it now, Lieutenant." SSgt Castro stepped forward, her eyes scanning the Hospitallers present. "Sergeant Maxwell? Good. Vacation's over. Let's get it all unloaded and make room for the rest."

By the time the last half of the supplies rolled into the station, several things had happened. With the help of the Juracanians, the supplies already on the platform had been shifted to other staging areas. Weapons and ammunition had been carried down one level and stored in a side tunnel. Uniforms, rations, and other supplies had been taken up to the top station where SSgt Castro was doing a quick inventory so they could decide how to distribute the equipment among the Juracanians.

Dewey had just returned from carrying a crate of ballistic shields as Lt Haynes entered the tunnel, riding on the leading handcart.

"Lieutenant Haynes," Dewey said. He stepped down the wood stairs this time. "I hope you've arrived safe and sound."

"Safe, sound, and the last of the supplies," said Haynes. She scanned the platform behind Dewey. "I was lured on by the promise of hot coffee and a tour."

"Coffee's on the top level." Dewey pointed up reflexively. "You can take a crate of supplies up where Lieutenant Gray has a third pot of coffee brewing."

"Third?"

"I'm afraid we've created a bunch of coffee addicts."

"Better than Synth-X."

"What isn't? Anyway, we got coffee. The tour will have to wait."

"Looking forward to it." Lt Haynes turned to the Hospitallers gathered around the front car. "Sergeant Simon? Sergeant Barrett? Let's get it unloaded."

Dewey stood by as the Hospitallers and the last of the Juracanians who'd helped clear the tracks carried crates and totes of supplies up the wood stairs. Alexander checked each container, telling the person holding it where to go. When it was a Hospitaller, he paired them up with one of the civilians, admonishing them to stay close and not get lost. It occurred to Dewey that Alexander was a good leader in training.

Once the last of the civilians and Hospitallers disappeared with their cargo, Dewey went down to the cars and selected a crate of grenades. This would allow him to visit the caches of weapons and ammo without calling much attention to his presence. Even though he knew where he was going, Alexander still stopped him to verify his container.

"Lower level," Alexander said. Then, with a mischievous grin, he asked, "You know the way?"

"Aye, Alexander, I know the way."

They separated, both chuckling.

On the way down to the lowest subway level, Dewey passed several of his people. With his hands full, he could only nod in return to their salute. He also had to hold tight to the crate, or any one of them would have taken it for him.

When Dewey got down to the platform, another Juracanian looked at the container.

"Grenades," said Dewey.

"Okay. The far side then."

Dewey walked across the platform, nodding to PFC Horton and Pvt Hart as they passed him. Dealing with the Juracanians was refreshing in some ways. Other civilians would have been deferential, sometimes overly so, because of his rank. He'd seen them become absolutely obsequious in the presence of a colonel or general. The Juracanians seemed unconcerned. Perhaps it was because of the more democratic way in which they chose their leaders? He wasn't sure. But he was certain that would be changing soon.

The Juracanians' centuries-long isolation was going to come to a crashing halt. Not, Dewey mused as he set the crate down, that it hadn't already been trodden upon.

Turning from the stacks of ammunition, Dewey discovered Lt Owen and Samantha approaching.

"There you are," Lt Owen said.

"I've been missed?"

"Trunks have been coming down the elevator," said Samantha. "Thought maybe you'd want to get working on this plan of yours."

"Indeed," Dewey said. "Let's gather up the officers, SSgt Castro, and the Juracanian leaders, and let's discuss what happens next."

The plan that Dewey laid out for the civilians and the Hospitallers was similar to what he'd already discussed with his people prior to shifting supplies into Atacama. They needed to take control of the communications on the base before Mr. Thayer or the mercenaries realized the Hospitallers were a threat. After that, they needed to free Sgt Parks and Cpl Mitchell's fireteam. Then they needed to subdue the mercenaries and take control of the base and the elevator.

And they had to do all of that while not attracting the attention of the ships and reinforcements above.

"Sounds like fun," said SSgt Castro.

Lt Owen nodded in agreement.

SSgt Castro would be having fun. Her idea of fun, as it were. She would be taking a group of hastily trained Juracanians to the edge of the city, closest to the wall's guarded gates surrounding the elevator and company buildings. The Juracanians, under Castro's tutelage, would provide a military-type diversion. If everything went well, it would draw the mercenaries' attention. Hopefully long enough for Dewey's teams to do their jobs.

The civilians needed more convincing.

Before the meeting, Dewey had Lt Owen and Lt Matthews configure extra helmets to run the civilians through the plan while in VR. This allowed him to zoom in on critical places and fast forward through the entire operation. It was something he was used to, as were the other lieutenants and SSgt Castro.

Samantha and the other civilians had never experienced VR, and that led to several complications. The biggest complication was that Franco kept falling out of his chair and was eventually strapped in with Lt Gray standing behind him for support.

"Let me see if I got all this worked out," Samantha said. She seemed the one who'd adapted easiest to the VR simulation. She reached out and touched areas of the map while she spoke. "You need to get into the comm building and secure it before Mr. Thayer or the military commander realize it and try to call for help. At the same time, my people have to move closer to the gate and the wall to provide a distraction, but they can't be seen before the comm is secured, or they'll call for help. And Alex has to convince those being used as forced labor to keep laboring, or else the people on the ships will get suspicious and send down help. That right?"

"You forgot freeing our people being held hostage," said Dewey. "But, yes, that's right."

"One misstep, and the whole thing falls apart," said Alexander. He was the one civilian with the most prominent role. He had to go with Dewey's platoon. Then, while they secured the comm building, he had to reach the civilians and convince them to keep acting normal, even when there was a battle nearby.

"Fun, right?" SSgt Castro asked in response to Alexander's concern.

The only people who seemed in agreement with SSgt Castro's appraisal of the situation were Lt Owen and a Juracanian, Emily Novarro, whom the staff sergeant had designated as one of the leaders of the military arm of the resistance.

"Not how I would describe it," said Samantha. "Still, it beats waiting for the invaders to enslave all of us or us dying of imported diseases."

"Speaking of which." Dewey turned to MedTech Chambers. "How are we looking?"

"The last set of blockers I gave everyone are still working," Chambers said. "But the keyword is last. Forty-eight hours and some of us are going to start feeling the effects of low-level radiation sickness."

"Fortunately, I don't plan on being here that long." Dewey turned and smiled at the Juracanians. "Not intended as an insult."

"None taken," said Franco. He seemed relieved to no longer have to operate in the VR scenario.

"Right." Dewey checked the time on his tablet. It was still set for ship time, but he didn't need to know the exact hour. "We've a few hours until sunset and a few more until it's dark enough to proceed. That gives SSgt Castro time to move the supplies she needs and then for her people to move into position. In two hours, Lt Owen, if you don't mind, I want everyone that's going to be down on the platform and ready to go. I'll pass the message on to the squad sergeants as well."

"We'll be ready," Lt Owen said.

Dewey turned back to the Juracanians. "Keep the helmets for comm purposes. Lieutenant Matthews will show you how to answer and how to end a connection. And let's get ready."

In the two hours before Dewey appeared on the station platform, he wrote a message that he would send via the comm station if things went pear-shaped. If it worked, it should reach HQ and the nearest Hospitaller ships. If it didn't, then things would likely go from bad to worse. Hopefully, it wouldn't come to that. Mostly, though, he was hoping his plans would work. Then, the message sent would be different and would go out after they'd accomplished their goal.

But as Dewey was a Hospitaller, he sent a copy of the message and directions to all the other officers. Just in case.

With that out of the way, Dewey gave his gear a once-over and ran a diagnostic on his helmet's systems. When everything was green and clean, he made his way down to the lowest platform. Along the way, he picked up company.

"Lieutenant Gray," Dewey said. "You bring coffee?"

Gray laughed. "The Juracanians drank it all."

"Not all," said Lt Haynes. The nod of her head cleared up the implication of who may have helped the Juracanians.

"Can't blame me," Lt Gray said with a barked laugh. "The beans are good."

A short discussion of the Juracanian coffee industry's future kept Dewey distracted until they exited the last stairwell and stepped onto the platform. The Hospitallers, already on the platform and formed up, popped to attention as Dewey arrived with Lt Haynes and Lt Gray in tow.

"Stand easy, everyone," Dewey said. As the platoon relaxed their posture, Dewey searched and then said, "Sergeant Barrett. We ready to roll?"

"Ready, Lieutenant Tyler," said Sgt Barrett.

Dewey nodded and then looked around. "Where's Alexander?"

An essential part of the plan required his presence. Dewey would be more than a little frustrated if they had to scramble for a replacement.

"Down here, Tyler," said Lt Owen.

Dewey found Owen at the end of the platform. When he caught Dewey's eye, Lt Owen pointed across his body and into the tunnel.

"There's a hard line down here. It's how Alexander communicates with his girlfriend."

From the tunnel came a loud response. "She's not my girlfriend, Lieutenant."

On the platform, Hospitallers within earshot chuckled and snickered as they relayed the conversation to those who hadn't heard. It sent a wave of humor through the platoon.

"Sorry," said Lt Owen, though it was clear he wasn't sorry. "It's how he communicates with our contact on the inside."

Alexander appeared at the edge of the platform. His face looked a little red, in Dewey's opinion. He chose not to comment on it. Instead, he asked, "Everything ready on the other end?"

"Guard changed a couple hours ago," said Alexander. "Mr. Thayer is engrossed in some vid he's fond of. And Ms. Lerner has everything else ready to go."

Dewey nodded and then scanned across the platform, catching the return gaze of many of the Hospitallers present. Once more, they were stepping into harm's way. This time, though, it was as much for the civilians as it was for themselves. Failure would have repercussions for them, but more so for the civilians. Mr. Thayer and his mercenaries would likely take their anger out on anyone left alive. People like Luc and the other Juracanians in the nearest towns, for example.

So, it seemed to Dewey like the best idea was not to fail.

"Sergeant Barrett," he said after he scanned the platoon. "Put a team on point with Alexander, and let's move out."

20

Dewey had anticipated a slog through waist-deep water, similar to his last excursion through the subway system. Instead, the walk through the tunnel resulted in splashing through water that barely wetted their ankles. If Dewey had to guess, and sometimes that's what it came to, he'd have guessed that the Juracanians had switched power over to this tunnel's pumps to drain it. Or maybe it was just more waterproof than the tunnel he'd navigated the last time he crossed under the river.

Also, unlike the tunnels that Dewey had been guided through under the city, this tunnel was littered with obstructions. Again, left to guess, Dewey assumed that debris had been left in place to give the impression the tunnel hadn't been used by escaping Juracanian slaves. The tunnel certainly looked unused.

It was the obstructions that slowed the Hospitallers. That and the steep climb from under the river and up to the hidden spaceport station. However, Dewey had based their time on the experiences of the Juracanians, not on the abilities of the Hospitallers. As such, they'd arrived earlier than they'd anticipated.

The station was more obstructed than the tunnel. Cpl Lena Wong had commed Sgt Maxwell, who'd commed Dewey to come forward. He joined Wong's fireteam and Alexander just past the mouth of the tunnel.

Dewey now understood why the mercenaries might have missed the presence of the port station. From the number of beams, crete slabs, and other debris, it looked like a giant hand had pushed the station into the ground, right into the station's underground platform.

"I can see one person getting through there," said Sgt Maxwell. She was standing just behind Dewey. "But an entire platoon?"

"We'll have to get up to the surface the same way the Juracanians got down here," Dewey said. He looked over his shoulder and smiled at Sgt Maxwell. "One person at a time."

"Kind of hard to surprise the enemy when your attack is one person at a time," added Cpl Wong.

"Very true." Dewey stepped past Cpl Wong and Alexander. He rested a hand on a rusted beam and leaned through an open space, looking upward as he did. Now he was glad they'd arrived early. "Tell me, Alexander, is there enough space above where we can regroup without being seen by the mercs?"

"Probably," said Alexander. "The station had a level above this where I guess they screened people for access to the port. There's a wide set of stairs that goes to the surface from there. Whatever was on top of that was destroyed, covering the stairs. It's not as cluttered as this."

"Cluttered?" scoffed Sgt Maxwell. "If this is cluttered, I'd hate to see a mess."

The Hospitallers nearby chuckled in agreement. Dewey didn't bother with silencing them as he was busy running through scenarios in his mind. "Is there more than one way to the stairs, Alexander?"

Alexander shrugged. "Probably. I'm not even sure how I got through it all. I just knew I had to go down until I found tracks."

Dewey nodded and tapped his comm. "Owen. We have the comm link to the city?"

As they'd come through the tunnel, Lt Matthews and Sgt Thompson had been setting out hands. The comms would be spotty over the distance from the spaceport to the city, especially when down in the subway tunnels. They would also run the risk of being overheard by the mercenaries. The comm would have been secured, the words spoken encrypted, but it would still be a signal that would have given away their presence.

Instead, they were using a directional signal with the hands serving as relays. A helmet left at the starting point served as the final relay, allowing Dewey to communicate with the Juracanian leaders and SSgt Castro.

"Thompson says we have a clean comm line," said Lt Owen. "You ready to use it?"

"I need to talk to SSgt Castro. We might have a small delay getting to the surface."

"Okay, give us a second."

Dewey switched the comm to general communication but dialed down the strength. "Okay, Hospitallers. We have a short break here. So, eat something now, do a last-minute gear check, but be ready to move when the order comes."

Dewey's comm beeped, and he switched comm channels.

"Good to go, Tyler," said Lt Owen.

"Thank you." Dewey tapped the comm for SSgt Castro.

"I hope you're not calling to move up the schedule, Lieutenant Tyler."

SSgt Castro's comment made Dewey laugh, drawing the attention of those around him. "Move up the schedule? You're not ready, Castro?"

There were smiles and nods from those around Dewey as they interpreted his comments.

"We're almost there," SSgt Castro said. "But I had to stop and do some quick lessons on loading weapons and how to move with some stealth. You know, like not complaining about how hard the work is."

SSgt Castro and Dewey had been doing this for more than ten years, not counting all the years in the orphanage. All the Hospitallers around Dewey had at least four years of training and experience since leaving the orphanages. The Juracanians had none of that experience. Until now, their resistance had been nothing more than observing the base, and helping others escape and return to their homes. Dewey was surprised that the complaining hadn't come earlier.

"Well, fortunately for you, Castro, we are running behind schedule. Or we will be very soon."

Dewey quickly summarized the situation and what he planned to do next.

"So another hour most likely," SSgt Castro said. "I'm sure we'll be ready by then. If not, I'll do it all myself."

Dewey didn't laugh at the comment. He was aware that not only would SSgt Castro do it herself if needed, he knew that she could.

"Remember, Castro, all they have to do is make a lot of noise and hit close to the target. Just enough to distract the mercs. You don't have to win the war."

"Make noise? Oh, we got that covered." SSgt Castro laughed. "Just let us know when you're ready for more."

"Will do, Castro. Talk to you soon." Dewey cut the comm. He turned to Alexander. "I've never seen a map of this station. Can you point in the direction of the stairs?"

Alexander pointed up. "There and back a little." He pointed to one side. "They lead out that way, toward the comm building. The view is blocked by the building, which is why it was easy for us to get in."

"Let's hope it's as easy to get out," said Dewey. He tapped the comm. "Owen, Haynes, Sergeant Barrett, to the front, please."

A few seconds later, the lieutenants and Sgt Barrett were present. They, like Dewey, took a moment to absorb the imagery of the tangle that surrounded them.

"This looks interesting," said Lt Haynes.

Sgt Barrett added the critical question. "How are we going to get through all that, Lieutenant Tyler?"

"With patience," said Dewey. "And effort. About four efforts, I think."

He laid out the plan. Everyone had a helmet, including Alexander. With strategically placed hands and running the helmets' locator programs, they could trace everyone's path through the maze of debris.

"We send four people," said Dewey. "Then, we see which paths are the most efficient. After that, we send the route, or routes, to everyone else's helmet and get topside as quick as we safely can."

"You should send Lieutenant Hall, too," Lt Owen said. "Hall was a climbing enthusiast at her orphanage and holds the record for best time on the climbing wall in the exercise bay."

"Get her up here," said Dewey.

While Lt Owen commed for Lt Hall, Dewey directed the placement of five hands to maximize data collection. With Lt Hall climbing, too, they would be recording five paths. Climbing with the lieutenant was Alexander because he'd been here before, Cpl Wong and two from her fireteam, PFC Webb and PFC Bryant.

"Remember," Dewey said as the five climbers started looking for handholds and paths, "it's not a race. We want the best and safest route for the rest of us."

The climbers acknowledged Dewey's reminder and started clambering up and into the debris. They were quickly out of visual. The only way to follow them now was through the VR map. With his shield down, Dewey was able to look at the debris and see lengthening lines superimposed on it. Each line had a label, showing Lt Hall several meters ahead of the other Hospitallers. Alexander was close on her heels, four meters to the left.

"I almost feel like we should have set odds and taken bets," Lt Owen said. His voice was a distracted whisper, like his comment was meant to be internal and not to be shared. Still, when several of the enlisted Hospitallers laughed, he didn't seem embarrassed by his statement.

Another two minutes and Lt Hall's line started to shrink. Next to her, Cpl Wong was now parallel and slowly passing.

"Is Hall okay?" asked Lt Haynes.

Dewey tapped his comm. "Hall?"

"Dead end," answered Lt Hall. "I've got it now."

On the visual, Lt Hall's line made a hard right for a meter and then shot up, passing Cpl Wong's line. To the left, Alexander's line was veering in Hall's direction and picking up speed.

"Photo finish?"

"Looking that way, Haynes," Dewey said.

Lt Hall's line was meters past Cpl Wong. PFC Webb seemed to have stalled, his line slowly shrinking as he worked his way back. PFC

Bryant hadn't moved in some time.

"Bryant?" Dewey asked after tapping his comm. "You okay?"

"No," said PFC Bryant. She laughed and then added, "I'm stuck."

As the best routes appeared to be worked out by Alexander and Lt Hall, Dewey commed PFC Webb.

"Webb, I'm sending you Bryant's location and her route. She's stuck. See if you can help her out."

"Will do, Lieutenant. My path wasn't any better."

"No worries, Webb, the other climbers have found us a way through." Dewey tapped the comm to close the connection just as Lt Hall's and Alexander's lines converged. Five seconds later, Dewey's comm pinged. He tapped the comm and said, "Nice work, Lieutenant Hall."

"Thank you, Lieutenant Tyler." Dewey could hear the pride in her voice. "It would have been more fun if there wasn't the urgency involved."

"Understood. We have room for the rest of the platoon?"

There was a pause of a muted comm, then Lt Hall was back. "Looks like it. Alexander says we're at one of two places where we can position everyone. The stairs take a ninety-degree turn. There's a crete slab partially blocking the stairwell, but it's passable."

"Expect company soon." Dewey closed the comm once more and turned to Lt Owen and Lt Haynes. "Can you two clean up those routes and start sending people? Private Russell and I will start now."

"You aren't going to try and beat Hall's time, are you?" asked Lt Owen. He had a mischievous grin implying he'd been thinking of trying.

"I'm just going to try and get up there in one piece." Dewey waved for Pvt Russell to proceed along Lt Hall's path. Once Russell was out of sight, Dewey grabbed the debris and pulled himself up. Before disappearing into the rubble, he looked back at Owen, saying, "See you at the top."

The very last to arrive at the stairs were PFC Webb, PFC Bryant, and MedTech Chambers. Chambers had been diverted to Bryant's location. While trying to extricate herself with PFC Webb's help, she'd sliced through her sleeve and cut her arm. Treating it hadn't been difficult, but guiding Bryant through, with her reduced to one arm, slowed the three of them down.

"Sorry, Lieutenant Tyler," PFC Bryant said as Webb and Chambers lifted her out of the last of the debris. Her arm was strapped to her chest, just above her rifle.

"Better late than never, Bryant," said Dewey. "But you're going to be on rearguard with MedTech Chambers and Lieutenant Haynes, for now."

"Understood, Lieutenant."

Dewey gave her a nod and then went forward, crawling under the crete slab to where three of the fireteams and three of the lieutenants waited. "How's it look?"

Lt Owen had his face shield down as he spoke. "We pushed two eyes onto the surface," he said. "That's got us a panoramic view of the back of the comm building. But we can also see left, right, and most of what's behind us. Ran a thermal, too. We're alone on this side of the building."

"At the moment," added Lt Matthews, who also had her face shield down, the edges giving the telltale glow of VR.

"Pessimist," whispered Lt Owen, just loud enough to be heard by everyone. He pushed up his face shield and turned to Dewey. "What's next?"

"Secure the perimeter," said Dewey. He turned to Sgt Maxwell. "Take Corporal Lopez and Corporal Chavez's fireteams and secure us a perimeter using the comm building as one side. Make sure everyone stays out of view of the other buildings."

"On it," said Sgt Maxwell. She signaled to Lopez and Chavez. "Lopez? Your team first, break left."

Dewey pulled his face shield down, accessing the two eyes on the surface. He watched as first one fireteam and then the next moved out, taking up firing positions to protect the rest of the platoon as they exited the stairwell. When the fireteams were in place, Dewey received a comm message from Sgt Maxwell. Dewey acknowledged it and shut down the outside view.

"Okay, Barrett, Take everyone else out."

After acknowledging Dewey's orders, Sgt Barrett gave his own. The rest of the Hospitallers flowed out in designated order, followed by the remaining lieutenants and their loadmasters. Dewey waited until PFC Webb was past the crete slab and on her feet before he joined the other Hospitallers on the surface.

Dewey pushed past some tough, pale bush that was low to the ground to reach the surface. He made sure not to uproot the plant as he went. It seemed best to keep the entrance hidden in case their mission was unsuccessful. At least the Juracanians would still have their escape route.

He joined Lt Haynes, who was kneeling next to Sgt Maxwell. "Everything look okay, Maxwell?"

"So far, Lieutenant," answered Sgt Maxwell. Then, "Now what?"

"Now?" Dewey took a moment to scan the area. The space elevator was still some distance away, but the trunks' loading cranes were visible and in motion. So far, the port seemed unaware of their presence. He turned back to Lt Haynes and Sgt Maxwell. "Now we send Alexander on his mission. Then we go secure us a comm building."

21

Dewey spent several minutes talking to Alexander, making sure he knew what to do and where to go. Once he was gone, the Hospitallers reused the two eyes from reconnoitering the subway's exit. Sgt Barrett rolled one to the left, out from the shadow of the comm building. Sgt Maxwell did the same, except she put a spin on it that not only impressed Dewey but put it closer to the hidden front side of the building.

"Neat trick," admitted Sgt Barrett.

"Came in handy during snowball fights," said Sgt Maxwell. "I'm surprised I still know how."

"Probably threw a lot of snowballs," said Dewey as he brought down his face shield.

They still didn't have a view of the front of the building. From Alexander's description, he knew that there was a steel door with a single lock they'd have to breach. There weren't any windows to see in. But there also wasn't supposed to be anyone inside, either. Hopefully, that remained true once they were in.

Dewey also hoped that the comm building was exactly as it was presented. It was a standard structure, pre-built at a factory on Nanabush, in the United Planets' Aayaase system. When Dewey had been a newly minted lieutenant, he'd been responsible for comms. That had sparked his curiosity, leading him to scan through hundreds of schematics for comm systems. He wasn't surprised to see this one here. It was used throughout most systems because of its reliability, low cost, and ease of purchase.

Most important, though, it meant that Dewey knew where everything was inside.

"Unless they made changes," said Lt Owen.

"Would you?"

"Well, no," Owen said in response to Dewey's question. "But I'm a Hospitaller. I like order."

"That won't be their reason," said Dewey. "It's easier to just leave things as they are, especially if you don't have anyone trained to reconfigure what already works."

"Great. So we go in and do what?"

"There should be three terminals along the back wall." Dewey then described the files and systems they had to quickly access. Once there, they had to flip digital switches that would disconnect outgoing ground comms from the space elevator while simultaneously shunting incoming comms to a terminal inside the comm building. That way, they would not only control what went out but what came in.

If the mercenaries at the space elevator platform announced they were sending reinforcements, it wouldn't be good for the ones on the ground to know they had help on the way. Especially if Dewey's Hospitallers had the mercenaries in a tough spot where they might surrender. Knowing help was on the way often gave a near-beaten group a sudden burst of motivation.

"Once we blow that lock, the ground mercs will come looking," said Lt Haynes. "I hope Staff Sergeant Castro is ready."

"She will be," said Dewey. "She's never let me down. Let's get into position. Owen, comm me when your team is ready on the other side."

With his fireteam, Sgt Barrett moved to the other side of the building, shadowed by Lt Owen and his flight crew. Dewey went the opposite way with Sgt Maxwell and the others. The eyes had shown them a clear path around the building. It also showed that several watchtowers on the wall a hundred and fifty meters away were visible. If anyone up there looked back into the base, they'd see the Hospitallers for sure.

The other side was exposed to the company office building's windows, the tallest of the structures. Four floors up, the level was lined with thick carbon-reinforced windows. Alexander assured them that even though that was where Mr. Thayer spent most of his time, he rarely looked out the windows. He didn't like to get too close to them, even though they were shielded from radiation.

As Sgt Maxwell's fireteams prepared themselves for the rush that would take them around the building to the front, Dewey's comm beeped.

"They're ready on the other side, Maxwell," Dewey said. "Go when you're ready."

"Here we go." Maxwell tapped Cpl Wong on the helmet. "Go time."

In her turn, Cpl Wong edged forward. Next to her were PFC Webb and Pvt Russell. They were both carrying deployed ballistic shields. Behind them was PFC Bryant, a shape-charge in a ballistic cup in her good hand. Wong held up one hand and counted down from three. When she made a fist, her fireteam rushed around the corner for the front of the building.

Dewey followed with Lt Haynes and MedTech Chambers.

Behind them came Cpl Lopez's team. Two of the team also carried deployed ballistic shields, facing outward toward the rest of the base and the watchtowers. Lt Hall and the remaining supernumeraries went last, the loadmaster, Sgt Simon, bearing a fifth ballistic shield.

By the time Dewey had reached the building's front corner, Cpl Wong and her team were at the door. Webb and Russell had turned so that their ballistic shields bracketed the door. PFC Bryant stepped into the space, pressed the ballistic cup over the door lock, and then retreated around PFC Webb's shield. Cpl Wong, behind Pvt Russell, reached out and touched virtual controls. In Dewey's face shield, he saw the warning for an imminent explosion.

The explosion was anticlimactic, as it should be. With his hand against the building wall, Dewey felt more than heard the explosion. The shield cup had contained the explosion, directing its force inward.

"Lieutenant," said Cpl Wong. She and Pvt Russell had pulled the door open, positioning themselves next to it and behind the shield, which now faced outward.

"Let's go, Haynes." Dewey sprinted around the corner, reaching the doorway just ahead of Lt Owen, who'd come from the other side. Owen pulled up short. Dewey dashed inside the comm room.

A quick glance showed Dewey that he'd made the right guess. Everything looked exactly as if it had come from a handbook schematic. All of the panels were exactly the same as the images he'd seen. Several still had tags that had been placed by the manufacturer. What it looked like to Dewey was that Mr. Thayer's company had bought the system and just turned it on, making only minimal programming adjustments. All of that made sense if someone was assuming they didn't have anything to fear. It also explained why it would be easy for Ms. Lerner to reinstate the protocols for sending messages.

"There." Dewey pointed as he took the middle seat. "Third menu, Owen. Should be easy."

Dewey was looking for a menu that would allow him to control incoming messages. He was looking for it when his comm beeped. It connected automatically, which meant he had SSgt Castro online. He continued to search the programs and menus as he talked.

"Go ahead, Castro."

"There's activity on the wall. They pulled the guards back from the gate and buttoned it up."

"They're onto us," Dewey said loud enough for everyone in the comm building and out to hear. To SSgt Castro, he added. "Time to make yourself known."

"Excellent." The comm went silent.

Dewey had found the application that controlled the incoming messages. He was setting up a new receiving file when he heard the first, distant explosion. SSgt Castro had gotten to work.

"Got it," said Lt Owen. He stepped back from the terminal as he clapped his hands together, followed by a quick fist pump.

"Lieutenant Haynes?" Dewey asked. He had his receiving folder established and protocols in place. He'd know when and from whom any messages arrived from up top and on the ground.

"Someone in the office building tried to send a message out," said Lt Haynes. She was leaning in close to the screen. At the same time, Dewey received a signal of an incoming message to his dead-end folder. "From Mr. Thayer, I guess."

Dewey checked the folder. He could hear the near-distant rumble of shoulder-fired rockets and the chatter of machine guns. While Dewey didn't think SSgt Castro would risk the civilians' lives, he still hoped they were safe.

"Right, here it is." Dewey touched the screen, opening the message. "Yep. Mr. Thayer is sending a request for help. Let's go give him some."

The room grew dim. Dewey turned to see that Cpl Wong's fireteam had pulled themselves into the comm room, blocking the doorway with their ballistic shields. Cpl Wong looked over her shoulder at Dewey as she helped to hold the top shield in place.

"Company," said Wong.

Her statement was confirmed by the sound of gunfire and the high-pitched thudding of small-arms fire against the shields. As long as no one started using heavy machine guns or high-velocity rounds, they'd be safe. Dewey took the time to drop his shield and call up the eyes, still lying on the ground outside.

The first thing Dewey saw was a body on the ground. Fortunately, it was some distance away and did not look like one of his people. Using his hands, he slid the image to show him the side of the comm building. He saw the wall, several ballistic shields, and a bristling of barrels pointing out from behind the shields. Switching to the other side of the building showed a slightly different scene as the Hospitallers on that side were pushing forward.

"Sergeant Maxwell? Sergeant Barrett?"

"Maxwell here, Lieutenant. Looks like a squad of mercs from the barracks. I don't think they expected to find us. I think we surprised them."

"Can you and Barrett button them up?" Dewey asked. He wanted the area secured as fast as possible.

"Yes," both sergeants said as one.

"Don't trip over each other's toes," Dewey said. "Maxwell, you take the lead out there."

"Will do, Lieutenant Tyler. We're going to push them back to their barracks and maybe convince them to stand down."

"You're not that smooth a talker, Maxwell," said Sgt Barrett. They both laughed as Dewey switched the comm. "Lieutenant Matthews?"

"Matthews, here."

"Sergeant Barrett and Sergeant Maxwell are going to deal with the mercs. I need you and the rest of the flight teams to watch their backs."

"Glad to do it, Tyler."

"What about us?" asked Cpl Wong as Dewey was tapping his comm.

"Sorry, Wong, you'll have to sit this one out."

"Bummer," said PFC Bryant. "I was certain I could take these guys with one hand tied behind my back. Or to my chest, I guess."

The self-effacing humor pulled a few chuckles as everyone trapped inside the comm room waited, listening to the firefight slowly fade from the immediate area.

While they waited, Dewey contacted Alexander, which did not go as smoothly as making a comm connection with another Hospitaller.

"What? Hello?" Several awkward noises hurt Dewey's ear. "Is this working?"

"Alexander," Dewey said loud enough to pull the Juracanian's attention. "It's Lieutenant Dewey."

"Hey, Lieutenant. Someone's firing weapons."

"That's right." Dewey noticed the other Hospitallers in the comm room looking at him. He shook his head and said to Alexander, "Someone is shooting. Us and the mercs. Did you talk to your people?"

"Yes."

There was an awkward silence where Dewey waited for more information, something he'd expect to receive from one of his own people reporting in. Once Dewey realized Alexander wasn't going to report automatically, he prodded the Juracanian. "And what did they say?"

"Say? Oh, right. They're still working. But they asked if you could get them some food? No one's sent them lunch today."

"Send them food?" The other Hospitallers chuckled. "Okay, soon as we have the base secure, we'll see about food. But they need to keep working."

"They said they would. But food will help."

"We'll get back to you," said Dewey. He quickly cut the comm. "The Juracanians are going to keep loading the trunks, but doing it on a full belly would be nice."

"I'm feeling a bit peckish myself," said Lt Owen, earning his own laughter response.

Outside, the firefight was still going but seemed to have diminished in intensity. The images through the eyes had shown the Hospitallers pushing forward. It was just a matter of waiting. Dewey took the time to check in with SSgt Castro.

"How you holding up?"

SSgt Castro harrumphed and said, "It's like spending time at the gun range."

"Boring," Dewey said. "But necessary."

"At least the Juracanians are enjoying themselves," Castro said. "I suppose you're having fun now, too, from the sounds of it."

Dewey laughed. "I'm stuck inside the comm building, Staff Sergeant Castro."

The conversation ended with shared laughter. Dewey turned his attention back to the scene outside the comm building. There were several more bodies on the ground. Zooming in allowed him to determine they were mercenaries. It also made Lt Owen groan in displeasure as he was suddenly pulled forward in VR without warning.

"Sorry, Owen," Dewey said. He slowed his movements as he continued to study the scene. He stopped when he saw MedTech Chambers treating someone on the ground. He tapped the comm to connect with her. "How bad?"

"Not bad," said Chambers. Dewey watched as she applied a seal to what looked like a hip wound. "Not great, either. Corporal Lopez here zigged when he should have zagged."

"Can he move?"

"Yes, Lieutenant, he can move. I had to tackle him just to take care of the wound." There was a pause, then, "Yes, Corporal, I am telling on you. Now, quit squirming. Anything else, Lieutenant Tyler?"

Dewey had to force a smile off his face so he could speak. "No, no, Chambers. Carry on."

He left MedTech Chambers to her duties and scanned the rest of the area. Besides Chambers and Lopez, there was nothing much more to see except the office building's exterior and the base perimeter's distant wall. None of which was interesting to look at. He considered comming one of the squad leaders when his helmet pinged a request for an incoming call.

"Sergeant Maxwell," Dewey said.

"The mercs in the barracks have had enough, Lieutenant. We have six under control, and we've cleared the barracks."

"Good work, Maxwell. Be there in a minute." Dewey tapped the comm and closed the VR with the eyes. He signaled to Cpl Wong. "Clear the door, Corporal, the area's secured."

Once they realized they were being pressured on both sides, the mercenaries at the gate and wall quickly folded, too. Dewey didn't blame them. They were being paid to fight and protect someone else's property. Dying was a hazard but not a requirement. They weren't going to throw down their lives on a lost cause.

"Lieutenant Owen," Dewey said as they left the mercenary barracks. "Take a fireteam, find the food supplies, and feed the Juracanians. We don't want them to stop loading the trunks."

"I'll take care of it," said Lt Owen. "What are you going to do?"

Dewey had waved Sgt Maxwell to follow him as he started walking. "I'm going to pay a visit to Mr. Thayer."

22

The office building, where Mr. Thayer was holed up, sat separate from the other buildings. Unlike the barracks for the mercenaries and the communications building, Mr. Thayer's domicile and headquarters was designed as a bulwark against radiation. Dewey could only imagine the extra expense used to bring all the sections down from space, assemble them, and then decontaminate them so that Mr. Thayer could hide in relative safety.

Dewey recognized some of the materials used in the building's construction. He'd read about them sometime in his past, and it was apparent that Mr. Thayer had a lot of pull with his company, or he'd gambled heavily on his success on Juracan. If it were the latter, he was going to be very disappointed by Dewey's presence.

To speak to Mr. Thayer meant having to get inside the building. A thick-walled airlock controlled access. Mr. Thayer was unlikely to open it himself and wave the Hospitallers in. Dewey was quite okay with blowing the lock with some shaped charges if needed. And that would only happen if Ms. Lerner wasn't able to assist.

"Well, that's a bummer," said Sgt Maxwell.

Dewey had brought the sergeant, along with PFC Stewart Murray. There wasn't any need to overwhelm Mr. Thayer with the presence of an entire platoon or even a fireteam.

Sgt Maxwell's verbal disappointment was understandable. As they'd rounded the corner to face the airlock's front, Dewey could see that the access light was green. The hatch was unlocked and cleared for entry.

"Maybe we should use the charges anyway?" suggested PFC Murray. "In case it's a trap."

"Good point," said Sgt Maxwell, not even bothering to hide her grin.

Blowing things up was just part of the child-like enthusiasm that the Hospitallers shared. Dewey chalked it up as part of the psyche of Orphan Corps members. They'd grown up together or in similar circumstances so that sometimes it felt like they were still playing in the fields and playgrounds around their orphanage homes.

"The Juracanians might need this building one day," Dewey said as he knuckled the green button to start the hatch opening. "So let's leave it as intact as possible."

The disappointment on Sgt Maxwell's and PFC Murray's faces was feigned, evidenced by their laughter that followed the fake frowns. They followed Dewey into the airlock, where Sgt Maxwell punched the button to close the door and start the cycle of admittance.

Dewey waited patiently as the air was circulated and filtered. He and the others pulled up their masks to filter the powdery mist ejected through nozzles in the ceiling and wall corners. The mist left a dusty coating of white on their skin and clothes, reminiscent of their past experience on the planet Wenshen. Another cycle of air and mist cleared away the powder, then the light for the interior door flashed green.

Past the interior door, Dewey found that he and his retinue were in a very typical corporate lobby. There were several chairs and couches arranged around low tables. There were digital art frames on the wall that even now cycled through scenes of different planet surfaces and various types of mining equipment. There was even a receptionist's desk, but no receptionist.

"You think the dispenser works?" PFC Murray asked as he made his way to it.

"I can't imagine it wouldn't," said Dewey.

He wasn't interested in the dispenser and wasn't concerned if PFC Murray tried it. He was more interested in the elevator that didn't have a call button. Could it be possible that no one knew they were in the lobby? With the dozen cameras mounted in the ceiling, it seemed unlikely.

And yet, here they were, alone.

Dewey went over to the receptionist's desk while Sgt Maxwell followed PFC Murray to the dispenser.

"It's got coffee," said Murray. He punched a button on the machine, waking it and causing a paper cup to appear.

"Don't tell Lieutenant Gray you've been drinking someone else's coffee," Sgt Maxwell said. "You'll break his heart."

Dewey examined the surface of the receptionist's desk. He was looking for a way to contact either Mr. Thayer or Ms. Lerner. Touching the desk brought the built-in monitor screen to life. It was barren of the numerous apps Dewey had seen on other desk monitors, including his own. He double-tapped it, thinking it might give him other menu options.

At the same moment, as Dewey tried a second time with the double-tap, he heard the click of a door latch behind him. He turned, his hand settling on his weapon's pistol grip, to see a door open where it had only looked like a wall panel. From behind the door, a young woman emerged. She looked at Dewey and smiled as her eyes scanned him and the desktop.

"It's bio-locked," she said. "You won't get anything from it unless you're me. Or Mr. Thayer, and he'd never come down here."

"Radiation?" asked Dewey.

"Not much. Not if you're not paranoid."

"And Mr. Thayer is paranoid," Dewey said.

"To put it mildly. I'm Tegan Lerner." She stepped forward, one hand out, clearly unconcerned about the radiation.

"Lieutenant Dewey Tyler, Hospitaller Orphan Corps."

"Alexander told me you could be trusted," said Ms. Lerner. She made her way around the other side of the desk, toward the elevator door. "I hope that my assistance with the Juracanians speaks in my favor if or when the Intra-Systems Courts get involved."

As Ms. Lerner stopped in front of the elevator door, a frame of light winked on, and the doors slowly parted. She stepped in, holding back the doors with one hand.

"Coming?"

"Maxwell, Murray," said Dewey as he stepped to the elevator, straddling the threshold as the other two Hospitallers hurried over.

"How's the coffee?" asked Ms. Lerner.

PFC Murray still had the cup in his hand as he stepped to the back of the elevator. "I've had better. Recently, as a matter of fact."

As the doors slid shut, Ms. Lerner laughed lightly. "Alexander mentioned something about that. Do they really have coffee beans here on Juracan?"

"It's the Juracan version of a weed," PFC Murray said. He sipped at the coffee in the cup once more, made a face, then shook his head. "This tastes more like weeds."

The doors to the elevator slid open. Dewey was surprised to see that they were looking at a different room. He hadn't even felt the elevator move. Impressed, he stepped out, followed by Ms. Lerner and then Sgt Maxwell and PFC Murray.

It was a large conference room, and they were on the fourth floor. Dewey knew the level because of the windows. He'd seen the band of them circling the fourth floor when they'd been outside. Two of the walls of the conference room were not windows. One was a solid wall, and that was where the elevator was. The fourth wall was glass, but it only looked onto another conference room. Dewey couldn't see a way to access it.

The other room's table butted up against the glass partition lining up with the table on Dewey's side. He imagined that it had all been a single room before. And he was pretty sure as to why it was now divided with a thick wall of glass.

"Mr. Thayer?" Dewey asked, turning to Ms. Lerner.

"Two minutes, thirty seconds," answered Ms. Lerner. "It's his thing."

"What's your thing?" asked Dewey, since they had to wait for Mr. Thayer's dramatically paused entry. "Why are you helping the Juracanians?"

Ms. Lerner's features took on a hard setting, her eyebrows reaching down and toward each other.

"Because they were being mistreated. I didn't know when I took

Abandoned on Juracan

the position that Mr. Thayer was forcing them to work as slaves. Not until I looked deeper into the accounting books. I'd been scheduling payments for the Juracanians as employees, not realizing that the money didn't exist and wasn't going to them. I heard a couple things from the soldiers when talking to Mr. Thayer. I got suspicious and started looking."

"That's about the time you met Alexander?"

The look on Ms. Lerner's face softened at the mention of Alexander's name.

"It was. I couldn't sleep one night after accessing the hidden accounting files. I have a corner apartment over there." Ms. Lerner pointed toward the opposite corner of the building. "I saw movement. Someone was climbing into the bushes and debris past the communications hub. When I realized it was one of the locals - one of the Juracanians - I hurried downstairs."

Ms. Lerner laughed and looked around. Dewey wondered if the sec-cams had mics as well. He couldn't imagine them not and pointedly looked at one of them.

"It wouldn't matter now," said Ms. Lerner. "But the audio is off, and Mr. Thayer is locked out of that system. Anyway. I followed Alexander into the debris. I wanted to talk to one of the Juracanians, so I could hear the truth from them. I got stuck and couldn't move, so I called out for help."

"I'm not surprised that he came back to help you," said Dewey. Alexander was a good representative of the kind of compassionate people the Juracanians were. At least those they'd met so far.

"I'm surprised he did," Ms. Lerner said. "But I was stuck, scared, and desperate. But he did come back and help me, and we talked for several hours. I thought he was escaping, but he'd apparently already done so months before. Now he was running messages back and forth for other Juracanians. We talked every time he came through the tunnel. He told me everything that he knew. I told him everything I knew. That's when I started helping."

"Quite a chance you took," Dewey said. As he spoke, there was movement on the other side of the glass partition. When Dewey looked in that direction, Ms. Lerner did the same. She pulled a small tablet out of a pocket and tapped it several times.

"Mr. Thayer," she said while putting the tablet away. "This is the Hospitaller officer, Lieutenant Tyler."

Tall and narrow-shouldered, Mr. Thayer stood at the far end of his side of the table. He had a small tablet of his own that he glanced at several times before putting it on the table surface.

"Mr. Thayer is paranoid that you and I being radioactive is going to get to him somehow."

"You're fired, Ms. Lerner."

She ignored him and continued talking. "I've never been in that room or his private quarters. Mr. Thayer has sealed himself in."

"You'll never work for this company again."

"I got it," said Ms. Lerner, her voice as sharp and quick as a snapped stick.

"Mr. Thayer," said Dewey. He stepped forward as he spoke, drawing some of the attention to himself. "As I'm sure you know, we've now assumed control of your base."

"Which is illegal, and you're in a lot of trouble for it."

"Perhaps, but I think the capture of our ship by your people will have some bearing on the outcome of any decision. As will the enslavement of locals."

"Locals." Mr. Thayer's voice was a harumph of annoyance. "There wasn't supposed to be anyone here."

"We can let the planetary governments address that situation. For now, all I'm interested in is getting my ship back."

Mr. Thayer looked down at the reader on the table as he spoke. "Well, good luck with that."

"You can call upstairs and direct your company and the mercs with them to stand down."

"Did you see the shipment yard?" asked Mr. Thayer. Dewey thought Mr. Thayer was about to change the subject. It proved to be otherwise. "I have twice the number of trunks ready to be sent topside than the freighter can carry. And I have enough reclaimed material for another hundred trunks. You and your ship won't be going anywhere until I move all of it off world. After that, you and your kind can go jump in the nearest black hole for all I care."

Dewey could see Sgt Maxwell and PFC Murray off to one side. They were more expressive in their dislike for Mr. Thayer and his behavior. Being a little more experienced in dealing with civilian leaders, Dewey had his emotions contained and not presenting themselves on his face.

"Mr. Thayer, if you will not help us regain our ship, we'll be forced to do it ourselves. That would make this a military action. People are likely to get hurt."

"You'll get hurt," said Mr. Thayer. He paused as he tapped the reader still lying on the table. Dewey was beginning to understand what Mr. Thayer was looking to find. If Dewey was right, Mr. Thayer wasn't going to see what he was hoping for.

"Perhaps," Dewey replied. "But so will many of your people."

Mr. Thayer pushed the reader away, looking visibly annoyed as he did. "Speaking of many people, how many do you have? A platoon? There are two companies of our military forces waiting up there. You might want to reconsider your actions."

"He's lying," said Ms. Lerner. Dewey wouldn't have been afraid to admit that he'd been worried until she spoke. "I have a copy of the manifests for all the ships. There are only two squads."

"You don't know that." Mr. Thayer had started stalking toward the glass partition, pulling himself to a halt after several steps and quickly backtracking. "Ship manifests are sealed and encrypted."

"Unless you're too lazy or too paranoid about doing the work yourself." Ms. Lerner pulled on a chain hanging around her neck. Dangling from the chain, like a gaudy bauble, was a security cube. They usually required a thumbprint to activate once connected to a computer system. "You told me to keep it after I did the work you didn't want to do on the manifests."

"I also told you to destroy it. Which you told me you did."

"I guess that makes us both liars."

"Doesn't matter," said Mr. Thayer. He waved off the exchange with Ms. Lerner. He picked up the readers as he continued to speak.

"They know you're here. If you attempt to take a crew trunk topside, they'll know you're coming."

The last point was valid and something Dewey had already taken into consideration. But, again, Mr. Thayer didn't have all the correct information.

"Your people may know we're on-planet, but they don't know we're on your base or that we have control of it."

"More the fool you," said Mr. Thayer. "As soon as I got the call from Lieutenant Young, I fired off a message."

"Lieutenant Howard Young," said Ms. Lerner in an aside. "He's in charge of the soldiers here."

"Fortunately, that message didn't go through," Dewey said. He signaled for Sgt Maxwell and PFC Murray to pull back to the elevator.

While Dewey's people moved positions, Mr. Thayer was busy swiping and poking his reader's screen. Triumphantly, he waved it and pointed the screen at Dewey.

"Wrong! It went through. I have the receipt."

In turn, Dewey took out his tablet and pulled up the messages that had gone into the dead-end file he'd set up. There was one message, repeated fourteen times, from Mr. Thayer. Dewey tapped on it and read the message verbatim.

"That doesn't mean you stopped the message from getting through," said Mr. Thayer. His paling expression implied he doubted his own words.

"We're about to go and find out," said Dewey.

23

The mercenary platoon leader, Lt Young, had just enough of a look in his eyes to signal to Dewey that this was not his first military action. The anger he expressed through clenched fists and jaws told Dewey the lieutenant wasn't used to being bested as thoroughly as he was today. He also wasn't used to someone else sitting in his seat behind the desk.

"Can we try again, Lieutenant Young?" Dewey asked.

Dewey and the young lieutenant were not alone in the office. Behind the mercenary, and just to either side of the doorway, PFC Burke and Pvt Becker stood watch. Lt Owen lounged in a chair off to one side where he appeared to be more interested in the view out the window.

"I don't have to tell you anything." The words were expressed with the same heat as the glare the young lieutenant gave Dewey.

Dewey's question was asked distractedly as he hadn't expected the lieutenant's answer to change. Instead, Dewey was busy at the portable terminal system on the lieutenant's desk. Like the comm building, it was fairly common equipment, sold to planet-side militias, colony security, and apparently to spendthrift mercenary units. Dewey knew the manufacturer, knew the model, and had read a report on the short-comings of this and other comm systems. He'd read the report the same time he'd received the update to his security disk.

The security disk Dewey carried was similar to the cube Ms. Lerner had displayed, except that it didn't have pokey corners. It was also more powerful, stuffed with layers of encryption-busting code. All Dewey had to do was know what part of the system's programs to access, then put the disc close enough and activate it. Fortunately, he could do the last two steps without revealing the presence of the disc.

"All right, let's try this again." Dewey was tapping rapidly, working through several more programs and files. "Your replacement is Lieutenant Frank Alexander. That right?"

Dewey knew it was, and based on the smallest muscle movements on Lt Young's face, he knew it, too.

"Only two squads." Based on a quick scan of the incoming unit, Dewey knew it was a little more than that. Still, the supernumeraries were a communications clerk and a medic. Lt Young had neither.

"You don't have a medic?"

"Not something I'm likely to tell you." The anger was lessened by several degrees. Dewey had the feeling the lieutenant was beginning to accept the situation.

"True, but it says right here that you don't." Dewey tapped the screen with one hand as he tapped his comm with the other. "Chambers, how's the wounded?"

"Couple wounded on our side. Any merc not dead is wounded. SSgt Castro's team must have really let loose on the gate guard."

"Very likely. Have you done a rad check on the mercs?"

"Hadn't," said MedTech Chambers. "Should I make that a priority?"

Dewey suddenly realized that having mentioned a rad check, he had Lt Young's attention.

"No," said Dewey, "but maybe as quickly as you can after patching up their wounded."

"On it, Lieutenant Tyler."

Dewey tapped the comm and turned his attention back to Lt Young. "You're worried about radiation? You've been here for six months."

"Someone shorted the supply of blockers. Half of us have been without for the last two weeks."

"You don't have a printer?"

"It malfunctioned the first month. Command said we'd be fine."

"But you disagree," said Dewey. "And you, yourself, haven't had blockers for two weeks? I get that right?"

Lt Young didn't answer, but he didn't have to. Dewey could tell by the way the mercenary had spoken that he was the kind of officer who put his men first, even if he was young for the job.

"Owen," said Dewey. "Could you go and have a look at their printer and see if we can fix it? Barring that, check the canisters and see if they'll work with Chambers's system."

"Oh, good," said Lt Owen, rising to his feet. "I was beginning to get bored."

"It took a lot of talking," said Alexander. "But they said they'll keep working. They think they've traded one invader for another."

"Hopefully, they'll give us enough time to prove them wrong," Dewey said. "Or at least enough time to get our ship back."

Dewey and Alexander were standing back from the cranes as the Juracanians deftly loaded them onto the sliders before setting them on the elevator rail. Twenty meters farther away, Cpl Chavez and her fireteam served up food from warmers pulled from the mercenaries' cafeteria. Several older Juracanians were helping serve and controlling the flow of other hungry Juracanians.

"Did you find everything you need?" Alexander asked.

Alexander referred to the supplies Dewey had been seeking before their surprise attack on the ships docked at the elevator platform. Dewey wanted a way to avoid using the passenger trunk and hopefully avoid detection. To do that, he needed EVA suits. While it was unlikely to find military-grade suits in a storage unit on the planet's surface, other kinds of suits would suffice.

"Still looking," Dewey said. He nodded in response to the nods sent his way by several Juracanians, their hands busy with trays of hot food. Dewey paused as he watched the Juracanians pass and then find a level area to sit cross-legged and eat their food without the pressure of time. "None of the mercs will tell us where to look, which is understandable in a stubborn sort of way. But, I've seen the manifests. They'll have them stored for return to the platform."

"But they travel in the trunk for people. Why would they need special suits?"

"Military procedure. Plan for the worst. In this case, it could mean a sudden decompression by accident or intent. Sometimes systems fail. I wouldn't want to be stuck in one when the power failed and the temperature started dropping."

"That happens?" asked Alexander with a visible shudder.

"It can. I've never experienced it. But it's a possibility, so we plan for it."

After a few seconds, Alexander asked, "What if the trunk falls off the elevator?"

Dewey laughed. "It won't. That being said, these trunks have parachutes that should deploy if they start to accelerate toward the ground faster than intended. There's a manual deploy, too, in case a human happens to be inside. However, I doubt the chutes would help much."

"So, you'd just die."

"That's the plan," Dewey said with a chuckle. It was like dropping to a planet's surface in a dropship. They'd only lost one parachute coming down to Juracan. If they'd lost them all, getting the engines back online and powered up to slow down the impact might have been possible. But either way, the impact was going to happen.

"Not a very good plan."

"You'll get no arguments from me on that," said Dewey. His comm beeped at that moment. He tapped it and responded, "Lieutenant Gray. What do you have for me?"

"I have several containers stuffed with emergency EVA suits. If you're interested."

"'Stuffed'?" asked Dewey. It wasn't what he would call a military or even an organized term.

"Remember when we were kids," said Lt Gray. "and we hadn't yet learned how to properly organize our lockers? That kind of 'stuffed.'"

"Send me the coordinates."

When Lt Gray said that the containers were organized as badly as their lockers when they were young, he was, in Dewey's opinion, being quite generous. Maybe the mercenaries had been in a hurry when they first touched down and planned to get back to the containers to organize the gear later and just forgot. But Dewey was hard-pressed to think of anything on the planet that would have demanded so much of their attention that they couldn't find the time to fold and properly stow emergency EVA suits.

Dewey pulled in all the officers and the recently arrived SSgt Castro. He started them going through each of the suits, running their internal diagnostics. Several suits had compromised seals. Several more had weak batteries. One had an oxygen leak, and one more smelled like someone had gotten sick in it and not bothered to sterilize it.

"To be honest, Tyler," said Lt Owen, "I don't think any of them have been sterilized. We might want to have MedTech Chambers give us a booster before we climb in these."

"We'll work with what we got," said Dewey. "Speaking of which, how many good suits do we have?"

"Twenty-five," said SSgt Castro. "Thirty if you want to live on the edge."

Dewey had more people than suits. That wasn't too great of a problem as he'd planned on leaving a few people planet-side to help the Juracanians.

"There's no reason to go risking lives any more than we already are," said Dewey. "Castro, check on Sergeant Parks. Let me know if her squad's good to go. If not, we're going to have to split up fireteams."

They'd found Sgt Parks and the other captured Hospitallers in one of the trunks used to haul people up the space elevator. They'd been given several buckets for relieving themselves and a case of emergency rations. Sgt Parks had said the rations were a form of torture, and they'd gone mostly uneaten.

"What," said SSgt Castro with a follow-up grin. "And miss out on all this fun? Oh, well, if I must." She quickly marched out of the container.

"Who're you going to make unhappy?" asked Lt Haynes.

"Maxwell," Dewey said. He'd picked up one of the suits and was examining it. It was construction-grade, United Planets manufactured, used for EVA construction of ships and stations. But it was about ten years old. It was missing several of the upgrades that increased the suit's survivability and the newer, more reliable batteries. These had less operation time, made even less so because no one had bothered to handle them properly and connect them to a refresher for oxygen and a battery charge. They'd get them to the loading platform. After that, they'd have to move quickly.

"Why Sergeant Maxwell's squad?"

Dewey put the suit on the catch where it should have been hanging. "She's got one injured. Sergeant Parks is probably itching to prove she and Corporal Mitchell's fireteam are good to go. If they aren't, I'll pull Corporal Wong's fireteam and put in Corporal Garner's."

"Either way, some of them are going to be disappointed."

"We can't all have fun all of the time," Dewey said. "Let me know when the suits are ready. I need to check on the situation with the trunk."

The acknowledgments of Dewey's orders quickly faded as the officers returned to the suits and Dewey rounded the side of the trunk. Not too far away was the comms building and the mercenaries' barracks. The team of Juracanians that SSgt Castro brought through the gate was now on guard duty. While the mercenaries had the training and experience to overcome those with less or none, Dewey had seen the look in the civilians' eyes. If the mercenaries saw it, too, they'd just sit and wait. This wasn't worth their dying for.

So, the mercenaries on the ground were buttoned up nicely and would stay put, even if they had disdain for the guards. The Hospitallers' eyes and hands would doubly ensure that the situation remained the way it was until Dewey could have them sent topside.

For now, Dewey had to get his people up to the loading platform. The thought drew his attention to the space elevator, which was truly impressive once a person had to tilt their head back to see all of it. The three tracks, running on the three cables, were held together every hundred meters by a triangle of girders. Running down the inside of the triangles were the communication and power cables. There wasn't a ladder. If something happened to a trunk that stalled it in place, it was stuck there until a service trunk could come up or down after it.

Sensors kept the trunks safely apart, and they were swiftly and efficiently moved off the track by cranes once they reached the platform.

The cranes worked inside the larger platforms, shunting the trunks to elevators or storage queues. The smaller platforms had the cranes bolted onto the undersides of the platform. They would remove the trunks and then attach them to the spines of the container ships. Tracks on the container ship's spine would allow the trunks to be pushed toward the back end of the ship. There were inspection hatches in the ship spines that allowed access from the ship to the containers if there was a problem.

That was their way in.

"Lieutenant Tyler." Sgt Barrett saluted as Dewey approached. Sgt Barrett and Cpl Chavez's squad were working on one of the trunks with several Juracanians assisting. Specifically, the trunk the Hospitallers were going to be taking up the elevator.

The bottom of the trunk, once it started up the elevator, would become a side. Everything would be tilted ninety degrees. The trunks for human transport had gimballed seats. Cargo trunks had tic-downs for crated cargo. The ones here were meant for raw materials and had nothing. So, while Cpl Chavez and one of the Juracanians made changes to the access hatch, the rest were bolting ledges onto the walls, ceiling, and floor.

There was going to be a lot of quick shifting of Hospitallers as the trunk began to tilt upward.

"Sergeant Barrett. How are things looking here?"

"More than halfway done with the platforms," said Sgt Barrett. He joined Dewey, walking around the trunk to where the rest of the squad was working. "I did take a look at the troop trunk, thinking maybe we could pull the seats. This is quicker."

It was something Dewey had anticipated. The manuals he could recall scanning years ago before his first ride down a space elevator had included details of the different types of trunks. Things changed with time, though, so he'd approved the check on the seats in case he'd been wrong. Apparently, some things never changed, and removing the seats would take more than a day.

"We can get moving soon?" Dewey wanted to be close to the ship's front but not be the last trunk to arrive. He wanted the ship docked when he took control of it. While it was possible to accomplish the mission either way, docked was simpler. Simple plans had fewer things that could go wrong, and this plan was already complicated enough.

"It's gone faster the more we've done," said Sgt Barrett. He paused long enough for Dewey to acknowledge the Hospitallers and Juracanians who'd stood upon seeing him. Once they went back to work, Sgt Barrett pointed as he spoke. "Once a couple more of the Juracanians learned what to do, I was able to leave them to work without one of us assisting. So this last section will take less time than the first."

"So you'll be done soon?"

"Thirty minutes, I'd guess."

Dewey clapped Sgt Barrett on the shoulder. "Good. Soon as your people here are done, I need everyone suited. Time for a ride."

24

Dewey climbed up the trunk's sidewall using his arm strength to pull himself along the ceiling. Once in position, he clipped himself into place with carabiners and a little help from SSgt Castro. He slowly relaxed against the webbing that had been attached to the back of his emergency EVA suit. Only once it took his weight did he relax his grip on the shelf from which he now hung.

"I don't think I could travel any other way after this," said SSgt Castro. She had her usual grin on her face. She, too, was hanging from webbing held in place by carabiners.

"Well, I'm sure it's already more comfortable than flying in a Martini, Staff Sergeant," said Sgt Barrett, who was resting on the deck directly below them.

"There's little that isn't more comfortable than flying in a Martini," said Dewey.

Martinis were atmospheric craft, designed and built by the Hospitaller system. They were rugged, could fly through most anything, but shook like the proverbial martini being made.

"How we looking?" asked Lt Owen. He'd entered before Dewey with Sgt Parks's squad. Like Dewey, he was hanging from the ceiling. It had been Dewey's decision that at least some of the lieutenants took the more difficult positions.

"Let's find out." Dewey tapped the comm of his helmet as he twisted to look at the last row where Lt Hall and Cpl Fleming's fireteam were buckling in. "Sergeant Maxwell. How do things look on the outside?"

The comm was scratchy.

"We're buttoning up the trunk now," said Sgt Maxwell. "You

should feel movement in five minutes. Crane's overhead and ready."

"Thank you, Sergeant Maxwell. And don't drink all the coffee."

"We won't," said Sgt Maxwell. "But I can't say the same for the Juracanians. They really like this stuff."

"I'll pass the compliments on to Lieutenant Gray."

"Compliments?" Lt Gray was below Dewey and one row down. "For me?"

"Hooking up now, Lieutenant Tyler."

Sgt Maxwell's words were punctuated by the bass-clatter of the crane grabbing the sides of the trunk. The sounds were followed by a shudder that caused the Hospitallers hanging to wobble erratically in their webbing. Dewey held the metal shelf overhead to stabilize his movement.

"Lifting now," said Sgt Maxwell through Dewey's helmet.

"Thank you, Sgt Maxwell. We'll comm you once we have control of the platform."

"Talk to you then, Lieutenant Tyler."

The comm clicked and went silent. The trunk swayed a little more as its position on the loading platform was changed. Dewey could visualize the crane turning, the trunk clamped in its metal claws, carrying the trunk to the rail car waiting for them. The previous trunk would already be on the upward slope ahead of them.

"No one above me better get sick," said Lt Gray. Several Hospitallers vocalized the sounds of retching. Gray laughed, adding, "I'll cut your coffee ration."

Dewey and SSgt Castro laughed as the retching sounds instantly disappeared with the threat. A loud boom and jostling of the trunk silenced further conversation. Dewey listened to the sounds of the trunk making contact with the railcar and the clicks and clacks of latches locking into place. A few minutes after that, there was silence, with only the breathing of the Hospitallers around Dewey serving as background noise.

When his comm beeped, he tapped it immediately. "Go," he said.

"You're locked in, Lieutenant," said Sgt Maxwell. "Departing in ten. Nine. Eight…"

Dewey listened to the countdown, displaying it with one hand as it reached five. At one, he paused and made a fist just as the trunk jerked and continued to move. A growl of wheels on a track filled the compartment with its noise, fading to a whisper as it transitioned to the main track that would take them up the elevator.

The shift in position came subtly at first. Dewey became aware of the pressure against the soles of his feet as the trunk began to angle upwards. With each passing second, more weight was transferred to them. The weight distributed across the webbing, holding him up, shifted. In mere minutes Dewey was standing, leaning back against the webbing to avoid having to hold the supports on the ceiling-turned-wall with his hands.

"Helmets," Dewey said. He removed his Hospitaller helmet, slinging it on a hook on the side of the EVA suit. He donned the EVA helmet, clicking it into place. A heads-up display gave him the status of the suit. Unlike riding in the trunk designed for human transport, the only oxygen available was what they had in their suits and the trunk around them. But the air around them would soon become too cold to breathe.

Dewey tapped at the exterior of the face shield where the buttons were projected from the inside.

"Comm check. Fireteams to leaders. Leaders to squad leaders. Squad leaders to Staff Sergeant Castro. Officers check in with me."

One by one, Dewey received an affirmative from the officers riding up with him. Besides Lt Owen and Lt Haynes, there were Lt Gray, Lt Matthews, and 2nd Lt Hall. No one would be barfing on Gray, now. Not with helmets in place. Anyone who lost their lunch when the gravity faded would be stuck with it floating in their helmet. There was a vacuum tube for such emergencies, but that rarely removed everything, and it never removed the stink.

A light blinked in Dewey's HUD. He tapped it as he looked over at SSgt Castro. "Everyone good?"

"Mostly," said SSgt Castro. "Corporal Garner's comm is glitchy. He can't hear, and broadcasting, he sounds like he's underwater."

"Okay, he'll need to take the rearguard position," said Dewey.

Once they secured the spine of the ship they were boarding, Garner's squad would have to keep it secured. Anyone they captured on that level would be Cpl Garner's responsibility, too. Dewey didn't anticipate failure and the need for a fallback position. Still, Hospitallers liked to be prepared for even the least preferred possibilities.

Of course, they still had to get there. It would take several hours to reach the platform. Until then, there was nothing that Dewey could do. He was okay with the waiting, even if it meant he had no control over the situation at the moment. He couldn't accelerate their climb. He couldn't even change his mind and send the trunk back to the surface. Everything he had done and would do was currently out of his control. And while this would drive some people a little mad, Dewey relaxed into it and accepted it.

"One-tenth credit for your thoughts."

"Oh, I don't think you really want to know, Castro."

"Try me, LieutenantTyler."

"I was wondering if I had time to read a book." Dewey grinned.

SSgt Castro laughed. "One mission at a time, Lieutenant. One mission at a time."

The only warning that the trunk was nearing its destination was the altimeter display on Dewey's HUD. Even then, they didn't have the exact number. Dewey was basing the height on the data from books about space elevators he'd read through one weekend during officer training. At thirty-eight thousand kilometers, the HUD reading flashed red. Seconds later, as Dewey was getting ready to alert everyone, he felt the trunk's deceleration as it reached the end of the line.

"That our cue?" asked Lt Owen over the suit comms.

"We're a couple kilometers from the end of the ride," Dewey said. "Make sure the person to your left and right are awake. Castro, you awake?"

"Awake and bored," said Castro. "Really need to stretch my legs."

"Soon enough." Dewey turned in the restraints to see as many of his people as he could. Everyone had strapped in as the trunk had begun its climb. Now, like Dewey, they were floating connected by their tethers. "All right, everyone. We should be at the platform momentarily. We still have to wait for the cranes to transfer the trunk to the ship. There could be a lot of jostling and shaking. Once we're secured, do not untether until you are given the signal. Corporal Chavez's team will take the lead with Lieutenant Owen.

"We need to secure the ship's comms as quickly as possible so that they can't warn the troopship. If we don't, this will get messy."

"We'll secure them," said Lt Owen.

The trunk shuddered, and everyone drifted to the ends of their restraints.

"Right, almost there. Check your gear. We continue with EVA helmets and comms until we control both ships."

Around him, Dewey's squad checked each other for properly stowed gear. The suits weren't designed to hold weapons. The Hospitallers had to modify the slings that were usually connected to their torso armor. Everyone carried a pouch of eyes. They worked not only as reconnaissance but could also be set to self-destruct. The damage they caused was less lethal than a grenade, which meant reduced chances of hull penetration. The rounds they carried had a short range, too. They packed enough punch for ten meters and then quickly fell off, reducing the chances of causing an accidental decompression of ships and stations.

Dewey held still while SSgt Castro tugged his straps, and then returned the favor. The trunk shuddered and then wobbled. The crane now had the trunk. The crane would be sliding along its tracks, linking up with the cargo ship before reaching out and connecting the trunk to the ship's spine.

By the inspection hatch, Cpl Chavez was talking on a closed comm with her fireteam and Sgt Barrett.

Fifteen minutes passed, and everyone looked toward the wall with the inspection hatch. Loud, metallic clacking hinted at the actions happening outside. The trunk was now connected to the spine. A jerk of movement indicated that the trunk was being shuttled down the spine to its final location.

Dewey commed Cpl Chavez. "Your team ready?"

"Ready, Lieutenant."

Dewey hadn't expected any other answer. His people were well trained, not only as soldiers but as Hospitallers. The work ethic, the teamwork, had been drilled into them since childhood. Sometimes Dewey wondered what the point of an officer was when the enlisted ranks knew so well what was expected of them.

While Dewey thought his thoughts, the trunk rumbled and shook before finally making a herky-jerky stop. A second later, the loud thud of shipping clamps locking on vibrated through the trunk's interior.

Cpl Chavez unhooked from the trunk and pushed off, gliding past her team, catching herself at the inspection hatch. Behind her, one at a time, the rest of the fireteam followed suit. They circled the hatch as Cpl Chavez looked back toward Dewey.

In return, Dewey nodded, setting the plan into action.

As one, the four members of Cpl Chavez's fireteam turned the catches that held the hatch closed. There were eight of the latches that, once turned, allowed the hatch to float free. They passed the hatch out of the way, where Sgt Barrett grabbed it and secured it to the trunk interior. Meanwhile, PFC Murray had been handed through the hatchway by the rest of the fireteam. They kept a hold of him until he found his balance on the gravity plates that ran the length of the spine.

The gravity plates were on because it took less power to keep them running than it did to power them off and on. Especially if they'd been off for a long time. And no one enjoyed doing a spot inspection of the trunks in zero gravity. It might be easy to glide down the spine, but most people didn't like how it made their stomachs feel.

PFC Murray was followed by Cpl Chavez. After her, Pvt Hart followed, along with PFC Horton. Sgt Barrett pulled himself over to the hatchway and slowly eased his head around for a peek. After several seconds, he tapped the comm for a direct connection to

Dewey.

Dewey responded to the comm request, asking, "How's it look, Barrett?"

"Empty, Lieutenant," said Sgt Barrett. "They probably don't come down here if they don't have to."

"Go ahead and send Corporal Fleming's team to the engine room. Comm me when that's secure."

"Will do." The comm went quiet. Dewey watched as Sgt Barrett communicated with Cpl Fleming. It was a brief exchange that ended with Fleming's team unhooking themselves from the trunk and then crawling over to the hatchway and then through it to enter the ship's spine. Sgt Barrett went last, behind Pvt Wells.

"Staff Sergeant Castro? If you don't mind?" Dewey asked over the comm.

"Finally," said Castro, the humor in her voice evident. "Something to do."

SSgt Castro unhooked and pushed to the hatchway. She turned and went through feet first, using the opening's lip as a handhold as her body was tugged by the spine's gravity. After she was absent from view for several seconds, Dewey's comm beeped. Tapping it, he got the all-clear from Castro.

"Parks," Dewey said after switching channels on the comm. "You and Corporal Mitchell's fireteam, please. You'll have Lieutenant Owen and Lieutenant Haynes on your six. Don't let them get distracted."

Sgt Parks laughed as she signaled to Cpl Mitchell. "I'll keep them on a short leash, Lieutenant."

One by one, Cpl Mitchell's fireteam made their way to and through the hatchway. There was some commotion that Dewey assumed was at least one of the team catching the gravity wrong. Then, they were gone, too.

When the comm beeped again, it was Cpl Chavez. "Lieutenant Tyler," she said. "We're clear to the forward hatch. I don't see any movement through the window. Permission to proceed?"

Dewey started unhooking from the trunk, signaling for everyone remaining to do the same. To Cpl Chavez, he said, "As soon as Corporal Mitchell makes contact with you, proceed. Stay off the command level until Lieutenant Owen is sure he has control of the ship's comms."

"Will do, Lieutenant."

Dewey pushed himself toward the hatchway, arriving at the same time as Lt Hall and Lt Matthews. He turned to locate Cpl Garner, who was just arriving with Lt Gray just behind. Setting his comm to a five-meter radius, Dewey pulled the corporal close enough that their helmets touched. He then spoke to everyone present at once.

"Lieutenant Gray, I need you to stay with Corporal Garner. If commands arrive that he doesn't hear, I need you to pass them to him via helmet-to-helmet contact." When Lt Gray nodded acknowledged the directions given him, Dewey continued. "Lieutenant Matthews and Lieutenant Hall are with me. When Corporal Fleming has the engine rooms secure and can proceed forward, Garner's team moves aft. Lieutenant Gray stays with Garner as his comm liaison. Questions?"

When it was clear that no one had questions, Dewey nodded his approval. He then tapped Cpl Garner's helmet. "Soon as we have the ship secured, we'll fix your helmet or replace it."

Cpl Garner nodded, obviously frustrated by the dead comm of his suit.

"All right, let's go."

25

After closing the comm, Dewey slipped through the hatchway. He could feel the odd tug of gravity on his legs before he felt it in his belly. It was a bit like vertigo. Dewey held tight to the edge of the hatchway until the queasy feeling passed. In some ways, it reminded him of dropping into or out of VR.

Behind him, the rest of the Hospitallers transitioned from the trunk to the spine and its gravity. Lt Matthews stumbled as she approached Dewey's position, catching herself before Lt Hall could lend a hand. She tapped her comm as she stood straight. Dewey connected with her, catching her laugh in his ears.

"I'm surprised how quickly one forgets how gravity works," Lt Matthews said.

Dewey acknowledged with a nod and closed the connection. He watched past Matthews as Lt Gray and Cpl Garner stepped across the corridor to make room for the rest of Garner's fireteam. Gray signaled to Dewey that they were proceeding aft. Dewey acknowledged with his own hand signal and then tapped Lt Hall on the helmet, pointing forward when he had Hall's attention. With a nod, Lt Hall started forward, Lt Matthews close behind. Dewey watched Lt Matthews fidgeting with her weapon as she kept up with Lt Hall.

The pilots still had annual infantry training, as did every member of the Orphan Corps. But occasional training was a poor substitute for constant, repetitive actions. Still, all the years of discipline would help if the time came to use the weapon. Dewey might be amused at Lt Matthews's discomfort, but he had no doubt about her ability to handle herself if things turned violent.

At the forward hatch, they found Pvt Foster. Dewey tapped his comm to check in with him.

"Corporal Mitchell is with Lieutenant Owen and Lieutenant Haynes," said Pvt Foster. "Corporal Chavez's team has gone forward to secure the billets on this level and to watch the stairs."

"Good work, Foster," Dewey said. He adjusted the comm to pull Lt Hall and Lt Matthews into the conversion. "Stand fast here, lieutenants. I'll be right back."

Lt Matthews nodded assent. Dewey clapped Pvt Foster on the shoulder before stepping through the hatchway. To the right, there was a narrow corridor, which Dewey was gratified to see. His directions to the other Hospitallers had been given under the assumption that he knew the schematics of the type of transport ship they were boarding. So far, it looked like his memory was still holding up.

The narrow right-side corridor took a hard left after several meters and then abruptly ended a few meters after that. A hatch in the floor had been raised and locked into place. It now served as a shield behind which PFC Gonzalez knelt, her weapon's barrel visible around the edge. Gonzalez nodded as she made eye contact with Dewey. Dewey returned the nod and then knelt to look into the opening the hatch customarily covered.

"Owen?" Dewey inquired over a narrow radius of communication. "How's it going?"

"Good," Lt Owen said. "Space is at a premium down here, though. I couldn't convince Corporal Mitchell to wait topside."

"He's doing his job, Owen," said Dewey. His voice was light with humor. He knew Lt Owen was jesting, teasing Cpl Mitchell to keep things light. "You have control of comms yet?"

"I'm about to. I'll give you a call when I do."

"I'll be listening." Dewey cut the suit's comm and stood. He gave and received a thumbs up from PFC Gonzalez before returning to the spine hatch. At the hatch, he signaled for Lt Matthews and Lt Hall to join him.

Lt Matthews followed Dewey as he went past the hatchway. The corridor here was broader and longer, meant for general passage and small cargo shifting. It took a hard right turn into a space that was more foyer than corridor. On the port side was the stairwell. PFC Horton had his eyes on it, watching over the sights of his weapon. To the right were several doors. These led to a small medical unit and private quarters for passengers who could afford it. Straight ahead was a wider doorway that led to a bunk room used by extra crew, standard fare passengers, or soldiers.

The only soldiers Dewey saw were his own. But they weren't alone.

As Dewey stepped into the forward bunkroom, he quickly noticed that besides Cpl Chavez, PFC Murray, and Pvt Hart, there were two civilians. The civilians were sitting side-by-side on a bunk, in their skivvies, and looking a little uncomfortable with the situation. The Hospitallers, on the other hand, looked amused.

"Lieutenant Tyler," Cpl Chavez acknowledged Dewey's presence as he stepped into the room. Dewey noticed she was trying not to laugh.

"What's going on?" Based on the lack of clothing and how the two civilians seemed to be trying hard not to notice each other, even though their thighs were touching, Dewey had a pretty good impression of the answer.

"Caught them with their pants down." Cpl Chavez had one hand, balled into a fist, and pressed against the faceshield of her helmet as if it might help muffle the giggles that were trying to escape.

"I believe you were once caught in a similar situation," said Dewey. "In the back of a dropship, no less."

"What? No way," said PFC Murray. His face shone with a broad grin, mirrored by one on Pvt Hart's face.

The two civilians were distracted by the admittedly odd conversation being had by soldiers boarding their ship unannounced. But Dewey also noticed that the woman kept watching him, only looking away when he shifted his attention to them.

"Do you want to get dressed?" he asked.

"Yes, please," the man, young in looks, said. Dewey nodded, and they scrambled for their clothes. Dewey signaled to Cpl Chavez to watch the woman. He stepped over to where the young man was shuffling through his pants and deck boots.

"Hold on," said Dewey. He managed to grab hold of a small comm set before the young man did. "You could get someone else hurt if you do what I think you wanted to do. Now, get dressed and sit."

"Yes, sir." The young man jumped into his pants, quickly yanking them up to his hips.

"Lieutenant Tyler."

Dewey turned to where Pvt Hart and Cpl Chavez were standing with the young woman. She had her pants on and was slipping a shirt over her head as Chavez waved for Dewey to join them. After signaling for PFC Murray to guard the other civilian, Dewey joined the three women, the civilian now sitting to strap on her boots.

"Chavez. What do you have?"

"This," said Cpl Chavez. She held out her hand.

Dewey expected to see another comm unit. Instead, he was presented with a red pocket knife.

Dewey picked up the knife, turning it as he did. There were lots of pocket knives in the galaxy. There were even lots of red ones. But, still, there was something about the Hospitaller pocket knife that made it instantly recognizable to any orphan who'd been presented with one after turning fifteen.

Most Hospitallers could be forgiven for not knowing every orphanage's name and location in the Hospitaller system. But Dewey wasn't most orphans and had seen the list when he was ten. "Chockmah," he said, looking at the young woman. "That's on Lavaur. The Ulgen system."

"That's right," said the young woman. She seemed impressed that Dewey so easily recognized the letters etched into one side of the knife.

Dewey offered his hand. "Dewey Tyler."

"Victoria Dixon." She shook hands with Dewey, then asked, "Why are you all here?"

"Stuck on the planet," said Dewey as he handed the knife back to Victoria. "Came looking for our ride."

Victoria snorted amusement. "They don't tell us anything. Get the trunks, move the trunks, stay away from the trunks. The trunks are radioactive. Did you know that?"

"The whole planet is," said Cpl Chavez. "When's the last time you got checked?"

"End of every trip out of here," said Victoria. "Are we in trouble?"

"You might not be." Dewey looked left. "Your friend might not be. Depending on what he knows."

"Mack? He knows engines. I know mechanics, hydraulics, life support. The captain and X.O., they know where we go."

"How many crew?" Dewey asked.

"Bare bones." Dewey looked at Mack. He was now fully dressed and continued to talk. "Captain Roberson does his own piloting. X.O. Turner handles navigation. There's me and Toby for engines, and Victoria, Satchel, and Meg for everything else."

Dewey nodded and looked at Cpl Chavez. "Seven. Should be easy enough, so long as no one gets any crazy ideas in their head."

"They won't," said Victoria. "Especially if I go first."

"How long have you been crew?" Dewey asked.

"Four years. I did vocational training through the Hospitaller programs." She shrugged, looked at Mack, and then added, "I did a year on a Hospitaller ship before deciding I wanted to try something different."

It might work. Dewey looked at Cpl Chavez, who seemed impressed by the idea. "All right," he said. "We'll go together."

The comm in Dewey's suit beeped for his attention. He held up a hand to pardon himself from the conversation with Victoria.

"It's Owen. I've got control of the comms. Messages will still be received, but none get out without my permission."

"You sound like you enjoyed that," Dewey said with a chuckle.

"Absolutely. So when are you storming the bridge, and can I come?"

"I'm going to disappoint you on several fronts, Owen." Dewey waved for Victoria to follow as he walked. Cpl Chavez shadowed her. "We may have an in with a member of the ship's crew. She's going to introduce us to the captain."

"Sounds boring," Lt Owen said. Then, "But safe. I'm for safe."

"As am I. I'll check in with you after I get to the bridge."

"I'll be listening for messages."

The comm clicked. Dewey turned to Victoria. "We'll follow your lead, Victoria."

"Thank you," she said as she stepped past Dewey. "I like the people I work with on this ship. I'd rather not any of them get hurt."

"Neither would I."

Dewey followed Victoria out of the bunkroom and toward the stairs. Behind him, Cpl Chavez still followed. PFC Murray and Pvt Hart remained behind with Mack at Dewey's request. At the bottom of the stairs, Victoria paused and appeared to take a deep breath that she slowly released. With a brief nod to Dewey, she started up.

With so few people, it was unlikely they'd meet anyone on the next landing. This was the bridge deck. The bridge was forward, with the captain's quarters aft of that, followed by the chow hall and kitchen. The crew was quartered up on the top deck, which had the least amount of space and likely explained Mack and Victoria's decision to sneak down to the passenger bunkroom for a little private time.

Victoria looked right and then turned left toward the bridge. There were sounds of dishes and cutlery in the chow hall, but the door was closed, hiding the identity of the person or persons eating. The captain's quarters were also hidden behind closed doors. The only door that was opened was the one they needed to access. Victoria stopped at its hatchway. Dewey stopped a meter behind her, staying out of sight but not hiding.

"Captain?"

"Victoria. What do you need?"

Victoria giggled. She was likely nervous about what she was doing. "I need you to trust me."

There was a pause, and then a second voice joined in. "We've never had a reason to not trust you. And you've never had to ask before. Did you do something to the ship?"

"No, X.O., I didn't do anything to the ship. We do have company, though."

"Company?"

Someone moved on the bridge. Behind Dewey, the barrel of Cpl Chavez's weapon came up. Dewey pushed it back down as a tall, broad man lumbered into view. He paused when he looked past Victoria.

"Who are you, and how did you get on my ship?"

"They're Hospitallers, Captain," Victoria said. "They're not pirates or anything like that."

The captain's eyes swiveled in their sockets and seemed to focus on Victoria. "Then why are they on my ship without permission?"

"If I may, Captain," said Dewey. "This was the only safe route to the troop transport across the platform. This company you're hauling for has taken our ship captive. I intend to free it."

The captain turned toward the bridge, looking at something Dewey couldn't see. The captain's head tilted quizzically, and then he was glaring back at Dewey. "You've hijacked my comms?"

"Temporarily. We were afraid you might do what I think you just tried to do. Again, Captain, we don't intend you any harm. We just need access to the platform. Once we have our objective, we won't need to bother you after that."

"What about my cargo? I get paid to deliver it. I lose money if I don't."

"The Hospitallers reimburse anyone they inconvenience," Victoria said hurriedly. "Even if we lose the cargo, they'll pay out for income lost. And they don't take anywhere near as long as the company we're hauling for."

Another man appeared in the hatchway, partially hidden by the captain. "Is there any guarantee that you'll keep your word?"

"My word as a Hospitaller," said Dewey. "It's all I have, but it's worth a lot to me."

"Hospitaller word," said the man behind the captain. "And we're not cooperating with them as they've taken our ship hostage."

"If anyone inquires," Dewey said, "that is what we'll tell them."

"We'd get paid and be done with this company," said Victoria. "I know you hate this run, Captain."

The captain stepped back and waved Dewey onto the bridge. "Decontamination eats into profits. I signed a contract in which they left the radiation part out. This'll break the contract for me, and I won't take a penalty. But you'll have to leave someone on board, you know, to 'hold us prisoner.' Just in case."

The captain smiled. Dewey returned the smile. "I don't think that'll be a problem."

"Oh, and you'll have to distract the guards."

The transport captain waved Dewey over to a general-use station and quickly did a few things to bring up an image. It was sec-cam vid of the interior of the loading platform. The interior was empty, devoid of anything that might be useful for defensive positions.

"They don't know we have it," said the captain as he manipulated the view to orient and zoom in on the opposite airlock. "At least I don't think they know. It's in our placard that we post outside the hatch wherever we dock. Was Victoria's idea, actually."

When the captain was done, Dewey could see the other airlock. Not only were two guards posted, but they were also positioned behind two wide podiums. Podiums, if Dewey was right, that hid dense synthetic plates that would stop weapons fire. At least they had a defensible position. And it was pretty much as Dewey expected.

"Thank you, Captain," Dewey said with a friendly clap on the shoulder. "Fortunately, I had another idea in mind."

"What idea?"

Dewey tapped the faceplate of his EVA helmet. "We're going to go through the back entrance."

26

Dewey's decision about who would be staying to 'keep the ship's crew prisoners' was being made for him. He'd pulled everyone down to the lower deck. Lt Owen stayed with the comms, but everyone else was now in the forward berthing area. They formed a rough circle around Cpl Garner, who had his EVA helmet off. Lt Haynes was prodding the helmet's electronics.

"I've tried everything I know," said Lt Haynes. She looked up from the helmet to Cpl Garner and then over to Dewey. "But, I still can't get the helmet's comm to work."

"They have suits on this ship, don't they?" asked Cpl Garner.

It reminded Dewey of a time when they hadn't been able to go on a field trip because the van had blown a tire. Spence, one of the kids in Dewey's orphanage squad, hadn't understood why they didn't just pull a tire off one of the other vehicles in the yard. They'd all learned about tire size, rotation, wear, and a slew of other things that day having to do with tires and transportation. Cpl Garner was looking for another tire, even if it didn't fit.

"The suits are sized for the person who owns them," said Dewey. "But even if we find one that fits you, they aren't good for anything but hanging out in space, waiting for rescue." Dewey held up his hand to stop Cpl Garner from asking the next obvious thing. "We've checked their maintenance EVA suit. You'd be better off with a rescue suit."

"So I'm stuck here," Cpl Garner said.

"Looks that way," said Lt Haynes, handing Garner's useless helmet back to him. "Sorry about that."

"I wouldn't say 'stuck,'" Dewey said. "We need someone to play at keeping the crew hostage. And we'll need a diversion soon enough. It'll include shooting at the mercs across the way."

Cpl Garner grinned. "You're just saying that to make me feel better, aren't you, Lieutenant Tyler."

"I am saying it to make you feel better, true. But I still need you to make a diversion when required."

"Seems unfair to the rest of the fireteam," said Cpl Garner. "Their suits work just fine."

Dewey nodded his agreement. "And that's why I'm going to make them Sergeant Parks's fireteam. It's a trade. We get Arnold, Burke, and Becker, and you get the ancillary officers."

"Ancillary?" Lt Haynes asked, eyebrows arched. Lt Gray and Lt Matthews looked equally horrified.

"I get to boss lieutenants around?"

After a short burst of laughter, instigated by the shocked look on Lt Haynes's face, Dewey said, "I wouldn't suggest bossing them around. Especially the one who knows how to make coffee."

"Good point," said Cpl Garner and Lt Gray, simultaneously.

"All right. Now that we know what we have to work with let's get to work."

Fifteen minutes later, Dewey and the rest of the Hospitallers, excluding Garner and the officers, were pulling themselves along the station platform's underside. The route was circuitous as they had to go a quarter of the way around the circumference to avoid the cranes still picking and loading the remainder of the trunks. Once they had a direct line on the troopship from the other side of the elevator cables, Dewey directed Cpl Chavez's team to take point.

The maneuver was risky. They were crossing the station without the aid of the electromagnets built into the emergency EVA boots. Instead, they were pulling themselves along, hand over hand, using pipes, handholds, and momentum to carry them forward. The only precautions were the tethers built into each suit. Every fireteam member was connected to the team member directly in front of them. If one person missed a handhold, they could be kept close by the tethers. Of course, if the entire team lost their grip, the story would be much different.

Dewey, like the squad leaders, was tethered to the end of a fireteam. He followed along in the wake of Cpl Mitchell's fireteam, five meters behind Pvt Hart, who was last in line for Cpl Chavez's team. Behind Dewey, with Cpl Garner stuck on the transport ship, Sgt Parks led Garner's fireteam. Further back, SSgt Castro followed along, attached to Cpl Fleming's team.

The two squads formed a wobbly line that no basic training instructor would ever have tolerated. The thought gave Dewey a moment of levity in an increasingly worrying situation. If they made it across the platform's underside without incident or detection, they would enter the troopship next. Then, they'd have to cycle the airlocks from the outside. That would alert the ship's bridge if anyone was paying attention. If they made it through the airlocks, there would likely be resistance from the crew or mercenary squads. Hopefully, Cpl Garner's actions would distract most of the mercenaries, at least until Dewey and the others managed to exit the airlocks.

No matter which way Dewey looked at it, there was going to be a fight. It wasn't the fight that worried him, though. It was the potential loss of Hospitallers here and perhaps even on the Graevya if Dewey's team made too much noise and attracted the attention of the third company ship. And that was the next problem. They were going to have to board and take the gunship currently attached to the Graevya.

Dewey's comm beeped, drawing his attention back to the moment. "We're here, Lieutenant."

Only then did Dewey realize that they'd all come to a stop. It had been an automatic reaction that he'd made without being aware. He checked the line of Hospitallers. Near the back, someone was floating free of the platform, slowly pulling on the tether to regain their position.

Dewey tapped his comm. "Everyone still with us?"

The fireteam leaders and squad leaders confirmed that everyone was still together. It was SSgt Castro who'd lost her grip, but apparently because Pvt Wells had forgotten the staff sergeant was there and lunged forward to keep with his fireteam.

"Having fun, yet, Castro?" Dewey asked over the comm.

"Like a walk in the park, Lieutenant."

"Good to know," Dewey said before changing the comm to connect with both squads. "Everyone stand by. Check your gear. Check the gear of the people nearest you." Then, he switched channels to connect with Cpl Garner. "How's it look from there, Garner?"

"They just changed guards," said Cpl Garner. "They don't seem too concerned about any uninvited guests. One of them has his eyes closed. The other is chatting to someone on their comm."

"Okay. We're about to crawl across the bottom of the troopship. I'll ping you when we start cycling the airlocks."

"We'll be ready."

Dewey switched the comm once more. "Okay, Chavez. Move out."

The platoon separated into two groups. Sgt Barrett, with SSgt Castro, led his squad to the aft airlock. Dewey and Sgt Parks took the rest to the forward airlock. Unlike the platform's underside, the ship had plenty of handholds, allowing for the squads to spread out into their fireteams, approaching the airlocks from two sides.

When Sgt Parks and Dewey reached their airlock, Cpl Mitchell's fireteam followed Dewey to one side of the airlock. The reassigned members of Cpl Garner's fireteam followed Sgt Parks to the other. When everyone was in position, Dewey pinged Sgt Barrett for an update.

Sgt Barrett's response was brief. "Ready."

Dewey looked across the airlock hatch and gave Sgt Parks a thumbs up, which she returned. Then, Dewey tapped the com before opening the cover that protected the external controls of the airlock. "Sergeant Barrett? Start now."

With one finger, Dewey poked the cycle button that would evacuate the airlock so they could enter. When the light turned red, signaling the start of the cycle, he tapped his comm again, sending a ping to Cpl Garner. There'd be no way to know if and when Garner started his distraction. There'd also be no way of knowing how well the distraction did or didn't work.

From this point until the end of the skirmish, they'd be out of contact, and it would all come down to training and luck. Dewey was hoping that luck favored his team.

In the amount of time that allowed Dewey to start second-guessing his plan, the red light for the cycle process flashed to green. Dewey punched the open button with his fist, eager to start moving. As the door swung open, Cpl Mitchell moved around Dewey, engaging the electromagnets of his boots and bringing his weapon up to sweep the airlock's interior. A heartbeat later, he lowered his weapon and signaled to Dewey that the space was clear.

The team flowed into the airlock with Dewey in the middle and Sgt Parks entering last. As she stepped in, she hit the controls with the side of her fist. The door began to swing shut.

On the other end of the airlock, Cpl Mitchell's team was unfolding four of the ballistic shields they'd brought with them. Usually, a single ballistic shield would stop small-caliber weapons and grenade blasts. But Dewey wasn't taking chances and had directed the teams to overlap the shields. They might not stop a heavy machine gun. Still, they'd slow the rounds down dramatically, and the body armor they wore under the EVA suits should be enough protection at that point.

Over the forward door, the light had turned green. Dewey tapped the control to open the door and stepped back, crouching behind the ballistic shields with Cpl Mitchell. The door was halfway open when they heard and felt the first hard strikes of short range rounds beating against the shields. Dewey looked back at Sgt Parks, who was ready with the grenade barrel on her MUW. When he gave her the go-ahead, she shouldered her weapon and quickly fired two grenades through the still widening gap.

Around him, the other Hospitallers hunkered down and rocked with the dual explosions. Then Dewey tapped his comm. "Return fire."

Two at a time, Hospitallers popped up, firing at the mercenaries on the other side of the airlock hatchway. The return fire was less aggressive than before the two grenades. As the door to the airlock opened fully, Dewey could see two mercenaries down a short corridor. On the deck between the Hospitallers and the mercenaries, three other mercenaries were prone and not moving.

Something slapped Dewey's helmet, knocking him onto his backside. Next to him, Cpl Mitchell came up, firing a short burst that went unanswered. After the growl of combat, the silence that followed rang like a bell in Dewey's ears. That or being hit on the head was causing the ringing.

"You okay, Lieutenant?" Cpl Mitchell was standing, offering a hand to Dewey.

"Think so," Dewey said as Mitchell pulled him to his feet. "I think I got grazed by a round."

Sgt Parks laughed and tapped Dewey's helmet. "Dead center, Lieutenant Tyler. If you hadn't had that helmet on, we'd be saying your name come morning."

Sgt Parks referred to Roll Call when Hospitallers across the second radial arm of the galaxy read out the names of those who had died the day before.

"That'll be another day," said Dewey. "Let's secure these two corridors. I need to get to the bridge."

"Let's move, people," Sgt Parks said. "Mitchell, you got left. I'll take forward."

Cpl Mitchell nodded before turning to his fireteam. They still carried the ballistic shields. "Bring one shield. Gonzalez is on point. Let's clear the hall."

With Pvt Foster right behind her, PFC Gonzalez moved to the hatchway and slowly rounded the opening, her weapon pointing left down the hall. At the same time, Pvt Foster watched the hallway facing the airlock. Ten seconds later, Gonzalez slipped out of the airlock, trailed by Foster, PFC Wong, and then Cpl Mitchell.

"Our turn," said Sgt Parks. She signaled to PFC Burke.

Burke nodded and crept forward, out of the airlock, and down the facing hall. Behind him, her weapon watching over Burke's shoulder, PFC Arnold followed close behind. Next went Pvt Becker and then Sgt Parks. When Burke reached the end of the hallway and checked where they'd seen the last two mercenaries, he gave a quick look down the corridors to either side and returned a thumbs up.

"We're good, Lieutenant," said Sgt Parks.

Dewey started forward, tapping his comm as he crossed the airlock threshold. "Staff Sergeant Castro, how are things aft?"

The response from SSgt Castro began with a laugh. "Boring, Lieutenant. We could hear you all up front. Sounds like you were having fun. I think they put everyone forward, not realizing we would split up. Surprised the two engineers, though. I told them I wouldn't tell anyone, but one of them started crying."

"Crying? Did you scare him?" Dewey was continuing down the hallway, passing Sgt Parks, who was signaling for Cpl Mitchell to pull back.

"Not on purpose," said SSgt Castro. She laughed briefly before adding, "He's young, though. Probably not used to having his ship boarded by a bunch of Hospitallers."

"Okay. Button up engineering. Tell Sergeant Barrett to leave a fireteam in charge and then pinch forward to clear the rest of the ship." Dewey turned to Sgt Parks, engaging her on the comm. "Parks, have Mitchell's team secure this corridor. We'll deal with the bridge as soon as I check in with Cpl Garner."

"You got it, Lieutenant Tyler." Sgt Parks switched her comm and started talking to her team.

"Corporal Garner? How're things?" asked Dewey after switching his comm to speak directly with Cpl Garner through the transport ship's comm.

"Token firefight," said Garner. "Soon as we started firing, the guards pulled back and secured the hatch. They didn't even shoot back."

Dewey looked down at the two mercenaries dead on the deck. "Was one of them tall and skinny? The other had red hair?"

"Sounds about right, Lieutenant."

Dewey looked back down the hallway, where the other mercenaries were sprawled across the corridor, lifeless. Less than a squad. That meant there was more to deal with.

"Okay, Garner, keep an eye on the airlock and let me know if anything changes."

"Will do."

Dewey cut the comm and pinged SSgt Castro. As he did, he heard gunshots, muffled by distance and the EVA helmet he was wearing.

"If you're looking for the rest of the mercs," said SSgt Castro, who wasn't sounding amused, "we found them."

"Everyone okay?" Dewey signaled for Sgt Parks to come closer.

"No. The mercs caught us in a crossfire. Horton's down for good. Cpl Chavez took a couple rounds, but she'll be fine once we get her patched up. A few of us took rounds across the helmet. I've got a lovely scratch across my field of view. Cheap gear."

"Okay, Castro. Tell us where they are."

As SSgt Castro described the corridor and doorway the mercenaries had used, Dewey dug up the schematics from his memory of ship layouts. There was a certain irony in using their sickbay for an ambush. Still, it meant there were two ways in, and maybe the Hospitallers could pull a surprise. As for the corridor, that was the one that ran the length of the starboard side of the ship. It had two sets of ninety-degree turns in it, forming zig-zags, for events such as what was happening now. But the protective corners were a double-edged sword. They provided defense for the ship's crew, but they also offered protection for boarders.

"Thank you, Castro," said Dewey as the staff sergeant finished her report. "Help's on the way."

They couldn't all go and provide relief. There was still the bridge to deal with, too.

"Parks," Dewey said once he had the sergeant on the comm. "Take Burke and Becker down the far corridor. Be careful. We don't know how many mercs are that way. You might only need to be a distraction for Sergeant Barrett."

"Will do." Sgt Parks signaled for PFC Burke and Pvt Becker to follow her as she moved quickly back toward the airlock.

"Corporal Mitchell. You take Gonzalez and Foster. Continue down this corridor to the sickbay entrance. The mercs are using it as their defensive position. Take it away from them. I'll be on the bridge with Arnold and Wong."

"On it," said Cpl Mitchell. Then, "Stay safe, Lieutenant Tyler."

Mitchell gathered PFC Gonzalez and Pvt Foster before hurrying down the corridor to sickbay.

"Okay." Dewey signaled for Arnold and Wong to follow him. "Let's go see how the bridge is behaving."

27

Dewey took the stairs down to the level where the bridge was located. While not precisely in the center of the ship, as it would be for a combat vessel, it was still on the middle deck and a third of the way back from the nose. As Dewey recalled them, the schematics showed a bridge with port and starboard entrances with the port side accessible by the upper deck and the starboard side by the lower deck. A third door to the rear led to the captain's office and private cabin.

Dewey had expected to be fired upon by the ship's crew as he came down the stairs. Instead, he encountered a sullen silence, punctuated by the presence of a closed and sealed hatch. Purely for fun, he poked the hatch release button and got the response he expected. Which was to say that the hatch didn't move.

"Staff Sergeant Castro?" Dewey asked after tapping his suit's comm button. "You copy?"

"Loud and clear, Lieutenant. We're just about finished mopping up here. The mercs just realized they've become the middle of a firefight sandwich. We're negotiating a surrender."

"That's good to hear." Dewey pushed the bridge access button again, just for something to do. "We still have control of engineering, yes?"

"We do. I can pop down there if you want."

"Won't be necessary," said Dewey. "Just tell me who's there right now."

"Corporal Fleming and Private Wells are manning engineering right now. You need me to send anyone else?"

"Nope, Staff Sergeant, two will be plenty. When you get the

surrender buttoned up, I'd like you and a fireteam to come to the bridge from the starboard side. You'll need to go down to the lower deck to access it."

"You got it," said SSgt Castro. "See you soon."

Dewey tapped his comm and then tapped once more to open a connection to the ship. Specifically, he was trying to reach the bridge.

"Hello," he said. "I'm looking for the captain of this transport ship. Any chance they are still on board?"

There was a pause, then a click, then another pause, and then someone was speaking. "I'm the captain of this ship."

"This is Lieutenant Dewey Tyler of the Hospitaller Orphan Corps. Does the captain of the ship have a name? Rank?"

Another pause before the voice said, "Anton Sullivan. Captain. Now, what do you want?"

Dewey looked back at PFC Arnold and PFC Wong. Into the comm, he answered, "Access to your bridge. Your surrender."

"Not likely," said Captain Sullivan.

"You sure? We've captured or killed the mercs onboard."

"I've already contacted the Amazia. They know you're here."

"Of course." Dewey nodded to himself. He'd hoped they hadn't contacted the other ship but wasn't surprised that they had. "I still need you to surrender."

"Maybe you should surrender."

"Right. Stand by." Dewey tapped the comm. He disliked these kinds of arguments. "Corporal Fleming, you copy?"

"Sure do, Lieutenant Tyler," replied Cpl Fleming. "What can I do for you?"

"You're in the engineering control room?"

"Yes, we are. Me and Private Wells."

"Good. On the starboard side, there's a cabinet between the two workstations. Do you see it?" Dewey was working with the memories of ship schematics for this series of ship. While it was unlikely that anyone had changed the layout or bothered with upgrades for something like a transport, he'd been wrong before.

"Right here, Lieutenant. 'Life Support Systems.'"

"That's the one." Dewey then explained what he wanted Cpl Fleming to do.

"Just turn the two dials?"

"That's it."

There was a pause, and then Cpl Fleming said, "Done."

"Great, I'll have PFC Arnold comm you when I want it turned back on." Dewey turned the comm off and gave his attention to PFC Arnold and PFC Wong. "They're about to realize they've lost airflow."

Arnold and Wong nodded before raising their weapons to their shoulders, ready to defend. Dewey did the same and then tapped his comm.

"Captain Sullivan," he said. "Would you like to reconsider?"

Dewey wasn't surprised when he didn't receive an answer. He also wasn't surprised when he heard the hatch to the bridge unlatching. The barrels of PFC Arnold's and PFC Wong's weapons came up, pointing directly at the small gap that began to appear between the hatch and hatchway.

When nothing else happened, Dewey sighed. The captain was going to be difficult, and time was becoming an issue.

"Staff Sergeant Castro?" Dewey said after comming the staff sergeant. "What's your location?"

"On our way." SSgt Castro's voice was shaky. Dewey assumed she was jogging toward her next position now. "We have the rest of the mercs wrapped up. Corporal Chavez is seeing to PFC Horton's body."

"When you get there, let me know if they've cracked open the hatch." Dewey switched the comm again. This time he reached out for Lt Owen over on the cargo ship. "I could use your help over here. I'll send PFC Wong to open the front door."

"On my way."

Dewey cut the comm. "Wong? I need you to pop down and let Lieutenant Owen in."

PFC Wong looked at the open hatch and back at Dewey, raising his eyebrows to project the unasked question.

"We'll be fine," Dewey said. "Hurry down. Hurry back."

Wong nodded and made for the stairs, quickly disappearing. As Dewey turned his attention back to the barely open hatchway, his comm beeped for a connection with SSgt Castro.

"You in place?" Dewey asked. His attention was split between the comm and a flicker of shadows on the other side of the hatchway.

"In place," said Castro. "The hatch is open here. Are we going to push forward?"

"Maybe," said Dewey. "Stand by."

Dewey signaled to PFC Arnold to keep an eye on the hatchway as he stepped forward. With one boot, Dewey pushed on the hatch. It started to swing open but came to a sudden, short stop. Dewey retreated, lifting his weapon's barrel to guard the wider opening.

"Captain Sullivan? I've got people on both sides of the bridge. Let's do this without anyone getting hurt. What do you say?"

Dewey's question was answered by three gunshots. PFC Arnold and Dewey brought their weapons fully up, ready to defend. As Dewey checked past PFC Arnold, he could see Arnold doing the same thing in his direction and then shrugging. Where had the shots come from? Where had they been aimed?

Their attention was drawn back to the open hatchway. A hand appeared, a pistol dangling off one finger.

"All right, we surrender."

Dewey and PFC Arnold tracked the hand as it moved toward the ground and then deposited the pistol there. It switched to grabbing the hatch and pulled, revealing an older man with graying hair. He was dressed in a typical ship's crew jumpsuit with the added gold piping of an officer.

Through the suit's external comm, Dewey asked, "Captain Sullivan?"

The captain nodded and stepped back, remaining in sight as he did.

"The rest of your bridge crew, please."

With a jerk of his head, Capt Sullivan pulled four other men, all younger, into view. They wore the same ship suits as the captain, with one of them sporting silver piping.

"Thank you," Dewey said. Then he switched to internal comms to speak with SSgt Castro. "I need you to sweep the rest of the bridge. I have five in my sights."

"Will do."

Though Dewey couldn't see SSgt Castro and the fireteam with her, he could tell they were on the bridge based on the eye movements of the ship's crew in his view. After thirty seconds, SSgt Castro appeared behind Captain Sullivan and gave Dewey a thumbs up. Dewey nodded and shifted his weapon into a less threatening position.

His comm beeped. Lt Owen was making contact. "Is it safe to come up? I heard gunshots."

"All clear, Owen."

On the stairs, Lt Owen appeared behind PFC Wong. Dewey signaled for Lt Owen to remove his helmet and then started unlatching his own. Communication with the ship's crew would be easier without having to activate the external speaker and mic repeatedly. The air smelled different outside the helmet. The sharp tang of gunpowder was fresh in the air, along with the smoke of burning plastic.

"Staff Sergeant Castro," Dewey said over the comm. "What did they shoot?"

The response was preceded by a snort of annoyance. "Navigation."

"Of course." Dewey crossed the hatchway threshold. He took a moment to scan the ship's systems, noticing the smoke and occasional spark from the console where navigation was handled. Dewey wasn't sure just how dumb the captain thought Hospitallers were. "That's like shooting yourself in the foot so you can't be taken prisoner, Captain Sullivan."

"What do you want?" asked the captain. His words were sharp with anger.

"My ship," Dewey said. "There's a few other things, too, but we can start with that."

"I don't have your ship."

Dewey walked the perimeter of the bridge. Capt Sullivan didn't have control of the Graevya, that was true. But the company he worked for did. Dewey wasn't sure if the captain of the gunship would go for an even trade. Not if they were aware of the illicit activities happening planetside. For that matter, did Capt Sullivan even know?

"Did you know the planet had a population on it?" Dewey asked as he began tapping through one station's screens, searching for data files on Juracan.

"The planet was abandoned during the Radial War." Capt Sullivan had taken a defensive attitude, his arms crossed over his chest.

The crew next to Capt Sullivan had adopted a different attitude. They looked frightened. Several of them took a small step away from their commanding officer. So, either they knew about the Juracanians, and were aware of the trouble they were in, or they'd just learned that information and understood the trouble they still were in.

"Right. I'm going to take that as a yes." Dewey was distracted by the files for Juracan and two other planets that were not in the standard registries. One of them he recognized from the appendix of the registry where known missing systems and planets were listed. Unfortunately, with the EVA suit on, he couldn't access his tablet to copy the data over. Instead, he scanned the files slowly, knowing that the information would stay with him.

"What are you doing?"

Dewey closed the files and turned around. He smiled and said, "Being nosey. Tell me about the captain of the gunship."

Capt Sullivan shrugged. "Don't know him."

The eyes of the crew implied differently.

"I'd like him to release the Graevya and stand down," said Dewey. "We can send for neutral forces to help sort out the situation."

That idea seemed to make Capt Sullivan nervous. Dewey was even more sure that the captain was aware of what was happening on the surface of Juracan.

"Well, let's contact the captain of the gunship and find out." Dewey turned his head and raised his voice. "Lieutenant Owen, if you don't mind."

"No problem," said Lt Owen as he stepped onto the bridge. His eyes scanned the room, his eyebrows arching as he noticed the damaged nav station. "I can repair that."

Dewey laughed, causing SSgt Castro to grin in turn. "No need, Owen," Dewey said. "I need a comm connection with the other ship."

"Right." Lt Owen moved to the designated comm section and took a seat. He spent several minutes moving through files and tapping controls before asking, "Make the request now?"

"Yes, please."

Lt Owen nodded and slipped on the comm's headset before tapping several more controls. He then turned and gave Dewey a thumbs up. Connection made.

"Greetings," said Dewey, speaking into the air, his chin slightly elevated. "This is Lieutenant Dewey Tyler, Hospitaller Orphan Corps. I'd like to speak to the captain of the gunship currently holding the Graevya hostage."

"This is Captain Webb."

Dewey waited for more and was mildly annoyed that the gunship captain hadn't given him more information. Not getting it, Dewey said, "You have control of the Graevya. I'd like you to release the ship and its crew."

"I'd like you to surrender."

Again, it was a short and abrupt response, seemingly devoid of emotion. Dewey signaled for Lt Owen to mute the mic. When Owen confirmed it was done, Dewey tapped his comm for his platoon.

"Listen up. I need all of the ship's crew removed from the ship. Take them across and put them in the trunk we rode up in. Staff Sergeant Castro, put two guards outside the trunk. Then all of our people need to return here. That includes Lieutenant Haynes and Corporal Garner. The other officers will remain behind with the trunk guard."

"Will do," said SSgt Castro. She waved to the Hospitallers with her and pointed at the bridge crew. They stepped forward and began to guide the crew off the bridge.

Capt Sullivan resisted. "What are you going to do?"

Dewey looked at the captain with feigned surprise. "Well, I'm not going to surrender, that's for sure."

Once all the crew was off the bridge and Dewey had confirmation that the rest of the ship's crew and the surviving mercenaries were being escorted across to the cargo ship, Dewey turned his attention back to Lt Owen.

"Okay, Owen, when you unmute the mic, I want you to do an inventory search. See what kinds of things the mercs brought with them."

"Anything specific?"

"Yes," said Dewey. "Things that go boom would be nice."

"Nice, indeed." Lt Owen turned back to the comm station. "Ready?"

"Ready." When Lt Owen signaled, Dewey resumed talking to the captain of the gunship. "How about we send for a mediator, Captain Webb? I'm sure we can get a flotilla of Allied Planet ships to come and work out a compromise."

"How about I space the crew? Starting with the privates and working my way up?"

The comm clicked as Lt Owen muted the mic. "I don't like this guy."

"Agreed. Find anything?"

"Shoulder fired rockets," said Lt Owen. "Grenades. There's also blocks of explosives if that'll help."

Dewey knew by Lt Owen's grin that he knew it would help. "Locate the explosives, make sure we have detonators, too. Send someone to get all of it. Unmute the comm."

Lt Owen turned back to the screen and tapped it a few more times. "You're on."

"Tell you what, Captain Webb, I think I have a better idea. Let's talk this out face to face."

There was a moment of silence. Dewey could imagine the captain of the gunship racking his brain to figure out Dewey's angle. Finally, he said, "How do you propose to do that?"

This time Dewey paused, but it was purposeful. "I'll come to you."

28

The mercenary troopship was better supplied than the cargo hauler and the mercenaries currently stationed on Juracan. This pleased Dewey almost as much as it pleased Cpl Garner. Garner now had a working EVA helmet.

"No barracks duty for me," said the corporal as he tapped the comm.

"Don't press your luck," said SSgt Castro in response. Her grin flashed through the clear face shield of her own helmet.

Dewey was only paying partial attention to the conversation. His primary focus was on the plans he'd laid out and then run past the other lieutenants and SSgt Castro. He didn't doubt the plan would work, but he was worried about the cost. They'd already lost PFC Horton. Dewey would like to not lose any more people if it could be helped. However, considering what they were going to attempt, he couldn't shake the dread of hearing another name or two that would have to be added to Roll Call come morning.

He'd run through several variations of the scenario. None of them ended without there being some sort of firefight. People were going to get hurt. Dewey just needed to minimize that damage as much as possible.

"Owen?" Dewey asked over the comm. "How's it look?"

"Coding's done. We have full navigational control of the ship from the escape pod." He paused and then said, "This'll work, Tyler."

"I know," Dewey said. He wished he could know in advance the price they'd have to pay. He tapped the comm, connecting with Lt Haynes. "Everything loaded?"

"Just about," replied Haynes. "We're getting the last of it into the airlock in engineering. Sergeant Simon has the remotes connected. Give us ten minutes?"

"Take fifteen," said Dewey. "Double check it all."

"Will do."

Dewey tapped the comm once more, connecting with everyone on the bridge. "Staff Sergeant Castro? How's it look?"

"Like I would know," said Castro. She laughed. "You want all these electronics taken care of? You'll need a different platoon sergeant. You want it all blown up? That'd be me. That being said, Parks and Barrett tell me that the ship is ready to release from the station. Sergeant Thompson assures me that Lieutenant Owen can handle navigation from the escape pod. It'll be crude…"

"But it'll work," finished Dewey as he nodded. Once more, Dewey tapped the comm. This time it was for all the Hospitallers onboard. "Ten minutes, people. Report to your positions ASAP."

The comm clicked off. Around the bridge of the troopship, Hospitallers began to move. Barrett and Parks saluted as they passed Dewey. Behind them, Cpl Garner and his fireteam followed. That left SSgt Castro and Sgt Thompson. Elsewhere around the ship, Dewey trusted that the other fireteams were moving to the escape pods on the ship's port side. PFC Horton's body had been bagged in his personal body bag and removed to the platform. If all went well, they'd be back to recover the body and eventually ship it or its ashes to Denhaag for interment.

Dewey fervently hoped that it was the only body bag they'd have to deal with this day.

"Thompson, go join Lieutenant Owen. Tell him we're on our way."

"Will do, Lieutenant Tyler." Thompson saluted as he hurried off the bridge. His boots on the metal stairwell quickly became a fading echo.

"Worried?" SSgt Castro asked. She was sitting at one of the comm stations, slowly spinning it in circles.

"When am I not?"

Castro laughed. "Good point." She paused in the midst of a spin and then used her feet to shuffle back around to face Dewey. "I just realized," she said. "Did you realize?"

"That I worry a lot?"

"No." Castro waved her arms around, almost falling off the seat. "This'll be the second ship we've destroyed in as many missions!"

SSgt Castro was referring to Wenshen, where the ship's commander had landed her ship on the planet's surface. A ship never meant for atmospheric operations.

"Wenshen wasn't my fault," Dewey said.

Again, Castro laughed as she mimed opening a book. "You sure?"

"Coincidence. And this ship isn't ours, so I don't think it counts, either."

"Two missions, two destroyed ships." Castro stood, joining Dewey, who'd also taken to his feet. "You can't argue those facts."

Together, they left the bridge and made their way down to the lower deck. There was an escape pod connected to the bridge. However, since Dewey wasn't sure it would survive what came next, he decided to leave it unmanned. Instead, they were using one of the larger troop escape pods. Hopefully, it would survive what Dewey was about to attempt. If not, his name would soon be etched on his commanding officer's wall.

"Welcome aboard," said Lt Owen as Dewey followed SSgt Castro through the hatch.

The escape pod was a rectangular box with rounded edges. Jumpseats ran the length of both sides with a third row down the middle. Modified pilot and copilot seats were near the entrance. The pod could hold several squads with emergency gear stored beneath the floorboards. For this mission, the pod held Cpl Fleming's fireteam, Dewey, SSgt Castro, Lt Owen, and Sgt Thompson.

"Everything ready?" Dewey asked. He took a position behind the pilot's seat and started strapping himself in. This included attaching the oxygen and power chargers to his EVA suit.

"Good to go," said Lt Owen. His answer was given quietly. His attention was focused on the controls and one panel he was making adjustments to. "Lieutenant Haynes has all the explosives in place and has locked down the aft escape pod. Lieutenant Matthews and Lieutenant Hall also have their pods secured and ready."

"Waiting for the green light, then?" asked SSgt Castro in her knowing tone. She was strapping in across the way from Dewey.

"On your mark, Lieutenant Tyler," said Lt Owen.

To SSgt Castro's right, Fleming's fireteam was already secured, their faces intent on Dewey and Lt Owen. They returned the nods that Dewey gave them. There was no doubt in his mind that they were as nervous as he was. However, while they were firm in their trust of him to see them through, Dewey could feel the cold dread of failing them.

But he always felt that way. Even when sending his people into a safe situation, there was still the chance something could go wrong, and he would have to recite one more name the next morning.

The only way to find out how things would unfold was to get on with it.

"Let's do it," Dewey said. He grinned, though he didn't feel the same excitement that SSgt Castro often displayed at times like this.

Next to Dewey, Lt Owen nodded and tapped the comm. "Stand by for separation."

Owen tapped a few more keys. Then, on an image of the ship's side on a screen, he tapped twice more where there were two red circles. The red circles pulsed and then snapped to solid green. Dewey felt a slight shift as the ship fell off the station, pushed by the releasing clamps. There was a passing wave of queasiness as the artificial gravity cut out.

"Separation complete," Lt Owen said. Dewey recognized the tone as one of a person talking more to themselves than to anyone else. "Engaging system thrusters. Here we go."

The ride was less exciting than a dropship entering atmo. There wasn't gravity to pull on the occupants as the ship banked or pushed forward. All Dewey had was the information given to them by Lt Owen and what Dewey could see on the screens. The gunship and the Graevya were less than a thousand kilometers away. Days of travel on the ground, but in space, it would take much less time than that.

"We're being hailed by the gunship," said Lt Owen.

"Ignore them." Dewey leaned back in the seat and feigned relaxation. He expected the gunship to fire on them, but not yet. They would wait. Dewey would do the same in Capt Webb's boots. There might be a chance that Capt Sullivan still had control of the troopship. Capt Webb would hold out as long as he could. Then he'd fire on the ship.

Lt Owen was piloting the ship erratically, even though Dewey couldn't feel it. They were attempting to make it look like the ship was damaged. In a few more minutes, one of the airlocks would blow. Then one of the ship's engines would fail. There'd be several final warnings and threats before Capt Webb finally relented and fired on his own company's ship.

All Dewey had to do was time it right.

As the passing minutes collected themselves into groups of ten, Owen updated Dewey. "The merc captain demands to know what we're up to." After a half-hour, when Lt Owen had moved the troopship within five hundred kilometers, the report changed to, "Captain Webb requests we stand down or he will fire on the troopship."

Dewey sat a little taller. He scanned the Hospitallers in the escape pod, pointing at a sleeping PFC Ramirez, earning a nodding laugh from the others. Finally, Dewey turned his attention to Lt Owen. "Have Lieutenant Haynes blow the first airlock," he said. "Then initiate unlock procedures for all the other escape pods."

By all the escape pods, Dewey included the ones the Hospitallers hadn't boarded. They were a necessary subterfuge.

"Doing it now," said Lt Owen. He tapped a comm button on his screen and started a conversation with Lt Haynes.

Less than a minute later, the troopship vibrated with the explosion from the airlock.

"Now engine one," said Dewey.

Owen passed the command along to Lt Haynes. Another minute

later and another shudder signaled that the troopship had lost one engine. Owen was busy making adjustments to the ship's motions.

"Drunk maneuvering," Lt Owen said as he began to make more adjustments to the controls.

The ship would wobble just from the explosions. Lt Owen had to perform extra actions to keep the ship turning in ways that shielded the escape pods occupied by the Hospitallers. The ship was going to be fired on soon. He and Dewey needed to keep the Hospitallers safe for as long as possible.

Three minutes passed. Lt Owen nodded his head, turning to look at Dewey. "He's given us his final order to stand down."

Dewey pressed against the restraints as he sat forward. "How far away?"

"Two hundred twelve kilometers."

"Blow the locks on the starboard escape pods," Dewey said. "Tell the other pilots to separate when they must, but try to hold on as long as possible. We want this to look like a desperate attempt by the ship's crew and the mercs."

"Of course." Lt Owen tapped several keys on the board in front of him. "We survive this, I'm going to suggest they add a training program for this sort of situation. I like adventure, Tyler, but this may be more than I'm comfortable with."

"Me, too," said Dewey.

SSgt Castro laughed and said, "I'm having fun."

Fleming's fireteam laughed. However, Dewey could see the looks on their faces. Looks that ran counter to the implied humor of their laughter.

"Final warning," said Lt Owen. His laugh was a snort as he added, "Again."

"Distance?"

"Hundred kilometers and braking."

"He'll be firing soon," said Dewey. "Tell the other teams it's time."

"On it." Lt Owen began relaying Dewey's orders then he cut himself off. His voice changed energy as he spoke to everyone.

"Missiles inbound."

Dewey tapped his comm. "Lieutenant Haynes, are we ready with the other explosives?"

"We are, Lieutenant Tyler."

"Owen, we need those explosives to go just before the missiles," Dewey said.

"Got it." Owen tapped the comm on the escape pod's pilot board. "Haynes. Ready. Set."

The pause was extended. Dewey imagined the rockets somehow missing the ship when he heard Lt Owen give the final word. The next beat came with the vibrations and sounds of the explosives in the other airlocks going off. Before they'd had time to fade, everything shook as the ship was shoved sideways. Several other Hospitallers reached out like Dewey to brace themselves.

"We're away," said Lt Owen. The shudder of explosions dulled to the vibration of the escape pod's thrusters. "Coming around."

"Everyone else?" They were now running on silent, relying on silent commands, brief blips of data to keep everyone together.

"Everyone has confirmed separation," Lt Owen replied.

The other pods would ping at regular intervals. If they stopped, then Dewey would know they had a problem. He fervently hoped that none of them had a problem.

Right now, though he couldn't see it, Dewey knew several things were happening. With the addition of the mercenary explosives stuffed into the airlocks, the ship's explosion would create a distraction. If anyone was paying attention after that, they'd see escape pods and ship debris drifting in the gunship's direction. The debris would thin as it approached, revealing the escape pods and their approach.

The situation would escalate from there.

"Twenty kilometers," said Lt Owen. "All pods are braking. Gunship comms are trying to make contact. They're threatening to fire on the pods."

"Emergency signals," Dewey said.

Lt Owen nodded. He tapped the screen that would release a

command to all of the unoccupied escape pods. They would begin their standard emergency broadcast. That would clog the comm lines. The question then would be whether or not the gunship captain would fire indiscriminately on the escape pods.

"Owen, is everyone shadowing the lead pods?"

"Stand by." Lt Owen leaned toward the screen while he made adjustments to the pod's position with his right hand. "We are. Haynes slipped out, but she's back in again. The others look good, too."

Without warning, the escape pod shuddered. Cpl Fleming looked alarmed as he turned to Dewey. In his turn, Dewey held up his hand, ordering calm.

"Our cover's been blown," said Lt Owen. He was tapping the control screen and adjusting the pod's movements. "Literally blown to bits."

"How close?"

"Three kilometers," said Lt Owen. "We're coming in warm. Brace yourselves."

Dewey turned to Cpl Fleming and his fireteam. Over local comm, he said, "Engage your boots, separate from ship supply. We make contact, we're blowing the hatch and moving."

"You got it, Lieutenant," said Cpl Fleming. He was already disconnecting the power and air supply umbilicals. Next to him, the rest of the fireteam was replicating his actions.

"Who's first out?" asked SSgt Castro. She was rolling up and storing the umbilical cord in her suit.

It was a fair question. Castro likely knew that Dewey was hesitant to put one of the PFCs on point in this situation. Dewey had the feeling that Castro was volunteering. While he didn't expect to meet resistance while on the skin of the gunship, he understood the concern.

Dewey laughed, trying to keep it sounding normal. "What? You think I'm going to let you have the first step on an EVA action? I call dibs on that."

"I thought you might," said SSgt Castro with a nod. "I'll be right behind you."

It was Dewey's turn to nod. "When aren't you?"

And now it was SSgt Castro's turn to laugh. "When I'm in front!"

"Here we go!" Lt Owen's voice was elevated with tension. "In four, three, two, one. Contact!"

The pod shuddered as it banged against the surface of the gunship. Dewey released his restraints and stomped over to the pod's hatch. "Thrusters holding, Owen?"

"They're on full. We should be good for ten minutes if we need them."

"We won't," said Dewey. He opened a panel and pulled on a bright orange lever. It came down ninety degrees. As it stopped, there were several muffled explosions, and then the hatch was drifting away. Dewey brought his weapon up as he stomped over to the hatchway. "With me, everyone."

Over the comm, Dewey heard SSgt Castro's determined voice. "Right behind you."

29

As Dewey stepped out onto the surface of the gunship, it felt like familiar terrain. It wasn't his first venture across the exterior of a ship that was moving through space. In fact, Dewey was confident that if he did a quick poll of his platoon, he'd find that every one of them had experiences similar to his. At least once in their years at their respective orphanages, they'd spent a weekend on an airless planet or moon, experiencing low gravity while wearing spacesuits. Most, if not all of them, had toured a space station from the inside and out to experience magnetic boots and zero gravity.

In the three years of basic training, they would have had additional experiences with ships and space. Everyone had been trained in rescue operations where they entered ships without crew assistance, sealing breaches, repairing airlocks so that more help could access the interior.

Likely as not, the mercenaries operating the ship had never practiced entering a ship unaided, or by force. Certainly, they'd never trained in boarding a ship from space. However, they must have had some idea of how it all worked. The troopship had carried the right equipment, sealed in hard plastic crates.

Now, the Hospitallers carried the equipment.

"This way," Dewey said over the localized comm. The connection included Lt Owen and Sgt Thompson, who were bringing up the rear.

Before leaving the troopship, Dewey had done a quick mental search and dredged up everything he had read and seen about gunships and then about the specific design. He'd marked four entry points. Two of those points were not airlocks.

Dewey's team was forward, making their way to an airlock one deck below the bridge. They would breach the lock once a distraction occurred. The distraction would come when Lt Haynes's team blew a surgically precise hole through the hull into the engineering section. And if that wasn't enough of a distraction, Lt Matthew's team would be doing the same forward, a deck above the fire control station.

The crew of the gunship would be very distracted. Then Dewey's team here, and Lt Hall's team on the other side, would make their entrances.

Dewey stepped back at the airlock, scanning the ship's surface for any surprises, like a counterattack, for example. Lt Owen and Sgt Thompson were on the other side of the airlock doing the same thing. Cpl Fleming and his fireteam were unrolling an explosive charge around the airlock hatch.

If Capt Webb had done an emergency lockdown of the airlocks, Dewey's team would enter the hard way, cutting out the airlock hatch with the explosives. Once they were inside, they could release an emergency seal that would expand and cover the hole. This would allow the team to cycle the airlock and enter the main body of the ship.

Dewey's comm chimed, twice short, twice long. He tapped the comm, keeping it just to his team. "Lieutenant Matthews is in place forward and ready to go."

"Almost done here," said Cpl Fleming. They'd unrolled, encircled the entire hatch with the explosives, and were now setting the fuses and blasting caps.

"Nothing personal," said SSgt Castro as she scanned her quarter of the perimeter, "but I'd rather be with Lieutenant Haynes."

"Don't fret, Castro," Dewey said as his comm chimed three short and two long. "This will be a nice explosion, too."

"If we get to use them."

"Fingers crossed then, Castro? Heads up, everyone. Lieutenant Haynes is ready."

Dewey's comment was followed by a third series of chimes, two short and three long. Lt Hall was also in place and ready.

"You sure you don't want to contact Captain Webb and see if he wants to surrender now?" SSgt Castro asked.

Dewey reached for his comm. "You want me to?"

"We've already got the explosives set," said Cpl Fleming. "Don't ruin the fun now."

"Don't worry, Fleming," said Dewey. "The staff sergeant is only joking."

"True," admitted Castro. "So?"

In response to Castro's one-word question, Dewey tapped his comm, emitting a single chime that lasted for five seconds. As it ended, the ship vibrated. Aft, debris could be seen ejecting from the ship as the teams with Lt Haynes and Lt Matthews set off their explosions. Dewey signaled to Lt Owen to hit the button to open the lock.

Owen bent down and punched the button that should either start the hatch opening or signal that the airlock was cycling out ship atmo so they could enter. Neither happened. With a shake of his head, Owen stood and backed away.

Simultaneously over the comm, Dewey heard the information from both teams on the gunship's aft end. "We're in."

"Our turn?" asked Cpl Fleming.

Everyone had backed away from the airlock hatch. Even through the face shield of two helmets, Dewey could see SSgt Castro grinning. To Cpl Fleming, Dewey said, "Our turn."

The ship vibrated with another explosion just before Cpl Fleming detonated the explosives around the airlock.

"Can't believe we're last," said Lt Owen, earning a guffaw from SSgt Castro.

Around his feet, Dewey felt Cpl Fleming's explosion. The hatch shuddered and drifted away, haloed by bits of debris. Fleming signaled his team. They flooded the hatch, weapons at the ready. Dewey didn't expect that the mercenaries were suited, armed, and waiting in the airlock. Still, he also wasn't going to expect them not to be.

As he followed the rest of the team into the breached airlock, he listened as the other teams entered the ship. There were several crew present in an aft corridor, but they were incapacitated by the sudden decompression. One looked likely to survive. The teams were also sealing the breach holes so that they could repressurize the space. When that was done, they could open the hatch that had automatically closed with the sudden drop in air pressure. It would bring any defense the ship had running in their direction.

Forward, Lt Matthews's team had already cycled through the airlock. They entered to find the space empty.

"How's it look?" Dewey asked over localized comm.

PFC Wallace, who was at the inner hatch, his helmeted head pressed to the small inspection window, flashed a thumbs up.

"All clear," he said. Then, "Wait, no. There's at least one person down the corridor. They're peeking around the corner."

"So we'll have company," said SSgt Castro. "Good."

"Okay, let's seal the breach."

Dewey stepped aside so Fleming's team could start sealing the breach. Cpl Fleming pulled a round disk from a package he'd carried over from the troopship. The disk unfolded several times until it was wider than the hole in the hull. A handle in the middle allowed him to pull the oversized disk tight against the ship. The rest of his fireteam opened canisters and dispensed a sealant that adhered to the hull and the disk. The sealant was fast-acting, and Cpl Fleming released his hold on the disk's handle after forty-five seconds.

Outside the airlock, Dewey had been watching the person down the corridor. They looked over their shoulder several times as if talking to someone else. As he continued to monitor the activities in the corridor, Dewey gave a signal to SSgt Castro. She pushed a large, round button on the interior wall, starting the airlock cycle.

Even with opposing forces down the corridor, they would have to exit the airlock fast. The seal would hold for a while, but if it separated while the interior hatch was open, it could suck Dewey's team out into space along with anyone unfortunate enough to be down the corridor.

"Thirty seconds," said SSgt Castro.

Dewey stepped back from the hatch and opened a ballistic shield. It was one of their own, so Dewey knew it would work. Next to him, Lt Owen was doing the same thing.

"Fifteen."

Dewey joined his shield to Lt Owen's. They knelt behind the shields as Cpl Fleming's fireteam took up position behind Dewey and Owen. SSgt Castro was pressed back against the wall.

"Zero," said SSgt Castro.

The red light above the hatch turned from red to green. The hatch clicked before starting to swing open into the corridor. With Lt Owen next to him, Dewey shuffled forward, filling the expanding gap with the ballistic shields. Dewey could feel the infrequent bump of one of the fireteam behind him as they moved to maintain their position close behind.

"They're not firing," said Cpl Fleming over the comm.

"They're waiting for the hatch to start closing," said SSgt Castro. She'd moved in behind the others as they passed the airlock threshold. "Reduces the chances of causing a decompression."

"And it blocks our exit," added Dewey. "Which means they're going to fight."

"Oh, good. Let me get the door then." SSgt Castro swatted the button that started the hatch swinging shut. Ideally, they'd cycle the airlock, so it was in balance with the exterior, but that wasn't a priority for now.

Dewey was beginning to wonder how far the ship's crew would allow him and the others to proceed when someone pointed a boarding gun around the corner and pulled the trigger. Fortunately, Fleming's fireteam saw it too, ducking just as the weapon fired oversized buckshot. SSgt Castro hadn't seen the gun.

"Stars and comets!" Castro dropped to the ground in a rough cross-legged position, difficult to do in an EVA suit. Her right hand was clasped over her left bicep. "That was rude."

Over Dewey's head, Cpl Fleming and PFC Ramirez returned fire with several short bursts that chipped the corner where the boarding gun had appeared.

"Castro? You ready to call it quits?"

"Me, Lieutenant?" Dewey paused to look back at SSgt Castro. She had a small can of suit sealant, the tip pressed into one hole. Several other holes were slowly leaking air and small droplets of blood. "All they did was annoy me. Wait until I get my turn."

"Waiting," quipped Cpl Fleming.

The fireteam shuffled forward another meter. The fireteam, operating in pairs, kept the boarding gun from firing by shooting short bursts whenever it appeared. Behind them, by a quick peek, Dewey saw SSgt Castro switching the barrels on her weapon, preparing it for grenades. When she was ready, she loaded a cylindrical cartridge and gave Dewey a wink.

"Waiting's over, Fleming," said Dewey. "Duck."

The fireteam took a knee behind Dewey. The boarding gun fired. Then SSgt Castro was up and returning fire. She stepped to one side and then the next. Dewey was able to peek over the ballistic shields and just caught sight of the grenades bouncing off the side corridors' back wall and then exploding. SSgt Castro unleashed the entire cartridge of grenades before she sat back down. One of the holes she'd sealed had begun to leak again.

"Everyone hold," said Dewey. "Private Wells? Give the staff sergeant a hand."

Pvt Wells paused long enough to earn a laugh from the slow clap he performed. Then he was kneeling next to SSgt Castro, sealing the hole a second time.

"Must have worked loose when you were firing," said Pvt Wells.

"Or I did a bad job of it," said SSgt Castro. "My dorm father would be very disappointed."

"Master Sergeant Gunder would have you running the hills for days," added Dewey.

SSgt Castro chuckled. "Yeah, he would. And I would have run them for him, too."

"Agreed. You have an eye for that grenade tube? I'd like to see around the corner."

Pvt Wells had leaned back, his head tilted like he was examining his patchwork. Seeming to find it acceptable, he gave Castro a clap on the shoulder and returned to his position. SSgt Castro shifted to better access a pouch attached to the outside of her EVA suit.

"I've a couple," she said as she displayed them.

"One should be enough. Everyone else, let's keep a sharp eye out in case they're faking."

They were about a third of the way to the end of the corridor for the airlock. Past the cross corridor would take them to the mess hall and crew barracks. Dewey hoped that Lt Hall was working her way inward and would draw attention that way so he didn't have to spend time clearing extra spaces. His goal was the bridge, and he still had to make it up one level.

The eye was launched by SSgt Castro. She'd bounced it off the ceiling to burn off some of the eye's momentum. It hit the ground, bounced halfway to the ceiling, and then rolled to a stop in the very center where the corridors crossed.

"You've redeemed yourself, Castro." Dewey sat and started to unlatch his EVA helmet. He'd kept everyone in EVA suits, helmets sealed just in case Capt Webb decided to do something extreme like evacuating the air from the ship's interior. The potential for losing artificial gravity was also part of his reasoning. It was a standard technique for slowing down boarders, cutting off their gravity when they least expected it.

Now, though, he needed to access the eye. To do that, he needed his Hospitaller helmet.

"Owen," Dewey said just before removing the EVA helmet, "you got comm."

With the EVA helmet off and his own helmet on, Dewey called up the VR program and located the active eye sent by SSgt Castro. The image was limited to one eye, so the program didn't put Dewey into a virtual landscape. Rather, it was like watching a giant vid screen. Except Dewey had total control. He panned the view to look down one side corridor and then the other. He counted five dead or wounded. From the blood on the deck and the wounds he could see, at least three of them were easily checked off in the dead column.

Before exiting the VR system, Dewey zoomed forward to examine the far ends of both side corridors. He was mostly interested in the corridor leading forward. Still, there wasn't any reason to leave their backsides bare just because he hadn't checked the opposite direction. Both corridors proved to be devoid of anyone but the dead and the wounded.

With the way currently clear, Dewey removed his helmet and secured the EVA helmet back in place. "It's clear down both corridors," he said over the comm. "Might be a couple wounded here that we'll want to treat and secure before we move forward. Lt Owen, take Fleming and his team forward and work on that while I check in with the others."

"Will do," Lt Owen said. Then, "Corporal Fleming, shall we?"

Fleming nodded and took over Dewey's ballistic shield. Then, he and Lt Owen proceeded forward with the rest of Fleming's fireteam.

"How's the arm?" Dewey asked SSgt Castro.

"Stings a little. I'm fine otherwise."

"Hope so." SSgt Castro was the type of person to hide their wounds to keep the team moving. Dewey tapped the comm for a closed connection. "Let's see how the others are doing."

As it turned out, Dewey may have seen the most action. Lt Haynes in engineering had managed to resuscitate one of the crew. He was feeling sick but grateful to be alive. Lt Matthews, forward, had encountered some resistance, but a lucky shot had wounded one of the ship's crew. They and the other crewmember with them had quickly surrendered. Lt Hall had yet to encounter anyone from the ship's crew. From the two prisoners held by Lt Matthews, Dewey knew the size of the crew. Counting the ones in engineering, the two Matthews had control over, and the five Dewey's team had dealt with, they'd dealt with more than half crew.

Dewey believed they'd find most of the others defending the bridge and bridge level.

"Hall," Dewey said once he had the lieutenant on the comm. "I need you to come up to the next level from your end. If anyone's in the corridors, maybe we can spread them thin."

"We're ready when you are."

"Go ahead and start. We'll be a few moments." Dewey closed the comm. He waved SSgt Castro to follow and went to check on the wounded.

"Two," Lt Owen said when Dewey joined him. "One of them, Fleming's not so sure about. I kind of agree. If we got him to their med unit, then maybe. Otherwise…"

"Okay. You and Staff Sergeant Castro stay here. Round up all the weapons and secure them. I'll take Fleming and his fireteam up to the bridge. If things get complicated, I'll send for you."

"Understood," said Lt Owen.

SSgt Castro wasn't so pleased. "Hey, I'm not that badly wounded," she said. Dewey knew she was joking around and wouldn't actually argue his orders.

Dewey turned to Cpl Fleming. "Let's move out."

"You got it, Lieutenant Tyler." Fleming signaled to his team. They started forward with PFC Ramirez on point.

Ten meters brought them to a broad space in the corridor. The corridor continued forward. But here there was a door to the right and the stairs up and down to the left. From his memory, Dewey knew that the room beyond the door had several purposes that ranged from small cargo to passenger bunks to a training room. Had there been a military unit on the gunship, Dewey would have figured them to be there. And he'd also be more reluctant to proceed without clearing everything. The door was too close to the stairs to take chances.

Cpl Fleming, with a signal from Dewey, moved his team to either side of the door. Dewey moved out of the way as Fleming gently took the door handle and pushed down on it. When it didn't move, he tried a little harder. Finally, he jiggled it.

"Locked," he said over the comm to Dewey. "Want us to force our way in?"

Again, Dewey was tempted to just leave it. But there was always that nagging chance.

"Boarding gun," said Dewey. He pointed to Pvt Wells and then back down the hall.

Wells hurried back to where SSgt Castro and Lt Owen were looking after the wounded crew. He returned with the boarding gun. The gun's grip was stained with drying blood.

Cpl Fleming took the weapon, positioned his team, and pressed the barrel against the door where the lock was located. When Dewey gave him the okay sign, Fleming pulled the trigger. The buckshot made quick work of the lock. The door slowly swung on its hinges as Fleming retreated away from the opening.

PFC Ramirez and PFC Wallace were bracketing the door. They took turns clearing their side before comming Dewey.

"Is it clear?"

"No, Lieutenant Tyler," said PFC Wallace. "People. Bound and gagged. I think it's the crew of the Graevya."

30

Dewey followed Cpl Fleming into the room. Pvt Wells remained by the door, scanning the corridor and eyeing the stairwell. The room was neither storage nor bunks. Though there were attachment points on the deck that could secure bunks, they'd either been removed or never installed. The only thing in the room was ten Hospitallers. They were gagged, and their arms, knees, and ankles were secured with quick-ties.

With several motions to indicate they should remain quiet, Dewey directed Fleming and his team to release everyone. Silently, as they were cut free, the Hospitallers of the Graevya stood, rubbing at sore wrists, walking feeling back into their legs, and moving their jaws to displace the discomfort of having a gag in place.

"Sergeant Stephens," Dewey said through the suit's external speaker as the duty NCO of the second bridge watch approached. "How long have you been here like this?"

"A day, I think, Lieutenant," said Sgt Bert Stephens. "As soon as the mercs boarded the Graevya, they pulled everyone not on duty over here and tied us up."

"They put all of you here?" Dewey didn't relish the idea of having to search for more captives. He needed to take control of the bridge. The mercenaries had likely already called for reinforcements.

Sgt Stephens nodded. "Everyone they brought over is in here. Unless they brought more later. I hadn't thought of that."

"No problem, Sergeant. We'll deal with that next. Right now, I'm going to need a few volunteers. I don't have EVA suits for you or even the usual body armor. But I do have a boarding gun here and several more weapons down the hall."

"It's almost been a year since my last training," said Sgt Stephens as he scanned the room. "But I think we can put together a reliable fireteam. What do you want us to do?"

Dewey explained what he needed, which included relieving SSgt Castro and Lt Owen of their current duties. He would feel a lot better about having Castro with him, especially considering her aim with a grenade launcher on her multi-use weapon.

"Guard the prisoners, protect the stairs. Got it." Sgt Stephens turned away and called for three other Hospitallers.

"Everyone else," Dewey said, "I'm going to need you to hold tight here for now."

There were good-natured grumbled agreements that Dewey could understand. No Hospitaller wanted to sit idle when there was work to be done. It had been such a large part of the Hospitaller philosophy as they'd grown up that it wasn't the sort of thing a person could just ignore. However, without weapons, they'd be good for nothing more than cannon fodder if it came to a fight. Dewey wasn't going to have any of that.

"I appreciate your understanding," said Dewey after the grumbles faded. "As soon as I can find weapons or an opportunity for you, I'll send someone down."

"Are there wounded?" asked one of the Hospitallers. It took Dewey a blink of time to recall his name.

"MedTech Ross Baker, yes," Dewey said. "If you'll go with Sergeant Stephen's fireteam, there's at least one wounded ship's crew. Two if you're talented."

"I'll do my best." MedTech Baker followed Sgt Stephens out the door.

"Again, everyone else stand fast." Dewey nodded to Cpl Fleming and left the room.

"We're going to shut the door," said Fleming. "I know you can't barricade it, but it'll look safer."

Cpl Fleming followed the rest of his team out of the room, pulling the door closed. The lack of a latch kept it from staying closed. Fleming looked at Dewey and shrugged.

"You always find a way," said SSgt Castro as she and Lt Owen arrived. "That's why you're my favorite lieutenant. Nothing personal, Lt Owen."

"I'm good," Owen said. "I don't know how you planned to have Graevya crew held captive on board, Tyler, but I'm impressed."

"Lots of planning," said Dewey. He turned and looked at the stairwell. "Care to pop another eye, Castro? Give us a view of the corridor on the next level? Entrance to the bridge is five meters aft of here."

"I'll see what I can do." She stepped over to the stairwell and began to examine the walls and ceilings.

Dewey stepped away, signing for Lt Owen to keep watch. Owen nodded and took a step forward. With Lt Owen overseeing the moment, Dewey tapped his comm to check in with the other teams.

"There's four outside the hatch," said Lt Haynes. "I've never considered myself a good aim, but these guys are terrible. Oh, hold on. Yeah, okay, there's three outside the hatch now."

"Don't let them overrun your position," Dewey said as he changed the comm to contact Lt Hall. "What's your position?"

"Almost to the other side of the bridge," Hall said. She sounded a little winded to Dewey, but it could just have been from the adrenaline. "Had a skirmish with a couple people before they surrendered. Felt like token resistance."

"We still have possession of fire control," said Lt Matthews when Dewey commed her. "We pushed back the crew. They've disappeared. Not sure where they went, but we've been clearing and securing rooms as we look for them."

"As long as you're keeping them distracted," Dewey said. "We don't need any surprises on our end. We'll be going up in a moment. Hall is on her way, too."

"Understood," said Lt Matthews. "Let me know if you need more. We're a deck away."

"Will do." Dewey closed the comm just as SSgt Castro was aiming up the corridor.

"She thinks someone is up there," Lt Owen whispered over the comm. "She says she's going to pop one grenade and put an eye up right after. I wasn't sure, but I'm not going to tell her what not to do."

Dewey could see Owen's grin through their face shields. He nodded in agreement. SSgt Castro was as good a Hospitaller as there was, but she did have a stubborn streak. There was little to complain about as it had saved Dewey more than once since they'd begun working together.

The muffled sound of the grenade exploding drew Dewey's attention. He looked at SSgt Castro as she fired again, sending the eye on the heels of the grenade. She stepped away from the stairwell and gave Dewey a thumbs up. Now he had to change helmets again.

The switch was more manageable now that he'd done it once. Soon enough, Dewey was looking at the upper corridor through the VR system. There were two people in the corridor at the end opposite the bridge. One was wounded, and the other was trying to deal with the wounds.

Dewey tapped the comm, allowing him to speak through the eye. "If you agree to stand down, I'll send medical help to you."

The two men twitched in surprise, scanning the corridor, looking for the source of the voice. They spoke in a quiet whisper that Dewey couldn't decipher. But after a few short exchanges, the uninjured crewman nodded, saying, "Yeah, fine. Just get some help. I can't stop the bleeding."

"Stand by." As he began to methodically and swiftly change helmets, Dewey signaled for Lt Owen's attention. Over the EVA comm, he said, "Call back MedTech Baker and send him up. I'm going ahead with Fleming's fireteam to secure the corridor."

"On it." Lt Owen switched his comm to locate Baker. He smacked the side of his helmet. "Baker doesn't have comms with the EVA suits."

As Owen trotted down the corridor to find MedTech Baker, Dewey replaced his EVA helmet before signaling Cpl Fleming to take charge. "They agreed to stand down," Dewey said. "But be ready."

Fleming nodded and then signaled his team to follow as he took point.

"When Baker gets here," Dewey said to SSgt Castro, "escort him up."

Dewey then followed Cpl Fleming's fireteam. PFC Ramirez was on the landing, watching down the corridor toward the bridge hatch. Pvt Wells was past the two crewmen, watching the other end. There was a door between Ramirez and the bridge. Based on Dewey's recollection, that should be the captain's quarters.

Cpl Fleming worked on the ship's crewman, applying pressure patches to several of the injured crewman's wounds. At the same time, PFC Wallace stood watch over them. There was a lot of blood on the deck where the injured crewman sat.

Dewey tapped the comm for the external speaker. "Medic's on the way."

The other crewman looked sideways at Dewey as he continued to push against an aggressively bleeding wound. "A grenade?"

"Would you have surrendered before that?" Dewey asked. As if his side was expected to be polite, even when being shot at.

The crewman seemed to understand, but he glared at Dewey for another two heartbeats before his eyes shifted to the side. Dewey turned to see MedTech Baker topping the stairs. He waved the medtech over.

Baker knelt next to Cpl Fleming. Fleming tapped the comm of his suit, activating the external speaker. Dewey didn't hear the conversation but didn't need to, knowing that Fleming was quickly describing the situation as he saw it. A minute later, Fleming stood and backed away, allowing MedTech Baker to take over.

"We going to go and let the captain know he has injured?" SSgt Castro asked over a closed comm connection.

"Might be a good idea," Dewey said. "Before someone else gets hurt."

Before proceeding down the corridor to the bridge hatch, Dewey checked on Lt Hall's position. She was on the opposite side with the prisoners in tow. Dewey told her to stand by before making a final check-in with Lt Matthews and Lt Haynes.

"Now we can go and talk to the captain," Dewey said. He started down the corridor, quickly followed by Cpl Fleming, PFC Ramirez, and Pvt Wells, who slipped past Dewey to clear the way. Dewey understood but still found it amusing as there was now nothing but a corridor and a closed hatch.

Dewey opened a general comm channel at the hatch. What he said should be heard across this ship and perhaps even on the Graevya if they were listening. "Captain Webb? I'm here to talk about that surrender."

After a count of thirty, Dewey repeated his request. The third time, Dewey waited a gracious minute but still didn't get a response.

"We going to blow the hatch?" asked Lt Owen over the EVA comm channel. "Those things are pretty thick."

It was an interesting idea, but the casualties on both sides might increase with the explosion. The amount of explosives it would take also might not be available on the ship. And the troopship was no longer an available source of supplies.

"Nope." Dewey turned around to face Owen and SSgt Castro. "We're going to do this in a way that will reduce the body count and probably really annoy Capt Webb. Which is fine because he's annoyed me. I don't think I've ever met anyone this stubborn."

"Hey, now," said SSgt Castro, earning a laugh from Dewey and Lt Owen.

"Well, let's get this plan in motion, then," Lt Owen said. He started laughing again when he went to wipe the laugh-tears from his eyes only to bump into the face shield of his helmet.

"Let's," said Dewey. He went back down the corridor to where MedTech Baker was still tending the badly injured crewmember. "How's he looking?"

MedTech Baker sat back on his heels. "I've got him stabilized for now. But if we don't get him into a med unit ASAP, I'm not sure he'll make it."

"Understood." Dewey turned his attention to the other crewmember. "How many are guarding the access point to our ship?"

The crewmember blinked several times before seeming to focus on Dewey. "Guards? None, I think. The captain said the rest of the crew would behave because we had some of their people here. I only signed up for this ship because it was a non-combat escort. Karl signed up because I said it was safe."

Dewey looked down at the injured crewmember. "This Karl?"

"Yeah. His wife is going to be so mad."

"Then we'll do our best to make sure he lives to take the brunt of her anger." Dewey looked around and pulled Pvt Wells's attention before speaking to the crewman. "Take Private Wells here with you to your infirmary. We need a stretcher. We have a full med unit on the Graevya and excellent medical help."

"Yes, sir," said the crewman. He gave an awkward salute before waving Pvt Wells to follow him forward.

"All right, people," said Dewey after adjusting the comm for the entire platoon. "New plan."

Dewey quickly laid out the evacuation plan, leaving Lt Haynes's team in place and having the other two teams sweep the ship for anyone not locked inside the bridge.

"That's two teams of two for each hatch to the bridge," Dewey said at the end. "And everyone else onto the Graevya."

Pvt Hall and the crewman returned as Dewey finished giving orders. He directed Fleming's fireteam to handle the wounded crewman.

"They'll bring your friend to our ship. You'll come with me for now."

The crewman looked at his friend, slowly being moved from the floor to the stretcher. He then nodded. "You want me to lead?"

"You may." On general comm for the platoon, Dewey also added, "Let's move, people. I want to get this over with."

Entering the Graevya was like entering a ghost ship. Though, to be fair, Dewey had only read about ghost ships in fiction. Unless entering a ship in a military action or rescue mission, there was normally someone at the boarding hatch. Dewey reminded himself as he stepped off the transit tube that this wasn't a normal day.

Behind Dewey, the crewmember, who finally gave his name as Ulaf, followed with PFC Wallace and Pvt Wells behind him. The rest of the platoon, the rescued Graevya crew, and the gunship's captured crew were just now entering the tube that connected both ships.

"Now, I wasn't part of any boarding party," Ulaf said. His voice sounded whiny, but Dewey presumed it was just the EVA suit's exterior microphone. "But I did hear that all those who'd been left here were confined to quarters. Except for eating and stuff like that."

Externally and over the comm, Dewey replied, "Then we'll start with the mess hall."

To reach the mess hall, they had to go up two decks. That was also where the med unit was located. One deck up were bunkrooms for Hospitaller units. There was plenty of empty space there as Dewey's platoon was the only one that had been on board.

Switching the comm to connect with just his platoon, Dewey began giving orders. "Lieutenant Matthews. You and your team will show the gunship's crew to an empty bunkroom and stand guard there. Lieutenant Owen, you and the rest of Lieutenant Hall's team will help MedTech Baker get the injured to medical. Staff Sergeant Castro, seal the hatch on both sides."

As he started up the stairs, Dewey had confirmation from everyone. There were ten Hospitallers still left on the gunship. Lt Hall had four of them guarding the two entrances to the bridge. Lt Haynes had her team buttoned up in engineering. Once the wounded were dealt with, and Dewey knew the Graevya was secure, he would deal with Capt Webb.

The number of feet following Dewey diminished as they passed one deck. He could hear Lt Matthews giving orders to the few uninjured and captured crewmembers. Behind him, further down, Dewey heard Lt Owen's team working with the stretcher and encouraging the walking wounded.

The next level brought Dewey to the chow hall entrance and the corridor leading aft where Lt Owen and MedTech Baker would access medical. Without waiting for Wallace and Wells to clear the room, Dewey pushed the door to the chow hall open and stepped inside.

31

The chow hall's wide-open space was as quiet as the rest of the ship, even with a half-dozen Hospitallers sitting at several tables. The Hospitallers were looking in Dewey's direction, not moving and not speaking. It occurred to Dewey that they may have heard the approaching footsteps and were wondering what would happen next. Then, like a scene from a Friday night vid, an unknown person in a non-Hospitaller EVA suit had burst through the doors.

But being Hospitallers, even ones who'd recently had their ship taken hostage, they were nonplussed by the sudden entrance.

"One sec," Dewey said through the external speaker. Methodically, he released all the latches to the helmet and removed it. He took a moment to enjoy the wide eyes and exchanged looks between the Graevya crew. Then, they all jumped to their feet, standing at attention because an officer had just entered the room.

"Hey, Sergeant McKenzie," Dewey said as he moved further into the room.

"Hey, Lieutenant Tyler," said Sgt McKenzie. "Nice to see you."

"You as well. Everyone doing okay?"

Sgt McKenzie shrugged. "For the most part."

There was nothing like having your ship taken hostage to make a crewmember question their career choice. Dewey understood. Though he'd never been on a ship that was boarded by hostiles, he had been aboard ships fired upon and on occasion wondered why he kept putting himself in those situations.

"Where would I find Captain Gregory and Major Hughes?" Dewey asked. He doubted anyone was on the bridge. "Their quarters?"

Sgt McKenzie looked back at the rest of the crew and then back to Dewey. "Captain Gregory's in sickbay. He'd been at the airlock when the mercs came through. Apparently, he wasn't compliant enough, so they shot him."

Dewey was beginning to like the captain of the gunship even less than before. "The captain will be all right?"

"He's patched and sedated," said MedTech Howard Fox from where he stood. "They wouldn't let me stay with him, though."

"Why don't you go check on him, then? Ship's ours."

"Thank you." MedTech Fox was up and striding quickly out of the chow hall, past the door hastily opened by PFC Wallace.

Dewey turned his attention back to Sgt McKenzie. "And Major Hughes?"

"Likely stalking the corridors," Sgt McKenzie said with a follow-up laugh. "He tries putting on a good-natured face when he sees us. He forgets some of us have been with him for years."

"Understood," Dewey said. Then, "Oh, we brought some people you might like to see."

Dewey turned and signaled to PFC Wallace. With a nod, Wallace turned and pulled the door open again. All of the Graevya crew that had been taken hostage filed into the chow hall. Their faces lit with happiness as they saw their crewmates. Names were shouted. Several people stumbled over bolted-to-the-floor seats and tables to reach their friends.

As he stepped back to allow the crew their moment, Dewey turned to PFC Wallace. He had to put the helmet on to speak as Wallace was still locked in his own suit. "You and Wells stay here," Dewey said. "I'm going to find Major Hughes."

"Understood, Lieutenant Tyler." Wallace stepped aside, allowing Dewey to pass through the doorway.

Dewey went up one more flight of stairs to the command deck. He passed the bridge, noting that the hatch had a weld on it. They'd have to clear that if they wanted to do anything with the Graevya. Two doors down were the private quarters of the ship's captain.

Dewey knocked and waited. He didn't have his Hospitaller helmet on, so he couldn't check the time. After an approximate minute, he knocked once more.

After another approximate minute, he was preparing to knock again when someone called out to him. Dewey barely heard the voice. The external mic was off, but he'd also not latched the EVA helmet back into place, so some sound whispered through the gap. He turned right and saw nothing. Turning left, he found Maj Hughes approaching, a quizzical look on his face.

Dewey quickly removed the helmet and snapped to attention with it under his arm. "Lieutenant Tyler reporting in."

"You're late," said Maj Hughes. His stern face lasted until he was within a meter of Dewey, then he grinned. "I wondered if you were going to try something. After Wenshen, I guess I shouldn't be surprised. Come in."

Maj Hughes opened the door to his quarters and waved Dewey through. Once inside, Dewey began opening his EVA suit, peeling back the seals and connections.

"I imagine there's a lot to say?"

"Yes, there is, Major," Dewey said. "We've taken control of the gunship. Well, almost. Captain Webb has locked himself on the bridge and won't respond to any comm requests."

"He's a hard case," said the major as he took a seat in one of the chairs on the guest side of his desk. "He seemed quite eager to fire missiles on us. That's part of the reason I surrendered so quickly. I had the crew to think of. Then he went and shot Gregory."

"I learned that from Sergeant McKenzie." Dewey was extracting a package from inside the EVA suit. "But you did manage to get off a message to us. What about to headquarters?"

Maj Hughes nodded as he watched Dewey. "We did. We just don't know if it was received. As you saw, they've sealed us out of the bridge and locked down our comms. What are you doing, Lieutenant?"

"This," Dewey said as he held forth a tightly sealed paper bag wrapped in layers of tape, "is freshly roasted coffee beans."

"You brought radioactive coffee onto my ship?"

"It's not radioactive, as it turns out," said Dewey. He paused and studied the wrapping holding the coffee. "Not the beans anyway. Maybe in the paper and plastic, but not much."

"Put it there. I'll have someone test it." Maj Hughes had pointed to a spot close to the door and not near him. "Now, tell me you have a plan for dealing with Captain Webb."

Dewey set the bag of coffee beans on the narrow counter near the door. "Yes, sir, I do. But I also expect him to react when it happens. I'm just not sure what he'll do."

"Well, why don't you start by explaining to me what you're going to do, and I'll tell you what I would do in response."

That had been Dewey's intention. His idea was elaborate but put on hold by someone in the corridor, shouting for his attention. Dewey stepped to the doorway.

"Over here, Private Wells."

Wells sprinted the three meters between him and Dewey. "It's Lieutenant Haynes. They've been trying to raise you on the comm."

Dewey was about to say he hadn't heard the comm. Then he realized he'd taken the helmet off and hadn't set the comm to alert him.

"Thank you, Wells." Dewey stepped back into Maj Hughes's office and grabbed up the EVA helmet, yanking it over his head. He tapped the comm. "Lieutenant Haynes? What's going on?"

"The ship's captain - or somebody else on the ship, I'm not sure - they've overridden the controls here and have locked me out of the controls for the ship's engines."

Dewey tapped the external speaker on his EVA suit. "Repeat that, please, Haynes."

"Someone's overridden the controls to the engines."

Maj Hughes stood. "Did they override the governors, too?"

Dewey relayed the question to Lt Haynes.

There was a pause. Dewey could hear Haynes muttering, then, "Uh, yes. Yes, the governors have been opened."

"You need to get your people off that ship immediately," said Maj Hughes as he started past Dewey. "I'll be down in our engineering until we get the welds off the bridge hatches."

"Yes, Major," said Dewey. He followed the major into the corridor. "Do you think Captain Webb is going to try and force control of his ship?"

"We wish, Lieutenant Tyler. But, no, he's turning his ship into a bomb. Get your people off." Maj Hughes clapped Dewey on the shoulder and then started running down the corridor toward the engine room as he tapped his comm piece and began shouting orders.

Dewey's comm beeped.

"The crew says they need to get to stations," said Lt Owen. "What's going on?"

Dewey turned in a half-circle. He didn't have a place to run toward to fix the problem.

"Captain Webb has rigged his ship to explode," he said as he marched toward the bridge hatch. "Get out of the way of the crew. Then find us a couple grinders and a welding system as a backup so we can get onto the bridge."

"On it."

Dewey tapped the comm again for general communication with his platoon. "Listen up, everyone. The gunship is being primed to explode. Everyone on that ship needs to get to an escape pod and jettison immediately. Staff Sergeant Castro, if the airlock hatch is sealed, you need to manually disconnect the transit tube. Use ship's comm to let Major Hughes know when we're clear."

Several people responded in the affirmative. Their words were jumbled and indecipherable, but Dewey could tell they were all acknowledging without question.

"Lieutenant?"

Dewey turned to face Pvt Webb, who'd asked for his attention. "Yes?"

"Would that captain actually blow himself up?"

"I don't think so," said Dewey. He turned again, examining the spot welds. The welds had been aggressively but sloppily applied. The grinders should make short work of them. If not, they'd be cutting through with the torch. And there was still Pvt Webb's thought that he also shared. "I think it's a diversion, Webb."

Before Pvt Webb could inquire, the deck vibrated with booted feet on the stairs. Lt Owen was leading a charge of Hospitallers, each of them carrying some piece of gear or other. Owen was brandishing an industrial grinder. It was large enough that it took two hands to carry.

"That should do the job," said Dewey. He waved a hand toward the hatch. "Have at it."

"My pleasure," said Lt Owen.

Ten minutes passed. Dewey now stood on the bridge of the Graevya. They'd have been through the welds sooner, but Lt Owen had been too aggressive and wore the grinding wheel down too quickly. Fortunately, they'd had two more waiting to take over. As soon as they had access to the bridge, Dewey had contacted Maj Hughes.

"Good to know," said the major. "You can use my seat to transfer controls to engineering. That'll be faster than me sprinting forward."

"Got it." Dewey had taken the major's seat and pulled up the screen that allowed him to switch control of the ship aft. At the same time, his comm beeped. "Lieutenant Haynes, I hope you're away and safe."

"No, Tyler. Not yet," said Lt Haynes. "We've got the pod ready. I wanted to monitor the engines while trying to override the override."

"You should have left. But since you're still there, how's it look?"

"Not good," said Haynes. "The stations in engineering have been locked out. I've been manually flushing coolants into the engine systems and engaged the fire control units. It's slowed the engines' overheating, but that's it. All I can do now is watch the energy readings for the engines as they rise to critical. You've got about eight minutes, twelve seconds, and counting."

"Right," Dewey said. "I appreciate your attention to details, Lieutenant Haynes, but now I am ordering you to get in the pod and get away from the ship. You might not have enough time to escape the blast radius."

"Good point. Exiting now."

Dewey commed Maj Hughes and gave him the time to detonation.

"Plenty, then," said Maj Hughes. "Stand by. Things might get bumpy. We're going to give the gunship a little nudge away from the elevator's loading platform, just to be safe."

Shortly after giving Dewey the details, Maj Hughes's voice boomed through the shipwide comms.

"Stand by for impact. Stand by for impact."

Klaxons punctuated the major's warning.

A half-second later, the Graevya shuddered. Dewey could feel and hear the boom and subsequent groan of metal as the Graevya made contact with the gunship. The torturous sound lasted for another minute and then went silent like a comm call cut off mid-sentence.

"Accelerating away," said another voice over the ship's systems. "Brace for shockwave."

"Well, this is fun," said SSgt Castro. She jogged onto the bridge and popped a salute for Dewey, then dropped into a seat at the nav station, belting herself in.

Elsewhere, Lt Owen was buckling in, as were the other Hospitallers who'd helped them get onto the bridge. Dewey used the EVA comm to warn anyone who might not have heard the warning over the ship's system. Then it was like holding one's breath, waiting for the moment.

They didn't have to wait much longer. There was one warning over the ship's systems. Then the Graevya vibrated and rocked. The hull rang as debris clattered against it. Several warnings popped up on the screens.

"Hull breach," said Lt Owen. "Ship's sealing off the damaged areas. No one seems to have been hurt."

The Graevya crew would have known to move toward the ship's core and would have dragged along any of Dewey's people if they hadn't already started moving. And then, almost as quickly as the battering of the Graevya began, it stopped. The hull stopped protesting, and the number of red lights for hull breaches stopped climbing.

Dewey connected to the ship's systems through the suit and called for Maj Hughes.

"I think we may have scratched the paint," he said.

Maj Hughes laughed. "You think? Have you checked in with your people?"

"Doing it now, Major."

Using the ship's systems and Lt Owen's assistance, Dewey reached out and spoke to the three escape pods that held his people. Lt Haynes had a broken arm. Several others had suffered abrasions. One of the pods had lost atmosphere, but everyone was already in EVA suits, so they would be fine.

"Search for other escape pods," Dewey said. "Let's see if we can round up Captain Webb."

"I already thought of that," said Lt Owen.

"And?"

Lt Owen turned to Dewey and shrugged. "There aren't any other escape pods."

32

Dewey was at the airlock as the escape pod with Lt Haynes on board opened. MedTech Robbins and MedTech Fox entered the pod and returned after a couple minutes. Between them, they had Lt Haynes, a temporary cast already on her arm.

"All right, there, Haynes?" Dewey asked.

Haynes nodded. "Now I remember why they say to be securely buckled before slapping the eject button."

"Could have been worse," said Dewey.

"Yeah," said MedTech Fox. "The lieutenant could be dead."

"What? And deprive you of the chance to browbeat and chastise me? Perish the thought."

Lt Haynes's comment earned a few chuckles from MedTech Robbins and the other Hospitallers following Haynes out of the pod.

"How's everyone else?"

"We're good, Lieutenant Tyler. We almost caught Lieutenant Haynes before the wall did."

"I'll note that in my report," Haynes said over one shoulder before disappearing with the medtechs.

"If everyone's okay," said Dewey, "then report to Staff Sergeant Castro in the platoon's bunk space."

"Will do, Lieutenant."

Dewey turned back to PFC Wallace as the other Hospitallers departed the area. "Go ahead and seal it up."

"You got it, Lieutenant Tyler."

Dewey's comm beeped. He was out of the mercenary EVA suit and in his own combat EVA suit, which fit better and was connected to the ship's comm systems.

"Captain Gregory," said Dewey after tapping to open the connection. "Everything okay?"

"Remains to be seen. There's a new ship in the system. Major Hughes thought you might want to come up to the bridge and join us for the entertainment."

"I'm on my way." Dewey turned to Wallace, who was securing the airlock. "Report to Staff Sergeant Castro. Tell her I'm on the bridge if she needs me for anything."

"Will do."

Dewey had to traverse half the ship's length and go up two flights of stairs to reach the bridge. By the time he'd arrived and requested permission to enter, they'd determined the new ship's designation.

"It's a merc ship," said Maj Hughes. He sounded annoyed to Dewey. "They've got their identity transponder on, but it's mostly garbled."

"Means we can't identify the ship name or the owner," said Sgt Bert Stephens, the bridge NCO.

"And they aren't responding to comm requests?" Dewey asked as he took a seat to the side of the portside bridge hatch.

"No." Maj Hughes's comment was hard with annoyance mingled with frustration.

They had no idea what the new ship was up to. Was it going to attack? Was it just the tip of an armada they were going to have to deal with?

"We have another signal." PFC Jon Dunn turned in his seat. "It just popped up on the screen. It's an emergency transponder."

"Where?" Maj Hughes sat straighter, his hands gripping the armrests of his chair.

PFC Dunn turned back to his workstation and took another look at the data on his screen. "Fifty thousand kilometers from us and moving away. Major, the pod has engaged engines. It's accelerating away from us."

"Toward the other ship?" asked Capt Gregory. He was tapping on his keyboard, streaming data on his screen as he spoke.

"Yes, Captain."

"Merc ship is accelerating now, too," said Cpl Carole Patton from her station. "Toward the escape pod."

"Captain Webb," said Maj Hughes. "That's what he was planning."

"He couldn't have known another of their ships would arrive so soon," said Dewey. "I wonder how long he was willing to wait."

"Until his air ran out," said Maj Hughes. He'd pulled out the touch screen terminal from the side of his seat, flipping it over so it covered his lap. He tapped it awake and began working on it. "Likely, he was planning to return to the station if no one came to his rescue. Unfortunately, the other ship will reach him before we can."

"Which means we'll have to wait to see what they do next," said Dewey. By the time they knew that, the other ship would have the advantage of speed. The Graevya had positioned itself over the space elevator's loading platform to protect it and the cargo ship, which was now unloading trunks and sending them planetside.

"I've never been a fan of waiting," grumbled Maj Hughes. Dewey noticed that several others on the bridge were nodding in agreement.

Dewey stood. "While we're waiting, I'm going to check on my people."

"We'll let you know if anything changes," said Maj Hughes.

Before going down to the platoon's bunkrooms, Dewey made a quick stop at medical to check on their injured guest from the no longer existent gunship. Inside medical, Dewey found MedTech Fox and MedTech Baker. They jumped to their feet as Dewey entered.

"Stand easy," Dewey said. He stepped over to the door leading to the inpatient beds. "How's our guest?"

"Grumpy," said MedTech Fox.

"Save a man's life and not even a thank you," added MedTech Baker.

"How ungrateful." Dewey returned the smiles of the medtechs and entered the inpatient room. The mercenary from the gunship was lying on a partially elevated bed. There was an IV attached to one of his arms. He'd been staring off into the distance until he turned to glare at Dewey.

"When can I go back to the Amazia?"

"The gunship? I wouldn't recommend it," said Dewey. "Your captain blew it up and made his escape."

"You lie."

"Rarely," Dewey said. He sat on the bunk next to that of the mercenary. "And not in this instance. I'm Lieutenant Dewey Tyler. I'd like to know your name."

"Sergeant Larry Anderson, Green Battalion."

"What organization?"

"Parthica."

"'Parthica'?" Dewey nodded while he dug through his memories. He'd read a list of mercenary organizations that had been compiled a little more than a year ago. Parthica wasn't one of them. But that really didn't mean much. What was current a year ago was different from five years ago and just as likely different from the present. Things change. Corporations reorganize. "I can't say I've ever heard of 'Parthica.'"

"And when will I be repatriated? You can't keep me hostage."

Dewey stood. "Oh, you're not a hostage. You're a prisoner. As far as repatriation, that remains to be seen. I think one of your company's ships is in-system. I'll let you know more when I do."

Dewey left the mercenary, who was now muttering to himself, and passed through the exam room.

"Cheery disposition," Dewey said as he made his way to the exit.

"You noticed, did you, Lieutenant Tyler?" asked MedTech Fox, a broad grin punctuating the end of his question.

The echo of laughter from medical followed Dewey to the stairs. He jogged down two levels and then headed aft toward the platoon's bunkroom.

"Officer on deck!" shouted Sgt Barrett as Dewey crossed the threshold. There was a short burst and clatter of noise around the bunkroom as Hospitallers jumped to their feet. Across the space, SSgt Castro appeared at the door to Staff NCO quarters as the sounds around Dewey abruptly ceased.

Dewey paused to look around the room. Some of the platoon was still on the surface of Juracan. Only PFC Horton had been lost. It was only one, but it was still one too many. A few others had contusions. Only Lt Haynes had suffered broken bones. All things being equal, they'd come through this in pretty good shape.

"As you were," Dewey finally said, dismissing the unit to return to whatever activities they were previously engaged in. For some, that was performing preventive maintenance. For others, it was a cat nap. Still others were in casual groups, talking amicably.

"News?"

"Sort of," said Dewey, turning his attention to SSgt Castro and Lt Owen, who'd suddenly appeared from officers' quarters. "There's another ship in the system. Captain Webb might be alive. An escape pod beacon came on shortly after the other ship arrived. They're on a converging path."

"So, wait and see?" asked Lt Owen. When Dewey nodded, Owen grumbled and said, "I hate waiting."

"You and the major," Dewey replied. "But for now, that's what we have to do. The other ship is still a few hours out, but I'd like everyone suited just in case."

"I'll see to it," said SSgt Castro. She nodded to Dewey and Lt Owen before turning back to the platoon's bunk room.

"Major try the coffee yet?" Lt Owen asked.

"Not yet," said Dewey. "He wants it tested for radiation first."

"Think he'd miss it if we promised to bring him more?"

"I'm not sure we need to get on his bad side right now," said Dewey. "But there's plenty of Insta in the chow hall."

"Guess that'll have to do."

An hour later, Dewey thought that Lt Owen had made do quite well with the Insta, having consumed nearly an entire carafe by himself. Dewey vaguely remembered getting a second cup from the carafe. Still, he'd been listening to Owen talk about the time he'd set his dropship down on a sinkhole. The dropship had been larger than the sinkhole by a few centimeters but still managed to slide down about twenty meters before it stopped. Even on full thrusters, all he'd managed to do was vaporize the water below, turning the whole place into a steam bath.

"I had to wait a day and a half before they managed to lift us out," Owen said. He was looking at the carafe in his hands, upended but not disgorging Insta like it had been doing shortly before. "Me, Lieutenant Matthews, Sergeant Thompson, and two squads, and no toilet. Couldn't even pop a hatch to take a leak."

"Telling tall tales again?"

Dewey looked and jumped to his feet, followed by Lt Owen, who'd been distracted by the carafe.

"Me, Captain Gregory? Never. They're more like medium tales."

"Of course they are," said the XO. "Anyway, the inbound ship is making contact with the escape pod, in case you want to come and watch from the bridge."

"Mind if I tag along?" asked Lt Owen as Capt Gregory retrieved two carafes of Insta from the galley.

"If there's an empty jumpseat, you're welcome to come."

Dewey and Lt Owen followed the XO up to the bridge. Once there, Dewey and Lt Owen grabbed seats along the back wall, out of the way. Capt Gregory made a circuit past all the stations filling no-spill cups with steaming Insta.

"You think they'll have any left over?"

"Sure, Owen." Dewey shook his head. He wasn't sure if Owen was joking around or if he hadn't yet had his fill.

Across the bridge, Sgt McKenzie turned his seat. He nodded to Dewey before speaking to Maj Hughes. "They're on docking maneuvers, Major."

"Keep monitoring," said the major. He accepted a cup of Insta from the XO before turning in his seat to look in Dewey's direction. "Lieutenant Owen, nice of you to join us. Lieutenant Tyler, as you heard, they are about to dock with the escape pod. I anticipate things will ramp up from there. Their communications have been secure, but there's been a lot of back-and-forth even if we can't hear what they're saying."

"Staff Sergeant Castro has everyone suited up," said Dewey. "We can post everyone to battle stations now if you'd like."

Maj Hughes took a sip of his Insta and then said, "Let them relax a little longer. If that ship comes in hot, they'll be busy soon enough."

"They're docked," Sgt McKenzie said over his shoulder.

"Here we go," said Maj Hughes.

His words were anticlimactic as nothing happened for a quarter-hour. It was just enough time for Lt Owen to mooch a cup of Insta from the XO and return to his seat.

"We have motion," said Cpl Alicia Lawrence. "Ship's accelerating."

"Might want to give Staff Sergeant Castro the command," Maj Hughes said over his shoulder.

"Ship's turning."

"Belay that last order, Lieutenant Tyler. Sergeant McKenzie, what do we mean when we say they're turning?"

"Turning away from us," said Sgt McKenzie. He'd stepped over to Cpl Lawrence's station. They were both examining the display, sharing a whispered conversation. McKenzie finally stood and turned to face Maj Hughes. "They're accelerating in a system outbound direction."

"There's nothing out there," said Lt Owen.

"They're going to jump," said Maj Hughes.

Cpl Lawrence tapped Sgt McKenzie's arm and pointed at the screen. McKenzie nodded and said, "You're right, Major. They just jumped out of system."

"That makes no sense," said Capt Gregory. "They have people on the station and on the planet. There's a corporation employee on the planet."

"Not their employee," said Maj Hughes. He'd pulled out his own screen and was scrolling through menus and opening windows.

"What about the mercs?" Lt Owen asked.

"They're mercs," said Dewey. "Their loyalty is only going to go so far. Corporal Anderson in medical is going to be very disappointed."

"Not to mention Mr. Thayer," said Lt Owen. "Oh, I want to be the one to tell him the news."

"You may get your chance," said Maj Hughes. "Sergeant McKenzie, plot a course. Let's dock with the station and talk face-to-face with Captain Roberson and whoever's in charge of the mercenaries. We have a mess to start cleaning up."

33

Dewey stood on his side of the meeting room. He listened to Mr. Ernest Thayer shout denials that could probably have been heard even without the two-way speaker.

"You lie!" Mr. Thayer was stomping about, holding a small sculpture of a planet held aloft by a backhoe. Several times Dewey thought he was going to hurl it across the room. Clearly, it had value, or Dewey was sure it would have already been smashed. "You're trying to trick me into giving away information. I know this scam."

"Done it a few times yourself, then?"

"Easy, Owen," Dewey said.

For his part, Mr. Thayer marched up to the thick glass divider, thought better of it, and took two steps back while continuing to glower at Lt Owen. "I'm a businessman, so yeah, I know the tricks to get information from others. And I know what to do with that information. So you won't get any from me."

"They're not lying," said Tegan Lerner from her position in a corner, close to the glass but still stuck on the same side as Dewey and Lt Owen. "I've seen the data. The Parania dropped in, recovered Captain Webb, and then left."

"I thought I fired you?"

"You hired me back because you can't run this place without me."

Mr. Thayer shared some of the glower for Lt Owen with Ms. Lerner before shifting his attention to Dewey. "I don't trust her either."

"No, I didn't think you would," said Dewey. "That's why I'm going to give you back access to the comms. You can call whoever you want and confirm for yourself what is happening."

A look of suspicion crossed Mr. Thayer's face. It was clear to Dewey that Mr. Thayer had learned to doubt everyone's motives over the years. Dewey found that to be a rather sad way to live one's life. It seemed easier to just live honestly and accept people for who they said they were until proven otherwise.

"You're just going to give me back complete access to the comm? Just like that?"

"Well, let's be sensible," Dewey said and smiled. "We're going to be listening in. We won't interfere, but we will be paying attention."

"What if I call for another gunship? Or three of them?"

"You can try," said Lt Owen, earning another glowering look from Mr. Thayer, "but I don't think you'll get any satisfaction."

Dewey tapped his comm, connecting to Lt Matthews in the comm building. "You can go ahead and open the controls, Matthews."

"One sec." There was a pause that exceeded one second. Then Lt Matthews was speaking again. "Okay, Mr. Thayer can now access the comm."

"And you'll be monitoring," Dewey said. It wasn't a question.

"Me and Sergeant Thompson, yes, Lieutenant Tyler."

"Thank you." Dewey tapped the comm and closed the connection. He spoke to Mr. Thayer and Ms. Lerner. "You have access to the comm now. When you're ready to talk to me, Ms. Lerner can make the connection."

Without waiting for a response, Dewey turned and entered the waiting elevator. Lt Owen followed, slapping the down button as he stepped inside.

"That was fun," Owen said after the doors had shut and the elevator began its descent.

"Not as much fun as it'll be when Mr. Thayer learns he's been cut loose."

"Like a dropship without engines." Owen laughed. "Or parachutes."

After leaving the admin building, Dewey and Lt Owen went to the mercenary barracks. Lt Howard Young, the officer in charge of the mercenaries on the ground, was more philosophical about his and his team's situation.

"No one's going to want to take responsibility for this mess," Lt Young said. He was holding a cup of coffee in his hands. Seated at the table with him were Lt Haynes and Sgt Simon. Several carafes borrowed from the Graevya sat in the center of the table along with a small pyramid of five cups. "And if you think you can track our employment back to our company, I can assure you that our names and records will have been purged from the systems."

"So what will you do?" asked Lt Owen, reaching for a carafe and a cup as he asked. "I mean, assuming you're free to go once an investigation is over?"

"Not sure," said Lt Young. "Probably go and sign on with another company. My records might not exist, but people know people, and I don't think anyone will say anything disparaging about me and my unit."

"You could hire on here," said Dewey. "The Juracanians are going to need training and a security force until then."

Lt Young laughed. "No offense, Lieutenant Tyler, but I don't think the Juracanians want to keep a reminder around. More importantly, I don't relish the idea of living on a radioactive planet."

"You got your radiation blocker, yes?"

As Dewey had promised, they'd brought down chems and parts to fix the mercenaries' med printer. Most of them were starting to show early signs of radiation sickness by that time. With Maj Hughes's permission, two of the medtechs had come down with a portable med fac. They were giving extended treatment to the most badly affected mercenaries. All of which was a surprise to the mercenaries. Conversations like the one they were in the middle of made it clear to Dewey why the mercenaries would feel that way.

"We did," said Lt Young. "But I don't want to depend on them to survive. But the idea of doing security for someone more reliable sounds like a good idea. We get out of here, I'll put out some feelers and see what bites."

They passed the next hour with an exchange of stories. There was a marked difference between the two, with Lt Young's stories sounding more like aggression. At the same time, those of the Hospitallers were more about their attempts to help people like the Juracanians. Based on how Lt Young kept looking off into the distance, Dewey believed that the stories coming from Owen and Haynes were having some effect on the mercenary.

"You know," Lt Young said after a long pause to pour coffee and taste it, "we hear stories of you all and what you do. Management tells us it's all propaganda to hide what you're really doing. Other people refuse to accept that anyone does anything nice in this universe just for the purpose of doing good."

Lt Haynes laughed. "We could be lying."

"No, I don't think so. I can't say I'm perfect at reading people, but it's too natural how you all are talking. You really are doing this for honest and good reasons. Even as an enlisted in the United Planets Forces, we rarely did anything helpful. And then it came with a hefty price tag."

"Hospitallers have a long history of helping others," said Dewey. "It began with the founders pooling their fortunes to care for all the orphans left after the Radial War. Then all the orphans needed something to do as they grew up. It has sort of grown from there."

"Right," said Lt Young. "But they could have created a military force to take control of planets. Instead, they chose to help."

"I'm not complaining," said Lt Owen. Dewey noticed Owen had the look of someone who needed to find the restroom. "I like helping people. I like a good dust-up, too. Not going to lie. But it's the helping that makes me feel good. Like I'm paying back the kindness done to me. I mean, what would I be like if I hadn't had the orphanage and my dorm parents to look after me?"

Dewey nodded. "I've sometimes wondered that, too. I don't think many of us would have survived childhood or even infancy."

"That what you officers do when no one's looking? Philosophize?"

"I'll never tell, Staff Sergeant," Dewey said. "How are things in the enlisted barracks?"

"Everyone's taking it in stride," said SSgt Castro. "The mercs are a little unsure what's going to happen to them, but other than that, they're happy to have the radiation blockers and Lieutenant Gray's coffee."

Lt Young stood. "I think I should go check in with everyone. See if I can tamp down any rumors that might start up."

Dewey's comm beeped for his attention just then. "Seems like we've all got someplace to be," he said, also rising to his feet. "I'll check in with you later, Lieutenant Young."

Young nodded and walked past a side-stepping SSgt Castro.

"Ms. Lerner?" Dewey said into his comm. "Mr. Thayer requesting my presence?"

"That he is, Lieutenant. He says, 'immediately,' but at your convenience."

"Understood." Dewey tapped the comm to close the connection. He turned to SSgt Castro. "How are the civilians doing?"

"Doing okay. Getting some decent food and medical attention. Samantha, Alexander, and some of the other Juracanians have come in from the city to talk and help."

"They're going to have some big decisions very soon," Dewey said. He was thinking of the future now that the galaxy knew they existed.

Unlike Wenshen, where the atmosphere was unbreathable to normal humans, people could survive on Juracan with the aid of radiation blockers. Who would come seeking fortunes? Mr. Thayer would only be the first. The radiation would help dissuade some. But others would gamble, just like Mr. Thayer had done. The Juracanians would have to decide who they would trust and who they wouldn't. Then, did they want to be part of the galaxy or stay apart?

Time would tell.

"Come along, Castro, let's go see what Mr. Thayer has learned."

What Mr. Thayer had learned did not sit well with him. Though his personal accounts and investments had mysteriously grown by substantial numbers, no one at the company he'd claimed to work for had any recollection of him. Passwords, company accounts, all of it had disappeared, looking as if they'd never been there in the first place.

"So, thanks to you, I may be rich, but I don't have my job anymore." Mr. Thayer was pacing angrily on his side of the glass wall. Dewey noticed that the sculpture that Mr. Thayer had been holding earlier was now on the ground, broken into tens of pieces. Some even looked as if they'd been ground into the carpet by an angry foot.

"They pushed you out the door and locked it behind you," said Lt Owen, who'd tagged along. "But I don't think you have an umbrella big enough to protect you from the storm that's coming."

Mr. Thayer stopped pacing. He looked at Lt Owen and said, "What does that even mean?"

"It means you still have to answer for the crimes you've committed here," said Dewey. "And it looks like you'll have to answer for them alone as we don't have a company to connect you with."

"Yeah? Well, that's where you and the company are both wrong." Mr. Thayer snapped his fingers and held out his hand. When nothing happened, he waved his hand. "Ms. Lerner?"

"Now I really don't work for you anymore," she replied. "Apparently, I don't work for anyone. And no, my accounts didn't bloom with creds, so pardon me if I don't feel like cooperating."

With a huff, Mr. Thayer stomped closer to Ms. Lerner, though stopping a meter short of the glass wall. Though he didn't glower at her, his look was still cold.

"Will you please show the lieutenant the folder I sent you?"

"Since you asked so nicely." Ms. Lerner flipped through several menus on her tablet and then double-tapped the screen before passing it to Dewey.

"I have kept every memo, email, directive, account, and file I've ever received or sent to the company from the first day I started until now," Mr. Thayer said. He now had a smile as cold as his stare. "All of it backed up to a private reader. I think that any government prosecutor who sets their sights on me will find striking a deal will open up a treasure trove of crimes. Crimes that will keep them busy until retirement, and probably their successors, as well."

"That's nice to hear," said Dewey. And it was, but he kept his face neutral. "But it's also very far above my pay grade. Major Hughes has assured me that representatives from the U.P. and A.P. are on their way here. You can tell your story to them and see if they're interested. My job now is to look to the needs of the Juracanians."

Dewey waved for Owen and Castro to precede him into the elevator.

"Hey!" Dewey turned at the shout from Mr. Thayer. "When will they be here?"

"A week?" Dewey wasn't sure.

"What do I do until then?"

"Same as you've been doing. Stay in here. Stay out of trouble."

34

It had been three and a half weeks since Dewey had last been to the town of Puchuncavi. However, he wasn't the first Hospitaller to return. Lt Gray's presence in the town was apparent by the smell of roasting coffee beans that seemed to permeate the air everywhere. There were also more people than Dewey recalled seeing the last time he was here.

"Welcome back," said Luc as Dewey came down the ramp of the RapRes.

Dewey shook Luc's offered hand. "Thank you," he said. "How are things in Puchuncavi?"

"Busy," said Luc as he laughed.

"I see that."

"Come along, and I'll show you why."

"I think we can smell why," said Sgt Parks as she came down the ramp with Cpl Mitchell and his fireteam.

They walked with Luc, but instead of heading toward the school where they'd initially bivouacked, they went the opposite direction. They arrived at a simple building past the town hall and down a side street, larger than an average home.

"Used to be a meeting hall," Luc said. "Come around back. Your lieutenant is there."

They went around the right side of the building. Doing so revealed a crete slab with a broad roof over the top. There were several picnic-style tables pushed to the edges. Near the middle were three large coffee roasters. They were crudely constructed and heated by burning wood. The roasters were tended by more than a dozen people who were also intently listening to Lt Gray, who talked while holding out bean-filled hands.

"Gray," Dewey said.

Lt Gray paused and looked over. "Lieutenant Tyler." He turned back to the people. "Keep the temperature constant. I'll be back."

After dropping the beans back into the cooling tray, Lt Gray joined Dewey and Luc. Sgt Parks and Cpl Mitchell had moved away several meters, conveniently close to several carafes and a plastic crate filled with coffee cups. Parks looked at the carafes and Lt Gray several times.

"Help yourself," Gray said. "Darker roast in the carafe with the green string on it. Love to get feedback."

"Will do, Lieutenant," said Sgt Parks as she quickly grabbed a cup and the carafe with the green string.

"I don't recognize most of these people," said Dewey. He waved a hand at the small crowd as he spoke. He'd seen everyone in the town before they'd left to take back the Graevya. Faces, like pages of books, never left Dewey's memory.

"There's two from Romerol," said Haynes, pointing at two people on a ladder, lifting buckets of raw beans to a hopper at the top of the third roaster. "Twins. Juan and Juliana. The rest are from other towns within a day's walk. If starting at dawn and walking until dusk counts as a day's walk."

"We invited them," said Luc. "Once Lieutenant Gray explained just how valuable the coffee beans were, it seemed important enough to teach other towns how to prepare their own beans."

"I've already talked to Major Hughes. He'll be taking a couple thousand kilograms of raw beans and a couple hundred kilos of roasted beans back with him," Lt Gray said. "He's contacted HQ, and they're going to send some business consultants to help the Juracanians with loans, equipment procurement, and marketing."

"Sounds exciting," said Dewey. He was being polite. Business and all the thousands of things they entailed didn't interest him. He'd rather build an emergency camp for displaced civilians than attempt to handle business things. Gray, though, was of a different mind. "And you'll be here for a while to help with the training."

"So my TDY request went through?" Gray pumped the air with one fist. "That's great news. How's the dark roast?"

Cpl Mitchell raised the carafe and gave it a shake. "Gone, Lieutenant."

"We'll get more." Gray turned to Dewey. "Anything else?"

"For the Juracanians, yes," Dewey said. "For you, just a hope that we'll see each other again, soon."

They shook hands as Gray said, "I'll be sure to bring coffee."

"You do that. Now, we'll leave you to your students." Dewey turned and started walking with Luc. To the side, Sgt Parks and the fireteam were quickly downing the coffee in their cups. Holding up a hand, Dewey said, "No rush, Parks. I'll be at the town hall. I'll comm you when I'm ready to leave."

"If you're sure, Lieutenant Tyler." Sgt Parks didn't seem to be sure and was caught between standing and sitting.

"I insist," said Dewey. That seemed to be enough of an order for Parks and the others. They settled back down as Lt Gray appeared with two more carafes of the dark roast.

With Luc for company, Dewey returned to the center of town and to the town hall. Inside, they met the other town elders. Several of them had coffee cups in their hands as Dewey arrived.

"Welcome back," said Constanza as she shook Dewey's hand. "We've had news of what happened at Atacama from some of our people. We're assuming you have other news."

"I do," said Dewey. "Maybe we could sit? This might take a while."

They convened to a conference room at the back of the building. After they all sat and Dewey accepted a cup of coffee, he caught the elders up on everything that had transpired from the moment Dewey and his platoon had gone up to the space elevator platform.

The battle was the quick part. What took time to explain was what was happening in the rest of the galaxy's second radial arm. Both the A.P. and U.P. governments were interested in Juracan. Numbers of planets mattered. The more planets they had, the more resources were available. The United Planets government was exceptionally eager to add a new world to their sphere of influence. Especially now that the Allied Planets had shown a willingness to snipe any planet that could be persuaded into joining them.

In the next week, the two organizations would send representatives to speak to the Juracanians. They'd have to travel to different regions and give their pitches to hundreds of groups like the elders in Puchuncavi. Then, those groups would have to decide what they wanted to do as a whole planet.

While the Hospitallers were impartial, being here only to help the Juracanians if they asked, Dewey had his opinions. The Allied Planets government had been aggressive in recruiting Free Planets and planets currently under the U.P. System's guidance. Aggressive to the point of using propaganda and fomenting rebellions on planets that already had internal issues. It was also true that the A.P. didn't like the Hospitallers, accusing them of meddling with their worlds.

As much as Dewey tried to deliver the information neutrally, he clearly hadn't done good enough.

"So, it seems like the A.P. System might not be best suited for us?" asked Valentine. She was sitting at the far end of the table and seemed a lot better now that Bennie had fully recovered.

"I can't say that for sure," said Dewey. He spent a lot of time looking at his cup as he talked. "They are as advanced as the U.P. System. They have a lot of the original planets from the beginning of the First Expansion in their government. They can provide a lot of assistance."

"It sounds like the U.P. could do as much for us, though," said Luc. He was leaning on the table with both elbows, his hands cupped together as he spoke.

"What if we don't want to join either?" asked Constanza. She wiped at her lap as she spoke, as if brushing away both options. "Is that a possibility?"

"Yes, it is," said Dewey. "You don't have to commit to anyone if you don't want to. But there are forces, mostly corporate, that will attempt to take advantage of that, too. Being part of one of the different coalitions offers protection."

"At a price," said Valentine.

From next to her, Jacobo said, "Everything has a price. What I want to know is if those are our only three options. A.P., U.P., or go it alone. That it?"

Dewey smiled. "No, there are two other options."

"Let's hear them, then," said Jacobo.

After another hour of questions and explanations, Dewey felt like they'd gotten nowhere.

When Luc sat back in his chair, a motion mimicked by several other elders, Dewey knew the meeting was over.

"We're going to have to talk to the other towns," said Luc. "That's going to take some time."

"Clock's ticking," said Valentine. She paused and looked at the other elders. "Lieutenant Dewey said we'd have company in a week."

"Not much time," Jacobo said. He shook his head, almost seeming to be defeated.

"We'll make it work," said Luc. He stood.

Dewey stood, too, understanding that he was no longer needed here. "We've done some work on the comm system at the elevator. You'll be able to contact us with the equipment I have in the RapRes. The Hospitallers will provide any assistance that you need."

"With no strings attached?" asked Jacobo.

"Well," Dewey said. He grinned before adding, "Maybe a cup of coffee."

Epilogue

Onboard the Graevya, Dewey had finished a meal in the mess hall. The dessert had gone down well with Juracanian coffee. Now, Dewey had time for himself. He'd retired to his quarters and indulged in a hot shower and fresh clothes before sitting himself in the straight-back chair at his desk. His tablet lay before him.

While Dewey didn't believe in fate or luck, he did wonder about what had transpired over the last standard year. Each time he'd tried to read a book, things had happened. Crazy things, in his opinion.

However, he reasoned, those events, the book, the lost planet, had happened at the beginning of the journey aboard each of the ships. This wasn't the beginning of the journey but the middle. They were currently back in route to join the rest of their battalion.

So that shouldn't matter, then, if he opened the tablet and relaxed with a good history of the origins of the Allied Planets government, right?

Dewey tapped the desk next to the tablet, not quite ready to touch it. SSgt Castro would enjoy seeing Dewey's dilemma. Of course, she would encourage him to do it, open the tablet, and open a book. She seemed to be tireless when it came to new adventures and life-threatening situations. For himself, Dewey would like a nice, basic, humanitarian aid mission. Maybe a flood or earthquake on a planet he already knew about.

"Middle of the journey," Dewey said softly. "And it's all coincidence. It doesn't mean anything."

Slowly, Dewey reached out and tapped the screen of his tablet, waking it. He pulled it a little closer and flipped several menus to find his library of unread books. There were hundreds of them. He found the one about the history of the A.P. and tapped it. When it opened, he looked away. Then, cautiously, Dewey turned back to the tablet and read the title, then the author, and then the first chapter.

From over Dewey's door, the small speaker chimed to inform everyone that an all-ship communication was coming. Dewey closed his eyes.

"Lieutenant Tyler to the bridge. Lieutenant Tyler to the bridge."

The End

Hi.

Abandoned on Juracan is my pandemic novel.

I began this story in February of 2020, just as the whispers of a pandemic began to evolve into shouts of concerns. Then, everything changed.

My daughter was now home every hour of every day. She now needed my attention and my help with her schooling as everything moved online. Suddenly, writing was shoved to the back burner.

I was slow to adapt to the changes and writing ground to a halt. In fact, the only thing that kept Abandoned on Juracan going was that I was sharing chapters weekly with my newsletter subscribers.

At least once, I had to pause the story to figure out what I'd done with the storyline. This is very much unlike me as I prefer to know where I'm going and what happens next. But there were weeks where I would sit down and write, only knowing where I'd been and hoping I knew where I was going. So strange things happened in the story.

Genders were swapped several times. Lt Haynes is female. Yet, she seemed to switch back and forth depending on what chapter. On top of that, she stole Lt Gray's spotlight as the coffee expert. That happened halfway through, and it took several readings on my part to untangle most of that.

Fortunately, I had help. Tim and Wendy provided lots of assistance in fixing threads that had become tangled or switched. I'm not sure if the story would have ever been published if it weren't for their help.

So, thank you, Tim and Wendy. And thank you to the newsletter subscribers who read the first drafts of the chapters, forgiving me my errors, and enjoying the story anyway.

Stay safe, everyone.

Earl T. Roske

29 March 2021

www.ingramcontent.com/pod-product-compliance
Lightning Source LLC
Chambersburg PA
CBHW052018240626
47153CB00006B/1856